A Fiery Siren

Once she had been Annabel Spencer, a proper British subject; now she is a coveted prisoner. But even Annabel couldn't imagine being offered to a fellow Englishman for a night of pleasure . . . a night that ignites a burning desire.

A Cynical Soldier

Charged with defending the glory of the British Empire far and wide, Lieutenant Kit Ralston views the women of the realm with a bitter smile. But when he meets Annabel, a scintillating, jade-eyed temptress, his hungry heart awakens.

A Bold Destiny

Vowing to rescue Annabel and make her his own, Kit abducts her—but can the power of their love protect them from what the future has in store?

Avon Books by
Jane Feather

SILVER NIGHTS
BOLD DESTINY
RECKLESS ANGEL
THE EAGLE AND THE DOVE

JANE FEATHER

Bold Destiny

AVON

An Imprint of HarperCollinsPublishers

AVON BOOKS
An Imprint of HarperCollins*Publishers*
10 East 53rd Street
New York, New York 10022-5299

Copyright © 1990 by Jane Feather
ISBN 978-0-380-75808-1
www.avonromance.com

First Avon Books paperback printing: March 1990

Avon Trademark Reg. U.S. Pat. Off. and in Other Countries, Marca Registrada, Hecho en U.S.A.
HarperCollins® is a registered trademark of HarperCollins Publishers.

Printed in the U.S.A.

10 9 8 7 6

Prologue

August, 1833

I t was that uneasy time of day, when shadows fell long from the craggy peaks, pooling in dark mass along the narrow track of the pass as it wound its tortuous way between crouching cliffs.

George Spencer glanced over his shoulder at the caravan moving slowly behind him. The camels, their panniers laden with the merchant's goods, plodded, heads high on their elongated necks, looking absurdly dignified as if to disassociate themselves from the ridiculous business of being beasts of burden. Their drivers clicked their tongues, and cried their strange encouraging sounds that camels were supposed to understand; cries that in this instance were intended to hurry them up as the shadows lengthened and the narrow throat of the Khyber pass through which they crept still showed no signs of emerging into the comforting familiarity of British India.

If Annabel had not taken it into her head to disappear from the camp that morning—following an ibex, she had maintained in excuse—they would have set out two hours earlier and would have been well onto British soil by dusk. Instead, they were journeying through this gray and threatening defile as the day drew to its close. The evening star had already shown its face, bringing not reassurance but alarm. The horsemen, riding in escort, caressed the

1

smooth wooden stocks of their rifles, shifting in their saddles as they glanced around them, along the narrow twisting track disappearing into gloom, and upward to the massive peaks that seemed to huddle, malevolently waiting.

"You seem uneasy, George." Rosalind Spencer, riding at her husband's side, spoke with customary calm. "It cannot be much farther."

George smiled down at her. As always, just the sound of her voice soothed him; the quiet brown eyes calmed his restless anxiety. "Something has to be done about Annabel," he said, but without conviction. They had been saying that for the last ten years. The only difficulty was that the child refused to have anything done about her. She continued on her own sweet way, and all the remonstrance in the world could not turn her from a course once she had set it.

Rosalind returned the smile, well aware of her husband's thoughts. Their daughter was an everlasting delight, a joy second only to the pleasure they had in each other. Of course, she was unruly, obstinate, thoroughly spoiled one would say with absolute truth, but that was frequently the case with only children.

"She will settle down again when we return to Peshawar," she now reassured her husband comfortably. "The familiar routine of lessons and riding and meeting with her friends will soon occupy her, and she'll forget about stalking ibex and haunting the bazaars."

Annabel Spencer wrinkled her small, well-shaped nose. They were talking about her again. She could always tell by the way they leaned toward each other, by a certain conspiratorial set of their heads. It was probably about this morning. Papa had been quite dreadfully annoyed, almost angry, really, just because she had delayed them for a couple of hours. The truth was that she could hardly bear to contemplate returning to the prim, orderly existence in the large white house at Peshawar, with its lush gar-

dens, armies of servants, rigorously executed social
life; the inane chatter of the little girls considered by
her parents to be suitable companions for their
daughter; their fond mamas smiling and nodding on
the verandah, where the hot air was stirred by the
punkahs energetically wielded by small, ignored
servant children.

She looked around her and found nothing in the
Afghan landscape to alarm. Instead, it stirred her
with its untamed grandeur. She had reveled in every
moment of the last six months, during which George
Spencer had made good his promise that after her
twelfth birthday, he would take her with him on his
next journey across the mountains into Afghanistan
and Persia. He had bought carpets, rich silks, silver,
and beaten gold, to be shipped to England and the
eager market that had made him a nabob.

But Annabel had little interest in the means by
which her father had amassed his fortune. For her,
the fascination lay in the people with whom he bar-
gained: the khans, lords of life and death in their
own tribes; the shrewd-eyed merchants, soft-voiced
yet implacable; the women who moved like shades,
enwrapped from head to toe; the hillmen, rangy,
turbanned warriors with pointed cleavers at their
sides, or Persian scimitars, so sharp you could see
the edge shimmer in the sunlight. She had lost herself in the exotic wonders of the bazaars; in the richness of the *aylag*, those wonderful summer pastures
high up in the mountains where the nomads took
their fat-tailed sheep, the goats, cattle, and ponies
to graze in the spring until the first snows of September. She had shivered in pleasurable apprehension at the howl of wolves, the spoor of black bear,
the great, grayish, clumsy bulk of the lammergeyers,
hanging over the landscape in search of decayed and
decaying flesh.

So absorbed was she in her reminiscent musings
that the first cry of alarm from one of the leading
horsemen failed to penetrate immediately. She
glanced up from her sightless contemplation of her

mount's braided mane . . . and was engulfed by terror.

Ghazi tribesmen were everywhere, swarming down the steep sides of the cliffs, jumping from rocks, those on horseback pounding down the track toward George Spencer's now screaming, milling caravan. Shot after shot cracked from their jezzails, as they aimed the long rifles into the panic-stricken group and men fell from horse and camel, to litter the track, where the wounded were slaughtered by the knives of their fanatical attackers.

Rosalind died with a bullet between her shoulder blades, knowing no more than an instant of pain before infinity swallowed her. George flung himself from his horse with a cry of outrage and despair, but the broadsword pierced his heart before he could reach her, and the breath left his body as he spoke her name.

The dreadful, unbelievable images tumbled before Annabel's transfixed gaze. She sat rigid on her little brown pony, the wild savagery of the hillmen's yells of triumph and exhilaration as they slaughtered the infidels, the feringhee dogs, battering against her eardrums so that the sounds seemed to be inside her head. Around her whirled, swirled, the hellish scene. Faces—brown, bearded, flashing white teeth—merged, then separated. Horses screamed, gun smoke fogged then cleared, and out of the fog suddenly materialized a face that she knew instinctively had her own fate written upon it. A small, pointed beard; long ringlets hanging beneath a skullcap; the glistening eyes of the fanatic. One arm raised high, the khyber knife poised at the top of the arc, poised to sweep the head from her shoulders.

Her mouth opened wide on a soundless scream of terror. Her hood fell back. Her eyes stared, huge, terrorized.

The Ghazi saw eyes the color and depth of jade, a complexion of the most delicate purity, hair like burnished copper, glowing in the dusk-gloom. A

look of speculation banished the glare of blood lust.
The cleaver was returned to his belt.

"Akbar Khan." She heard the inexplicable mutter
even through the horror that rendered her mute and
immobile. Then she was swinging upward, through
the air, as a pair of huge hands caught her beneath
the arms and lifted her from the pony. Her terror
found expression in a wild, unearthly shriek. Her
captor laughed, dumping her on the saddle before
him, twisting her cloak about her so that her arms
were trapped at her sides. He yelled something over
his shoulder at the confused carnage behind him,
but if he was answered, Annabel could not tell
amidst the cacophonous shrieks still rending the air.
Then they were galloping along the track, a winter-
threatening bite to the wind whistling past her ears,
raking through her hair, making her eyes water, so
that she could not tell during that long ride when
the tears of overpowering grief finally began, sub-
suming her terror.

Chapter 1

September, 1841

As hangovers went, this one certainly qualified for the superior category, Christopher Ralston reflected painfully, and if anyone was a good judge of such matters, he was. The sun seemed unnecessarily shiny in that bright blue mountain sky, glinting in unfriendly fashion off the eye-hurting dazzle of the snowcapped peaks.

Ordinarily, the majesty of the Afghan landscape could stir him despite his general malaise, but today was a particularly bad day. Smiling plains, stark mountains, busy streams, bravely winding tracks pursuing their rocky, devious course despite all the odds thrown up by the terrain—all failed to ease the persistent throb at his temples, to lift the numbing heaviness of depression, to lubricate his dry mouth, soothe his frying eyeballs, quiet his uncooperative stomach.

As always, he wondered why he did this to himself. Why play the last hand . . . and the last hand . . . and the very last hand? Why have the last brandy . . . and the last brandy . . . and the very last brandy? Why fall, night after night, onto his cot, cursing his batman, who struggled with hooks and buttons and boots, as he put his near-insensible officer to bed?

Silly question. Who wouldn't seek oblivion, banished to this godforsaken outpost of the civilized

6

world? Banished to the mediocrity of a lieutenantcy
in the East India Company's Cavalry?

God, what an irony! His lip curled in self-mockery.
The Honorable Kit Ralston, society's darling despite
his rakehell reputation—or perhaps because of it—
the dashing captain of the Seventh Light Dragoons,
cast into outer darkness because of a drunken impulse!

"Your pardon, sir, but we've been riding for four
hours. The men will be better for tiffin."

The soft tones of Havildar Abdul Ali fell like rain-
drops, but the reminder, for all its gentleness, was
none the less an imperative. Kit nodded brusquely
to the sergeant, trying to appear as if the reminder
had been unnecessary. "I have it in mind to halt in
those trees. We'll be less exposed." He gestured
with his whip to the lee of the mountain, where a
small copse offered a jewel of lush green in the bare
sandy plain.

"Of course, sir," murmured the ever-tactful havildar. "A perfect choice."

Kit wondered if he could detect irony in the man's
tones, and decided he didn't much care either way.
Lieutenant Ralston's disaffection from his present
service was no secret to the men or officers; but then,
none of them was overjoyed to be part of an army
of occupation with not the slightest legal or moral
excuse for the role, using British bayonets to force
upon the unwilling Afghans a ruler whom they
loathed . . . and loathed with good reason Shah
Soojah was that species of oppressor whose tyranny
had its base in his own lack of spirit and excess of
fear. He was no ruler for the fiercely independent
Afghan tribal chiefs.

Lieutenant Ralston gazed wearily around the
landscape, speculating idly on what he and his patrol would do if they came face to face with a war-
ring party of Ghilzai hillmen. Turn tail and run for
it, probably. The Ghilzais were hardly civilized foe,
although more so than the Ghazi fanatics, but they
were all zealots when it came to their determination

to engage in guerilla warfare against the feringhee invaders and their puppet ruler, who presumed to tax them and dictate to them; who denied the hillmen their immemorial right to levy charges for safe use of the mountain passes; whose arrogance ignored the self-determination of the Afghan tribes and their khans.

He touched spur to his horse. "Let's stop dallying, Havildar."

Abdul Ali permitted himself the slightest lift of an eyebrow before calling an order to the five sepoys behind him and following his commanding officer at the gallop across the plain.

The cool green copse was one of those delightful surprises with which this generally inhospitable landscape was dotted. It was more extensive than had appeared from the distance, and they found a clearing floored with a carpet of thick green moss sprinkled with golden buttercups.

The prospect of food revolted Lieutenant Ralston and he left his men cheerfully preparing their tiffin, himself wandering on foot further into the trees. The path began to slope gently downhill, and he followed it without much thought, venturing deeper into the wood. The lake, when he came upon it quite unexpectedly, took his breath away. It was a perfect circle within a necklace of trees, large, flat stones at the bottom glistening through the translucent water. He took a step toward it, out of the trees, intending to cool his aching head in the inviting water, when something caught his eye and his step faltered. He moved back instinctively into the trees and stood still, staring.

Someone was swimming in the lake. A bare white arm curved, cleaved the surface. At this distance, he could make out no distinguishing features, but his eye fell upon a pile of material some feet from the water's edge, quite close to where he stood. The swimmer's clothes, he presumed. The little heap offered nothing that could identify the dress as European. Curious, he stepped from the screen of trees and moved to the pile, bending to examine it.

He heard nothing, until the tiny prick in the soft vulnerable spot behind his right ear froze him, rigid with alarm. Someone was standing behind him, holding the point of something very sharp against his skin. A voice, a female voice, spoke harshly in Pushtu. He swallowed, trying not to move his head in case he might inadvertently drive the point into his scalp.

"I speak a little Persian," he said in that language, "but no Pushtu. I mean no harm."

To his relief, the pricking pressure was lifted, but he remained still, not daring to turn. It seemed incredible that he might have come upon an Afghan woman, unattended, taking a bath in the lake. These people guarded their women with all the care decreed by Koranic law. It was fair to say they did not accord them consonant consideration in their daily life, but their women most certainly did not go around taking baths in public lakes, however secluded such lakes might be.

"We will speak the language of the feringhee, if you prefer," the voice amazingly said. "Turn around very slowly."

Christopher obeyed with the utmost caution. Surprise and alarm, he found, were wonderful stimulants. His head had cleared, although his heart was racing in response to the knife's threat. Once he had turned, however, the speeding of his heart had a quite different cause.

He was never sure what he noticed first. Was it the jade-green eyes, slightly almond-shaped, tilted at the corners? Was it the extraordinary whiteness of her skin? Was it the deep, glowing copper of her hair, massed damply on her shoulders? Or was it that she was quite naked—slender, lissom, delicately curved . . . and quite naked?

A naked white woman, water glistening on her body, stood before him, holding a wicked stiletto in

the manner of one who knew how to use it and
would have no hesitation in doing so.

"Who the devil are you?" he heard himself demand, somewhat hoarsely.

"And who the devil are you?" came the prompt
response. The green eyes darted around the lake,
glanced toward the trees. "Feringhee soldiers do not
ordinarily travel singly. It is a little dangerous, is it
not, these days?"

The taunt in her voice was unmistakable, and he
felt his hackles rise in annoyance. However covertly
sympathetic he might be to the Afghan's rejection
of the British military presence, he was still an officer in that army and accusations of cowardice,
implicit or no, were not to be tolerated.

But just how did a gentleman express his annoyance with a stark-naked woman armed with a
stiletto?

He was still struggling with the dilemma, uncomfortably aware of the glint of mockery in the green
eyes, when she spoke again. "You had best leave
here. They will kill you if you are discovered."

"Who will?" He was swamped with confusion,
conscious that he was at an appalling disadvantage,
yet feeling that he should not be—a lieutenant in
Queen Victoria's army at such a loss. Surely it ought
to be possible to wrest that dagger from her. But to
do that, he would have to touch her, and he did not
think he could do that with any objectivity in the
present circumstances.

"That is none of your business," she replied. "But
you may take my word for it that if they find you
here with me like this, they will kill you. And it will
be a singularly unpleasant death—something at
which they are expert." Her tone was matter-of-fact,
but he became aware of a sudden tension in the lithe
body. "Go," she said.

"Now just a minute!" He discovered an imperative if belated need to assert himself. "I do not know
who you are, or what right you have to be here when
I do not. But I see no reason on earth why *I* should

run away. It seems to me that *you* are the vulnerable one at this moment." He allowed his gaze to drift pointedly down her body and felt a prickle of satisfaction as a tinge of pink showed against her cheekbones. "Make no mistake, I am not denigrating your charms, but English ladies do not make a habit of exposing themselves to strange men. And if you are not an English lady, what are you?"

She moved so fast, he did not know how it happened, but the point of the stiletto pricked his throat, drawing a bead of blood, and the jade eyes were cold as stone. "Who I am and what I am are nothing to do with you, feringhee dog!" she said softly. "I do not live by your rules or bear your labels."

"Goddamn it! But you are as much a feringhee as I am," he said, abruptly grasping the wrist of the hand that held the blade to his throat. He was too angry to calculate the risk he took, but it paid off. She did not drive the point deep into his flesh, as she so easily could have done. Instead, her eyes widened in surprise and with an element of chagrin. They stood thus for an instant, his fingers banding a narrow, fragile wrist, her naked body drawn so close to his that her breasts brushed his tunic with her sharp indrawing of breath.

"You are no Afghan, no Persian, no Indian," he said, pressing his advantage with great deliberation. "And that, miss, makes you as much a European infidel as I. And I tell you that young ladies where I come from do not stand around in their bare skins flourishing knives at innocent strangers." He released her wrist as suddenly as he had grasped it and stepped back, straightening the manhandled collar of his tunic, watching her warily.

A look of uncertainty had crept into the jade gaze. She opened her mouth to say something, then her body stiffened. The uncertainty vanished, replaced with a mixture of determination and alarm. "They are coming. You must go. There is no time to lose."

Kit could hear nothing beyond the background noises of the copse, but the urgency in her voice could not be gainsaid and he found himself striding toward the concealment of the trees. Once out of sight, however, he stopped. A thick screen of bramble offered a vantage point from which he could see the lakeside, whilst remaining hidden himself.

Out of the trees on the far side of the small lake surged a twittering flock of black-shrouded figures. Their voices in anxious and scolding Pushtu filled the small clearing as they scurried toward the figure of the copper-haired woman, who stood beside the pile of discarded clothing, squeezing water from her hair with apparent insouciance.

The watcher in the trees stared, spellbound and bemused. What *was* this? Who the hell was she? An English girl . . . woman . . . How old was she? Nineteen, twenty perhaps . . . certainly no more than that . . . an English girl being treated with the utmost familiarity by a flock of Afghan women. Familiarity, yes, but he could detect something else, as the twittering continued unabated while the women busied themselves drying and dressing the girl, who received both the undeniable scolding and the attentions with seeming indifference. They were behaving toward her as if she were a very special charge . . . a very precious charge. Knowing the fierce reputation of these tribal women, Kit Ralston felt not the slightest inclination to show himself, and understood with considerable gratitude why the girl had sent him into hiding with such urgency.

He watched as she stepped into the wide full *chalvar*, encasing the long slender legs that still filled his internal vision. Her attendants dropped an embroidered tunic over her head, pushed her feet into curly-toed slippers, bending to attach the toes to the bottom of the trousers. Then they enwrapped her in a voluminous chadri, veiling her from head to foot. Only her eyes were visible behind the *ru*-band, a mesh insert of embroidered white silk. Apart from the fact that her clothing was of soft, white silky material, as compared to the darker, coarser stuff of her attendants; she was now indistinguishable from the other women; her white skin and burnished hair were hidden from temptation.

Kit shivered slightly at the thought of what would have happened had he been discovered with her in her nakedness. Whoever she was, she seemed as much subject to Koranic law as any woman of Islam—and such women were not for the eyes of infidels. But she must belong to some man, in that case. The idea of an English girl bound to one of these hillmen was not one he could begin to encompass. He knew that the khans were lords of life and death in their own parishes. And as far as he was concerned, that was their own business with their own people. But this was an Englishwoman . . . a citizen of the greatest empire in the world.

Good God! It was inconceivable. Whatever the circumstances, it could not be permitted—not, at least, by any Englishman deserving of the title! Infused with an impetuous new energy that chased away his earlier jaded depression, he strode back through the trees to rejoin his patrol.

The havildar stood up hastily as his officer appeared in the clearing. "Thought the Ghilzais had got you, sir," he offered in heavy humor that could not quite disguise the element of truth in the jest. In Abdul Ali's experienced opinion, men as disaffected and generally blue-deviled as Lieutenant Ralston could not be trusted to take proper precautions in enemy territory. It made them unpopular officers, unless they had a sergeant like Abdul Ali to circumvent the thoughtlessness.

Kit gave him a sharp glance, then, to the havildar's astonishment, a slight grin quirked the previously forbidding mouth, a glint of wry humor flickered in the heavy-lidded gray eyes. He took off his plumed shako and ran his hands through his thick, slightly curly fair hair. "They almost did, Havildar. But not in the way you mean. . . . Is that tea the men are brewing?"

"Yes, sir. Do you good, it will." The sergeant called in Hindi to one of the sepoys, who brought over a tin cup of steaming liquid, its reddish-brown color indicative of its strength.

Kit gulped, shuddered, gulped again, and began to feel human. "We're some four hours out of Kabul," he said, pulling a map from his saddlebag. "In the heart of Ghilzai country." He shook out the map with one hand, taking another gulp of tea. "Our orders are to attempt to pinpoint the whereabouts of Uktar Khan and his hillmen."

"Or Akbar Khan," said Abdul, pursing his lips. "Seems to me, sir, that it's Akbar who's the real menace."

"I'm sure you're right. But seven men aren't going to find the commander-in-chief in these mountains unless he wants to be found. He's living a nomad's life and hasn't shown himself in months."

"Only through his influence," Abdul pointed out. "He's behind every raid, every plot, every skirmish, every murder."

"I don't doubt it." Ralston peered into his empty cup, wondering whether a second dose of that exceedingly vigorous brew would undo the effects of the first, or simply double the benefit. It occurred to him that food might not be a bad idea. "What was there for tiffin, Havildar?"

"Just bread and cheese, sir. We're traveling light."

"Of course." He should have known that. It was his responsibility to give the supply orders to the patrol—iron rations in keeping with this supposedly undercover mission. If he had managed to do so in the aching fog of the night's excesses, he had forgotten. But Abdul Ali would have seen to it, anyway. He'd make a much better commander of this little patrol of sepoys than Lieutenant Christopher Ralston, who had never been more than a Hyde Park soldier, smart in his regimentals, popular in the mess, a devil with the women who all loved a uniform. . . . That sour wash of self-disgust threatened his newfound enthusiasm.

"Here, sir." The havildar was holding out a wedge of goat's cheese and a hunk of bread.

Kit took it with a grunt of thanks and turned back to the map. Those women must have come from some village nearby. But it could not be an ordinary peasant village. The English girl's clothing was too rich for the ordinary villager, and the duty and attention she had received from such a large group of women indicated an establishment of great importance—the establishment of a khan.

He chewed on the dry bread, then swallowed more tea, his brain moving smoothly, no longer addled and weary. It was surely in keeping with his present mission to identify the particular khanate. Who was to say it wasn't the stronghold of Uktar Khan? It would certainly be a dereliction of duty to ignore the possibility, now that it had occurred to him.

The women had appeared from the far side of the little lake. He and his patrol would explore from there. He refolded the map, hearing the paper crackle satisfyingly as if in tune with his own sense of decision-making. "Tell the men to pack up, Havildar. I've a hunch I want to follow."

Abdul Ali politely hid his skepticism and surprise at this briskly authoritative tone from one whose lassitude and scorn for the entire enterprise they were engaged upon was usually barely concealed. He gave the necessary orders, and within a quarter of an hour the little group was making its way through the trees to the lake.

The lake lay peaceful and deserted, with no sign of its recent visitors. The noon sun shone through the gap in the trees, dancing across the surface of the water like a mischievous imp. For once, Kit found nothing disagreeable in either the light or the fanciful imagery it created. He directed his troop around the lake, where the grass had been depressed by footprints into the semblance of a track. They followed the track into the trees, then found themselves climbing steeply.

"Seems to be going up into the hills, sir." Abdul

drew alongside Kit. ''It looked from the plain as if the wood was only at the base of the cliff.''

Kit nodded. ''The light plays strange tricks in this place.'' They rode on in a gradually deepening silence, until not even the cry of a bird could be heard, only the crackle of the horses' hooves as they broke twigs underfoot.

The women could not have had more than an hour's start on foot, so where the devil were they? Kit peered around, his uneasiness growing. Abdul was sitting his wiry pony, sniffing the wind, his eyes darting ceaselessly, trying to catch some warning of the danger they all knew lurked somewhere. And then it found them.

The trees stopped without warning, and the small patrol almost fell on top of a nomad encampment. The black tents huddled on a sandy flat high above a deep gorge in the lee of a jagged cliff.

''Dear God,'' Kit muttered, even as he cursed himself for not having the forethought to have sent one of the sepoys ahead as scout. The nomads were not usually warlike, but these days you could rely on nothing, and robbers abounded throughout the land.

Men were appearing from tents, in black head-cloths, their long loose *chapans* of white homespun with wide sleeves flapping around them.

''Wait!'' Kit ordered sharply as the soldiers raised their muskets. ''See what they do first.''

The nomads seemed to glide toward the group. They had staves in their hands, knives in the folds of their *chapans*, but no firearms that Kit could see. He could afford to wait for them to get closer in order to judge their intentions. But as they drew nearer, the naked hostility in eye and posture became apparent. He was about to give the order to fire and retreat when a voice—a very familiar voice— called sharply in Pushtu through the menacing silence that had fallen over the encampment.

The figure in the silky white chadri came swiftly toward them, and the men hesitated, although their antagonistic eyes remained fixed on the intruders. Ignoring the patrol, she spoke to the nomads, her words low and rapid. There were frowns, mutterings, but for the moment no one made a move toward the group of soldiers.

She turned at last toward Kit and spoke in Persian. "What business do you have here?"

He looked at the swathed figure, his eyes seeking the green gaze behind the embroidered insert of her veil . . . seeking and finding. "I was looking for you," he replied steadily, hoping that no one but themselves spoke Persian. Did he imagine the flicker behind the *ru*-band?

"That was a foolish quest," she said in a tone of cold indifference, before turning back to the cloaked and bearded men. She spoke again, and the name of Akbar Khan was clearly distinguishable. Kit felt Abdul stiffen, and with sudden inspiration he spoke in English.

"My business lies with Akbar Khan," he said clearly. "I would talk with him. I believe that the son of Dost Mohammed would welcome the opportunity for discussion at this stage."

She stood very still, examining him. "You have a message from Kabul? From General Elphinstone . . . or from Shah Soojah?" The derision he had noted before invested her voice as she spoke the names, and he could not really blame her. Elphinstone, the general in charge of the British army in Kabul, was a weak, enfeebled, indecisive disaster waiting to happen. And the nominal ruler of Afghanistan was no better. But it was disheartening, not to say alarming, to realize that the Afghans themselves had no illusions about their opponents' strengths.

"I would talk with Akbar Khan," he repeated curtly.

"And it is possible he would talk with you," she replied. "But if you come in peace, then you must lay down your arms and eat the salt of these people. Only thus will they trust you. And you will need their escort."

"It's a trap," Abdul hissed. "Tricky bastards they are, sir. Can't trust them further than you can see them, even the ones who speak the Queen's English like this one."

A scornful laugh came from beneath the chadri, but she made no attempt to dispute the accusation, and Kit did not know what to believe. She appeared to have some authority with these nomads, but what Afghan woman had authority over the men? Of course, he knew she was no Afghan . . . at least not in body. But in spirit . . . ? And Abdul was right about the treachery. These people saw things differently, drew different distinctions. But to eat their salt would ensure a guest's safety . . . if he could survive long enough to do so.

"You know where to find Akbar Khan?" he asked her.

She laughed again. "None better, feringhee."

The puzzle was beyond unraveling, at least in the present circumstances. The girl held all the cards, and if he was really determined to lay hands on an ace or two of his own, then he had no choice but to go along with her. The one thing he knew he could not do was to walk away from the mystery surrounding this extraordinary creature.

"We will not lay down our arms," he said in careful Persian, directly addressing the circle of men. They might not understand him exactly, but they would recognize the courtesy in his attempt to communicate with them. "It is not our way as soldiers to go unarmed, but we will dismount and walk with you."

The men turned to the girl, who translated swiftly. There was a murmured confabulation, then one of the men walked forward and took the bridle of Kit's horse.

"They will lead you into the camp," the young woman said. "You must manage without an interpreter until we leave in the morning. I am not permitted to consort with the men."

"By whose order?" he heard himself demand,

uncomfortably disturbed at hearing pronounced in his own language by a member of his own race this ritual proscription that could not be permitted to apply to such a one as she.

A ripple of laughter tinged her voice, as if she understood and ridiculed his rigid chauvinism. "Akbar Khan's. Without his permission, I may have no social dealings with men, and he is not here to give it." The chadri quivered about her shoulders, although he could not see the shrug and could only guess at the movement. "On the journey tomorrow, I will be able to interpret for you if you need it." She turned aside.

"Wait!"

She stopped, looking over her shoulder at him. "Yes?"

"Who the devil are you?"

"Ayesha," she replied. "And who the devil are you, feringhee?"

"Christopher Ralston," he said.

"I am honored to make your acquaintance, Christopher Ralston."

"The pleasure is all mine, miss."

This time there was no mockery in her laughter. It was a clear, infectious chime that brought a grin to his mouth as he watched her move smoothly toward a group of tents pitched to one side of the main encampment.

"Something very queer going on here, sir," Abdul muttered, grimly relinquishing his hold on his own bridle to an expressionless nomad.

"Very queer, Sergeant," agreed Kit. "But I've never cared for riddles, and I've a mind to unravel this one."

Chapter 2

Lieutenant Ralston passed an unquiet night. He and his men had established their own campground, around their own fire, and he set sentries throughout the night. But the sense of lying in the enemy's jaws, waiting for the mouth to close, was not conducive to restful sleep. He knew that Abdul Ali and the men did not understand why he was pursuing this dangerous and unnecessary course, folowing the notorious Akbar Khan into his own den. But the lieutenant could hardly explain that more than the interests of the British army in Kabul lay behind the impulse.

Where was she now? Sleeping soundly in one of those black tents, watched over by black-swathed women, presumably. Who was she? What was she? Where did she come from? And how in the name of all that was good had she ended up here? The long night provided no answers.

Dawn brought him out of a light and unrefreshing doze. The nomad encampment bustled with life as tents were struck, ponies loaded . . . and not just ponies. Women set off on foot up the narrow winding track weighed down with burdens and babies. Ignoring their struggling womenfolk completely, the men, unladen, strode ahead of them, talking amongst themselves, using their heavy staffs to aid their progress. Children, whistling, ran amongst the herds of sheep and goats, prodding and encouraging them on their way.

The three tribal elders, whom he had identified the previous evening, rode up to the small troop of soldiers. Gestures sufficed to communicate the message that they should mount and accompany the elders, who would ride at the head of the tribe.

And Ayesha? He could not ask, of course, but his eyes roamed the scene. Surely she would not be walking, another beast of burden, with the other women?

Then he saw her, mounted on a neat, high-stepping gray horse that clearly had Arabian lineage. She was still enveloped in the white chadri, but the voluminous garment appeared not to impede her mobility as she sat her cantering mount.

"*Salaamat bashi,*" she greeted, reining in before them. "It means 'May you be healthy,' " she translated with a chuckle, seeing Kit's blank expression. "You should respond, '*Mandeh nabashi. Zendeh bashi.*' It means 'May you never be tired. May you live forever.' "

"Thank you," he said somewhat feebly. "I will do my best to remember."

"It is an elementary courtesy," she said in reproving tones. "If you go amongst the hillmen, then the least you can do is learn a word or two of their language."

"Does Akbar Khan not speak Persian?" Kit asked, swinging onto his horse. "His father does."

"Yes, of course he does. He speaks English also. But he may not choose to do so," she told him. "He may not even choose to see you."

"But I am assuming that with your vouching for me, he will be only too happy to hear what I have to say," Kit returned blandly. "You are clearly a person of some influence."

"I am only a woman," she retorted. "You must know what that means in this land. I hope for both our sakes you are not as stupid as you seem to be. Akbar Khan does not suffer fools, and if he does not approve of your arrival, I can assure you *I* will be the one to bear the consequences."

"Then why are you taking me to him?"

She did not reply immediately, but he found himself most eager to hear how she would answer him. Finally, she spoke. "There will be a massacre if nothing is done to prevent it. With the passing of each day, it becomes more inevitable. Only Akbar Khan can stop it, but he will need to be persuaded that it is in his and his father's interests to do so."

"But his father is in voluntary exile in India," Kit pointed out.

"His father decided that he could best serve his people by yielding the fight himself at this point. But make no mistake, Christopher Ralston, Dost Mohammed knew well he was leaving behind his son to continue the fight for him. Akbar Khan is not as delicate in his methods as his father; the Dost is well aware of that. And this is not a fight to be fought with delicate methods. When it is won, and Dost Mohammed is once again shah of Afghanistan, he will wish to be on good terms with his British neighbor in India, and if he is implicated in the wholesale massacre of the occupying army, then he will find it hard to be so."

Kit stared. It was the first sensible analysis of the situation he had heard since arriving in Kabul from India two months ago. "It is true then that Akbar Khan is fomenting the rebellion of the tribes?"

"You do not expect me to answer that question, do you?" She looked across at him, and her jade eyes glinted through the mesh of her veil.

"Then tell me about yourself. You cannot deny my right to be curious."

"In Afghan society, women are defined in terms of the men who own them," she said. "I belong to Akbar Khan. That is all you need to know . . . and all you *may* know."

"You are an Englishwoman! Englishwomen do not *belong* in that barbaric fashion. Do not talk such arrant foolishness!" he exploded, then realized his mistake. The robed men who were riding with them drew rein as one. A harsh exclamation accompanied the sudden appearance of their khyber knives. Fierce black eyes glared their menace.

Ayesha spoke swiftly to them, and Kit heard a note of placation in her voice. She was answered by the chief elder, and a low-voiced argument ensued. At the end, she shrugged, saying softly to Kit, "I may not ride beside you. They do not care for a conversation between us which they cannot understand, particularly when it leads to shouting. They sense a threat, but cannot identify it, and it is their duty to watch over me."

Any argument he might have made died on his lips as the ferocious glares continued in his direction, and hands moved over the knives. He was aware of Abdul Ali and the sepoys riding behind him, knew that their hands would be on their rifles, knew that they were already jumpy, knew that one shot would ensure all their deaths. He inclined his head pacifically, and dropped behind to ride beside Abdul. The elders relaxed, but changed position so that Ayesha was now riding in the middle of them.

"Tricky bastards!" Abdul muttered again. "Thought they were going to spit you, sir."

"So did I," he said sourly. "But it seems that one must tread very carefully around Akbar Khan's woman."

"How is it that she speaks English like a native?" Abdul wondered aloud. He, of course, had not had the inestimable pleasure of seeing the lady without her clothes. Kit decided not to enlighten him for the moment, and merely shrugged the question aside.

They rode throughout the morning. Despite the September sun, the air carried a bite to it, the first intimations of a mountain winter. The track grew rougher and they were obliged to pick their way over stones and boulders. Once or twice, Kit looked behind to see how the burdened women were faring, but the riders had far outstripped the pedestrians within an hour or two, except for a few of the men whose speed easily matched that of the walking horses. They could hear the calls of the youthful shepherds bouncing against the cliff side, resounding in the rocky gorges.

It was a landscape so barren and hostile that Kit thought it could form the backdrop to his own construction of hell. He had now far exceeded his orders, which were to reconnoiter for two days and report back to brigade headquarters in Kabul on the third day. There was no possibility of his doing that, even if they did not die a gruesome death at the hands of Akbar Khan. But, on the other hand, if he could report on the whereabouts of the rebel leader, could report a conversation with him, then he would have pulled off a considerable coup. And if he succeeded in returning a captive Englishwoman to her own people, such an honorable, chivalrous act could only enhance his reputation. It was an enticing prospect, made all the more inviting by his certainty of the rightness of the mission. Whoever she was, whatever her history, she did not belong with these people, and Lieutenant Christopher Ralston fully intended to return her to her own.

"Notice the scout, sir." Abdul Ali drew his attention from this preoccupying reverie, pointing to a rocky escarpment ahead. A figure, jezzail held on his shoulder, stood looking down on the path. "We must be close," the havildar said. "They seem to be providing an escort."

Indeed, horsemen were appearing, silent and shadowy in the rocks alongside the path. The nomads showed no interest in the escort, although they kept pace, still at a distance, with the little procession. Kit wanted to ask Ayesha if this was normal practice, or was it in honor of the British troop? Had the news already reached Akbar Khan of the unexpected visitors? He urged his mount forward, until it was nudging the tail of her companion's horse. The man made a threatening gesture with his whip and snarled something.

"I just wish to speak with the lady," Kit said in his halting Persian, smiling and nodding in vigorous, innocent friendliness as he gesticulated toward the shrouded figure of Ayesha, riding just ahead. "A question for Akbar Khan," he ventured. The name appeared to have some magic attached to it. The man eased his mount sideways, permitting Kit to draw alongside the gray Arabian.

Ayesha did not look at him, but kept her face forward. "We are being watched by those with considerably more influence than these nomads," she said quietly. "You should not be speaking to me."

"Will Akbar Khan be expecting us?" he asked, barely moving his lips and keeping his eyes on the track ahead. "These scouts will report to him?"

"Yes, he will know. He will not know why or how you come to be with us, and I think he will reserve judgment until he does."

"And if he does not reserve judgment?"

"Then you are all dead men."

Her ability to state so blandly such an extremely unpleasant fact struck him as both unwomanly and unfriendly. Of course, that was if he was judging her as an Englishwoman. As an Afghan, there would be nothing callous about such an attitude. It was simply the pragmatic acceptance of a way of life. He fell back again, feeling the first uncomfortable prickles of misgiving about his grand rescue design.

The great stone fortress appeared suddenly, seeming to hang over the defile they were traversing, perched precariously on a rocky outcrop at the far end of the narrow pass.

Their shadowy escort closed around Kit and his men; silent, bearded, turbanned, they made no gesture of acknowledgment. They passed through a group of mud-walled huts clustered before the great iron gates of the fortress. People came out of the huts and stood gazing at the strangers with the almost prurient curiosity that folk at home evinced toward the more grotesque exhibits in the fairgrounds. Kit felt the hair on the back of his neck lift, his spine tingle. What craziness was this? He, who until that wretched business in London had never done anything that would jeopardize the comfortable, accustomed, pleasure-oriented course of his life, was following some idiotic, foolhardy whim . . . out of chivalry, blinkered imperial patriotism, and just plain fascination with a woman. You'd think he would have learned after his last trouble over a woman . . . and he couldn't even blame the demon drink on this occasion. Good God, he'd be the laughingstock of Horseguards Parade, if the tale ever got back. The debonair Kit Ralston falling victim to a woman's wiles! Except that there were no wiles to speak of.

They passed through the gates, inside the battlements. It was a fortified village, with barracks and stables, a great stone keep; there were a number of robed figures, some wearing steel helmets with vertical prongs, all hurrying about a clearly warlike business. The gates clanged shut behind them, and Kit felt the tension arrow through his men. He had no right to involve them in a personal quest that was rapidly becoming an obsession, had he? But they were soldiers, and this was a war. Forget the girl, he told himself, and concentrate on the war prize to be garnered from this expedition.

"Let's show them what the British cavalry is made of, Havildar," he said briskly.

Abdul Ali grinned. "With pleasure, sir." He shouted an order to the sepoys behind him. There was a crackle and jingle of harness. The horses stepped out, their riders smartly at attention, and the British Empire, in this small representation, prepared to go eye to eye with Akbar Khan.

Their escort simply matched the increased speed until they reached a square house, set behind a stone wall and standing in an incongruously pretty garden. They rode into a courtyard at the rear of the house. Kit signaled his troop to draw rein, and they sat, still at attention, watching and waiting.

Two women, veiled but not enwrapped in the street chadri, emerged from an arched doorway at the side of the building. The men around Ayesha moved aside and the women came over to her, rais-

ing their hands to help her dismount. Scorning the
proffered assistance, she slipped easily to the
ground. She cast a glance over her shoulder to where
the lieutenant and his men sat their horses; seemed
to hesitate; then, coming to a decision, took a step
closer to Kit.

"If you would treat with Akbar Khan, Christopher Ralston, be bold and truthful."

One of the women flew up her hands and let loose
a stream of protestation as Ayesha spoke to the infidel. She seized the girl's arm and hurried her toward the arched doorway.

Christopher watched the white-wrapped figure
disappear. Only then did he become aware of the
eyes upon himself. He turned his head toward another doorway, set square in the middle of the back
wall of the house. A man stood there, stocky and
broad-shouldered, dressed in a plain brown coat, a
saber thrust into the sash at his waist. He wore neither turban nor skullcap, and his hands were pushed
deep into the pockets of his coat. A bright blue gaze
rested in gentle speculation upon Lieutenant Christopher Ralston and his men. Then he turned and
went into the house.

Akbar Khan approached the entrance to the zenana, his expression still thoughtful. The two guards
salaamed as he passed through the rich beaded curtain into the women's apartments. He enjoyed the
sounds of the women, their soft trilling, the occasional chime of laughter, the warm moving mystery
of them in their secret, scented seclusion. They were
gathered around Ayesha, now divested of the
chadri, sitting unveiled upon a low divan. She
looked up as he entered, rose slowly, salaamed with
the rest of the women, who vanished in a twittering
cloud at the slight dismissive movement of his hand.

"So what have you brought me, Ayesha?" He
tapped the tips of his fingers together, regarding her
pensively.

Ayesha was not deceived by the calm question,
the apparent relaxation of the powerful body. After

nearly eight years in Akbar Khan's zenana, she knew every facet of this passionate, contradictory man. If he did not like her answer, or suspected the least falsehood, those men would die, and she would have to take the consequences of her own bad judgment.

The encounter by the lake must be buried deeper than the earth's core. And that strange prickle of excitement she felt when in the company of Christopher Ralston must be buried with it, even beyond her own acknowledgment.

"I trust you are not displeased," she said, turning to a side table where stood a bowl of sherbet. "You will take refreshment?"

"My pleasure or displeasure awaits your explanation," he said, waving aside the goblet she held out to him. He sat on the divan and gestured to the ottoman at his feet. "Why would you bring the feringhee into my castle?"

She took her place on the ottoman and picked her words carefully, starting from the precipitate arrival of Lieutenant Ralston and his troop in the nomad encampment. As always, she was alert to every indication of Akbar Khan's mood or attitude, every shift of position, every flicker of an eye, flutter of an eyelash, twitch of a muscle. She thought she knew how he would react to her suggestion that no harm could come from hearing what Kabul had to say at this delicate moment in the hostilities, when the rebels seemed to have the upper hand, but one could never be certain of Akbar Khan. It was his unpredictability that made him such a dangerous foe, and such a quixotic lord.

When she had told her tale and fallen into an expectant but uneasy silence, he stood up. "I shall judge this Christopher Ralston for myself. Let us hope that his mission is an honest one, and your own instincts without fault." He strolled to the curtained doorway, then paused, turned, and examined her, stroking his small pointed beard, as she stood quietly waiting for his departure to release her.

Something flickered in the bright blue gaze, a gleam that sent a shiver of apprehension down her spine. "You will join us for the entertainment after we have dined, Ayesha. I am interested in seeing how the Englishman behaves in the company of one who is of his own, yet not of his own."

The curtain rustled softly at his departure and she stood, chewing her lip. The danger was far from past. In fact, it could be said to be just beginning. He had detected something in her explanation that did not satisfy him, but it was not sufficiently suspicious to convince him of some misdoing, either on her part or on theirs. So he would continue to withhold judgment, watching and waiting until he found what he sought, or was persuaded that the mission was genuine. But what was the significance of that last order? That uncomfortable little gleam? What was he going to be testing? Or should it be whom? Herself . . . or Christopher Ralston?

The women came back into the room, chattering, but she turned from the questions and attentions, threw a veil over her head, and stepped into a small, enclosed garden. A parakeet screeched noisily from the perch where he was chained. She picked up a handful of sunflower seeds and fed them from her palm to the bird, who squawked and danced excitedly. But when she had no more seeds in her palm and had neglected in her absorption to take away her hand, the sharp beak pecked viciously at the soft mound at the base of her thumb, drawing blood.

She snatched her hand away with a cry of pain that brought one of the men guarding the garden running across the grass toward her, his knife raised to decapitate the errant bird.

"No!" she exclaimed in horror. "It was my fault."

The man regarded her in surprise, but he thrust the knife into his belt and returned to his post.

Ayesha lifted her veil slightly so that she could suck the wound. Treacherous bird, biting the hand that fed it. If Christopher Ralston merely looked upon Akbar Khan's Ayesha with interested eyes,

then he would stand accused of a similar treachery.
She wandered restlessly around the small space.
What had he said, when she had asked him his business? She could still hear his voice, quiet and steady.
I was looking for you.

She shivered. Did he understand anything of
these people? And if he did not understand, or
would not accept, the nature of a khan's power over
his subjects, particularly his own women, then they
were both in the gravest peril. Was it simply a mischievous, taunting game that Akbar intended to play
with Christopher Ralston? Or was there a grimmer,
more menacing purpose behind it? And whatever it
was, how was she to ensure that Christopher Ralston behaved with circumspection?

Akbar Khan, the son of the deposed shah, might
be a fugitive rebel, but he certainly knew how to live
well, Kit reflected, looking around the comfortable
chamber into which he had been escorted by an expressionless, heavily armed gentleman, who had indicated the porcelain jug of hot water, the towels,
the carafe of fruit juice, the plate of sweetmeats, and
the basket of fruit, before bowing himself out, leaving Lieutenant Ralston to his own devices.

Abdul Ali and the sepoys had been escorted in a
different direction, but neither threat nor discourtesy had been offered any of them so far, so he assumed they were receiving the hospitality consonant
with their position. If he was to be granted audience
with Akbar Khan, he had better concoct some convincing message. Should it come from Elphinstone?
Or Macnaghten, perhaps? The Envoy, as the latter
was titled, was the chief political officer in Afghanistan from the East India Company's Civil Service.
Yes, definitely Macnaghten. Everyone knew it was
the Envoy who made all the decisions in Kabul, over
both General Elphinstone and Shah Soojah. But
what would that pompous, self-important, complacent idiot wish to have conveyed to this rebel warrior? Threats? Promises? Conciliation?

If you would treat with Akbar Khan be bold and truth-ful. Ayesha had taken a risk to give him that advice so publicly. Why not tell the truth, as far as it went: he was sent from Kabul on a reconnoitering mission. Where better to explore than the lion's den? He wished to hear Akbar Khan's views on the present situation, and would gladly answer any questions directed to him. You couldn't get bolder or more truthful than that, he decided. But how did it advance the main goal of this suicidal expedition? How was he to get Ayesha out of this fortress, two days' ride from Kabul?

Circumstances would have to offer the answer to that one. He could make no plans when he had no idea of the layout or of what was to happen next. Perhaps he would not see her again while he was here. No, that was an altogether unhelpful specu-lation, the product of a sleepless night. He flung himself down on the cushioned divan beneath a low window and fell instantly, dreamlessly asleep.

Akbar Khan stood outside the window, examining the fair sleeping face. It was a face that carried all the insignia of his class and race, and the Afghan's lip curled contemptuously. In a few years, the marks of dissipation and self-indulgence would rub out the clear lines of his features, thicken the aquiline nose, slacken the sculpted mouth, coarsen the smooth skin stretched taut over high cheekbones. The muscle would turn to flab as the pursuits of the gaming ta-bles, boudoir, bottle, and dining room took prece-dence over the energetic activities of youth. It was not an unintelligent face, however. Perhaps he did have some understanding of the realities of the sit-uation, unlike the majority of those idiots, purblind in their arrogance, huddling in the ill-protected can-tonments outside Kabul, confident that the majesty of the British raj would prevail without the least as-sistance from themselves.

But what dealings had this Ralston had with Aye-sha? Akbar stroked his short black beard, a frown

appearing between his unusual blue eyes. They had
spoken English together . . . natural enough . . . but
her escort had assured him that the woman had been
correctly covered from head to toe the entire time.
Could she have told him her history in the short
time they had spoken together? If the reports he had
received were accurate, and he had no reason to believe they were not, then she could not have had
time for any detailed explanations. But the Englishman must be intrigued. And what of Ayesha? Had
she also been intrigued by her first encounter with
one of her countrymen in eight years? Of course she
had been. It had been her attempt to hide that that
he had detected earlier, when he had sensed a lack
of forthrightness in her account.

Akbar Khan turned away from the window. He
could hardly blame her for such a natural reaction,
but she must learn not to dissemble with him. Maybe
he would play a little game with them both, one that
would make all their relative positions perfectly
clear. A smile tugged at the corners of his mouth. It
was not an unpleasant smile: capricious, rather.

He glanced up at the sun. It was still early afternoon, and he could afford an hour or so in the pursuit of pleasure before turning his attention to the
lieutenant and his business. It had been four weeks
since he had left Ayesha in the fortress at Madella—
four weeks of hard campaigning—and a little of her
softness would not come amiss this afternoon. It was
strange how no other woman would do when he felt
this need. After three or four weeks' absence, he
would find himself sending for her from wherever
he had last left her in his present nomad existence.
She had had this hold on him for the last five years.

Akbar Khan strolled in the direction of the zenana.

"Ralston, *huzoor.*"
The low voice finally penetrated Kit's sleeping
brain. He opened his eyes onto a bewilderingly unfamiliar scene, and for a few seconds could not ori-

entate himself. A brown face, skullcap set over ringlets, dark eyes, the soft-spoken courtesy title, all were unfamiliar. Then his head cleared. He sat up, recognizing that for the first time in months, he had woken without a hangover. He did not count this morning, since he had barely slept all night. He felt amazingly fit.

"The sirdar awaits you, Ralston, *huzoor*," the man said in Persian, using the same soft, polite tone.

Kit felt fit, but he also felt filthy. He had a two-day growth of beard, and the dust of the plain caked his skin and clung to his tunic. He needed no circumventable disadvantages when he met with Akbar Khan.

"I must wash and shave," he said. "And my clothes need to be brushed." He made appropriate gestures, but his attendant seemed not to need them. He nodded and gestured that the lieutenant should follow him.

They walked through an arched corridor, open on one side to a mosaic-paved courtyard, and turned through another archway into a steam-wreathed chamber.

"Please . . . " His escort indicated the square tiled bath set into the floor, before raising one of the heavy metal cauldrons set over braziers along the far wall of the chamber. Hot water hissed onto the tiled bottom of the bath, to be followed by the contents of the second cauldron.

Ayesha bathed in cold mountain lakes. The memory, disconcertingly arousing, yet perfectly apposite, caused Kit some embarrassment. He yanked off his boots and stockings, then, turning his back on his attendant, shrugged out of his tunic, peeled off his britches and drawers, and stepped hastily into the hot water. The simple comfort of hot water effectively banished the awkward manifestations of arousing memory, and he lay back with a deep sigh of pleasure.

His attendant gathered up the discarded clothing and soundlessly left the room, returning in a short time with a razor, comb, and hand mirror. He stood stolidly by the window while Kit bathed, shaved, and combed his hair. As he stood up, stepping out of the bath, Kit heard the sounds of laughter outside. It was women's laughter and he found himself straining to identify the merry, infectious chime that he had heard only once before. But it was not to be heard now, any more than was the uncomfortably mocking chuckle that angered as it provoked.

Perhaps she was with Akbar Khan.

He scrubbed his skin dry with rough, almost punitive vigor. If he was to get himself and his patrol out of the stronghold of the chief sirdar in the Afghan resistance, let alone rescue the woman, he must concentrate on the important issues. Ayesha's congress with the rebel military chief was an irrelevant distraction just at the moment.

"If Ralston, *huzoor*, would be so condescending . . ." His attendant spoke in that same soft, almost obsequious tone, holding out a white *chapan*.

Kit took the cloak-like garment with a nod of thanks, wondering why the tone did not convince. But, of course, there was no need on God's earth for this man to play the servant to a feringhee dog who was in essence a prisoner. His unease deepened as the sensation of playing mouse to an unseen cat became undeniable.

His own clothes were waiting for him in the room allotted to him. They had been brushed, pressed, the buttons polished, his boots shined. They would pass muster even before Harley's eyes, he reflected, thinking of his conscientious and fastidious batman, presumably enjoying a little leisure, safe and sound in Ralston's bungalow in the cantonment.

Clean skin and tidied clothing did give a man a degree of much-needed confidence, Kit found, as he followed the still expressionless attendant through more corridors. The sense of being in an armored fortress was made constantly manifest. Large, powerful men, heavily armed, stood at doorways, outside windows, marched across briefly glimpsed courtyards. Yet the richness of tapestries, mosaics, Bokhara carpets belied the essential function of the place. Was Akbar Khan as much of an enigma as his palace-fortress?

A heavy tapestry hung across an arched doorway. The tapestry was drawn aside. Lieutenant Christopher Ralston of the East India Company's Cavalry stepped into the presence chamber of Akbar Khan, son of the deposed Dost Mohammed, sworn enemy of Her Imperial Majesty, Queen Victoria, and all her representatives.

Akbar Khan rose from the cushioned dais as the soldier entered. "Ralston, *huzoor,*" he said, smiling, stepping forward, hand outstretched in welcome. "This is indeed an honor."

Kit took the hand, felt the strength in the grip, and found himself wishing he were a million miles from this mountain stronghold, even as he wondered at the demented, chivalrous impulse that had led him here.

"I understand you have business with me," the sirdar was saying, drawing his guest toward the dais. "Let us discuss it now, if you are willing, then we will eat and enjoy a little modest entertainment."

Kit banished everything from his mind but the need to match wits with his stocky, powerful, apparently genial host. They sat on the cushions, and Kit was offered a drink of some mild spirit, Akbar Khan saying blandly that he hoped his guest would find it palatable. He himself did not touch alcohol, of course, but would not impose the rules of Islam upon an honored guest.

Kit took a token sip, found it pleasant, but decided that he would join his host in abstinence. He could afford no preventable disadvantages, as he had already concluded. "I am most grateful that you would do me the inestimable honor of receiving me, sirdar," he said formally. "Sir William Macnaghten is most anxious to have some exchange of views with you. I have been so deputed."

"I see." Akbar Khan nodded thoughtfully, stroked his pointed beard, sipped a little sherbet. "And what does Macnaghten, *huzoor*, wish to hear from me, would you say?"

Kit looked at him, and smiled. "I am certain, Akbar Khan, that Sir William would wish to hear that you had withdrawn your opposition to Shah Soojah. I am certain he would like to hear that your occupation of the passes between Kabul and Jalalabad would now cease, and that you and your fellow sirdars would no longer interfere with our communications and supply lines with India."

Akbar Khan laughed, a wonderful, rich laugh that sounded entirely genuine. "Ralston, *huzoor*, I like you," he stated. "I have time only for those who are prepared to be bold and truthful, as you will discover. You may take that message to your Sir William."

Ayesha had stood his friend, Kit reflected thankfully. He relaxed a little, leaning back into the cushions. "If we restore the subsidies to the tribal chiefs, Akbar Khan, would you make some concession in return?"

"There will be no concessions, Ralston, *huzoor*, not while an alien yoke lies upon our land; not while one drop of blood still runs in our veins." The calmness of the tone merely added to the resonance of the words.

Kit heard again Macnaghten's voice, lightly contemptuous as he dismissed the inconvenient insurgents. What had he said? *The people are perfect children, and they should be treated as such. If we put one naughty boy in the corner, the rest will be terrified.* Dear God! The man had clearly never met Akbar Khan.

The khan's bright blue eyes held a glint of amusement now as they watched the young lieutenant's expression. "What more have we to discuss, Ralston, *huzoor*? Will you tell me that Macnaghten and General Elphinstone intend to accompany Sir Robert Sale on his return with his brigade to India? Will

you tell me that they intend to subjugate the Ghilzais once and for all on that march?''

Christopher shook his head. ''No, sirdar, I will
not tell you such things. If your information is correct, then you must know that for yourself. If it is
incorrect, then it is no task of this envoy to amend
it.''

''But I have given you something to take back to
Kabul, my friend. Have I not?''

The extent of the rebel's knowledge of British
plans? Yes, he had been given that, just as he had
been given a glimpse into the physical strength of
the rebels, and the cohesion of their command.
Christopher smiled again.

''Indeed you have, Akbar Khan. But am I to be
permitted to take that information back to Kabul?''

The military chief looked injured. ''You have eaten
my salt, Ralston, *huzoor*. Do you doubt my honor?''

''I cast no aspersions on your honor, sirdar. Your
hospitality is most gracious,'' Kit said smoothly. ''I
assume it is in your interests that I report to Kabul
on what I have learned.''

''I will not question your assumptions. Let us
dine.'' Akbar Khan clapped his hands, and the servants standing around the chamber went smoothly
into action. Great bowls of succulent, savory stew
and rice were placed on low tables drawn up to the
cushioned dais, and other men came in to join them.
They were clearly warriors of some standing in Akbar Khan's military court, their coats smart and
close-fitting, their sabers shiny, their pointed beards
well-groomed. They offered salaams to both their
sirdar and his guest, and sat down on the cushions
around the table.

The conversation, out of deference to Kit, was
conducted in Persian, and Akbar Khan courteously
translated whenever he saw his guest in difficulties.

''You speak English with great skill,'' Kit complimented, dipping his fingers into the stew and scoop-
ing up a mouthful in emulation of his hosts.

Akbar Khan smiled with a hint of mischief. He

trailed his fingers in a finger bowl where dried rose petals drifted, and wiped his hands clean with great deliberation. "I had a rather unusual teacher."

Kit stiffened, but made no overt sign of particular interest. "Indeed?" he queried politely.

"Yes, I think you have made her acquaintance." The heavy-lidded eyes ran lazily over the lieutenant's face. "I understood from Ayesha that you and she had some conversation."

How did he know he was now approaching a most perilous edge? What had Ayesha said of their meetings? She would not have mentioned the encounter by the lake. He took a tiny sip from the spirit in his goblet and shrugged easily. "She interceded for us with the nomads. I think that without her intervention they would have attacked us."

Akbar shook his head sorrowfully and tutted. "They do not always welcome strangers, Ralston, *huzoor*, particularly in the uniform of the feringhee. It is most regrettable, but they are ignorant men." He smiled blandly. "I am certain you understand."

Kit nodded, responding with equal blandness, "Of course. But I was nevertheless most grateful for the lady's interest. It averted what could have been a most unpleasant incident for all concerned. I explained that I wished to meet with you, and she seemed to think that you would perhaps not be unwilling." His eyebrows lifted in query.

"No, I was not unwilling," Akbar Khan said, passing his guest a bowl of mulberries. "These are a great delicacy, Ralston, *huzoor*. We call them *tut*. The nomads bring them up from the plains."

Kit scooped a handful into his mouth. They were delicious, small and sweet, and he made the correct appreciative responses, all the while wondering if the subject of Ayesha was now closed for good. He certainly could not revive it.

Akbar Khan said something in Pushtu to a hovering servant and the bowls of stew and rice were removed, baskets of mulberries and apricots remaining. A tray of sweet cakes was brought in, and goblets of sherbet that tasted to Kit like honey. The men belched their satisfaction and settled back into the cushions. Akbar Khan smiled at his guest.

"We will have a little music now, if it would please you, Ralston, *huzoor*. And a little dancing. There are one or two of our women who are most accomplished."

Kit acquiesced with decent enthusiasm, then froze. A graceful figure, clad in a cream-colored satin *chalvar* clasped low on her hips, a richly embroidered, sleeveless turquoise tunic, and a cream-colored veil drawn over the lower half of her face and fastened with a glinting emerald at her ear, glided through the archway. He could not see her hair, but those jade eyes were unique. . . . They would be unique anywhere, not just in this mountain fortress.

She came over to the dais, salaamed to Akbar Khan, and said softly to Kit, "*Jur hasti, huzoor.*"

Akbar Khan chuckled. "She is asking if you are harmonious, Ralston, *huzoor*. It is a greeting of our people."

"*Zendeh bashi,*" Kit responded promptly.

His host applauded admiringly. "I am honored that you would trouble to learn some words of our language. The feringhee, in general, consider it unnecessary."

The feringhee, in general, did not receive advice from such a one as Ayesha, Kit reflected, trying not to devour her with his gaze. He was not supposed to have seen her in anything but the enveloping chadri. She had just spoken to him in Pushtu, so perhaps he was not supposed to realize who she was. He looked merely polite and waited.

If Akbar Khan was disappointed at this lack of reaction, he did not show it. "You must have wondered how Ayesha became so proficient in your language," he said, with another chuckle.

Kit looked him in the eye. "She spoke as an Englishwoman, Akbar Khan, not as someone who had learned the language as a foreigner."

The heavy-lidded eyes narrowed, hiding their expression. "How astute of you, my friend. Ayesha, remove your veil."

She unclipped the emerald pin, and the veil fell away from her face. It was Akbar Khan who rose from his cushion and drew the filmy material from her head, revealing the rich burnished copper mass hanging in a heavy plait to below her waist.

He was not supposed to have seen her before, Kit reminded himself fiercely, even as he gazed at the entrancing countenance, the incredible whiteness of her skin, the vibrant curve of her mouth, the deep green depths of those almond-shaped eyes.

Akbar Khan looked at them both . . . and then he smiled. "It is the custom of our people, Ralston, *huzoor*, to share our most treasured possessions with honored guests . . . to ensure our guests' comfort and pleasure at all times." The smile broadened. He laid a hand lightly on the girl's bare arm. "For tonight, my honored friend, Ayesha is yours."

Through his own stupefaction Kit saw shock, followed rapidly by anger, spring into the jade eyes. She swung round on Akbar Khan and said something fiercely in low-voiced Pushtu. His response cracked through the room like a ringmaster's whip, and she stepped back as if he had struck her. The sirdar turned back to Kit, and the blue gaze was now cold and sharp as a hawk's.

"You do not refuse the gift of hospitality, do you, my friend?"

Kit glanced around the room, seeing only hostility and menace on every face. No one moved so much as a muscle. If it was a trap, he had no choice but to spring it. He must think like an Afghan. He bowed to Akbar Khan.

"I am deeply honored, sirdar, and accept the gift most willingly." His eyes flicked toward the motionless Ayesha, who looked straight through him.

Akbar Khan rubbed his hands together with the air of one who has achieved a happy resolution. "Good. Let us listen to some music."

Without a word, still expressionless, Ayesha moved to sit on a cushion beside Christopher. Taking up the bowl of mulberries, she offered it to him with lowered eyes, before refilling his goblet.

Chapter 3

Kit kept his eyes on the floor before the dais. A group of musicians played strange and sometimes arousing music with reed pipes and rhythmically thudding drums. The girls who danced for them were a mere blur of golden limbs and swirling veils. Their eyes were heavily outlined with kohl, their skin shimmering with sweat as they whirled and quivered to the insistent demand of the music. But he was conscious only of Ayesha at his side. She said nothing, sat as if graven in stone, except when she attended to his wants, offering fruit, sherbet, and the sticky cakes, holding the finger bowl for him, handing him the towel, all these services performed with lowered eyes. Yet, despite this, he could feel the furious energy surging through her, the depths of her rebellion, and he could feel Akbar Khan's eyes on them both; eyes that were speculative and mischievous in a completely unplayful fashion.

Finally the sirdar abruptly called a halt to the music. The girl who was dancing came to a panting, quivering standstill, salaamed, and vanished from the chamber, the musicians at her heels. Akbar Khan turned to his guest. "I hope you are not in too much of a hurry to leave us, Ralston, *huzoor*. I would show you another of our customs in the morning, which you might find entertaining. We are to have a game of *buzkashi*. Do you perhaps know of it?"

Christopher shook his head. "I do not."

"Then, my friend, you have much to learn. It is our game of life, and will tell you much of the Afghan character." He patted Kit's arm in avuncular fashion. "You will amuse yourself, I trust. And you must not hesitate to tell me in the morning if Ayesha fails to please you in any way at all."

A tremor ran through the slender body at Kit's side, but she remained silent, merely touching her hands to her forehead before gesturing that he should follow her. She moved ahead of him unerringly through the corridors, across a courtyard, and paused at the door of the chamber that had been allotted to him. Here she stood to one side, waiting for him to precede her.

He did so, and the door closed behind her. "In what way may I please you, Ralston, *huzoor?*" she asked in wooden accents.

"Don't talk such nonsense!" he whispered fiercely. "What was I supposed to do? If I had refused, they would have slit my throat on the spot."

Instead of responding, she moved swiftly to the window, drawing the shutters together tightly. Then she went to the door, gently, soundlessly, shooting the bolt across. "There are guards everywhere, and they have large ears."

He stood looking at her. The soft yellow light of an oil lamp touched the high cheekbones with a golden glow, caught the luster in the burnished copper of her hair. He felt the most heady sense of unreality. She had been given to him . . . and that appalling, barbaric gift excited him shamefully. He fought down the excitement. "What is behind this? Do you know?"

"Akbar Khan is a man of powerful passions," she said slowly. "And strange caprices. He loathes the British, with a loathing so deep it should strike terror in the heart of every one of you in this country." She began to pace restlessly around the chamber, straightening a cushion, peering into a jug to check its contents, fiddling with the cakes and fruit laid out upon the table. "Do not ever be deceived by his geniality, Christopher Ralston."

"My name is Kit," he heard himself saying. "Can you not be still for a minute?"

She came to a stop. "Whatever you command, Ralston, *huzoor*."

A flash of anger prickled his spine. "Let down your hair."

Surprise flared in her eyes. Then very deliberately she did as he said, unplaiting the rich mass, loosening it with her fingers. It was long enough for her to sit on, he noted dreamily.

"I still wish to know more of what is behind this," he said, trying to sound calm and businesslike. "Why would Akbar Khan give you to me? You, who are guarded so closely, and treated with such care. Why would he do it?"

"To humiliate you," she said simply. "He would strike at the base of your pride by forcing you to acknowledge the power of an Afghan over one of your own race . . . and over you. You had no choice but to pick up the cards he laid down." She shrugged. "He is a man of many paradoxes, as I said. But hatred of your race and all you stand for is the most powerful force in his life."

"It is your race too," he reminded her.

She shook her head, saying with a hint of mockery, "No longer, Ralston, *huzoor*."

"It is!" He strode toward her, taking her shoulders, feeling the fragility of the collarbone, the soft curve of her upper arms. She looked up at him, and gave him that taunting little smile.

"I do not bear your labels or live by your rules, feringhee," she said as she had done once before.

It infuriated him, but it was as if she were insulting herself as much as him and everything he represented. And deep down, he knew his anger came from misgiving . . . from the incredible idea that she might not respond to the possibility of rescue. His fingers tightened; his gray eyes hardened. "So why would Akbar Khan do this to you, Ayesha? He would humiliate me by offering me an English-woman as my bed slave. Is he not also humiliating the Englishwoman in *you?*"

"I am being reminded that I must not make a habit of taking too much upon myself," she said with another shrug of indifference. "I overreached myself in bringing you here. He is unsure why I did so, but if it had anything to do with my feeling any interest in you . . . as a man . . . as an Englishman, perhaps . . . then he has demonstrated that I may feel what I wish, but I know where and to whom I belong."

"And do you feel any interest?" he asked without volition, the question whispering in the soft, lamplit night. He moved a hand to cup the curve of her cheek, to trail a finger over her cheekbone, to trace the firm line of her jaw. And he felt her tremble. "I should feel shame," he whispered, "but I do not. Any more than I feel humiliated by Akbar Khan's gift. I want to take this that has been given to me. I want it more than anything I have ever wanted. You have filled my every thought, waking and sleeping, since I saw you in the lake."

"The gift is yours to take," she said, but there was a catch in her voice. "It is an Afghan's gift of an Afghan woman. You need feel no shame in the taking."

"It is *you* I want," he said with sudden savagery. "Neither Afghan nor English . . . *you.*"

"But *I* am not to be given or taken," she replied, her eyes steady, although he could feel the heat of her skin beneath the tunic, the tremors that quivered through her. "Not where I am unwilling. This—" Her hands drifted down her body. "This can be given and taken, but *I* cannot."

Slowly he brought his mouth to hers.

To what lofty concept had she been paying lip service? Ayesha could summon no resistance to the insistent pressure of this kiss. Her head fell back, exposing the soft vulnerability of her throat, and as if in acceptance of the invitation his mouth moved down to press in heated adhesion against the wildly beating pulse.

She *did* want this . . . had wanted it in some recess of her self since he had told her, surrounded by threatening tribesmen, that he had come in search of her. Such a foolhardy quest . . . yet it had sent shivers of excitement and a far from unpleasant apprehension firing her blood and setting her nerve endings aquiver. She had lived so long in her shrouded, guarded seclusion, her experiences limited to and by one man. Now she inhaled greedily of the clean-washed scent of this man, felt the smoothness of his cheek against her own, the distinct hard pliancy of his lips when he brought his mouth back to hers. His hands spanned her back, molded her waist, slipped to hold her buttocks, drawing her against him so that the hard shaft of his wanting throbbed against her thigh.

His voice, guttural, whispered the words of desire, words in this language she had never heard before. She leaned into him, yielding to the passion she knew so well how to feel and to inspire, ceasing to question her motives, or the basis for this vibrant, thrilling longing that gripped them both. It was sufficient unto itself.

He drew back from her, his eyes heavy with desire. "I must see you again . . . as you were by the lake."

She drew the tunic over her head, tossed it to the floor. The bright copper mass fell forward over her breasts, glowing against the whiteness of her skin. Her hands moved to her hips, unclasped the band of the loose, flowing trousers. They slipped to her ankles and she stepped away from the puddled cream-colored satin, standing in the lamplight, offering her bared beauty to his hungry gaze.

He was wandering in a spellbound country, only dimly recognizing that some illicit quality to this encounter heightened his passion beyond any previous experience. It was illicit by any rule he knew—the situation of which he was so shamelessly taking

advantage, barbarous—yet, by some other rules,
ones that did not normally apply to himself, it was
entirely permissible. He did not know whether Ayesha was obeying those other rules, or whether she,
too, felt the wonderful, awful sense of moving beyond experience. Was she Afghan or English? Was
she *herself*? That was the only question that mattered, and he knew the absolute imperative of discovering the answer, of knowing that the woman he
was loving would be responding from her self to his
self.

He raised one hand, gestured with the tips of his
fingers, and she stepped toward him. Slowly, he
touched her forehead, drew his fingertips over her
face, tenderly tracing the curve of her mouth, brushing the slender length of her neck, slipping sideways to follow the curve of her ears. With breathless
wonder, he allowed his hands to drift over her
shoulders, to part the luxuriant strands of hair, to
reveal the tight pink crowns of her breasts. He heard
her swift, indrawn breath and he smiled in soft satisfaction as the nipples hardened beneath teasing
fingertips. He held the rich, warm swell of her
breasts in his palms, felt the jarring thud of her
heart, dropped slowly to his knees, laving the firm
roundness in his hands with hot damp strokes of
his tongue, catching the erect crowns between his
lips, heard her low groan of pleasure.

The softness of her belly invited his kisses, and
his tongue dipped into the tight whorl of her navel.
Her skin rippled against his mouth, the muscles of
her belly contracting involuntarily as his thumbs
pressed hard against the sharp points of her hipbones. His hands slipped around to clasp her bottom, and she leaned away from him, her weight
resting in his grasp as a deep quiver of anticipation
ripped through her.

He moved to press apart her thighs, to caress her
with long strokes, to taste the inimitable essence of
her, to feel her shudder with joy at the crest, to fall

limp against him, languid and formless in the aftermath of the joy he had given her.

Only then did she whisper his name. She spoke his name, "Christopher," lingering over the syllables, as she knelt with him. Her fingers busied themselves with the shiny buttons of his tunic, her mouth danced against his, tasting herself, teasing him to new heights of arousal. She drew off his tunic, kissed his nipples, trailed fire down his chest as she unfastened his britches, sliding them off his hips, her lips searing the flesh as she uncovered it. He was aching with longing, beyond the possibility of greater stimulation, but she pushed him down onto the rich carpet, lay alongside him, exploring, teasing, pleasuring as he had done for her, and he discovered that all limits could be extended.

She moved away from him for one yearning minute, kneeling up to lift the lid of a marquetry box resting on a low table. His face revealed his surprise as he looked at the little slip of lambskin she held in the palm of her hand, and she smiled softly, touching his lips with hers. "Akbar Khan's guest rooms are equipped for any eventuality. If I were not here, some other woman would have been offered to you, and she would have been no more anxious to conceive than I; pregnancy is for wives."

For a minute he did not know how to respond to this shockingly matter-of-fact statement. A little glimmer of uncertainty lurked in her eyes. "You do not mind, do you?"

He was not unfamiliar with the simple prophylactic, but he was not accustomed to its being proffered by a woman. But this was no ordinary woman, in no ordinary place or time. Accepting it as simply another manifestation of this forbidden landscape over which he was wandering with such uninhibited joy, Kit shook his head, reaching up to stroke the curve of her mouth. "How should I?"

Delicately, her fingers a caress, she slipped the sheath onto him, making of the act a further loving arousal, so that he closed his eyes on an exhalation of delight.

Drawing her beneath him, he held himself above her, looking down on her face. Her eyes smiled up at him. A pearly blush mantled her cheeks, her mouth curved with the pleasure of giving and receiving.

"Who are you?" he whispered.

"Annabel," she said.

He bent to kiss her eyelids, thrust deep within her, felt her body convulse in glory, and was lost himself.

For long moments they lay, still locked together, in the utter silence of the lamplit room, then slowly Kit hitched himself on his elbows, looking down at her with a rueful smile in his eyes. "Oh, dear," he said softly. "I was as precipitate as a virgin lad. But I have never been so inflamed, beyond all possibility of control."

Her head moved in languorous denial on the rug. "It was the same for me." She reached up to touch his face. "We have all night, Kit. There'll be time enough to take our time."

He turned his mouth into her palm, tasting the salt-sweet dampness of her skin. "Annabel," he murmured, lingering over the sound. "Annabel." Gently, he disengaged, rolling away from her and sitting up. "Now, will you tell me about yourself, Annabel?"

"I have not heard that name spoken for eight years," she said, rising gracefully to her feet. She went over to the table where the jug and basin stood, pouring water on a towel and coming back to him. Kneeling beside him, she ran the soothing cloth over his body, encouraging him to lie down again as she cleansed and freshened his skin.

He lay back, enjoying attentions to which he was quite unaccustomed. The women he had known hitherto were more inclined to receive than to give. But then Ayesha had been taught in a different school. He was no longer lost in the wild and

thoughtless realms of passion, and this time the reality jarred. He sat up abruptly. "That is enough."

She looked startled. "Does that not please you?"

"It reminded me of a fact I would prefer to forget," he said frankly. "Give me the towel." She
handed it to him without a word, and he went himself to the basin, dampened the cloth and came over
to where she still knelt on the floor. "Stand up."
He held his hand down to her, pulling her upright.
Globing the soft mound of one breast, he gently
sponged the translucent, glistening skin. "Let me
do it for you, now, while you tell me, Annabel, how
you come to be in this place, with these people."

Annabel shook her head and shivered suddenly,
her arms wrapping around her body in some reflex-
ive gesture of defense. "It's just a story . . . not important."

"Not important! How could you possibly say such
a thing?" He took her hands and held them away
from her, saying in sudden wonder, "You are
frightened."

She was, she realized. The prospect of digging up
those early memories of the petrified child, memories she had buried so deep they had ceased to
bother her, brought a cold shiver of remembered terror prickling her flesh. She tried to pull away from
his hold, turning her head aside from the steady
gaze. "I do not wish to talk of it."

Kit experienced what was for him a most unusual
reaction. He wanted to care for this woman in her
pain, wanted to soothe and comfort and reassure her.
He could not recall ever being stirred in quite this
way before, ever wanting to be bothered in quite
this way before. He released her, picked up a blanket from the divan, and wrapped it securely around
her. "There is no need to be frightened," he said
softly, taking her in his arms, lifting her onto his
knee as he sat on the divan, cradling her tightly.
"Tell me about it, Annabel."

"My name is Ayesha," she said, but the statement lacked conviction.

"Tell me," he pressed, stroking her hair as if she were a child in need of reassurance.

She sat silent for long minutes, allowing him to hold her, all the confidence and certainty with which she had faced him in the past quite evaporated. "We were on our way back to Peshawar, through the Khyber pass," she began in a strange, tight voice.

He listened, saw through her words the violent deaths of her parents, heard the dreadful screaming, the wild tribal yells, felt the appalling terror of the abducted child. "Then what?" he prompted when it seemed she would not continue. "Was it Akbar Khan who took you?"

"No." She shook her head. "It was many dreadful weeks before I came to Akbar Khan." She stared into the abyss of memory, then sat upright. "Let me up."

"May I not hold you?" he asked, amazed at the wash of tenderness he felt.

"I am not accustomed to being held in this way," she said with perfect truth. "Such gentleness is not the Afghan way."

"I did not realize it was mine, to be honest," Kit said.

She smiled suddenly and slipped back into his embrace. "The Ghazi who took me kept me for many weeks. I did not know then that he was waiting for Akbar Khan to come to his fortress at Madella. I was to be given to the sirdar as tribute that the Ghazi owed his leader. He decided that I would be a suitable tithe, more interesting than goods or cattle . . . and cheaper, too," she added, finding the story grow easier with the telling.

"I did not know this, of course, so assumed I was doomed to live forever with the man's family in a mud hovel."

"How were you treated?" asked Kit, feeling another tremor run through the slender body he held.

"Cruelly," she said baldly. "By the women, not by the men. I suppose they did not know what to make of me. I could not speak their language, did not understand anything. They ill-treated me, I think, because they were so accustomed to ill-treatment themselves. Victim became persecutor . . . it's a seductive role.''

Kit thought of the women he had seen that morning, struggling beasts of burden, toiling up the mountain. He tried to picture a twelve-year-old English girl, gently nurtured, grown in love, subjected to the torments of such an existence, and a powerful rage surged through him.

Annabel felt it in the broad frame at her back, in the sudden tightening of the arms around her. ''You cannot judge them by your standards, feringhee,'' she said with that hint of mockery he had heard before. ''They have much to endure.''

''Don't call me that again,'' he said, and there was no mistaking the warning in his tone.

She twisted in his hold to look at him, a speculative gleam in the jade eyes. Then she shrugged. ''But you are, and like the rest of your kind make no attempt to understand the Afghan. If those in command in Kabul had made the slightest attempt, you wouldn't be in this mess now.''

''We seem to be drifting from the point,'' he said stiffly.

''Are we? I don't think so.'' She got off his knee and began pacing around the room. ''Anyway, when Akbar Khan arrived at Madella, I was taken to him . . . a filthy, emaciated scrap in the tattered remnants of the clothes I'd been wearing when I was abducted. But by that time I understood and spoke a fair amount of Pushtu. So that when the Ghazi tossed me down in front of this man, who was dressed in helmet and chain mail, and said I was a gift to his sirdar, I understood—'' She bit her lip. ''I understood that I was in a hell, and there was no way out except death. I called the Ghazi a 'son of swine,' and several other of the worst epithets one can use to a Muslim. He knocked me to the ground, but before he could do anything else, Akbar Khan ordered him from the room.''

She took an apricot from the basket on the table and bit deeply into the golden flesh. "So that is how I came to Akbar Khan's zenana. I taught him English, and he taught me Persian. I asked for books, and he provided them, both in English and in Persian."

"And he taught you other things," Kit said, as dry as the summer plain, shrugging into the *chapan* he had worn that afternoon.

She made no pretense of misunderstanding him. "Yes, he did. But not until I was fifteen. He is connected by marriage to several of the chief tribes among the Ghilzais, but he keeps me apart from his wives, for which I am thankful. And I have a great deal of freedom for an Afghan woman."

"God Almighty! You are not an Afghan woman!" Kit exploded, outraged at this calm statement. "You are Annabel Spencer."

"I am Ayesha," she said calmly. "And content to be so."

"When I leave here, you are coming with me," he declared. "I do not know how it is to be achieved, but I will restore you to your own."

Her laughter chimed through the room. "If you could hear yourself," she said. "Such grandiose words! The Englishman will restore the captive to her own people. . . . You would play Knight of the Round Table, would you? Take the blinkers from your eyes, feringhee, and look at the situation clearly."

"Goddamn it! I told you not to say that!" He sprang across the room toward her. Where had this anger come from, banishing the wondrous passion of a bare half hour ago? Banishing the surge of tenderness he had felt; his need to hold and protect her. Now he wanted to shake her until she acknowledged the truth of who and what she was, denying whatever identification she seemed to feel with the Afghan.

She stood her ground, simply drawing the blanket more tightly around her. "There is no possible way

I could leave here, even if I wanted to," she said, slowly and carefully. "*You* will not leave this fortress if Akbar Khan decides that you may not. And I do not believe that any one of you will leave Afghanistan alive."

He stood, shivered into stillness by her words and the utter conviction they held. "What do you mean, you do not wish to leave here?" he asked. "You cannot possibly wish to remain a prisoner in some zenana."

"Why not?" She shrugged. "I am not sure that it differs too much from being a prisoner of the social and moral laws of an army cantonment in India. I grew up in such a society, remember? At least here I have horses and hawks, the mountains, and the company of those who are not hypocrites, however strict their laws. My life is far from dull, Christopher Ralston. I travel with Akbar Khan across the length and breadth of this country, and he denies me only what Koranic law forbids."

Kit felt the world as he knew it tip on its axis. How could she be saying these nonsensical, heretical things? And not just saying them . . . she meant every word of it. The truth shone from those jade-green eyes. To her, he was simply a blind, arrogant feringhee, and the world he would offer her, a stale and drear place of stuffy etiquette and hypocritical rules. And, if he were honest, that was the way he saw it himself. He played with that world, despising it, finding it shallow and unsatisfying. Why else did he fall into a drunken stupor night after night? Lose a small fortune regularly at the tables? Why else had he provoked those ridiculous duels that had earned him banishment into the outer darkness of the East India Company's Cavalry?

"You must have family in England," he said lamely.

She shook her head. "What if I have? They mean nothing to me. I have never been there. My life here has meaning. Even if I wished to, can you imagine how such a one as I would fit into that society? No,

Christopher Ralston, go back to your own, and leave me with mine."

"You called me Kit before," he said, still struggling to make some impact on this wall of conviction off which his words just seemed to slide, flat-surfaced, without the grip of his own belief.

"An error," she said, dropping the blanket. "A slip of the tongue in a moment of passion. I no longer use the intimate language of the feringhee."

He wrung his hands. He wanted so much to use them to break through this barrier that denied everything he had been brought up to believe in; to make some impact on the wall of superiority she had erected between them. "Was that all it was? How can you say that was all it was?"

She turned from him, bent to pick up her clothes. "Do you have need of me again tonight, Ralston, *huzoor?*"

If she would play that game, then he would play it too. "Yes, Ayesha," he said. "I do. You are Akbar Khan's to bestow on whom he chooses. He has given you to me tonight. And the night is but half over."

The clothes dropped from her hands, a soft silken pile of cream and turquoise. Slowly she straightened, keeping her back averted. "What would you have of me?"

He looked at her, the long, clean sweep of her back, the shoulder blades sharp-pointed, the indentation of her waist, the flare of her backside, the seemingly limitless length of leg. And he was lost in a welter of bewildering emotion. He desired her, wanted her body, wanted the skill with which she used her body to pleasure his own. But there was more . . . much more. There had been a moment when she had given him her self, but now she had withdrawn it, and he wanted that back.

He caught the thick mass of her hair, twisting it into a heavy rope, lifting it away from her as he bent to kiss her neck. Her skin danced, supremely responsive, beneath his lips. The tip of his tongue slipped warmly up the groove of her neck, found the soft spot behind her ear . . . the spot on his neck where she had held the tip of her stiletto, he remembered with a low chuckle that sent warm breath tickling into her ear.

Ayesha wriggled. He held her shoulders and she became still, poised.

"Did I not hear you say that we had enough time to take our time, my Anna?"

Her head bent in mute acknowledgment and she made no demur at the soft, loving intimacy of the name. He drew her backward to the divan, pressed her into the cushions. Her body gleamed white, fingered by gold as she moved in the lamp-glow. There was a moment when she tried to hide the light in her eyes, veiling them with heavy red-gold lashes, but he nibbled her earlobe and the lashes swept up, revealing laughter and the deep, smoky glow of resurgent passion. And once again, she gave him her self, without restraint.

Chapter 4

$\sim\!\!\circlearrowright\!\!\circ\!\!\sim$

Ayesha left his side in the translucent, pearl-pink light of early dawn.

"Must you go?" Kit smiled sleepily, hitching himself on one elbow, propping his head on his hand. "There are so many things I still want to do with you."

Her eyes scrunched up at the corners, giving her an air of mischievous speculation. Then, disappointingly, she shook her head. "The night is finished, Christopher Ralston. I was given to you for a strictly defined period."

"Don't talk in that fashion!" He sat up, reaching for his *chapan.* "How are we to get out of this place?"

She said nothing for a minute, watching as he stood up. He had the lean, muscular body of a horseman and athlete, slim-waisted, narrow-hipped . . . and all the ardor and energy of youth. They had enjoyed each other during the long hours allotted them, enjoyed each other with the vigorous, uninhibited pleasure of lovers who had found a perfect fit of body, imagination, and spirit. But Annabel Spencer was as much a realist as Ayesha. She had grown into adulthood in an environment where the stuff of dreams was unknown, where hopes were based strictly upon the planks of reality, where pleasure could yield to suffering without warning.

"You will leave after the *buzkashi,*" she said. "I do not think Akbar Khan will wish to detain you

57

after that demonstration. He will have made his point."

"But you are coming with me." He tried to infuse calm determination into the statement, to make it sound as if there was no question, but she laughed, and it was that mocking sound that so dismayed him.

"No, Ralston, *huzoor*. As I have said, even if it were possible, and it is quite *im*possible, I would not come with you."

"But how can you say that, after the night we have just passed?" He was uncomfortably aware that his voice resembled that of a bewildered child, a relatively accurate reflection of how he felt.

Ayesha struggled for patience. "Kit, I would not denigrate what has passed between us. It gave me pleasure beyond description . . . beyond any I have known. But you must see things clearly, distinguish between serendipity and the hard facts. I will never forget last night, and—" She paused, reached up to his forehead where a lock of fair hair flopped untidily. She twisted the lock around one finger, smiling gently. "And I will live in the belief that you will never forget, either . . . not even when you are married and the proud father of a tribe of children. You will remember our loving. Even when it has become only a dream-memory, it will warm you in the coldnesses of the spirit that touch us all from time to time."

"I will not leave you here."

She stood on tiptoe and lightly brushed his mouth with hers, trying to mellow the hard set of his lips with her own softness. "I may not see you again. Women do not attend a *buzkashi*. Kiss me in farewell, Christopher Ralston, and be thankful for what we have had. Do not let me go from you remembering anger at the last."

In the past forty-eight hours Kit had learned the wisdom of apparent compliance. He said no more, but held her to him, running his hands down the smooth, warm skin of her back, savoring the curve of her bottom and the firm thighs, imprinting her shape on his hands' memory, her scent in his nostrils, the taste of her lips on his own.

With one last lingering touch of her mouth on his, she slid from his embrace, slipped into her clothes, and glided to the door. She drew the bolt and was gone from him.

The guards outside the door glanced at her with the incurious eyes of men who saw no need for interest in the activities of a woman, since those activities were male-dictated. She moved with the leisured, graceful step she had learned over the years. Akbar Khan did not care for an impetuous pace, an overhasty remark, a thoughtless gesture. This most passionate and unpredictable of men insisted on the most peaceful and orderly behavior in those who peopled his leisure time and ministered to those of his needs not directly related to warfare.

Ayesha reached the zenana and was immediately enclosed in the familiar seclusion, lapped by the established rituals of this feminine sanctuary. The mysterious telegraphy of the palace had operated throughout the night, and the women all knew where she had spent the hours of darkness, and at whose command. The knowledge was not declared, but very little was openly declared in this place of secret understandings.

She had no wish to talk, and no one attempted to intrude upon her reserve as they undressed her, bathed her in hot, scented water, gave her green tea out of a delicate porcelain cup. She drank gratefully and retired to her divan in the private chamber off the main living area. There was a little hovering, straightening of sheet and quilt, closing of shutters, then the tapestry over the door swung back into place, the door closed gently, and she was left to sleep.

But sleep eluded her, despite her bodily fatigue. She was filled with a curious yearning, mingling with the deep elation that comes from having been, for however short and temporary a period, transported by ecstasy, out of mind and body. The appetite for loving was definitely one that grew whereon it fed, she thought, tossing restlessly, her mind filled with images of the night, her body hungering for more. She knew, of course, that if there were a certainty of more, the hunger would die down, permitting the peace of satiation. But there could be no repetition of those glorious hours. It was high time she reassumed the mantle of acceptance that she had worn without apparent difficulty for the last few years. On which bracing instruction, she fell asleep.

She awoke several hours later to the instant awareness that she was not alone. She opened her eyes onto the steady regard of Akbar Khan, sitting in complete, meditative stillness on the divan beside her. He reached out and touched the corner of her mouth.

"So, Ayesha, you passed a pleasant night, I trust."

"Was I intended to?" she countered boldly.

There was a moment of tense silence, then Akbar Khan laughed. "I confess that was not my chief motive. But I have no objection if you took some pleasure from the lesson. The lesson itself still stands."

She stretched languidly, yawned deeply. "I should not, then, have brought Christopher Ralston to you?"

The blue eyes narrowed. "You should not have attempted to hide from me that you found the feringhee intriguing. You must think me a fool, if you believed I would not know. It is only natural that you should react in such a manner." He stood up. "But now you have had the opportunity to satisfy your curiosity, you may put it behind you." He walked to the door. "The *buzkashi* will begin at noon. Your presence will add further spice to the demonstration."

Ayesha sat up, staring at the tapestry, still swinging slightly in the aftermath of Akbar's departure. She nibbled her lip. His intention had been even more complex than she had thought. Had she not enjoyed the night, then he would have been satisfied that the reminder of the absolute nature of his dominion had been well given. If she *had* enjoyed it, then he had shown her most effectively his power to give with one hand and take away with the other. Having teased her, whetted her appetite so to speak, he would deny any extension of that experience.

She shrugged in resignation. He was an imponderable man on occasion, but she had accepted that a long time ago and had long ceased to resent his whims. There was no such thing as perfection in this world. In general, he gave her the life she wanted, and if he pulled on her chain once in a while, then she could live with it. She was much more interested in the prospect of attending the *buzkashi*. It was a rare treat that she should be permitted to watch this quintessentially masculine spectacle. Was the permission offered as an olive branch? Or did Akbar Khan have an ulterior motive for her presence, as he had done last night? Impossible to tell! And it didn't matter, anyway. She would have the pleasure of Christopher Ralston's company for a short while longer. It would be tantalizing, but half a loaf was better than none at all.

The cliché reminded her that she was ravenous. She rang the little silver bell on the table beside the divan and swung her legs to the floor with a renewal of energy.

"You wish for something, Ayesha?" An elderly woman appeared in answer to the summons.

"*Nan-i-roughani,*" she said, her mouth watering at the thought of the thin, flat wheat bread crisply fried in clarified butter. "And eggs, please, Soraya."

The attendant nodded, pursing her lips slightly. "I'll have them prepared for you while you dress. You must wear the chadri for the *buzkashi*, otherwise you will offend." She did not add that Ayesha's very presence at the masculine rite would offend, but her disapproval was evident in the pursed mouth.

"I merely obey our master," Ayesha said demurely.

Soraya sniffed. She was all too well aware of the scandalous license Akbar Khan permitted this unusual member of his zenana, but not a word of criticism of the sirdar would pass her lips.

Ayesha dressed in the *chalvar* and tunic and for one minute had the strangest sensation. She remembered vividly what it was like to wear the boned bodice, the petticoats, stockings and garters, the voluminous skirts of her own people. It was almost as if she could feel both the slight pinch of the whalebone that she had worn since her eleventh birthday, and the dragging weight of her skirts in the heat of an Indian summer. How could she ever have endured such restriction? Just the thought of such clothes made the enveloping chadri seem like the most liberating garment. And it had one great advantage. It concealed not only her body. Her expressions were as securely hidden from observation, and she need fear no inadvertent betrayal of her emotions . . . something for which she would be grateful, when in the company of Christopher Ralston, under the eyes of Akbar Khan.

A wide shoulder above the mountain pass supported a broad, sandy, upland arena. Lieutenant Ralston and his patrol were escorted from the fortress by a silent party of turbanned, warrior hillmen mounted on magnificent Badakshani chargers, huge, sleek, arrogantly majestic beasts with wild eyes and flaring nostrils. Kit, gazing at them with unconcealed envy, was aware that Abdul Ali's expression mirrored his own.

"What could a man not do on such an animal?" the havildar murmured. "Mount the British cavalry on those, and we'd be invincible."

"I thought we were," Kit said sardonically. "At least, that's what I have been led to believe. We wouldn't be here otherwise, would we?"

Abdul Ali cleared his throat but made no other

response, since he could neither agree nor disagree with any propriety.

"What is this *buzkashi*, sir?" he asked after a minute.

"It means goat-grabbing," Kit said, having asked Ayesha the same question. "It's a trial of strength, I gather. They have to pick up the carcass of a goat or calf while on horseback, and carry it free and clear of all the others trying to do the same." He frowned. Ayesha had told him that this bald description could not begin to convey the flavor of the contest, and looking at their escort on their splendid mounts, he could believe her.

"*Salaamat bashi*, Ralston, *huzoor!*" Akbar Khan, on a Badakshani charger even more magnificent than those they had seen, hailed their arrival cheerfully, galloping across the upland toward them. The sirdar was clad in a rich, fur-edged jacket and loose britches tucked into riding boots, a round fur hat upon his head. He was bright-eyed and genial, yet Kit detected an undercurrent of excitement, or anticipation, in his posture and in the curve of his mouth. The Englishman did not find it in the least reassuring.

"*Mandeh nabashi*," he responded correctly, offering his host a courteous salute that Abdul Ali and the sepoys instantly imitated.

"Come, you must position yourself on that ridge over there." Akbar Khan gestured with his whip. "You will have the best view of the proceedings from there."

"Do you also take part, then?" inquired Kit.

"Oh, but of course. I was taught from the age of twelve the skills necessary for a *buzkashi* player—how to pick up anything from the ground when riding at high speed, for instance. Also, my father would plant a silver marker in the ground, and I would ride at it at full gallop and shoot at it with my bow and arrow." Akbar laughed merrily. "One learns a great deal of control and accuracy, Ralston, *huzoor*, from such exercises."

"I believe you," Kit said truthfully, looking around the natural arena where some thirty men jostled on horseback, all with the same air of impatient expectancy, of barely leashed energy and determination. Then he saw the figure in the white chadri, mounted on her gray Arabian, atop the ridge toward which they were riding. His heart turned over.

Almost as if he were aware of his guest's reaction, Akbar Khan glanced slyly at him. "Yes, Ayesha is also a spectator. She will be able to interpret the game for you. Like all Afghans, she has a perfect understanding of its significance."

Kit bit his tongue. Nothing would be gained by rising to provocation, and he knew all too well the degree to which Annabel Spencer had adopted the attitudes and behaviors of the Afghan Ayesha.

She offered no greeting as the party reached the crest of the ridge, did not even look in Kit's direction. Akbar Khan smiled broadly.

"Ayesha, I leave my guests in your hands. You will be able to answer any questions Ralston, *huzoor*, may have on the proceedings."

Permission having been granted, she turned toward Kit and offered the ritual greeting. He responded blandly, although his hands felt clammy in his gloves and his mouth felt strangely stiff as he formed the words. He could see no more than the jade glint behind the insert in her chadri, yet his mind's eye was filled with the image of her as she had been for him, sinuous and white in her nakedness.

"It is said the game originated with the horsemen of Genghis Khan," she informed him calmly, as Akbar Khan rode off toward the milling horsemen. "One man must succeed in grabbing the carcass of the goat . . . you see it over there?" She pointed with her whip to a large shape lying in the center of the arena. "Once he has grabbed it, he must hold on to it and gallop free and clear of the rest." A chuckle entered her voice. "All the rest, of course, are intent on grabbing the carcass back."

Kit nodded, absorbing this information. Some thirty magnificently mounted, superb horsemen all after the same prize . . . and all fierce in their determination to gain it. "Free and clear?" he queried.

"Exactly, Christopher Ralston," she declared with a laugh. "You have grasped the point. How free is free, and how clear is clear? There are no spatial demarcations on the ground."

She was talking to him as if they had never spent last night in each other's arms. He knew why, of course. They were not alone; the arena was surrounded by eager, cheering men from the fortress, and present on the ridge were three tribal elders, armed to the teeth, their eyes never moving from Lieutenant Ralston's patrol, making manifest the fact that they were well within the reach of the long arm of Akbar Khan's malicious mischief. Again the sensation of playing mouse to an unseen cat assailed Kit. Except that now he knew the nature of the cat, just as he knew that the all-consuming hatred Akbar Khan bore the English provided motive for his taunting little games.

"You *must* leave here with me," he heard himself say in a fierce involuntary whisper.

"You should pay particular attention to the *jorchi*," she said in neutral tones, as if he had not spoken. "When it is decided that a player has achieved freedom with his prize, the *jorchi* will sing in his honor, making up the verses as he considers appropriate. He is like a minstrel, a balladeer, whose task is to provide impromptu entertainment for the crowd. I will translate for you when the time comes."

"Thank you," Kit said dryly. "Your assistance will be invaluable."

"It is my pleasure, Ralston, *huzoor*."

"I could wring your neck!" he hissed.

"They are beginning. Watch carefully now."

He gritted his teeth in frustration and forced his

attention to the arena. Then he forgot all else but the excitement of the drama being played out before him.

Akbar Khan was easy to distinguish by the fur trim of his garments and his richly caparisoned horse. For a moment, everything seemed confusion. Wild yells accompanied frenzied forays into the seething melee as each man fought to get close enough to the carcass and correctly positioned to reach down and seize it. Suddenly, out of the violent jostling mass, Akbar Khan appeared, breaking free of his pursuers, one leg of the dangling carcass held by both hands, the reins gripped tightly between his teeth. The strain of the weight he was carrying was etched on his face. As three men bore down on him, yelling in frantic excitement and threat, he whirled his horse at breakneck speed away from them, shielding the carcass with his body as he bent low over the saddle and raced across the arena.

"Oh, do not drop it!" Ayesha gasped, impassivity vanished as she jumped up and down in her saddle. "Is he not the most magnificent rider?"

Kit wanted to resent the fervency of her praise, but could not. He could only agree with the sentiment. He himself had a considerable reputation as a horseman, but was under no illusions that he could compete with Akbar Khan in such an instance as this. The thrills of fox-hunting across the best country in England seemed tame beside the furious pace and endurance of this *buzkashi*. And the skills of a huntsman would be of little practical use here.

A great roar went up from the crowd as Akbar Khan was momentarily surrounded by rivals, but again he broke free, still hanging on to the prize, driving his great black horse across the upland, outstripping his pursuers.

"He is free and clear," Ayesha said, slumping suddenly in her saddle. "The crowd has said so."

Indeed, the crowd of spectators was cheering, applauding, some even firing rifles into the air. Akbar

Khan reined in his horse, turned back to the arena. His rivals fell back and the *jorchi* rode into the ring, lifting his voice in a resounding tribute to the victor.

"He is saying that Akbar Khan has the speed of the antelope, the spring of the leopard, the heart of the black bear," Ayesha translated swiftly. "Will you tell me it is flattery?" Again that mocking laugh was in her voice. "In the *buzkashi*, Christopher Ralston, you see the true strength and power of the Afghan. They will fight to the death, and will give no quarter. The British army in Kabul must believe very strongly in itself, if General Elphinstone thinks he is going to subjugate the Ghilzais."

Kit grimaced. "How can you despise your own people?"

"They have done nothing to deserve my respect," she replied shortly. "This . . . " She gestured toward the arena. "This is deserving of respect. It may be uncivilized, barbarous even, but it is honest and true. They value strength, courage, and determination. You will find no hypocrisy here."

"And what of treachery?" he demanded. "You would deny the treachery of the Afghan, the broken pledges, the stab in the back, the ruthless cruelty, the indiscriminate murders of innocent women, children, merchants?"

She shrugged. "They do not see it as treachery. They are honest about their lying." A chuckle entered her voice. "It is permitted if it will save a life, patch up a quarrel, please a wife, and deceive in war the enemies of the faith. Their dealings with the feringhee fall into the latter category. They are untouched by your so-called civilization, Ralston, *huzoor*, and they will pour out their blood to resist an alien yoke. You will never master this nation."

"Goddamnit, woman, one day I will master you!" Kit exploded, pushed beyond bearing by this blind allegiance to savagery.

"How like an Afghan," she mocked. "You see how easy it is to pick up their customs."

His face darkened; his hands curled impotently

around the reins. He knew he had sounded ridiculous; he felt the same way Annabel did about the vaunting, posturing idiots in Kabul; but they were still his people. As they were hers, if only she could be brought to acknowledge it.

Akbar Khan had thrown the carcass back into the center of the arena, and the horsemen were gathering for a renewed foray. Suddenly, the sirdar held up a hand and turned toward the ridge, his voice in ringing challenge echoing off the cliffs.

"Ralston, *huzoor!* Do you care to match the horsemanship and strength of the British cavalry against that of the Afghan?"

"No!" Ayesha whispered, all mockery gone from her voice, a thread of panic in the one word. "You cannot, Kit."

He turned to look at her, and felt the cold emptiness that comes from making the only possible decision. "Do you doubt me?"

"They will humiliate you, if they do not injure you," she said. "You cannot outride them."

"It is about time you realized, Annabel Spencer, that there is some backbone to the race of your birth," he declared icily.

"Sir." Abdul Ali moved his horse forward. "We're with you."

Kit glanced at his men. Not a flicker of emotion showed on the brown faces, not a hint of alarm in the steady eyes. "Very well, Havildar." He shook the reins and his horse broke into a canter, then galloped down the ridge toward the milling crowd of horsemen and the triumphant Akbar Khan.

Annabel felt sick. If she had not taunted him, he would surely not have accepted Akbar's absurd challenge. Why did she needle him? But she knew why. It was an effort to pierce the complacency she assumed he shared with all the other British in Afghanistan. She had grown up imbibing with every breath the violent contempt and loathing for the feringhee. But she could not also imbibe the easy, automatic acceptance of a wholesale massacre as the

only possible weapon against the invader and vengeance for the invasion. Her very soul revolted
against the idea in a way that she knew betrayed
her essential alienation from the people who had
adopted her. She did not believe the Europeans
could all be as bad as Akbar Khan made out, or as
the arrogant laxity of the British administration in
Kabul seemed to confirm. She had adored her parents, was convinced they could not have fitted the
mold presented to her by Akbar. But then she would
feel a stab of doubt. After all, she had been but a
child then. Spoiled, precocious, difficult. How often
had she heard the description in long-suffering pa-
rental accents. How could she trust the memories
and judgments of such a child at such a distance?

So she had tried to force upon Christopher Ralston some understanding of the true nature of the
enemy. And because of the conflict between her
learned loathing of what he represented and her instinctive revulsion at the fate Akbar Khan and his
fellow sirdars had decreed for them, her attempt had
been clumsy. Instead of compelling him to recognize
the danger, she had driven him with her mockery
into its arms. In the arms of that danger, he would
certainly come to the acceptance of the realities she
had been trying to instill. But it would be a hard
lesson.

She did not believe that Akbar Khan intended Kit
any serious physical harm. But he did mean to humiliate him, as he had tried to do last night. He
would send him away from here with his tail between his legs to report on the strength, the indomitable courage, the invincible purpose, the wild
savagery of the enemy. And she did not think she
could bear to watch that humiliation. But even as
her heart shrank with anticipated pain, she could
not drag her eyes from the arena.

Kit acknowledged Akbar Khan's gesture of welcome with a cool smile as he assessed his rivals. A
ferocious bunch, he decided, but what else had he
expected. The now somewhat mangled carcass of the

goat lay at some distance. It must weigh anything
from sixty to eighty pounds, he thought with a dis-
passion that surprised him. He could not possibly
succeed in getting free and clear with the prize. His
horse was no match for the Badakshani chargers,
and he had not the peculiar equestrian skills and
training of these *buzkashi* players. But he could ensure that he and his men put up a good show. He
glanced over his shoulder at Abdul Ali.

"We work as a team, Havildar. We're entitled to
that advantage, I believe."

The sergeant nodded and the sepoys drew together. A great cry of challenge ripped through the
still mountain air, and suddenly they were engulfed
in movement. For a second, Kit was thrown off bal-
ance, then he fixed his eyes on the carcass and forced
all else from his sight and mind. The swirling,
shrieking mass of horses and men spun around him,
but he rode hard, whipping his horse into the middle of the frenzy, aware that Abdul and the others
were behind him. Someone was leaning low to grab
up the prize; for a breathless second, he had it, was
pulling himself upright; then another competitor
swooped down, seized the goat; there was a brief,
fierce struggle before the carcass slipped to the
ground again. And in that split second, Kit was upon
it. He swung low, was conscious that Abdul Ali had
seized his reins so that he could use both hands to
hold the prize. His head hung below the belly of his
horse and all he could see were pounding hooves
and the rock-encrusted ground. His hand locked
onto the tail of the goat; his knees gripped his saddle with a savage strength he had not known he
possessed. If he could just get his other hand onto
the goat . . . He did it . . . got a grasp on a foot,
hauled the monstrous weight off the ground, himself upright in the saddle. Then they were off, Abdul
still holding his reins, guiding his horse so all he had
to do was concentrate on keeping hold of the carcass. The sepoys were clearing a way through the
seething, screaming throng struggling to wrest the

prize from them. There was one glorious moment when Kit could see only bare terrain ahead, could hear only the thundering of his own mount across the rocky ground.

How free was free? How clear was clear? He could hear Ayesha's laughing explanation of the ultimate catch in this game. With one almighty movement, he hurled the carcass from him, to land with a thud and a spray of sand onto the ground ahead. He would make his own rules. And retire gracefully and with honor. There was a pause, as of a collective catch of the breath. "*Juldi*, Havildar!" he instructed, taking advantage of the grace period.

The patrol obeyed the Hindi order to move quickly, and the seven men galloped away from the fray, back to the ridge, honor intact.

Kit was conscious of the most immense exultation as he rode up to Ayesha, who was sitting her horse, a veiled wraith, completely immobile. "Well?" he demanded. "Were we humiliated?"

She shook her head, and her eyes met his. It was hard to read their expression through the mesh of her veil, but they held his challenging gaze steadfastly. "You were magnificent, Kit. I owe you an apology."

The words were the sweetest balm, a triumph much greater than that he had achieved on the field. "We are not without resources," he said quietly.

She inclined her head in acknowledgment, saying only, "I fear you will need them."

"Well, Ralston, *huzoor*, you are to be congratulated." Akbar Khan rode up the ridge. "There is skill in using the resources at one's hand in an imaginative fashion, and great wisdom in recognizing the battles one cannot win." He smiled benignly. "In recognition, the host begs his guest to ask anything that is within his humble means to grant." He gestured expansively. "A horse of Badakshani, perhaps. You are a worthy rider for such a mount."

Kit looked out over the upland, across to the steep peaks beyond the pass below them, standing out bold, black, and snowcapped against the brilliant blue sky. He looked sideways at the still, veiled figure beside him. "I would have another night with Ayesha, Akbar Khan," he said.

In the deathly hush, the dingy, gray-white bulk of a lammergeyer loomed, hideous and prehistoric, over a narrow gully. Kit found himself watching it intently, as if Akbar Khan's response could not be of particular importance. The figure beside him had not moved a muscle. Where had she learned such immobility? he wondered absently.

"Christopher Ralston, you try my hospitality," said Akbar Khan.

Danger pricked the air like so many nicks of a knife tip. Kit felt his men close rank behind him, just as he felt the Ghilzais on the ridge ready themselves for the word from their sirdar. That word would ensure that they all died a bloody, messy, unnecessary death because Lieutenant Ralston had allowed his present obsession to override caution. He continued to watch the lammergeyer.

"If Ayesha is willing, then I grant your request," Akbar Khan now said, his voice as dry and brittle as old bones.

Kit turned to her, devouring her with his hungry eyes, certain of her response.

Her words fell bell-like into the stillness. "I think, Akbar Khan, that Ralston, *huzoor*, intended to ask that he be granted safe conduct from here, and an escort to the Kabul road."

There was nothing he could do but accept his dismissal. He had hoped, blindly, that in one more night of glory, he would persuade her to leave with him, would concoct a foolproof plan, would ride off with her . . .

"I must bow to the lady's wish," he said in level tones. "We will need no escort, Akbar Khan."

"A guide, however," the sirdar said, suddenly all geniality again. "No . . . Ralston, *huzoor*, I insist. You do not know this territory, and there are many pitfalls." He beckoned to one of the hillmen and spoke rapidly in Pushtu. The man grunted and ranged himself alongside Kit and his men.

"Good-bye, Annabel Spencer," Kit said.

"Good-bye, Christopher Ralston." She did not look at him. "May your God go with you."

She did not look at him, but she felt every yard of the distance growing between them like a gaping abyss. She had had to answer as she had in order to save them both. By offering her that spurious choice, Akbar Khan had been putting her to the test. He would never have forgiven her defection. And if Kit had possessed her, this time on his own terms, the sirdar would have decided that the guest had violated the laws of hospitality and had thus freed the host from the obligations of hospitality.

Kit and his men would have died with the stealthy knife in the back, and no one would have been any the wiser. If only she had had more time to teach him the ways of these people. There were so many traps for the unknowing.

"Return to the zenana, Ayesha." The curt instruction broke into this frustrating reflection.

She had presumably played her part in Akbar Khan's sport with the Englishman, a sport that had not gone entirely according to the Afghan's design. "As you wish." She set her horse toward the fortress, her own escort forming around her, and rode back to the whispering, cloistered world of the zenana.

Chapter 5

"**Y**ou have most flagrantly exceeded your orders, Lieutenant," General Elphinstone quavered from the depths of his armchair, where he sat swathed in blankets, a deathly pale figure, so frail it seemed a puff of wind would blow him away.

"I had hoped, sir, I would be excused, since I bring valuable information," Kit said, standing rigidly at attention since he had not been invited to stand at ease.

"Can't imagine what you think's valuable about a piece of scare-mongering, Ralston," snapped Sir William Macnaghten, Envoy of the East India Company's Civil Service and political advisor to the general. He swung away from the window, where he had been in morose contemplation of the autumnal garden outside Elphinstone's headquarter's bungalow in the British cantonment. "You spend two days with that rebel Akbar Khan, and all you can say is that he's a well-armed savage with a force of equally savage tribesmen. Damn it, man, he's no match for our forces. Colonel Monteath will have 'em by the heels in no time. He's gone to free the passes, clear the communication lines, and we'll have the news of his success any day now. You mark my words."

The surge of anger he felt at this blindness surprised Kit. He thought he was inured to the idiocy, and he thought he had been a deal more explicit than Macnaghten so contemptuously implied. "With all due respect, Sir William, I believe Akbar Khan to

74

be an opponent to be reckoned with. I do not think he will be easily defeated. When someone is driven by such a fierce—"

"Oh, be quiet, man!" Macnaghten interrupted irascibly. "What kind of croaker are you, for God's sake?"

Kit flushed angrily. "I am neither a coward nor an alarmist, sir. But I am capable of using my eyes and ears and drawing conclusions from what I see and hear. Akbar Khan knows that Sir Robert Sale's brigade is to return to India, and that they intend to deal with the Ghilzais en route. He knows that you and General Elphinstone are intending to accompany them." Here Kit paused. It was manifestly absurd to think of Elphinstone accompanying a fighting force in fighting fettle.

"Sale has already left," Elphinstone twittered feebly. "He has taken his brigade to assist Monteath in freeing the Khyber route." He plucked restlessly at his blanket. "It's to be hoped he clears the passes quickly, that I may get away; for if anything were to turn up, I am unfit for it, done up in body and mind."

This was the man who was to maintain British supremacy in Afghanistan! Kit fought to keep the mingled compassion and disgust from his expression. Elphinstone had not always been such a pitiable reed; the fault surely lay with Lord Aukland, the governor of India, who had appointed this broken, debilitated creature to the most arduous command at his disposal.

"So your omnipotent Akbar Khan does not know everything," Macnaghten declared with an air of triumph, seemingly oblivious of the general's last pathetic plea. "I take it mighty ill in you, Ralston, an officer in Her Imperial Majesty's cavalry, that you should run squealing at the bragging of a brigand."

Kit heard Ayesha's mocking laugh; heard the intensity of her conviction that the British would never leave Afghanistan alive; heard both and understood them as never before. And he wished with a passion fiercer than he had ever experienced that he could hear them again, and this time he would feel no need to deny the truths, no obligation to pay lip service to this lunacy.

Stiffly, he saluted, making no attempt to defend himself against the charges of this overstuffed civil servant. "Am I dismissed, General?"

"Yes . . . yes," said Elphinstone, waving irritably toward the door. "Off you go, Lieutenant, and resume your normal duties. Lady Sale is giving a soiree this evening, I understand. Take her my respects and ask if there's anything the mess can provide. Wonderful woman . . . wonderful woman."

"Oh, indeed, General Elphinstone," concurred Macnaghten. "Not a woman to be daunted. Her husband's fighting the damned Ghilzais and she keeps the flag flying . . . tends his vegetable garden, won't hear a word of despondency." He directed a look of derision at the hapless lieutenant.

Kit saluted again, turned smartly on his heel, and left the fetid room, where the smell of sickness seemed catastrophically mingled with the dank odor of suicidal delusion and inevitable disaster.

He strode through the cantonment, bitterly contemplating the role he played in this absurdity. On the general's staff, his main task seemed to be running Elphinstone's social errands for him. "A personable young man," the general had called him when he had first reported for duty—personable enough, presumably, to be preserved from the rough and tumble of soldiering and usefully employed as the general's courier and social secretary. Kit was not unaware that his impeccable lineage, his previous service in the elite dragoons, and his possession of a not inconsiderable fortune were also considered powerful qualifications for the job. They had also been powerful qualifications for his position in London society, a position he had cast away in such cavalier fashion. It wasn't as if the woman had been worth such a grandiose gesture . . . but even as he thought that, he could see Lucy's china-blue eyes, her golden curls, her innocent dependence upon him, this godlike creature who had entered her life, transformed her drab future. He *had* owed her his protection, but perhaps in less flamboyant fashion.

Christopher Ralston swore viciously under his breath, putting the pointless self-recrimination behind him. A series of errors had led him to this doomed situation and futile employment, but they had been his own errors. He could do worse than live with them. Again, the image of Ayesha-Annabel intruded. If anyone was an example of making the most of fate, she was. She had carved out a life and a place for herself in that utterly foreign society; so much so that she would not contemplate returning to the life she would have led if destiny had not intervened.

But she *had* to return! Her opinions and attitudes were informed by the people with whom she had lived since she was just a child. She had to learn the other viewpoint, accept who and what she really was. This one thing he knew: he was not leaving Afghanistan without her.

Such a goal could compensate for his present ineffectual, supremely unimportant position in the scheme of things. He approached Lady Sale's bungalow with something resembling a spring in his step.

"Why, Christopher, this is a pleasure. I had thought you on some mission." Lady Sale straightened from the parterre where she was dead-heading rose bushes and greeted him cheerfully. "You find me in my dirt, I am afraid." She came down the driveway toward him, wiping her hands on her apron. "But there is always so much to do in a garden. I promised my husband I would ensure his kitchen garden was kept in order while he was away, and I have barely had time for my own flower parterres." She gestured at the neatly turned earth behind her. "Not that I expect to see the fruits of this work. I shall be on the road to India as soon as the passes are cleared . . . within the week, I should imagine."

"Indeed, ma'am." Christopher bowed. "Kabul will be the poorer."

"You always had a smooth tongue, Kit," her ladyship declared. "Even as a child." She shook her head. "But come and see Robert's artichokes. And the cauliflowers are better than they've ever been."

Christopher dutifully followed her to the rear of the bungalow, where he admired the rows of vegetables so diligently planted by Sir Robert Sale when he was not out fighting the Afghans. "You are leaving Kabul before your husband then, ma'am?" he inquired as they went into the house.

"It seems I must. He is busy dealing with this latest Ghilzai outbreak. Such a nuisance . . . the mails are just not getting through with this blocking of the passes." She rang a bell in the hall. "So uncivilized of them, don't you think?"

"Most," Kit agreed dryly.

"Ghulam Naabi, tea, please." Lady Sale gave the order to the white-coated servant who appeared in answer to the bell, and sailed into the drawing room. "I am having a soiree this evening, Christopher. Someone has to do something to keep people's spirits up. A loo table, some music . . . probably a little tame for you," she added with a quirked eyebrow, "but it wouldn't do you any harm to spend an exemplary evening for once. I feel I owe it to your mother to keep an eye on you. Poor Letty," she murmured in a disconcertingly loud afterthought.

The days when his beleaguered mama had expected her friends to keep an eye on her errant son had long passed, Kit reflected with an inner smile. Not that it had done much good. The reports so faithfully presented by a series of interested matrons had merely driven his peaceable and slightly scatty mother further into herself, and his irascible father had declared for the thousandth time that his only son was no son of his . . . until he'd arrive on the doorstep in need of a little rustication and his scandalous exploits on the town would be forgotten.

"I am charged with General Elphinstone's respects, ma'am," he said, as if he had not heard her. "Also, if there is anything you need from the mess for the soiree, then we will be happy to supply it."

"Well, how very thoughtful of the general," Lady Sale declared, turning to the samovar, carefully placed on a side table by the servant. "Tea, Christopher?"

Since anything stronger was clearly not on offer, he accepted politely and sat down, prepared to spend the obligatory half hour of a morning visit.

"You will come this evening, Kit, won't you? I would like you to squire Millie Drayton. She's quite a taking little thing, but very shy. The Draytons arrived in Kabul last month, and Millie is much in need of diversion."

Kit thought of his night with Ayesha. And he thought of Millie Drayton. The contrast was so absurd he felt about to burst into a most unseemly and quite unexplainable fit of laughter. "I had planned—" he began tentatively.

"An evening of debauchery and idleness," interrupted her ladyship briskly. "I am not in the least surprised. But you could surely do a favor for one of your mother's oldest friends?"

Kit could only accede gracefully. He had known the old battleax since he was still in petticoats, and there was something about her that he could not help but admire, a certain indomitable side to her nature. He found he did not really resent her comments and interference, and resigned himself to an evening of crashing boredom in the company of the simpering and ingenuous Millie Drayton.

He made his escape as soon as he decently could, walking briskly through the chilly, early October air. He glanced up at the looming mountains ringing this city, perched a mile high in the most inhospitable terrain. Within a couple of weeks, those mountains would be snow-covered, and soon the flat plain around Kabul would be buried beneath drifts, the canal and the Kabul river icebound. The cantonment stood just outside the city itself, and again he became overwhelmingly conscious of how defenseless it was. Apart from the barracks, the mess, and the cavalry riding school, it was a mere suburban huddle of bungalows, each with its little garden, with no walls or fortresses, and separated by the canal and the river from the plain, the mountains, and their passes to safety; the canal and the river each crossed by a single, vulnerable bridge.

In the city itself, the massive fort of Balla Hissar, occupied by the puppet Shah Soojah, and a substantial force of British troops, dominated the landscape. It would surely make better sense to move the entire British contingent—troops and families—out of the cantonments and into the safety of the fort, Kit reflected. But to do that would be to admit to the possibility of danger from these rebellious savages, and such an admission was quite impermissible, an example of croaking. His lip curled as he directed his steps toward the city. His restlessness would not permit a return to his own bungalow, and he decided to wander the bazaars to get some sense of the atmosphere.

It was not a reassuring exercise. Even with only a word or two of Pushtu, he had no difficulty understanding the menace in the glares, the whispers, the occasional shouted insults. Women in their dark chadris flitted from stall to stall, but when they saw the infidel in his pristine uniform, they ducked into side streets or under awnings, pushed out of sight by their glowering menfolk. There were women, of course, in the bazaars who would not hide from him; women who for a certain number of rupees would be more than willing to show themselves. Kit knew where to find them, had done so in the company of his friends often enough, but he had no stomach for the thought now. Something had happened to him in the last three days. He wasn't sure quite what it was as yet, but he seemed to see the world around

him with a new pair of eyes, sharper somehow, yet
less cynical; as if he saw truth and reality without
the overlay of boredom and indifference.

A loud hail from across the street intruded on his
musing. He looked over and saw Sir Alexander
Burnes gesticulating. Burnes was Macnaghten's chief
lieutenant. Unlike the other British, he eschewed the
cantonments and lived in the British residency in
Kabul itself, a house opposite the British Treasury.
He maintained he preferred the company of Afghans, hostile or no, to the tedium of the social
round in the cantonments. Kit was in sympathy with
this, although he found the man a tedious companion. Weak and vacillating, he complained endlessly
of his anomalous position, subordinate to a man who
would give him no specific duties and treated him
with utter contempt. There was certainly no love lost
between Burnes and Macnaghten, a fact which did
not aid the smooth running of the political office in
Kabul.

"Morning, Burnes." Kit crossed the street.

"Heard the news?" Burnes took his elbow, turning him away from the bazaar, dropping his voice
although it was unlikely any of their fellow pedestrians would be able to understand them.

"I doubt it," Kit said. "I have had a most
unpleasant interview with Macnaghten and Elphinstone, and a wearisome half hour with Lady Sale,
but no news was imparted on either occasion."

"Chewed you out, did they?" Burnes said sym-
pathetically. "Well, I shouldn't take much notice of
the old man. He doesn't know what he's saying
most of the time."

"Sir William does, however," Kit said with a gri-
mace.

Burnes offered a barnyard expletive. "He may
know what he's saying, but he doesn't know what
he's doing. Take this latest business."

They had reached the residency, set behind high
stone walls and heavy iron gates. Nothing further
was said until they were indoors, out of earshot of

the sepoy guards and Burnes's household servants. Since this was a household where the samovar made infrequent appearances, Kit thankfully accepted a large brandy and took an appreciative sip.

"News has just reached us that Monteath has been routed by the Ghilzai at Tezeen," Burnes said without preamble.

Kit whistled softly. "And what of Sale?"

"Went to Monteath's support, and his advance guard ran from a Ghilzai skirmish." Burnes sounded as if this grim news afforded him some satisfaction. "Macnaghten's sending him an order to return to Kabul."

"Without clearing the passes," Kit mused.

"Oh, I gather Macgregor, the political officer with Monteath, has negotiated a settlement with the tribes . . . a return of the subsidies in exchange for clearing the passes."

Kit frowned. "You think they'll honor it?"

"Macnaghten says so," Burnes pronounced. "According to Sir William, a stable settlement has now been achieved."

Kit thought of Akbar Khan's declaration that there would be no concessions as long as an alien yoke lay upon the land. He remembered the *buzkashi*. He remembered Ayesha's cold, pragmatic conviction. And he shook his head.

Burnes chuckled. "Not croakin', are you, Ralston?"

"I fail to see why a refusal to subscribe to this cloud-cuckoo-land should be considered croaking," Kit snapped, putting his empty glass on the table. "Thanks for the brandy, Burnes." He stood up, straightening his tunic. "Are you attending Lady Sale's soiree this evening?"

Burnes offered another colorful expletive. "Catch me at that insipidity," he declared. "No, got other plans." His eyes narrowed lasciviously. "Care to join me, Ralston? Found a couple of fillies in the bazaar . . . by God, do they know some tricks!"

"No," Kit said shortly. "I'm promised to Lady Sale."

"Not like you to play the courtier," Burnes observed. "Turning prudish on us, are you?"

Kit laughed, but it sounded hollow even to his ears. "You should know better than that, Burnes."

"Aye, I should." He accompanied his guest to the front door. "Well, when you decide you've paid your debt to society, come and join us. It's going to be a long night, and you owe me a chance to recoup my losses of the other evening."

"Two hundred guineas, as I recall," Kit said, slipping into the old rhythms without volition. "A mere trifle! But if you're setting up the macao tables, then I'll be along."

"Until tonight, then."

Kit walked back to the cantonment, acridly reflecting that it didn't take much for him to revert. What point was there in holding to the truth against such blanket opposition? It wasn't as if he had any power to alter the opinions of those who made the decisions. That had been demonstrated to him with painful and mortifying force. And how the hell did he think he was going to reclaim Annabel Spencer for her own people? Such arrant, prideful foolishness! He was no less ridiculous than those he ridiculed. Mount an attack on Akbar Khan's fortress and carry off the lady across his saddle bow.

So faithful in love, and so dauntless in war . . . There was never knight like the young Lochinvar.

The refrain mocked his romantic imagery, although he supposed Sir Walter Scott had intended no mockery in the tale. Somehow, though, it didn't sound convincing in this mountain-enclosed trap. The umbrella of cynicism went up, and he slid beneath it with barely a whimper of protest. It was comforting in its familiarity, and the barrier offered asylum from hard-edged self-knowledge.

"Oh, Lieutenant Ralston, I do believe you are looed again!" A girlish giggle accompanied the statement, and Kit looked absently at the cards in his hands and those on the table. His thoughts had been so far from Lady Sale's drawing room and the loo table that he had failed to take the trick for the third time during this interminable evening. He shook his head irritably but attempted a light response.

"How foolish of me, Miss Drayton. I cannot imagine how I could have missed it." He placed half a sovereign into the pool. Only limited loo was played at Lady Sale's, for which, in his present state of abstraction, he could be thankful, he reflected caustically. With unlimited forfeits, he could lose a fortune if he continued in this fashion.

"I thought you were an accomplished card-player, Lieutenant," Millie Drayton essayed, batting scanty eyelashes over nondescript eyes. "Your reputation is legendary."

Kit decided abruptly that he could take no more of this fatuous simpering. He pushed back his chair. "I cannot imagine where you received such a false impression," he said, making no attempt to disguise his weary boredom. "If you will excuse me . . . " He bowed to the table at large, pretended not to see Millie Drayton's expression of hurt bewilderment, and went off in search of his hostess. It wasn't really the girl's fault, of course. She was a product of her upbringing, carefully schooled to accomplish the one goal of her sex—a respectable marriage. And all eligible men were fair game. He had been dodging pursuit for the last eight years and had taken a degree of malicious pleasure in the hunt, but for some reason the exercise had lost its savor.

"Oh, Kit, are you really leaving so soon?" Lady Sale looked up from her embroidery in the circle of similarly occupied matrons. "I had thought you young people would enjoy a little dancing; just a set or two. I know Mrs. Bennet would be happy to play." She nodded toward the drab wife of an elderly colonel, who hastened to assure her ladyship that she was entirely at the service of the young peo-

ple. "Yes, of course you are," her ladyship said
briskly, it not having occurred to her that anyone
might hold a differing opinion to her own. "I will
instruct Ghulam Naabi to roll back the carpet."

"I wish I could stay," Kit lied smoothly, "but I
have regimental duties, I fear."

"At this time of night?"

"It is barely ten o'clock, ma'am," Kit said. "I must
receive my orders for the morning."

"Oh, well, if you will not stay, you will not." Lady
Sale abandoned the lost cause, waving a dismissive
hand at him.

Kit bowed over her hand and made his escape
with heartfelt relief. The night air was sharply cold,
the stars bright in the mountain sky, the ground
scrunching frostily beneath his booted feet as he
strode through the darkened cantonment, his
thoughts centered on the prospect of brandy punch,
macao, and the relaxing company of like-minded
friends.

Burnes greeted him with exuberant enthusiasm,
his scarlet complexion, bloodshot eyes, and thick-
ened speech ample evidence of the way he was
passing the evening. In the smoke-wreathed library
at the back of the house were to be found six of Kit's
intimates, all in a state similar to their host's, loung-
ing with tunics unbuttoned and feet propped upon
the hearth. They hailed Kit's arrival with flattering
pleasure.

"Haven't seen you in days, m'dear fellow," Captain Markham stated, bending over the punchbowl.
"Thought you were supposed to be back from that
patrol a week ago." He ladled the steaming, fra-
grant liquid into a goblet and handed it to the new-
comer.

"I was . . . Thanks, Bob." Kit drank deeply.
"That's better. If that excuse for punch at Lady
Sale's had seen more than a whiff of a wine bottle,
I'll be damned."

"What were you doin' at that gathering?" demanded another, setting a taper to a small cheroot.

"Not your usual form of entertainment, doin' the pretty with the matrons, is it?"

General laughter greeted this undeniable truth. Kit undid the top button of his tunic and flung himself onto a couch. "Lady Sale's a friend of my mother. Couldn't really say no." He grimaced. "I was supposed to squire little Millie Drayton . . . insipid child that she is."

Someone nodded in solemn agreement. Social obligations to friends of one's mother really could not be avoided. "So what delayed you on patrol, Kit? Some delectable little Afghan filly?"

There was renewed laughter at this manifestly absurd sally; such entertainment would hardly be found during a routine patrol in the mountains.

Kit closed his eyes dreamily as the potent liquor warmed his belly, relaxed his toes, and created a gentle fuzziness in his brain. "No . . . not quite, but I've a tale to tell, my friends; one you'll find hard to believe . . ."

The tale was a long time in the telling, since Kit omitted only the part about his night with Ayesha. His impressions of Akbar Khan, the *buzkashi*, and most of all his impassioned conviction that Annabel Spencer must be brought back to her own people were dwelled upon with a fervent intensity, made the more so as his glass was frequently replenished by an attentive host.

"Lord, that is a story," Bob Markham breathed into the stunned silence. "An Englishwoman in Akbar Khan's zenana! You quite sure, Kit? Hadn't been dippin' too deep, had you?"

"What on?" Kit's scornful laughter cracked in the warm room. "Mussulman hospitality is conspicuously short of the demon drink. Besides, I wasn't inclined to risk losing my wits," he added. "Not in that company."

"Well, I'll be damned!" muttered a bewhiskered lieutenant, peering into his goblet as if some answer might be found there. "It's not right." He looked up, twirling his moustaches restlessly. "What are we goin' to do about it?"

"I wish I knew, Derek," Kit said. "I've been racking my brains trying to devise some plan for winkling her out of there, but that fortress is sewn up tighter than a Christmas goose." He did not add that the lady in question had refused point-blank any offer of rescue. In fact, any description of her at all had defeated him. She was so far outside the experience of anyone in this room; quite unlike any category of womanhood with which they were familiar.

"It's always possible Akbar Khan will show himself," Alexander Burnes said. "I don't think he's likely to remain holed up in the mountains for much longer. He's just waiting for the right moment to strike."

Kit nodded. "He's not the man to play a waiting game longer than necessary."

"If he leaves his fortress, then we could mount an attack and bring off the lady," declared an immaculate young officer in the tones of one who has had an idea of surpassing brilliance.

No one took any notice of this clearly impractical suggestion. William Troughton was renowned for such schemes, particularly late at night. Receiving no response, the young officer lapsed once more into ruminative silence.

"Well," pronounced Burnes, "I for one would like a hand of macao. I've a mind to recoup my losses of the last time."

This suggestion was received with favor, and the troublesome matter of an Englishwoman in the clutches of an Afghan rebel was forgotten for the time being by all except Lieutenant Ralston, who found his ability to concentrate on the cards unusually impaired.

Chapter 6

The hawk flew from Ayesha's gauntleted wrist, soaring into the limitless depths of the sky, diminishing to a mere black speck against the white-capped mountain, blushed with the rising sun.

Ayesha gazed upward, striving to keep the bird in sight. At her side, no less anxious, the falconer stared, his eyes narrowed against the sun's red glow as he waited in trepidation to see whether or not this latest pupil would prove a credit to the long and patient hours of his schooling.

"I've lost sight of her," Ayesha said at last. "Can you still see her, Shir Muhammed?"

The falconer shook his head. "But she'll be back."

"I trust so." Akbar Khan loosed the jesses on his own tiercel and tossed him upward. "I paid Badar Khan a good price for her."

The falconer shifted uneasily in his saddle, wondering if his lord would demand repayment in some measure if he had loosed the falcon prematurely. One could never tell with Akbar Khan. He could as easily shrug off the loss as have the incompetent punished. He glanced at the shrouded figure of the woman at the khan's side. Those jade eyes glimmered a message at him through the *ru*-band, and he felt a measure of reassurance. The hawk was hers, the gift of Akbar Khan, and she would have some say in the consequences attendant upon the bird's loss.

"See, here she comes." Ayesha pointed upward

to where an indistinct blur gradually became defined. She held out her wrist, smiling as the hawk swooped down, a sparrow in the wickedly curved beak, to alight daintily, her claws gripping the leather gauntlet. "Shall I let her keep the sparrow, Shir Muhammed?"

"No, not the first time. Take it from her." He opened the neck of the game bag at his saddle, and Ayesha pried the barely mutilated prey loose from the hawk's beak and dropped it into the bag. She whispered to the magnificent creature as she refastened the jesses, scratching the proudly lifted neck.

"Isn't she beautiful, Akbar Khan?"

He nodded, a shadow of a smile on the incisive mouth. "You'll have little enough opportunity for hawking in Kabul, Ayesha. You'll have to amuse yourself in the bazaars instead."

It was typical of the man that he would spring this surprise upon her at such an unlikely moment. "I am to come with you, then?" She kept the excitement from her voice, continuing to caress the hawk on her wrist.

"I see no reason to deprive myself of your company," he replied calmly. "I do not envisage any danger. But if you really dislike the idea, I daresay I will manage." He was watching her closely, and she was again grateful for the concealment of the chadri.

"No," she said carefully, "I do not dislike the idea. It has been two years since I was in any city, and I have a hankering for the bazaars."

"We leave tomorrow." He turned his attention to his own returning bird.

The newly trained hawk was to be flown only once that day, so Ayesha handed her over to Shir Muhammed and took a peregrine instead. In the absorbing business of flying the birds, she was able to control her bubbling speculation, apprehension, and excitement, but her heart was beating with a febrile speed. She had known Akbar Khan was to go to Kabul, where he intended to put spur to the insurgents at the very heart of the enemy camp. She knew that the British in the city were weakened by the absence of Sale's forces, and by the settlement with the rebels they believed had been achieved by Macgregor. She knew quite well that no truce had been reached, and that the concessions made by the British had given the rebels everything they wanted whilst failing to guarantee anything in return. If the British believed otherwise, they were deluding themselves. Winter was coming fast now, and with its arrival Akbar Khan would strike the coup de grace.

In Kabul, pinned to await this coup de grace, was Christopher Ralston. Maybe, in the same city, she would lay eyes on him. To dwell on such a thought was as dangerous as it was forbidden, yet she could not help herself. Just as she could not help the thought that if she was at Akbar Khan's side, she might wield some softening influence. He listened to her, although she was under no illusions as to the extent of her influence; it was unpredictable, but definitely limited.

The sun rose, spilling fire over the mountaintops, but it brought no consonant warmth. Ayesha shivered at the bite of a dawn wind stabbing through the gorge.

"Yes, it is perhaps time to return," Akbar Khan said, as aware of the shiver as he was of the inner turmoil she thought so well-concealed. He wasn't sure why he was taking her to Kabul, unless it was because he wished to see how she would behave in close proximity to the feringhee. She was different since that night with Christopher Ralston. The difference was indefinable, but none the less pronounced. Sometimes, he would shrug it off, accepting that when a woman shared a night of love with another man, there would be some effect. She would be changed in some way. And then he would wonder if the change ran deeper than he believed, and he would regret the impulse that had led him to press the experience upon her. It was not that she was in any way deficient in her attentions, in any way absentminded when he was with her, but he was now conscious of an inner spring that the girl he had educated in the ways of his people had not possessed . . . that the woman he possessed had never before evinced. And it disturbed him.

He turned his horse, his tiercel safely secured on his wrist. "Come, Ayesha. Shir Muhammed will secure the peregrine." The Badakshani charger surged forward.

Ayesha nudged her mare into a gallop. The falconer and his attendants were more than capable of handling her two hawks, and Akbar Khan had clearly indicated that his interest in hawking had for the moment ceased. It was an abrupt change of mood, but that was not unusual.

Once back at the fortress, she slipped from her horse and waited for some indication of his further wishes, but he strode into the house without a word for her. Frowning, she turned aside, through the arched doorway leading to the zenana. She had done nothing to offend, so what had caused his discomposure?

Still puzzling, she pushed through the beaded curtain into the women's apartments. Maybe he was preoccupied with Kabul and the *shura* he had convened with the other sirdars. It was bound to be a divisive council; they always were. There were too many leaders and too many agendas. Yes, that was the only possible explanation. She turned her attention to the morrow's journey and the necessary arrangements, only to find that they had already been made in her absence.

Soraya had the pursed-mouth look she wore when matters in the zenana were not proceeding according to her preferred path. She did not care for travel, but if Ayesha was required to accompany the khan, then Soraya must go, too, in her capacity as chaperone and handmaid. She would not question the decisions of her lord, but neither would she master her irritation with those who had no redress against it.

Ayesha recognized the pattern and resigned herself to the general discomfort of disturbance in the accustomed calm waters of the zenana. She set herself to soothe Soraya's exacerbated nerves and thus protect some of the younger members of this tight-knit community of women from undeserved sharpness.

They left the following dawn, a small party of warrior hillmen and four women. The women, Ayesha included, rode behind the men and were to all intents and purposes ignored by them. In defiance of custom, Akbar Khan generally kept Ayesha at his side on such journeyings, although her women would keep to the rear, and the lack of invitation on this occasion caused her further disquiet. She could not imagine why he should be annoyed with her; but if he was, why was she accompanying him to Kabul?

At noon, they came upon a *chaie khana*, and Soraya's muttered grumbles ceased at the prospect of tea and rest. The mule she rode like a sack of potatoes appeared no less eager to be rid of his burden as they halted outside the teahouse. The men went into the little building, escorted by a wizened and bowed old man who had appeared at their arrival. A shrouded woman darted out, beckoning to the female members of the party, and they followed her into a small, mud-floored room at the rear, where they would not disturb the men's relaxation. Even had she been riding beside Akbar Khan, Ayesha would have been subject to the customary public segregation and discrimination, and was far too used to it to remark upon it. The samovar bubbled as merrily in the back room as it did in the front, and that was all that mattered.

But she did find it irksome throughout the long afternoon to be obliged to keep her spirited mare to the pace of the mules on which rode, or rather slumped, the other women. For a moment, she toyed with the idea of riding boldly up with Akbar Khan, but recognized ruefully that she did not dare. He might be amused by her boldness, but he could as easily be angered by it. Resigned, she let her mind wander and her horse amble.

"Ayesha? Ayesha!" At the imperative repetition of her name, her head jerked up and she came out of her reverie. Akbar Khan had halted just ahead and was summoning her. She urged the mare forward.

"I beg your pardon, I didn't hear you."

"So I noticed," he observed. "You looked as if you were asleep."

"At the pace I must maintain in order not to outstrip the mules, I may sleep quite safely." She risked just a hint of acerbity.

The blue eyes narrowed, and he stroked his beard in silence for a moment. Then abruptly he laughed. "Come, if you wish to gallop, we will do so." He was away along the narrow, treacherous mountain track before she could get her wits together. What an unfathomable man he was! She shrugged aside the puzzle, as always, and set her mare in exultant pursuit.

They had soon left their escort far behind, and Ayesha needed all her wits and skill to keep the mare from stumbling on the hazardous rocky path at the speed set by Akbar Khan. At times, the track wound along a dizzying edge over a deep gorge, and a wave of terror would flood her as she clung desperately to the plunging back of her horse, all the time recognizing that this crazy ride was decreed by Akbar Khan for some purpose of his own. It was a test of her courage and endurance, and she was determined that she would not fail to keep up with him; she would not stop until he did. He had challenged her in such fashion several times in the past, almost as if he wanted to see how different she was from a woman of his own race and culture. Such women endured slavery, brutality, and unremitting toil in silence, but it was the silence of a broken-spirited beast of burden, not the silence of courage. Courage was a masculine virtue, yet Akbar Khan would have his Englishwoman evince it in masculine trials. She thought sometimes that it excited him when he tested her in this way. When she passed the test, as she always did, a night of passionate ardor invariably followed. And sometimes she wondered what would result if she failed. Would he become bored with her? And if he did, what future did she have . . . a lifetime's abandonment in a zenana?

The wind whipped her, tugging at the chadri as it flowed around her, and she gave herself into its grip, losing that last unthinkable thought in the wild, elemental rushing around her ears. Then she saw him draw rein, way ahead of her, at a point where the track widened and the challenge died. He sat his horse, watching as she careened toward him, not slackening her speed until she, too, reached relative safety.

The mare's breath came in great sobbing gasps, whistling through her flared nostrils, and, despite the cold, her flanks were lathered. Ayesha met Akbar Khan's gaze steadily, a glint of triumph in her eyes behind the mesh. Slowly he nodded, and a tiny smile quirked the corners of his mouth. But he said nothing, and they sat waiting in contemplative silence until the others came up with them and Ayesha's mount had recovered her breath.

They found shelter for the night in a hill village where the clustered houses of dried mud clung to the mountainside and a watchtower stood sentinel at the entrance. The head of the community, the village *aksakai*, came to greet them, bowing his venerable old head in acknowledgment of the khan. They were ushered into his one-roomed hut, where a fire of sheep's dung smoldered sullenly. The village mullah came bobbing through the low doorway, and Ayesha resigned herself to the long ceremonies of greeting in which the women would take no part. Until the ritual was done, there would be no supper, and she was famished. Her only comfort was that the men would also be starving, so with luck Akbar Khan might hurry things along a little.

Patience was a strength she had learned long since, and she now stood with the complete immobility that had so struck Kit, while the talk continued and the fire belched its noxious smoke. The men took green snuff, placed under the tongue, and the holy man's speech went on in almost hypnotic cadences. But at last his voice ceased, and Ayesha felt the ripple of relief in the women around her. Now, surely they could eat.

As was to be expected in such a poor village, the hospitality offered was hardly elaborate, and Ayesha was well aware of how much of a strain on his limited resources this large party of visitors was placing on the *aksakai*. But other villagers appeared with their own offerings: *talkhan,* a cake of dried mulberries with walnuts; round flat loaves of wheat bread to mop up bowls of *gaimac,* the thick yellowish crust that formed on cream; strips of dried antelope meat; and salt, shaved off a precious block. There was only *dugh* to drink. Ayesha found the boiled and watered milk a poor substitute for the tea she craved, and her spirit revived remarkably when she saw Akbar Khan offer his host as gift a bar of tea, flavored with red pepper. But would such a luxury be offered to the women? She waited, salivating in a fever of anticipated disappointment.

The samovar was brought forth with much excitement and hand-rubbing. The tea was made, communal bowls filled and passed around the men. Ayesha felt tears prickle ludicrously behind her eyelids. It was absurd to feel so painfully deprived over a cup of tea. But it had been a long, hard day, and the strain of her mad ride with Akbar Khan was taking a belated toll.

Akbar Khan glanced at her. She no longer wore the enveloping chadri, but, in deference to mixed company, her unveiled face was turned away from the room. Nevertheless, he could feel her plaintive disappointment across the small, smoky space that

separated them. Sometimes, he was amazed at how
finely tuned he seemed to be to her emotions, even
over something as trivial as this. He spoke to the
aksakai, who made haste to refill the khan's bowl.
He took the tea himself to Ayesha.

"Thank you," she said softly, lifting her eyes to
his face for the barest moment.

"I know how much you enjoy it," he returned, as
quietly. "And after such a ride, you have need of
something restorative, I think." He looked around
the crowded little room, and a rueful smile played
over his lips. "There are other pleasures we must
forgo, I fear, Ayesha . . . until we reach Kabul."

She bowed her head in acknowledgment and buried her nose in the rich, peppery fragrance of the
tea.

"I do not understand what has happened to General Sale," Elphinstone fussed, plucking in habitual
fashion at the blanket on his knees. "He has orders
to return to Kabul without delay, if the safety of his
sick and wounded can be assured." It was the last
week of October.

"I suspect, sir, that the general is unwilling to
trust the Ghilzais." Kit looked up from the map he
had been studying and spoke in the calm tones he
had learned eased his fretful commander. "He will
probably not take the route through the Purwan
Durrah pass, in case of ambush. If he takes the
mountain road to the south of that defile, it will take
him longer to reach the Jugdulluk valley, from where
he can send on a runner."

"Why should he not trust them?" demanded Sir
William. "They are our allies now. The truce has
been agreed. The passes are now free."

Kit sighed, but made no attempt to engage the
Envoy in argument. It would be a fruitless exercise,
and would only leave him foaming with frustration.
His head already ached.

"General, may I make a suggestion? Do you not
think it would be sensible to bring the commissariat

stores within the cantonment?'' The question had been troubling Kit and others for some time. The commissariat was housed in a fort on the plain outside the cantonment. Supplies were brought into the cantonment when necessary. It was relatively well-garrisoned, but an Afghan-held fort stood in direct line between the commissariat and the cantonment, and it took little imagination to foresee the potential threat this implied to the British access to their supplies.

"Oh, but surely we have taken all necessary defensive measures," protested Elphinstone. "We have dug a ditch around the cantonment, have we not, Sir William? And an earthwork."

Over which a cow could scramble, thought Kit sourly. "But the cantonment is surrounded by occupied Afghan forts, sir. Why do we not attempt to destroy them, if we cannot take them?"

"You are exceeding your brief, Lieutenant," Sir William said coldly. "Decision-making is not the province of an adjutant."

"I beg your pardon, Sir William." Kit wondered how long he would be able to contain himself as the knowledge of impending disaster . . . willful disaster . . . grew ever stronger. The defensive position of the cantonment was contemptible; Afghan fortifications massed in the surrounding plain. But Elphinstone had at his disposal an equipped and well-ordered force of four infantry regiments, two batteries of artillery, three companies of sappers, and a regiment of cavalry. And in the Balla Hissar, Shah Soojah had a considerable body of soldiers and guns. Such a combined force should surely be able to occupy the Afghan forts, ensure the safety of supplies, and strengthen the defenses of the cantonment. But no one would do anything; no one would even admit that there was a semblance of threat.

"I will have these dispatches sent to Brigadier Shelton," Kit now said, as if he had never made the previous suggestion. "Then I will give your instructions to Captain Johnson in the Treasury." He gathered up the papers, straightened his tunic, adjusted the position of his sword, saluted smartly to the general, and left the room. He sent a runner to Shelton, who was in camp with his brigade on the Seah Sung hills about a mile and a half from the cantonment, then he left the headquarters bungalow and rode into Kabul, to the Treasury.

Captain Johnson received him gloomily. "Macnaghten knows the coffers are all but empty," he said, reading his instructions to supply the shah with a further lakh of rupees. "And now that we've had to reinstate the subsidies to the chiefs, we're in even worse shape. Where does he think I'm going to lay hands on this sum?"

Kit shook his head. "I'm not in Sir William's confidence, sir. I am merely an adjutant who delivers messages."

Johnson cast him a sharp, shrewd glance. "Do I detect a note of irritation with our esteemed envoy, Ralston?"

"Of course not, sir. It's not my place to criticize," Kit responded smoothly.

"Balderdash!" the other declared. "We all know the man's a blinkered fool. He only sees what he wants to see. Don't know what's goin' on in the city at the moment, but the atmosphere out there sets my skin crawling. How about a noggin?"

Kit accepted a brandy with gratitude. The first drink of the day usually put paid to the ill-effects of the previous night's excesses, and his headache was worsening by the minute. Half an hour of shared grousing and a second brandy later, he took his leave of Captain Johnson and went out into the city streets, feeling much restored.

He left his horse at the Treasury and set off on foot through the narrow streets. Johnson had been right. The very air in the city seemed to vibrate with unease, with a barely suppressed violence. He was accustomed to the hostility of the inhabitants, but this mood was different. There was an insolence in the eyes that met his, a challenge in the way a man

would step aside as he approached, as if he would
not be contaminated by contact with the feringhee
dog.

He turned into the noisy, bustling bazaar, realizing that one hand was resting unconsciously upon
the sword hilt beneath his riding coat, his other on
the pistol in the deep pocket. Around him, the
crowd of buyers and sellers and gossips milled, but
the rapid bargaining jabber died an instantaneous
death at his approach, and dark eyes glared their
challenge and their threat.

Kit suddenly decided that he didn't wish to be in
the bazaar any longer. He turned on his heel . . .
and then he saw her. The blood seemed to still in
his veins, the breath to pause in his lungs. The silky
white chadri stood out as it had done before amongst
the surrounding sea of dark homespun, but even
without that identification, even had she been
dressed identically with the other women, he would
have known her. It was the set of her head, the way
she held her body. She was fingering bolts of material on a carpeted stall, the stallkeeper standing to
one side, watching and waiting. She said something
to one of the women accompanying her, and the
woman spoke to the stallkeeper. A rapid exchange
took place, in which Ayesha remained silent.
Clearly, her companion undertook the bargaining on
Ayesha's instructions.

Kit wanted her to see him. He needed her to see
him. The need to catch a glimpse of those jade eyes
meeting his from behind her veil became uncon-
querable. Deliberately, he made his way toward the
stall, no longer conscious of the mutters and the
glares, of the unconcealed menace surrounding him.
He stepped around the stallkeeper.

Ayesha was listening intently to Soraya's progress
in the bargaining, although protocol demanded that
she appear completely indifferent. She was gazing
off into the middle distance when the hairs on the
nape of her neck lifted. She jerked her head around

. . . and met the intent, demanding scrutiny of Christopher Ralston.

A cold sweat bathed her skin and trickled down her rib cage beneath her cashmere tunic as she held herself immobile, resisting with every desperate fiber of her being the urge to touch his body with hers. Her head moved infinitesimally . . . was it in negation or appeal? But she could not lower her eyes. They drank him in, as if she would absorb him, body and soul, through her vision.

She realized that Soraya was speaking to her. Her companion must not notice her charge's peculiar absorption. In a moment, she would also become aware of the English soldier, standing rapt a mere five yards away, and she could not fail to detect the current flowing between them. It was almost palpable, so that the air between them seemed to vibrate like a plucked string. Akbar Khan must not know of this . . . this . . . could one call it a meeting? Hardly that, but he must continue to believe in her indifference to Christopher Ralston, continue to believe that the night she had passed with the Englishman had disappeared into the mists of memory. If he suspected the truth, he would cease to trust her, and she could not risk the consequences of his loss of trust. Her life would become unendurable.

She dragged her eyes away from the lodestone of his gaze. "Have you concluded, Soraya?"

"He insists on a hundred rupees," the woman said, irritated with her failure to get her own price.

"It is well worth it," Ayesha said, fingering the material, trying to control her hand's tremor. "I did not expect to buy it for less. It will make a most beautiful tunic. If it is lined in lambswool, it will be warm enough for the winter."

They were talking in Pushtu, and Kit could not understand more than a word or two, but he did understand that she had as effectively dismissed him as she had done after the *buzkashi*. But in that moment of intensity he had felt the power of her wanting, and he was satisfied. He walked casually away,

rounded a corner into a dark, noisome alley, and
waited until she and her companions, business accomplished, left the bazaar. Then he followed, still
casually and at a safe distance.

The house stood in the middle of a row of similar
houses in the center of the city. It was an affluent
neighborhood by Afghan standards, but it was the
armed guards at the entrance who most concerned
Kit. They carried scimitars and jezzails, wore chain
mail and pronged helmets of the kind he had seen
in Akbar Khan's mountain stronghold. There was
no possible way an intruder could get past them.

He stood in the shadow of a doorway across the
street and watched as the women were admitted.
He looked up at the facade of the house. Windows
and verandahs lined the upper floor. Did he imagine
that glimmer of white crossing one of the windows?
He stared until black dots danced before his eyes. If
he *had* seen her up there, she was in a room to the
left of center. But what good did that do him? It had
a verandah. Perhaps he could shin his way up there,
pry open the window, slip inside. . . . But how was
he to get them both out again? And besides, she was
always accompanied by her shadowy entourage. Perhaps she slept alone, though. Perhaps in the dead of
night he could achieve entrance, spirit her away . . .
Oh, he was being ridiculous! It would be as easy to
abduct her from the streets of Kabul in full view of a
hostile populace as to gain undiscovered entrance and
exit to that house.

Without much hope, he strolled to the back of the
row of houses. They had high-walled courtyards
with barred gates set into the walls. And guards
stood again at the gate to Akbar Khan's house. There
was neither help nor inspiration to be gained from
that aspect.

Kit turned aside and made his way back to the
Treasury. Despite his dismally unproductive recon-
naissance, he was infused with an energy and determination that somehow made light of the
difficulties he faced. She was here, in Kabul. And

she was as much stirred by their proximity as he was. With those two factors in his favor, how could he fail?

"I have reason to believe Akbar Khan is in Kabul," he told Captain Johnson without preamble.

Johnson whistled softly. "That would explain the atmosphere. But try telling that to Macnaghten. He's convinced the man's still skulking in the Hindu Kush."

"He's here," Kit said firmly.

"Of course, you've met him, haven't you?" Johnson regarded the younger man curiously. "I heard tell of your interesting patrol. Didn't please the powers that be, I understand."

"No," Kit agreed aridly. He knew that Johnson's information about the lieutenant's encounter with Akbar Khan would include nothing of Ayesha. What a man told his intimates in confidence would remain so. "Warnings are considered croaking. But I daresay I had better inform the general and Sir William of Akbar Khan's arrival."

"I wish you luck." Johnson accompanied him outside to fetch his horse. He glanced up at the ring of mountain peaks and the lowering sky. He drew a deep breath. "If we're still here when the snows come, Ralston, we won't have a cat in hell's chance of getting through. They'll pick our bones clean."

"I didn't realize we were intending to leave," Kit remarked provocatively. "Does Shah Soojah no longer need British bayonets to safeguard his claim?"

Johnson's laugh crackled, sharp and bitter in the cold air. "Once we withdraw, the shah will be a dead man, as well you know. But the entire country outside this city is rising against the feringhee. Nott is struggling to hold Kandahar; Sale, you can be sure, is having to fight every step of the way back to Kabul. They're closing in on us from all sides. The Treasury is almost empty, the commissariat little better, and there's little enough chance of supplies getting through from Peshawar or Quetta. We're going to have to withdraw . . . sooner rather than later. And now you say Akbar Khan is in Kabul." He shook his head gloomily. "Haven't got a prayer, Ralston, and you may accuse me of croakin', if you like."

"I'm glad to have a fellow offender," Kit said grimly, mounting his horse. The two exchanged friendly salutes, and Lieutenant Ralston rode back to the cantonment to face the unenviable task of attempting to convince his superiors of a fact they would prefer not to hear.

Ayesha huddled into her fur-trimmed shawl. She stood in deep shadow in the small antechamber of the room where the *shura* was convened. The oil lamps sent grotesque shapes writhing against the plastered walls. In her complete immobility, she could feel her blood coursing through her body. The stone floor beneath her bare feet was icy. A bitter night draught tongued its way through a crack in the window behind her and set swinging the tapestry over the door to the council chamber. The voices within rose and fell. Occasionally, there would be an angry exclamation, the rasp of a chair on the stone floor, then Akbar Khan would say something, softly soothing, and the angry speaker would fall silent.

But every time Akbar Khan spoke, Ayesha was touched by the menace underlying the soft, seemingly conciliatory tone. He was inciting this incohesive group to concerted attack. He didn't say it, but she could hear it in every word and every pause. How could the feringhee be trusted? They made promises, but they maintained their forces in fighting readiness. Of course, they were seriously weakened by the closing of the passes. Of course, they did not appear to be taking elementary precautions against the possibility of attack. Of course, they probably despised the Afghan so thoroughly that it did not occur to them to prepare a defense.

A hiss of rage greeted this seemingly careless observation, and the voices rose now in agitation. And this time Akbar Khan made no attempt to quiet and soothe.

Ayesha slipped from the antechamber, her feet numbed with cold, but it could not match the deadly chill in her soul as she faced the absolute recognition of the path about to be taken . . . unless she could work some magic on Akbar Khan.

It was October the thirtieth.

"How could Sale have lost upward of one hundred and twenty men?" exclaimed Sir William, for once bereft of his calm superiority. "It's a bare three miles from Jugdulluk to Gundamuk."

"Three miles of mountain tracks, winding between commanding heights," Lieutenant Ralston pointed out with his customary accuracy. "The general says in his dispatch that the rear guard was attacked continuously by Ghilzais, who trapped them in the pass."

"I can read, thank you, Lieutenant," the Envoy declared icily. "And it reads like a piece of gross mismanagement to me. Why did not the main body of his army wait for the rear to close up on them before making the descent into the pass? What happened to his flanking detachments? Just tell me that. They should have been posted to protect the column."

"Oh, how can we know?" wittered General Elphinstone. "If one is not there to see the situation, it's very hard to pass judgment, Macnaghten."

"The fact is that General Sale must now be at Gundamuk, awaiting further orders," Kit put in. "What should I send to him?"

"Why, that he should return to Kabul immediately, of course!"

"Very well, General." Kit saluted punctiliously and closed the door very softly behind him. With each new disaster, each new piece of bungling, his sense of unreality increased. In many ways, the entire gruesome fiasco had become a joke, he thought.

A grim joke . . . none grimmer . . . but without a degree of gallows humor one would never retain one's sanity in this house of delusion.

The subaltern deputed to make the hazardous journey across Afghan-held territory to Sale at Gundamuk received his instructions with fortitude. "You'd be advised to adopt Afghan dress," Kit said, "and your men as well. You'll have a better chance of avoiding unwelcome attention."

The advice was acknowledged with a stoical grin, and the young man went off to gather his escort. Kit returned to his bungalow, where, under the disapproving eye of Harley, his batman, he donned Afghan costume himself, darkened his face with boot polish, shrugged into a fur-lined sheepskin coat, and set off on horseback into the city.

It had been easy enough to acquire the tunic, the turban, the loose trousers now tucked into the tops of his boots, and he felt immeasurably more comfortable thus attired as he rode through the city streets. There were no Europeans to be seen. Indeed, there were few people around at all; those there were gathered in knots at street corners or in doorways. An air of dread expectancy hung over the city, raking his spine with the now familiar chills.

Leaving his horse at Burnes's residence, he went on foot, as he had done for the last seven days, ever since he had seen her in the bazaar, to Akbar Khan's house, where he stood in the concealment of a facing doorway, keeping silent vigil, wrestling with the problem that still refused to admit of solution.

Nothing seemed to matter anymore but this mission he had embarked upon. It consumed his every waking moment. He had discussed it endlessly with his friends, but their enthusiasm and inventiveness tended to diminish in direct relation to the diminishing level of brandy in the bottle and the lateness of the hour. He could hardly blame them. It wasn't as if they had his knowledge of Ayesha-Annabel to feed the obsession. But as the collar tightened around the British presence in Kabul, so his determination hardened . . . became the only reality in this crazily deluded existence.

It was the afternoon of November the first.

Ayesha stood to one side of the window, looking down onto the street, down on the still figure in native dress, watching the house. What did he hope to achieve by this watching? It was a question she asked herself every time she saw him. And she wished passionately that he would go away, would leave her to live her life, would allow her to return to the peace and acceptance she had had before he had leaped into the calm waters of her existence. And she was afraid for him.

"We must allow no one to pass between the cantonment and the city." Akbar Khan's voice came from the corridor outside. "As a first step, we will isolate them in their encampment."

"But what of Burnes in the residency, and the men in the Treasury?" It was the voice of Badar Khan, and Ayesha knew that the two men were going to the council chamber where yet another *shura* was convened. She moved closer to the tapestry-shielded doorway.

"Forced to remain in the city, they will be cut off from their fellows in the cantonment," Akbar Khan replied. "We will begin to puncture the confidence of the feringhee dogs, create a degree of unease as they see we have the power to restrict their movements."

"But perhaps we should do more than that," Badar Khan said slowly.

"What do you have in mind?"

"A show of strength."

"A direct attack?"

"The people are restless," the other responded obliquely.

Ayesha shivered. She knew that the sedition amongst the citizens of Kabul had been carefully fostered by Akbar Khan and his fellow sirdars. If they unleashed the ferocity of the mob upon the enemy, the resulting horrors were not difficult to imagine.

"Perhaps we should just leave the people to make their own decisions," Akbar Khan was saying casually. "Go into the *shura*, my friend. I will follow you in a moment."

Ayesha stepped hastily away from the tapestried doorway, just as Akbar Khan entered the room. He regarded her shrewdly. "Were you listening?"

She blushed. "I could not help but overhear."

He stroked his beard thoughtfully. "I think, on occasion, that you position yourself in such a way as to *ensure* that you cannot help it."

"Why do you encourage this incitement?" she said with sudden passion, thinking of the man outside, below the window. "What benefit will accrue if there is violence?"

"What makes you think I am encouraging it?" he said with a careless shrug. "What the people do is their business."

"You know that is not so!" Agitated, she stepped toward him. "You know you can prevent an insurrection, if you choose. Does it amuse you to play with people in this fashion? To watch someone else do your killing for you?"

"You overreach yourself, Ayesha," he warned softly. "The feringhee must learn the nature of the Afghan, and the nature of the Afghan's revenge for insults done him. They must be taught to fear us."

As she had been taught, she recognized bleakly. She did fear them. She feared Akbar Khan. He had never treated her unkindly, never threatened her, never so much as punished her occasional childhood offenses, but the knowledge of his absolute power was sufficient intimidation. She touched her hands to her forehead in a graceful salaam of submission.

"I came to tell you to remain within doors," he said in his usual calm voice, as if the last exchange had never taken place. "Until I can be certain there will be no disturbance, I do not want you to leave the house."

"As you wish," she said without expression.

He left without further words, and she returned to the window. The watcher was gone. Night was falling, and the winter wind rushed through the deserted streets, setting a door to banging with forlorn, hollow resonance.

Chapter 7

<hr/>

"**D**amned impertinent savages!" Burnes exploded, later that night. "Who the hell do they think they are? Refusing to let anyone pass between the city and the cantonment!" He glared at the sepoy messenger who had just returned to the residency, having been turned back by a hostile crowd when he attempted to leave the city with a message from Burnes to Macnaghten.

The sepoy wisely made no response, correctly assuming that the question had not really been asked of him. The tirade continued to fall upon his head, however, until William Broadfoot, Burnes's secretary, coughed awkwardly. "Not really the man's fault, Sir Alexander. He couldn't help being turned back."

Sir Alexander shook his head disgustedly and waved a dismissive hand at the sepoy, who beat a relieved retreat. "I don't suppose it means anything," he said, rather more moderately. "Just a touch of unrest. It'll die down by the morning. If it doesn't, Elphinstone'll send in a brigade, just to show 'em who's in charge here."

"But how can he do that, Alexander, if we cannot get a message through to tell him of the situation?" Burnes's younger brother spoke up, turning from the window where he had been looking out onto the night-dark garden.

"Oh, don't you worry, Charlie," his brother reassured him. "Once it's light, we'll get a message through; there's no need—" He stopped at the sound of voices in the hall outside. "Hell and the devil! Is that Kit Ralston?" He flung open the library door. "Kit, what the devil are you doing here? I thought you'd left the city hours ago."

Kit came into the room, blowing on his hands. "Dear God, but it's cold out there. No, I decided to wander the bazaars for a while, see if I could deduce anything useful. I can pass amongst them unnoticed in this guise." He gestured expressively at his native costume.

"You look just like one of 'em," Burnes declared. "Apart from no beard. Did you hear the impudent bastards are preventing anyone going from here to the cantonment?"

Kit nodded gravely, shrugging out of the heavy goatskin coat. "It's ugly, Burnes. There's a head of steam out there just waiting to blow."

"Oh, rubbish. A few of our troops will soon put paid to their nonsense!"

"If you'll take my advice, you'll have the guards doubled," Kit said bluntly. "Both here and at the Treasury . . . oh, no thanks." He declined William Broadfoot's offer of his cigar case. "But I could do with a brandy. I'm chilled to the bone."

The drink was instantly forthcoming, and a lowering silence fell on the room. Kit paced restlessly, kicked at a slipping log in the hearth, frowned into his goblet, his thoughts with Ayesha. He could have sworn he had seen her at the window this afternoon . . . and that she had seen him. But another figure had come into the room. He had seen the bulk move past the window, and it required little educated guesswork to recognize the sturdy, powerful shape of Akbar Khan. What dealings had they had up there? The speculation simply fed his obsession, and he struggled to close his mind to it, returning his attention to his companions' newly resumed discussion.

"D'you think they know in headquarters that we're confined to the city?" Charlie Broadfoot asked tentatively.

Kit shrugged. "Hard to say. But it's all blown up so quickly, I doubt it. Until nightfall, things were as normal as they ever are in this place."

"Think you could get through, Ralston? Dressed like one of 'em?" asked Broadfoot.

"Probably, particularly as I'm riding bareback. They'd recognize a British saddle at the drop of a hat." He went to the window and drew aside the heavy curtain, peering into the unyielding darkness. "Let's see what happens in the morning. Maybe Alexander is right, and the atmosphere will calm down. Night shadows can embolden a braggart, but the first light of day will serve to deflate him."

"It's that damned Akbar Khan, you mark my words," Burnes declared savagely. "If I could get my hands on him, I'd see him hanged for a traitorous rebel."

Kit contented himself with a raised eyebrow. "If it's all the same to you, I think I'll get some sleep. If the situation hasn't improved by dawn, I'll make a break for the cantonment."

"Yes, yes, of course, my dear fellow. I'll get Abdul to show you to one of the guest rooms." Burnes went to the door. "I daresay you'll want to wash off that . . . that . . . well, whatever it is on your face," he suggested with a fastidious curl of his lip, stroking his own neat moustache. "Doesn't seem fitting for a British cavalry officer to go around lookin' like a bloody native."

"You'll be glad enough of it in the morning, if someone has to try and get through to headquarters," Kit responded without heat. "On occasion, expediency requires certain sacrifices, Burnes. It's fortunate I don't object to making them."

He followed Burnes's servant upstairs to a large, comfortable chamber at the front of the house, declined all offers of refreshment and hot water, pulled off his boots, and lay down fully clothed on the bed. He intended to catnap for what remained of the night, and be ready to leave at first light.

It was barely light on the morning of November

the second, however, when he came to full awareness with an uncanny sense of impending danger.
He lay in the darkened room, straining every sense
to identify what had woken him so abruptly. At first,
he could isolate nothing out of the ordinary. Slipping from the bed, he padded to the window and
drew aside the curtain. A thin gray light from an
overcast sky was encroaching on the night-dark.
With instinctive stealth, he pushed open the case-
ment, leaning out into the frigid air. Then he heard
the sound. It was coming from beyond the walls of
the residency. The sound of feet, an ominous hum
of voices . . . a hum that swelled like storm-tossed
waves on a pebble beach.

Hastily, he drew on his boots, checked his pistol,
and ran downstairs. In the hall, he found Broadfoot
and the Burnes brothers. Sir Alexander seemed un-
perturbed, and was as immaculately dressed as if he
were about to pay a morning call. Broadfoot and
Charlie, on the other hand, looked as rumpled as
men who had just tumbled from their beds.

"Looks like a little riot," Sir Alexander said,
brushing down his frock coat, straightening his cravat. "I'll have a word with 'em from the upstairs
verandah . . . soon send 'em packing."

"Did you double the guards?" Kit asked, going
to the barred front door. "Open up," he instructed
the alarmed servant.

"Couldn't see the point, dear fellow," Burnes
said. "Can't imagine what such a rabble would want
with me."

"An attack on the residency would be a powerful
spur to the rebels, and a powerful rallying point,"
Kit declared curtly, shrugging into his coat. He
stepped into the courtyard. The growing light cast
chilly shadows, enfolding the bushes and plants
adorning the courtyard. He crossed to the great
barred gates. Guards stood upon the high stone wall
with drawn arms. Through the bars, he saw the
slowly gathering crowd. They pressed toward the
gate, but made no particularly threatening move at

the sight of the brown-faced, turbanned man in his goatskin coat, or at the sepoy guards, who were, after all, not feringhee.

Kit said nothing, realizing that once he opened his mouth his disguise would be punctured, and he was now absolutely certain that he was going to be glad of his costume before many more hours were up.

He returned to the house. "I'll get word to Macnaghten."

"I'll speak with them first. Don't want to start squealing unnecessarily." Burnes progressed with measured step upstairs and marched onto the verandah overlooking the courtyard and the street beyond. At the sight of the feringhee, in his dark frock coat, his leather spats, his fawn beaver top hat, a great bellow went up. Fists were raised, staves flourished, and the wicked blades of scimitar and khyber knife gleamed dully in the half light.

Kit shivered at the depths of menace expressed by that lowering, threatening mob. The last restraints had somehow been ripped away, and the hatred and need for vengeance now loomed monstrous and unhindered. This fierce, proud people had been subjected to an alien yoke, and they were now going to throw off that yoke and avenge the insult.

Burnes raised his voice above the crowd, and for a moment they fell silent, listening to his fluent Pushtu. Kit had an instant's hope that this skilled linguist would be able to calm them, then his heart sank. The political officer's harangue became increasingly patronizing, expressing the sorrow and annoyance of a father when faced with a child's tiresome insubordination.

A stone flew through the air and struck a front window. The sound of breaking glass brought the mob surging to the gate, screaming insults. Some leaped for the wall, and one of the sepoy guards discharged his musket the instant before he was dragged down into the howling mob, his scream rising shrill in the air.

Burnes stepped back hastily into the house, slam-

ming the verandah door behind him. He threw the
bar across it before turning to the silent trio behind
him. His expression had lost some of its assurance,
and his usually dapper moustache seemed to droop.

"We'd best arm ourselves," he said. "Do you
think you can make it to the cantonment, Kit? We're
going to need reinforcements."

"I can but try. I wonder if they're covering the
stable gates." He didn't wait for an answer, but ran
from the room, down the stairs and down the corridor to the rear of the house. "Bar the door behind
me," he ordered the sentry, knowing that once that
was done, he was on his own in the open.

The door clanged shut, the bar fell with a heavy
thump. The yells of the mob were growing more
powerful. The sepoy guards on the wall were shooting, and Kit now heard shots coming from the front
of the house. Presumably his companions had begun their defense. It was getting lighter by the minute. He ran across the stableyard, skinned his fingers
in his haste to draw back the frozen bolts of the stable door. His horse greeted him with a restless
whinny. The other animals were all shifting in their
stalls, nostrils flared, whickering their unease. Kit
grabbed the halter hanging on a hook in the stall
wall, slipped it over the horse's head, and sprang
up on the broad back. The horse leaped for the door
the minute he felt his rider's weight, and they burst
out into the now-full daylight.

The back gate was sparsely guarded, the street behind miraculously empty. Kit bellowed at the sepoys
to fetch reinforcements as they bolted the gate behind him; and in the same moment a screaming
mass poured around the corner, heading for the rear
entrance to the residency. He could not possibly
withstand them, or add any useful support to the
guards. His task was to alert the cantonment. He
swung his horse away from the mob and galloped
down the street.

It was as if all human life in the city had been
drawn forth and concentrated on the square yards

around the residency. No one was to be seen. Doors
stood open to the street. His horse pounded over
the straw-littered cobbles, swung into the street
where Akbar Khan's house stood.

Kit had not been aware of deciding on this route.
In fact, this street was as good a way as any of reaching his goal—the city gates. But Akbar Khan's door
stood open and unguarded. After that, Kit was not
aware of making any choices. He simply acted.

Flinging himself from his mount, he stepped into
the dark, stone-flagged hallway. The empty silence
in the house seemed to take on solid form, as if he
were enwrapped in a wet and heavy cloak. He
mounted the stairs, cautiously yet without hesitation. It was as if he had always known the way.
Unerringly, he turned to the left at the head of the
stairs. A tapestried doorway stood exactly where he
expected it to be. He pushed through.

Ayesha stood in the center of the room, transfixed
as if frozen in mid-step. Her hair poured down her
back, burnished copper in the gloom. She was unveiled, dressed simply in a cream-colored woolen
tunic and flowing trousers, and her eyes still wore
the shadow of sleep. The whiteness of her complexion took on a deathly pallor as she saw him.

"Dear God! Are you mad?" she breathed. "Get
out of here, *quickly.*"

"Not without you," he said with perfect calm.
"There is no one here."

"Of course there is," she hissed fiercely. "The
women are all here. I have just woken, and any minute now, Soraya will wake and—"

"Then come quickly." He took a step toward her.
"The guards are gone from the door . . . gone to see
the fun, I daresay."

"Akbar Khan will have them crucified for desert-
ing their posts," she whispered, terror standing out
in the jade eyes as the image of what he would do
to Christopher Ralston if he discovered him here rose
in all its dread reality. *"Please, Kit, you must go from
here."*

He folded his arms and stood very still, looking at her. "I will not leave without you. The choice is yours."

Ayesha had no idea what was happening, except that as she had feared something momentous and horrendous was taking place in the city. She had been told nothing, but the sounds of the mob had woken her . . . that and the empty stillness in the house. And suddenly, Christopher Ralston had materialized. How? Where from? She could not begin to guess, and it did not matter. What mattered was that in his eyes she saw the same burning fanaticism exhibited by any Afghan zealot. She had seen it many times since that first time in the Khyber pass, and she knew how unvanquishable it was. Reasoning with him would be as pointless as reasoning with a lunatic. He was laying his life upon the line, forcing her to act to prevent his being torn limb from limb . . . or even worse. The sweat of terror broke from her pores, coldly damp, at the nightmare possibilities.

She moved swiftly past him to the doorway. If she could just get him out onto the street again, then she could jump back inside and bar the door. Once outside, he would be safe enough, dressed as he was. She began to run down the stairs, her heart pounding sickeningly at the thought that any moment could bring the guards back . . . could produce Akbar Khan. . . . If the guards caught her fleeing, fleeing unveiled in the company of a feringhee intruder, they would have no compunction in dealing with her. Her own fate would be as grim as Kit's.

"Do you have a cloak?" Kit followed her, speaking as if this madness were the most normal, ordinary occurrence; as if he had no understanding of what they were risking. "You'll freeze without something."

She made no response, having absolutely no intention of venturing more than a step beyond the door.

A heavy, fur-trimmed mantle hung from a hook in the hall. He yanked it loose and stepped after her,

into the deserted street. His horse still stood at the
door, but he was sniffing the air uncertainly, pawing
the cobbles with clear anxiety.

With a sudden movement, Ayesha darted back,
behind Kit to the door. Again without conscious
thought, he reacted, seizing her arm, hauling her
against him. There was a short, fierce, soundless
struggle, both of them knowing that the first cry
would bring disaster. Kit had only one thought. For
days . . . weeks . . . he had been wrestling with the
seemingly insoluble problem of his obsession. Now
the solution was in his hands. He had her, outside
in the street, free and clear. How free was free? How
clear was clear? The *buzkashi* catchphrase swam into
his head, to be instantly dismissed. He had her. He
had his horse. The other contenders were nowhere
in sight. The fact that the prize was resisting him
was an irrelevance he would deal with later. For
now, he would make his own rules.

Catching her around the waist, he lifted her clear of
the ground and tossed her forward over the bare back
of his horse. Shock rendered her motionless for the split
second he needed to jump up behind her. He flung the
cloak over her prone body, covering her completely,
before leaning forward, holding her securely with one
hand and the weight of his own body. His horse sprang
into an almost instantaneous gallop.

In the next street, there were people, running,
shrieking. The sight of a wildly plunging horse and
a wild-eyed, dark-skinned, turbanned rider seemed
entirely in keeping with their own rampage. The in-
ert bundle in front of him was unremarkable. But
Kit knew that if she called out, he would die here.
She didn't, but suddenly began to struggle, pushing
upward against the pressure on her back.

The smell of smoke, thick and acrid, filled the air.
Flames shot up from the direction of the residency,
and the savage yells battered against his ears as he
galloped madly toward the city gate. He had left the
residency no more than twenty minutes earlier, but
in that time, it sounded as if the mob had broken

through. With sudden dread, he changed direction, turning toward the street in front of the residency.

The scene was straight out of hell. The stables behind the house were burning merrily, the great gates of the courtyard flung open to admit the screaming horde. The bodies of the sepoy guards lay, broken and contorted. The front door splintered under a battering stave, and with a wild shriek the mob poured into the house. Then came a sound from the garden behind the house that stilled his heart, sent ice through his veins. It was an exultant shout of triumph, swelling to a roar. He straightened, his hand on Ayesha slackening. In instant response, she twisted violently.

"Goddamn you, keep still!" he hissed furiously, as if she did not have the right to protest the appalling discomfort of her position, and, indeed, in this moment of horror and violation, he associated her with the butchery he knew was taking place. He increased the pressure of his hand in the small of her back and stared into the flame-shot inferno.

The torrent of humanity boiled into the courtyard from the rear garden; still screaming exultantly, they held something aloft. Vomit rose in Kit's throat, filled his mouth. He kicked his horse into a gallop and left the scene, the image of Alexander Burnes's disembodied head scorched into his internal vision.

Ayesha ceased her struggles out of exhaustion. She was jolted unmercifully, her ribs screaming their protest, the heavy folds of the cloak constricting her breathing. Her rage now was so vast that it seemed all-consuming, so that she was aware of no other emotion. Even her physical discomforts were subsumed under this blazing outrage. She could guess where they were going, and when Kit slackened speed momentarily at the gate to the cantonment, she heard without surprise his imperative demand in English to the guard.

The gate swung open, and the horse galloped unerringly to Kit's bungalow and the prospect of his own secure stable. People in various stages of dis-

array and morning deshabille stood in the small front
gardens of the bungalows, staring toward the city
from whence came the dreadful sounds of riot and
carnage. The smoke from the fired residency and
Treasury now hung dense in the sky. People called
out to Kit as he passed, only some of them recognizing Lieutenant Ralston of the East India Company's Cavalry in the burning-eyed, wildly galloping
horseman. He made no response, drawing rein
abruptly at the door of his own bungalow.

Harley came running out. "Oh, my God, sir,
you're safe. What the 'ell's goin' on?"

"In a minute," Kit said shortly, flinging himself
to the ground. He reached up to lift Ayesha down,
but she pushed herself to the ground with a resurgence of strength and turned on him . . . like some
green-eyed lynx, he thought, when he could think
at all through the stream of abuse she flung at him
in Persian and Pushtu, as if English failed her in
such an extremity.

Harley stood dumbstruck, staring at this amazing
creature. Then someone hailed them from across the
street, and Bob Markham came running, talking as
he came.

"Have you come from the city, Kit? The old man's
screaming for you. He—" He stopped both speaking
and moving as he took in the sight before him. "In
the name of the Almighty!" he cried. "You got her
out!"

Ayesha spun around as his words penetrated her
fury, then she raised her hand and struck Kit with
the full force of her arm. "So you have talked about
me, too, have you, Ralston, *huzoor*? Mess talk, I
imagine."

Kit came to his senses. His cheek stinging from
the blow, his ears ringing with her insults, his brain
still reeling with the rioting images of horror, he
picked up the fallen cloak, threw it around her, and
bundled her into the bungalow, out of sight and earshot of any more inquisitive passersby.

Bob and Harley followed, both of them wide-eyed with surprise and curiosity.

"Annabel, I have to go to headquarters," Kit said urgently, pushing her into his bedroom and kicking the door shut on their audience. "When I return, we'll talk about this . . . we'll arrange something—" He pulled off his turban, running his hands through his hair in distraction.

"I am leaving, *now*," she declared, but more temperately than she had yet spoken to him. "Stand aside."

After everything he had gone through to get her here, she couldn't really imagine that he would calmly permit her to return, Kit thought incredulously. "Don't be ridiculous, Annabel. You're back with your own people now. Everything is going to be all right, I promise."

He had completely lost his wits! Ayesha stared at him, utterly nonplussed, as if she had just come face to face with a mad dog.

Taking advantage of her stunned silence, he moved swiftly to the door. "Harley will look after you. He will get you anything you want. I'll be back as soon as I've reported to the general."

Once on the other side of the door, he leaned weakly against it, facing the fascinated stares of his friend and batman. "You have never seen such carnage," he said, rubbing his eyeballs as if to dispel the searing images. "They've butchered Alexander and Charlie Burnes, and Broadfoot; fired the Treasury. I don't know what has happened to Johnson. The entire city is in arms and on the rampage. We must send troops in immediately."

Bob pointed wordlessly to the closed door at Kit's back and raised an eyebrow before saying deliberately, "The lady didn't seem too happy to me. *What* are you going to do with her?"

"Keep her here for the moment," Kit said crisply. "Harley, you will attend to Miss Spencer. She will be glad of food and tea, I am certain. Oh, God, I can't deal with this now. I *have* to go to headquarters," he added, the crispness vanished, a note of desperation in its place. "Will you stay here, Bob, and keep an eye on things?"

"You mean make sure she stays put?" the other demanded. "Lord, Kit, you do ask a lot of a friend."

"Thanks." Taking the statement as consent, Kit ran from the bungalow, swung onto his horse again, and rode at speed to headquarters.

In the bedroom, Ayesha examined her surroundings. The window was barred. A precaution, she guessed, to keep intruders out, rather than the occupants within, but it served the dual purpose. She could hear male voices outside the room. She turned the door handle. To her surprise, it opened.

Two apprehensive faces stared at her as she stood in the doorway. "Can I get you some breakfast, miss?" Harley ventured. "A nice cup of tea?"

"No," she said icily. "You can both stand aside and let me out of here."

"Can't do that, ma'am," Bob said, coughing awkwardly. "Promised Kit, you see. He'll make all right and tight when he gets back, just you wait and see."

Ayesha stamped a slippered foot in frustration. "I have no desire to wait and see, you idiot! Get out of my way!" But when she made to push past, Bob Markham, albeit apologetically, proved a very effective wall.

She could not possibly evade both of these rather bulky men; one, maybe, but not both. She threw a Persian oath at them and stormed back into the room, slamming the door so that it shivered on its hinges.

"D'you think a nice cup of tea would do the trick, sir?" ventured Harley.

"Doesn't seem that kind of lady to me," Bob mused. "A bit too fierce for tea." He shrugged helplessly. "But it can't hurt to try. You go and make it, Harley. I'll watch the door."

In ten minutes, the batman reappeared, a tray bearing tea and a plate of buttered toast in his hands.

"I thought she might be 'ungry, sir. A little toast might be soothing."

Bob looked doubtful but opened the door.

"If you do not leave me alone this instant, I shall strip naked," announced the lady in fierce and unmistakably genuine threat.

Harley nearly dropped the tray. "I . . . I . . . just brought you a little . . . little . . . breakfast, miss," he stammered, standing in the doorway, holding his offering.

For answer, the lady seized the hem of her tunic and began to pull it up. Both men gasped and fled the room.

"Lord," murmured Bob, wiping his brow.

"What 'as the lieutenant gone an' done, now, sir?" Harley set the tray on the hall table. "I know he 'as his frolics, a bit wild-like sometimes, but nothin' like this. Lost 'is wits, I shouldn't wonder."

Bob was all too well aware of his friend's obsession with the mysterious Englishwoman in Akbar Khan's zenana; although he had taken it no more seriously than anyone else, had assumed it was fed by brandy and the all-pervasive dissatisfaction and boredom of life in Kabul. Now, however, it rather looked as if it were a very serious matter indeed. Kit had clearly acted without thought for the consequences, and without any planning for the woman's future. He had never intimated, either, that the woman would be so fiercely resistant to rescue, should it be possible to effect.

Absently, he poured himself a cup of tea from the spurned breakfast tray, and nibbled a piece of toast.

"Oh, I don't think much of it," Macnaghten said, peering into his coffee cup. "Just a few of those damned rebels getting above themselves."

"Sir William, they have butchered the English in the residency, and the sepoys as well," Kit said, wondering when the last frayed tether of his temper would snap. "The residency and the Treasury have been fired. Prompt and vigorous military action are needed if the insurrection is to be quashed.''

"Well, it is a damnable shame we have lost Burnes and the Treasury,'' Elphinstone quavered. "I do feel we should do something, Sir William.''

Kit wondered if this were really happening. He had described as vividly as he could the scenes in the city, and these two had listened, at first as if they did not believe him, and then as if he must have exaggerated.

Sir William went to the window and stuck his head out. Faint sounds continued to come from the city, and the smell of smoke still hung in the air. "I suggest we order Shelton to march into the Balla Hissar from the Seah Sung heights, General. He can reestablish order in the city from there. Just the sight of his brigade will probably be sufficient to send the rats scuttling back to their holes.''

At least it was something. Kit went off to send the order to Shelton, but when he returned to the general's office in the hopes of being dismissed in order to change out of his unconventional garb, he was told by a wavering Elphinstone to send another runner to Shelton countermanding the first order.

"I think we should wait a little longer,'' the general said. "Just to see if things quiet down by themselves.''

"Akbar Khan is in the city,'' Kit said. "He will not permit things to quiet down, sir ''

"Lieutenant, were you never taught to obey orders?'' testily demanded the general.

Kit saluted and left to send the second dispatch. He decided that from here on, he would play the good soldier, obeying orders, however inane, without the least attempt to moderate idiocy with common sense. It would be less frustrating in the end, and it just might get him released from duty all the sooner and free to tackle the ever-pressing matter of Annabel.

Chapter 8

It was an hour later, however, before Kit was finally given permission to return to his bungalow and the attentions of his batman. In that hour, Shelton had again been ordered to march to the Balla Hissar, but when Kit left, Elphinstone was still wittering wretchedly as to whether the decision had been overhasty. Perhaps, after all, he should send to Shelton and tell him to halt his march, and await further orders?

Kit fled, leaving his alternate adjutant to muddle through the conflict. He found Bob and Harley sitting glumly outside his bedroom door.

Bob sprang to his feet at first sight of Kit with a heartfelt "Thank God!"

"Why, what has happened?" Kit's eyes went in alarm to the closed door. "Annabel is all right, is she not?"

"As far as I know," Bob said, straightening his tunic. "Wouldn't let either of us in there."

"I tried to take miss a nice breakfast tray," Harley contributed, "and she told me to leave 'er alone." Two red spots glowed on his weathered, leathery cheeks. "Threatened to take 'er clothes off in front of me, she did, sir. You couldn't expect me to—"

"No . . . no, of course not," Kit interrupted hastily, even as a bubble of crazy laughter edged its way into his voice. He turned into the sitting room, poured himself a large brandy, and drank it down in one swallow.

Bob regarded him rather as one might watch a close friend who has just run amok. "My dear chap, are you sure you know what you're doing?"

Kit shook his head, wiped his mouth with the back of his hand. "Not in the least. I only know I won't let her go . . . not again."

Bob pulled at his chin. "What did you think of doin' with her, Kit?"

Kit gave a short laugh. "Ridiculous, I know, but I had thought to solicit Lady Sale's protection for her . . . an orphaned, abducted girl of good family, returned to the bosom of her own people after horrendous experiences. I was sure the old dragon would assume the charge with the utmost enthusiasm."

"I'm sure she would, if the charge were of a different character," Bob observed. "But with the lady in her present mood, it's a preposterous idea."

"I know." Kit fortified himself with another slug of brandy and turned resolutely to the door. "I'd best go and sort things out."

"Yes, I think you had," agreed Bob. "And I'd best report for duty. What's Elphinstone doing about the riot?"

"Dear God." Kit groaned, pausing at the door. "He doesn't know what to do. It's been nothing but orders, and countermanded orders, and repeated orders. And Macnaghten isn't much better, just as indecisive, although he doesn't make it so obvious. If Ayesha is right, and I begin to think she is, we'll none of us get free and clear of Afghanistan."

"Ayesha?"

"I thought I said before: in Akbar Khan's zenana, Annabel is known as Ayesha," Kit replied. "And for the life of me, Bob, I don't know whether to approach Ayesha or Annabel at this moment."

"Ayesha," said his friend firmly. "Ladies called Annabel Spencer don't threaten to strip naked before two strange men. Mind you," he added, "I'm not sure inhabitants of zenanas do either."

"This one doesn't seem to fit any particular mold." Kit remembered how he had first met her, and the memory brought inspiration. He would meet confrontation with confrontation until she was prepared to talk in the way he knew she could and would, eventually, once she stepped back and looked at the realities. And once she began to talk with him, *then* he could begin to build.

"I'm excused duty until this evening. Keep me informed of what's happening, will you, Bob?"

"Of course. And for what it's worth, I wish you luck."

He was going to need rather more than luck, Kit reflected, as an added precaution locking the front door after his friend before taking the high road to his bedroom. How did one convince someone that she had been rescued, not abducted?

At the sound of the doorknob turning, Ayesha said loudly, "If you take one more step into this room, I shall take off my clothes."

Kit closed the door behind him. "A prospect that can only afford me inestimable pleasure, Annabel."

"Oh, it's you." She got off the bed, where she had been lying staring up at the ceiling. "I thought it was one of your cohorts. Could we stop this nonsense now?"

"It's not nonsense." He came toward her, smiling, holding out his hands. "I told you I could not leave you—"

"By what right do you interfere in my life? I told *you* I wanted nothing of your feringhee blundering. I do not live by your rules, and I do not bear your labels. How many times must I tell you that?"

"Annabel—"

"That is *not* my name!"

Kit took a deep breath and reached for her hands. "Ayesha, listen to me."

She stood very still, her hands resting limp in his. Her nose wrinkled, and for an instant her eyes closed. She had not smelled that pungent aroma on a man's breath since she was a little girl. It took her back to another world . . . when her father had lifted her for a welcoming hug, or had leaned over her in her neat childhood bed to give her his good-night kiss.

"My father always said that a man who drank before noon could never be relied upon," she said distantly, removing her hands from Kit's.

Kit felt the hot flush of discomfort rush to his face. He swung away from her. "I had a brandy . . . after the last few hours, a man's entitled, for God's sake."

She shrugged. "I wouldn't know. But I do know that your Afghan opponents will not be facing you befuddled with alcohol."

"What are you? Some kind of Puritan?" he demanded, as the ground slipped beneath his feet and he found himself pushed to the attack on a completely nonrelevant issue.

"You forget where I come from, Ralston, *huzoor*," she taunted, in control of this exchange for all her essentially captive state. "I abide by the laws of Islam, and I do not find them in the least distasteful."

"Don't talk in that fashion!"

"I will talk in whatever fashion I choose, Christopher Ralston! I do not obey your orders or your whims."

"But by your own admission you obey the orders and whims of men," he threw at her. "By the laws of Islam, is it not so?"

Ayesha was abruptly engulfed with the rage that had consumed her during the mortifying, painful ride to which he had subjected her. She slapped him; and then again, while he was still reeling from the first blow. But as her hand drew back for the third time, he grabbed her wrist. He was now as lost in the essence of battle as she was; as much at the mercy of the primitive, elemental reactions usually so well hidden beneath the veneer of polite congress.

"No! Not again, Ayesha. Strike me one more time, and so help me I'll wallop you right back!" The declaration bit into the air. His fingers tightened around her wrist. For a long moment, they stood thus, both breathing heavily, locked in a contest of wills. Then he felt the slowing of her pulse, the gradual relaxation as she brought herself under control.

"That would not surprise me in the least, Christopher Ralston," she said with an icy calm that matched her complete immobility. "I would not expect a gentlemanly restraint from you. Brutality and abduction are hardly acts of chivalry."

"Brutality?" The word shocked him from his brief sense of ascendancy.

"How else would you describe the way you forced me from my home and dragged me here?" The jade eyes were now filled with scorn.

He could not dispute it. "You gave me no choice," he said. "I would not hurt you for the world, Annabel, but there was no other way to get you here. You would not come willingly."

"And I suppose, following the laws of Islam you purport to despise, you decided that I must go where you wished." She sounded simply weary now. "Let us have done with this silliness, Christopher. I will go back to Kabul. I cannot have been missed for more than two, maybe three hours. I will say I wished to see what was happening and became caught up in the crowd and could not get back to the house." Even as she said this, she knew such an explanation would have no credence in Akbar Khan's household. He would never believe she had deliberately disobeyed him. He knew too well his own power and her recognition of it.

Kit shook his head. "You would never have left the house unveiled, Ayesha. How would you explain that?"

She shrugged, improvised, even though she recognized the futility. "I will say I lost my veil in the rioting." But Akbar Khan would have the truth from her. She could not possibly conceal it from him. And when he had the truth, he would not rest until Christopher Ralston had paid the penalty according to Koranic law.

"Why would you do this to me?" she said, her shoulders sagging in sudden defeat. "I told you I did not wish to be a part of this disaster. I do not belong here. I could never belong in your world."

"But you can," he said with passion. "I will teach you to belong."

"Such arrogance!" she exploded, swinging away from him. "Feringhee, you can teach me nothing! You saw what happened in Kabul. Do you think that is the end of it? It's but the beginning of the end! You will have no world soon."

Kit's features set into hard lines of stubborn determination. "You are an Englishwoman, Annabel Spencer. That is the only reality that concerns me. When you've come to terms with that, then we can discuss how best to proceed." He marched to the door and bellowed for Harley.

The batman appeared instantly. "Yes, sir." He stood attentively, but his wary eyes were fixed upon the slender, copper-haired creature fulminating by the window.

"I want to bath," Kit said, "and get this muck off my face. Also, I could do with some breakfast. You must be hungry, too, Annabel," he added, politely, dispassionately considerate.

"I will not eat your salt, Ralston, *huzoor*," she snapped.

He shrugged. "Please yourself. Fill the tub for me, Harley."

"Yes, sir." Harley hauled a brass hip bath from a cupboard and dumped it before the fire. His expression was a study in shock and disapproval barely restrained. He went off, reappearing shortly with two jugs of steaming water. He filled the bath. He looked at his officer, and then at the woman who had not moved a muscle, it seemed, in the last ten minutes. He cleared his throat. "Should I show miss to the sitting room, sir?"

"Good God, no," Kit said, sitting on the bed to pull off his boots. "I'm not letting her out of my sight."

Ayesha's breath was expelled in a low hiss. It seemed the battle lines had been drawn. But if he thought she was going to take the slightest interest in his toilet, he was much mistaken. Somehow, though, she delayed turning her back on the scene by the fire just a fraction too long, and when she did so, her memory of that broad-shouldered, well-muscled body, slim-waisted and narrow-hipped, had been recharged.

Kit had been well aware of her surreptitious gaze as he stepped naked into the bath, and he did not misinterpret the haste with which she had swung away to face the wall. It afforded him a modicum of satisfaction in this generally unsatisfactory situation. That current of passion still flowed between them. He had known it since that moment in the bazaar—a moment when nothing had existed but their own selves, reaching for each other, the shared longing naked in their eyes. From then on, he had known that only one course was open to them. She must enter his world since he could not enter hers. He wanted her, and she wanted him. If he could establish her in his world, then what was between them could develop at its own pace.

But first she had to be brought to acknowledge the passion openly. And she would not do that while she fought him. He turned his head against the rim of the tub to look at her through half-closed eyes. "Annabel?"

A quiver rippled through the still figure, but she neither turned nor responded.

Kit sighed and began to scrub the boot polish off his face. Harley's return to the bedroom with the lieutenant's freshly brushed uniform broke the silence, and Kit, resolutely ignoring the third person in the room, engaged his batman in customary conversation as he shaved and dressed. Harley was less successful at pretending Annabel was not there, so the conversation was somewhat stilted, but he did volunteer the information that since Kit had left headquarters, a runner had come from the Balla Hissar to say that the shah, on his own initiative, had

ordered one of his own levies, under Colonel Campbell, to engage the rebels in the city.

"With what result?" Kit asked, buttoning his tunic.

"Too early to say, sir. Captain Markham's servant
just brought me the news. The captain thought you
might be glad to 'ear it." He dipped a jug into the
tub, drawing off the dirty water, then glanced uneasily at the woman. "Will I lay breakfast in the dining room, sir? Or in 'ere?"

"In the dining room, please. For two," Kit said.

"I will not eat your salt," Ayesha said again, still
without turning to face the room.

"You are being childish," Kit said, waving Harley
toward the door.

"You dare to accuse *me* of childishness!" She spun
around on him. "You are behaving like some blindly
willful, spoiled brat, just like the rest of your mis-
begotten colleagues in this place. Refusing to acknowledge realities, firmly convinced that you can
ride roughshod over anyone—"

"Annabel, that is not so," he interrupted. "Now,
please—" He came over to her, holding out his
hands. "Please, cry peace. Think of the opportunity
we have. Only Bob and Harley know you're here.
We won't have to present you to Lady Sale for a
little while. Until then, we could enjoy ourselves—"

"Is that all you can think of? " The expression in
the jade eyes was incredulous. "At this moment,
with murder and mayhem all around you, all you
can think of is lust. You abduct me from my home
and force me into yours. I suppose ravishment is the
natural conclusion!"

"Do not be absurd," he said softly, sure of his
ground this time. He caught her chin, tilting her face
to meet his desirous gaze. "Yes, I want you . . . yes,
that wanting has fed my obsession to get you away
from Akbar Khan. But I can offer you a better life,
Annabel, than any he could offer you, if only you
would stop spitting for a minute and think about it.
When we get out of this godforsaken country—"

"You will never leave Afghanistan alive," she interrupted flatly, but the heat had gone from her voice, and he could detect a hint of uncertainty swimming in the depths of those clear eyes.

"You want me, too," he said, softly insistent. "Say it, Annabel."

"Breakfast is served, sir."

Kit swore under his breath. He released his hold on her chin. "Come and have breakfast."

She shook her head. "I have already told you—"

"That you will not eat my salt," he supplied wearily. "Very well, it is up to you. When you're ready to discuss this rationally, just let me know. I'll be waiting." He turned and left the bedroom, closing the door firmly behind him. "Harley, make sure that all the outside doors of the bungalow are kept locked at all times, and that the keys remain on your person," he instructed, marching into the dining room. "Miss Spencer is to have the freedom of the house when she chooses to take it."

"Yes, sir," Harley said woodenly.

Annabel examined the room that she had designated as her own prison cell. There was a carafe of water, a chamber pot in the commode cupboard beside the bed; the basic necessities. It was simply a question of how long she could hold out.

She flung herself on the bed again, staring up at the ceiling. Of course she would not be able to hold out indefinitely. Escape was as pointless as it appeared impossible. While Akbar Khan would be unlikely to punish her involuntary part in her disappearance, he would be revenged upon Christopher. And it was inconceivable that she should expose Kit to that danger. However angry she might be with him, she could not deny to herself how important it was for her peace of mind that he stay safe and well.

She had been tormented by fear for him during the weeks since he had ridden away after the *buzkashi*, her nights haunted with images of his inevitable fate if he could not find a way to leave this embattled land. In many ways she believed the feringhee invaders had brought their end upon themselves. She understood the Afghan, knew and understood their need for vengeance, for all that she recoiled from its inevitable savagery. But she would protect Kit from it as far as she was able. Why that should be, she had so far chosen not to examine. The question and its answer seemed to lead down a blind and frustrating alley. It was an alley Kit seemed determined to explore . . . passion . . . wanting . . . yes, she felt all of that. But the years of her growing had taught her to subjugate any emotion that might hinder the clarity of judgment necessary to steer her path through the complexities of Akbar Khan's zenana. And all-consuming desire for another man was definitely an interference.

Yet acknowledging that desire did nothing to lessen her sense of outrage at the position in which she now found herself. And Christopher Ralston was going to come to a recognition of the justice of that outrage. Since she did not believe the Afghans would permit the British to leave Afghanistan alive, her own future seemed academic. She would be with them and would therefore suffer the same fate. But she would not yield passively to the new existence decreed for her by Lieutenant Christopher Ralston. When all was said and done, *he* was not an Afghan khan. On which thought, she fell asleep.

Kit ate his breakfast, but without much pleasure. It was simply a necessary refueling. He was hungry, and the thought that Annabel must be also didn't aid enjoyment. He reached for the brandy decanter; then his hand stilled, as he recalled Annabel's lightly scornful tones. It was past time he exercised a little moderation where that sop and strengthener was concerned. He refilled his teacup instead.

His appetite satisfied, he paced the dining room restlessly; went into the sitting room and did the same there; he wandered into the small hallway; apart from his bedroom, Harley's quarters and the kitchen, that comprised the entire accommodation in this unmarried officer's bungalow. He hovered outside the bedroom door. He had said he would leave her alone until she indicated that she wanted both company and sustenance, but his hand found its own way to the doorknob. He turned it slowly and pushed open the door. He didn't need to go over to the bed to verify that her sleep was not counterfeit. The complete relaxation of her body, and the deep, rhythmic breathing, were sufficient. Soundlessly, and with disappointment, he closed the door again and put his head into the kitchen.

"Harley, I'm going to headquarters to find out what's going on. If Miss Spencer wants anything, see that she gets it . . . and lock the front door after me."

Harley, wearing the long-suffering air of the uncomplaining martyr, accompanied him to the front door, solemnly locking it on the lieutenant's departure. He tucked the key into his jacket pocket and returned to the kitchen.

An atmosphere of chaotic gloom hung over the headquarters bungalow as Kit saluted the sentry and entered the adjutant's office. Lieutenant Watson looked up in distraction from the sheaf of dispatches on the table. "Oh, Ralston, thought you weren't on duty until this evening."

"I'm not, but I couldn't sit twiddling my thumbs. What's happening?"

"Just chaos," Watson said glumly, indicating the dispatches. "The general has been shilly-shallying about Shelton ever since you left, and Sir William has now ordered Shelton into the Balla Hissar with instructions to use his own judgment, in communication with the shah, on how he proceeds from there."

Kit grimaced. "What of Campbell?"

Watson shrugged. "The last we heard, he was attempting to push his way to the residency through the center of the city and meeting fierce resistance on every street."

"He's trying to take a fighting brigade through those alleys?" Kit exclaimed. "Why the hell didn't he go around the city? At least he'd have open spaces in which to maneuver."

"Don't ask me," the lieutenant said. "Not my job to question." A querulous call came from the adjoining room and he sighed. "Our commander calls."

Kit went in search of Bob Markham, and found him in the map room, bent over the chart table. "Oh, hello, Kit. Come and have a look here. I've been told to recall Major Griffiths from Kubbar-i-Jubbar. Do you think he can get through this country?"

Kit examined the map. "Griffiths is a good man," he said bluntly.

"Good enough to make it through these passes? The Afghans will be holding them. He'll have to fight every step of the way."

"What about Sale?"

"Fallen back on Jalalabad; says he can't get through to Kabul. Elphinstone's sent a runner to Nott at Kandahar, asking him to send a brigade to Kabul."

"I don't give much for his chances," Kit said grimly. "Lord, Bob, what a hole we're in!"

"And getting deeper by the minute," his friend agreed.

"Has anyone found out what's going on with Colin Mackenzie? He's in charge of the other commissariat fort containing Shah Soojah's supplies."

Bob inhaled sharply. "Damn, I don't think anyone's given him a thought. He's completely exposed out there on the outskirts of the city."

"Got a good many women and children in the fort, as I understand."

The two men looked at each other, each imagining the hordes of Ghilzais and Ghazis attacking Mackenzie and his small garrison, with its vulnerable inhabitants.

"I'll talk to Elphinstone and Macnaghten. See if they'll authorize a force from here to go to his aid." Bob left at a near run, and Kit bent over the maps again.

Kabul was such a tiny isolated spot; Jalalabad so near yet so far through treacherous Ghilzai-held passes; Kandahar and Quetta an impossible distance for any but a fighting force in perfect condition. Women, children, camp followers, and all the baggage attendant upon the mass exodus of an army could never make it—not in winter, and not under the continuous harassment of warrior hillmen with their long rifles.

Would Akbar Khan permit them to leave unmolested, supposing Elphinstone and Macnaghten could be persuaded to negotiate? Annabel did not think so. And from what Kit had seen of the Dost's son, he did not think so, either.

"God Almighty, Kit! Those bungling asses won't lift a finger for Colin." Bob charged into the room, his face pink with indignation, fire in the usually mild blue eyes. "Captain Mackenzie must fend for himself." He offered a fair imitation of Sir William's pompous tones. "We don't know that he's under attack, after all," he went on, sounding as quavery as Elphinstone.

Kit could not help a ruefully appreciative grin, despite the desperation of the message. "You should have gone on the stage, Bob."

"I can think of worse careers," his friend returned. "The army for instance. What are you doing here, anyway? You're not on duty. I rather assumed you'd be busy sorting out that other matter."

"She's asleep," Kit said. "And she's so bloody stubborn! She'd make a good match for Macnaghten." He flung himself into a chair by the window. "I'd rather stay here, quite frankly, than pace around at home, chewing my fingernails, wondering what new tack to take when she wakes."

Bob shook his head wonderingly. "You've been bitten by a powerful madness, Kit. But in present circumstances, it seems curiously fitting. Only lunatic responses are appropriate, seems to me."

* * *

Annabel woke up to an imperatively appetizing aroma. It was familiar, but it belonged to life before Akbar Khan, and she could not identify it. Her mouth filled with saliva, and her empty belly grumbled in sympathy. Starving herself was clearly ridiculous. She would have to find some other means of expressing her anger with Christopher Ralston.

Springing from the bed, she brushed down her tunic and trousers, both of which had suffered on the mad ride from Kabul, and glanced in the mirror over the dresser. Her hair was in some disorder, but she used Kit's comb to reasonable effect, then left the room, following her nose.

It led her to the kitchen. "What is it that you are cooking?"

Harley, standing at the stove swathed in an enormous apron, jumped. "Gawd, miss, you startled me!"

"Oh, I beg your pardon. I am used to moving quietly." She smiled. "May I come in?"

"If you like, miss." Harley looked awkwardly around the small kitchen that he was accustomed to considering his private domain. "Shall I cook you up a bit o' bacon?"

"Oh, it's bacon . . . of course," she said, perching on a stool at the table. "I haven't smelled it in eight or nine years and I could not remember what it was. . . . Yes, please, I would love some. I am famished."

"You'd like an egg with it, then. And a piece o' fried bread, I daresay," Harley observed. His tone was hardly welcoming, but he no longer looked at her as if she belonged to some strange and definitely dangerous species.

"Mmmm," Annabel agreed with hungry enthusiasm. "And a cup of tea now." She smiled at the stolid figure wielding his spatula. "I am sorry I was so discourteous earlier. But I am afraid I was so angry with the lieutenant, I wasn't really thinking clearly. It was very kind of you to bring me tea."

Harley flushed, cleared his throat. "It's none o' my business, miss, what the lieutenant gets up to.

I've found it best to keep me own counsel. There's a cup o' tea in the pot if you'd like to pour.'' He indicated the fat teapot wrapped in a cloth to keep it hot.

This Englishman clearly didn't hold with samovars, Annabel thought. He also clearly did not approve of certain of his officer's activities, even if he did keep his own counsel.

Cups were to be found hanging on hooks in the wall. She poured the strong brew into two of them and took a deep, revivifying gulp. ''Do you know where Lieutenant Ralston is at the moment?''

''Gone to 'eadquarters, miss,'' Harley informed her. ''He's not on duty till this evening as I understand, but there's a deal goin' on at present.'' With an expert twitch of his wrist, he flipped the egg over in the bacon fat and then back again before sliding the contents of the frying pan onto a plate. ''There you are, miss. I'll take this into the dining room for you.''

Annabel was about to say that she would be quite happy to eat in the kitchen with the batman, but it occurred to her that the happiness would not be shared, either because he disapproved of her, or because it would offend his sense of social propriety. Probably a bit of both, she decided, following him into the dining room, carrying her mug of tea.

''Have you been with Lieutenant Ralston for many years, Harley?''

Harley put the laden plate on the table and took cutlery and linen from a drawer in the sideboard. ''Five years, miss. I was 'is batman when he first joined the Seventh Light.'' His lips drew together in a thin line of disapproval. ''Never expected to find ourselves out 'ere, we didn't. But I suppose, the way the lieutenant was carryin' on, it 'ad to 'appen. But a long way from Horseguards Parade it is, out 'ere among the 'eathen.'' A sudden flush darkened the leathery, rubicund countenance. ''Meaning no offense, miss. I know you're dressed like one of 'em, but it's clear as day you're not one of 'em.''

Annabel considered this as she sat down. "No, strictly speaking I'm as English as you. Only I don't think of myself as such. I've lived among the Afghans since I was twelve."

Harley's jaw dropped, and he stared. "Well, I never!"

"That's rather how the lieutenant reacts," she said with a slight smile. "It seems to strike to the heart of his patriotism."

"Not just the 'eart of 'is patriotism, I'll be bound," Harley observed darkly, putting a cruet before her. "It's that rovin' eye of 'is . . . always getting 'im into trouble." On which profundity, he left Annabel to her solitary breakfast.

So the lieutenant had a roving eye. Annabel took a mouthful of bacon and egg. It didn't exactly surprise her. But what had happened in London to earn him this sentence of banishment, as Harley had implied?

Dismissing the questions for the time being, she turned her attention to the deliciously familiar yet unaccustomed taste sensations on her plate and the contemplation of a bath before the bedroom fire to follow. But making plans for her day in these unfamiliar surroundings inevitably provoked other questions.

What was happening in Akbar Khan's house in Kabul? What had they made of her disappearance? How energetically would he pursue the investigation? Or was he now so deeply immersed in building the avalanche about to fall upon the feringhee invaders that he would have no time to concern himself with the fate of one who was, when all was said and done, simply an expendable female?

It would be so much easier if the latter were the case. Easier . . . and safer.

Chapter 9

Akbar Khan sat as still as if he had been sculpted.
His eyes seemed to look through the weeping
Soraya on her knees before him and way beyond the
circle of soldiers and servants lining the room.

"You are certain that only a mantle from the hall
is missing?" He spoke finally, his voice even, lacking so much as a trace of annoyance. But no one in
the room was deceived. They were all to a greater
or lesser extent guilty, and this stocky, powerful man
in his smart green tunic and lace-edged shirt would
pass just and appropriate sentence on every one of
them.

"Yes, khan," Soraya answered. "All her belongings remain in her room. She must have dressed,
because her nightclothes are upon the divan. . . . If
only I had not slept so soundly!" She began to wail,
calling upon the Prophet to punish her laziness and
lack of vigilance over such a precious charge.

"The fault was not yours," Akbar Khan said,
breaking into her caterwauling. "You slept no later
than you were accustomed to doing. The fault lies
with the guards who deserted their posts and the
servants who failed to bolt the doors. Ayesha did
not leave here of her own free will." The vivid blue
gaze swept the room, and in its wake even the brav-
est trembled. "Someone entered this house and took
her from it."

"But there was no sign of a struggle, sirdar. And

140

if Ayesha had cried out, then someone would have heard her,'' his chamberlain pointed out.

"That is true." The sirdar frowned. "Soraya would certainly have woken had Ayesha called for her."

So why had she not summoned help? He stroked his beard. Ayesha would not have left on some whim of her own. That was a fact beyond dispute. It was not a possibility worth considering. But she *had* left, it would seem, without overt protest. Which would seem to imply that she knew her abductor and was not afraid of him . . . or had she been afraid *for* him?

Gently, he nodded. If she had been afraid to alert the household to the presence of this intruder for fear of the consequences to him, then it would explain much. But the only British in Kabul who were not in the Balla Hissar that night had been massacred by the mob. There had been no traffic between the cantonment and the city for many hours before the attack on the residency. Or so he had believed.

His gaze snapped into focus. If Ayesha was now in the cantonment with the British, she was being held as safe for him as if he had her under his own roof. He could retrieve her easily enough when the time came to force the feringhee to abandon their position in favor of retreat. That time was drawing ever closer, and this personal affront would make the reckoning all the more satisfying. But now he had to deal with the negligence and desertion of certain members of his household. His eyes ran slowly around the room again, and they were hard as agate.

"Campbell has been forced back to the Balla Hissar." Watson emerged from the general's sanctum with this gloomy report. "A runner has just come from the shah. Shelton attempted to cover the retreat, but they still abandoned their guns outside the fort."

Bob Markham swore. "Leaving them to those savages!"

"Apparently there's mayhem in the city," Watson went on. "The people are on a rampage, looting, raping, butchering; only their own people at this point, but it's certainly keeping them fired up."

"So Kabul is now entirely in Afghan hands," Kit mused. He sat sprawled in a chair by the window, one leg thrown carelessly over the arm. "And no one can do anything about it."

"You think you can do better than Brigadier Shelton and Colonel Campbell, Lieutenant Ralston?" Sir William stood in the doorway of the adjutant's office, puffing out his chest.

Kit rose in leisurely fashion to his feet. "Not in the least, Sir William. The time when we could have succeeded with vigorous military intervention is past. Early this morning we might have achieved something, but the city is too securely in rebel hands now."

"It seems extraordinary to me, Lieutenant, that your brilliant analyses and well-timed advice have failed to earn you the promotion I am certain you richly deserve," said the Envoy with icy sarcasm. "General Elphinstone is feeling most unwell and is taking to his bed for the rest of the day. There is no more to be done here, so I suggest you all return to your quarters and hold yourselves in readiness should you be called." He turned and strutted off.

"Did I hear aright?" Bob Markham blinked. "Have we just been given a holiday?"

"That's what it sounded like to me," Kit said. "Afghan rebels are amusing themselves with a little rape, a little looting, a little murder in Kabul, and we shrug our shoulders and take to our beds."

"And meanwhile, Colin Mackenzie is stuck out there—Goddamnit, Kit! I need a drink." Bob slung his cape around his shoulders. "I'm going home to drown my sorrows." He stalked out of the room, and Kit followed him out into the bitter November afternoon.

The cantonment seemed to be in a state of shock, he thought. The bungalows were shuttered tight; there was none of the usual activity in the narrow streets, no one in their gardens, no children with their nursemaids. There were no servants to be seen making their usual rounds from bungalow to bungalow, bearing invitations and messages. Smoke curling from chimneys was the only sign of occupation, and that would not continue for long, he reflected grimly. Not unless they were able to replenish the fuel supplies—something that could only be done outside the cantonment in the open plain where Afghan tribesmen were massed, waiting.

He reached his own front door and turned the handle. It wouldn't budge, and he remembered his instructions to Harley. He knocked loudly. How would he find Annabel now? Still angry, still resistant? Or had she reached some acceptance in the hours since his departure? Eager anticipation prickled his spine, reverberating in his voice as Harley pulled open the door.

"How is Miss Spencer?"

"Havin' a bath, sir," the batman informed him in wooden accents. "She asked me to prepare it for 'er twenty minutes ago."

Kit stepped into the hall, shrugging off his cape. "Has she had anything to eat?"

Harley took the cape and hung it on a waiting hook. "'Ad a good breakfast, sir."

Breakfast and baths had to augur well, Kit decided.

"Is there any news, sir?"

Kit paused long enough to bring Harley up to date with the news from Kabul and the Balla Hissar before heading for his bedroom. He knocked but did not wait for invitation to enter.

She lay in the hip bath before the fire, her copper hair piled high on top of her head, her skin white as milk in the firelight.

"Am I to have no privacy?" Her voice did not match the warm, glowing room. She turned her head against the rim of the bath. Her eyes, cold and polished as green quartz, appraised him.

"I'm sorry. I was just so anxious to see you," he said with what he hoped was disarming candor. "Shall I go away again?"

The smooth milky shoulders lifted in a nearly imperceptible shrug, as if his presence were a matter of complete indifference. She raised one shapely leg high out of the water and began to soap it with an air of absorption.

Kit's hands moved as if they were performing the task of her own and his breath came swiftly. "Could I do that for you?"

"No." The flat denial seemed to admit of no negotiation.

He went to sit on the bed, where he could watch her. "I thought you might be interested in the news from the city."

She switched legs. "Has the might of the British raj quelled the riot, then? Avenged the murder of its citizens?"

Kit winced. "No, on the contrary."

She returned both legs to the tub and sat up, hugging her knees, regarding him now with interest. "They must have done something?"

Kit told her the events of the day and she shook her head in disbelief. "No Afghan could believe that you would not avenge your dead. They will despise you even more."

Kit could not find the words of argument on this score. Besides, he was losing interest in the conversation. In fact, if the truth were told, he had only begun it as a means of overcoming the chilly indifference of this entrancing bather. She was leaning back again and her breasts rose enticingly out of the water, rose-crowned, smooth and full as he had remembered them so vividly in the last weeks. He came over to the tub, dropping to one knee.

"Annabel . . . ?"

"No. Unless I have lost free will in *everything*."

Kit sighed and stood up again. "I'm sorry. I'll

leave you alone." He started to leave the room just as there came a knocking at the front door. "Who the hell's that?" He went into the hall, closing the bedroom door carefully behind him.

Harley was already unlocking the front door. "Good afternoon, Captain . . . Lieutenant Graham . . . Lieutenant Troughton." He stepped aside to admit Bob Markham, Derek Graham, and William Troughton.

"Thought we might drown our sorrows together," Bob stated, flourishing a bottle of claret. It was obvious that he was already well on the way to achieving that happy goal, and his companions were not looking exactly miserable.

Kit frowned. Surely Bob hadn't forgotten about his friend's "guest." "It's a little awkward," he began, and then changed his mind. Annabel had made it very clear that she did not wish for his company, so why should he sit in miserable solitude staring into the sitting room fire?

"Come in. Harley, open a couple of bottles of the thirty-five claret, will you?"

He ushered the three into the sitting room. "I could do with some cheering up." He threw more wood onto the fire and went to pull the curtains across the window, shutting out the bleak approach of evening. "Whist?" He rummaged in a drawer for cards.

In the room next door, Annabel heard the murmur of voices through the thin interior wall. Stepping out of the bath, she dried herself, all the while straining to distinguish words and voices from the generalized murmur. How many visitors did he have? She thought she could make out the voice of the man she had met that morning—the one who had appeared to know all about her. Were Kit's other visitors also party to the mess gossip? It was reasonable to assume so. He had clearly not thought Ayesha's part in his adventures deserving of a gentlemanly reticence when recounting the story. For some reason, the thought hurt as much as it angered, and provoked both the desire and scheme for retaliation.

She dressed in her trousers and tunic, slipped her feet into the curly-toed slippers, hooking the toes to the hem of the trousers, and plaited her hair, letting the heavy braid fall down her back. All she lacked was a veil.

Christopher's dresser drawers yielded shirts, underclothes, handkerchiefs, and cravats. She took one of the latter, shook it out of its neatly ironed folds and nodded her satisfaction. It would make a perfectly serviceable veil draped over her head and drawn across her face, leaving only her eyes visible. A small enameled box on top of the dresser offered a diamond-headed pin. Reasoning that since Kit had removed her from her own belongings without thought or consideration, he had the obligation to make good their lack, she used the pin to fasten the makeshift veil at her ear.

The dresser mirror showed her Ayesha.

Quietly, she left the bedroom, paused outside the door to the sitting room, listened to the laughter and the voices, some of them sounding a trifle thick, then she turned the knob and opened the door.

The four men looked up from the card table expecting to see Harley. They saw an Afghan woman in the door. Her hands touched her forehead in a salaam of greeting before she moved as smoothly as sunlight across the room and sat on the floor before the fire. Folding her hands in her lap, she sat with lowered eyes, quite motionless.

Kit recovered first. "Annabel, what are you playing at?" he demanded uneasily.

Her eyes lifted to his. "Am I permitted to speak in front of your guests, Ralston, *huzoor*? I had thought that maybe you might wish me to entertain them in some way. You are aware, I believe, that I have some skills." There was such pointed insolence in her voice that for a moment he was speechless, until he realized what she meant. His chair clattered to the floor under the vigor of his rising.

"You dare to suggest—"

Bob sobered dramatically as his friend, white with anger, descended upon the seated woman. "Steady on, Kit. Keep your temper, old man."

"Keep my temper!" Kit exclaimed. "Do you realize what she's suggesting?"

"Why should it trouble you?" Ayesha inquired, more calmly than she felt. For some reason she had not expected Kit to evince quite this degree of fury, had rather assumed he would be rendered mute with shame and embarrassment. "I'm sure your friends are well aware of the entertainment an Afghan host offers his guest . . . if only by listening to your experiences. You have taken possession of me, in the manner of any khan. It is customary for a host to share his possessions. I assumed you would wish to do so."

There was an instant of shocked silence, then Bob Markham coughed awkwardly and stood up. "Really sorry, Kit, I forgot all about this . . . this other matter. Should never have come . . . we'll be on our way."

Kit waved him back to his chair, without taking his eyes off Ayesha. The wave of blind anger had receded, leaving an icy calm in its wake. He did not know what lay behind this extraordinary scene, but he had a feeling it was not pure mischief. "No, there's no need for any of you to leave. Let me make formal introductions." Reaching down, he took her hands and drew her to her feet. "Miss Spencer, may I introduce Bob Markham, Derek Graham, and William Troughton." Deftly, he took the diamond pin from the makeshift veil and flipped the cravat aside. "Ingenious," he remarked dryly. "Gentlemen, Miss Annabel Spencer."

"Damn, Kit! You got her out then," observed William Troughton in much the same tone as Bob had used that morning.

"What a brilliant deduction," Annabel said acidly. "I should be flattered, I'm sure, to be a subject of such interest. Have you been laying bets on the matter?''

Kit closed his eyes for a second. ''All right,'' he said quietly. ''You've made your point . . . hammered it, one might say. Now, let's go into the other room and sort this out.''

''I cannot imagine what there is to sort out—''

''Well, I can,'' he interrupted. ''Excuse us a minute. The wine's on the table.'' He gestured toward the side table before planting a hand in the small of Ayesha's back and pushing her toward the door.

She went unresisting, since she suspected that resistance might result in an undignified rout.

In the bedroom, Kit kicked the door shut. ''What are you implying, Annabel?''

''I'm not implying anything,'' she said, stepping away from him. ''It's perfectly obvious that I've been the subject of mess gossip. You must be deriving great satisfaction from being able to show your friends the woman from Akbar Khan's zenana who gave you such pleasure for one—''

''You cannot possibly believe that I have discussed you in such terms.'' Two bright flags of color flew on his cheekbones. ''As if you were some back-street harlot! How dare you insult me in such fashion.''

''Insult *you*?'' she exclaimed. ''I am the one who has been insulted. Those men out there knew all about me. Deny that, if you can.''

''What kind of man do you think I am?'' He caught her arm, his fingers bruising the skin beneath the thin wool of her tunic. ''Yes, I told them of the presence in Akbar Khan's zenana of an Englishwoman abducted as a child. Yes, I said that you could not be left there . . . that no Englishman worthy of the name could leave you there. They all agreed with me. But if you think I would have said anything about the night we passed, or what I feel for you, then you do me the gravest injustice.''

Annabel stood looking at him, hugging her breasts with crossed arms. Then she offered him a tiny smile, her head tilted to one side. "If that is so then I apologize, Christopher Ralston."

"Of course it is so!" He was for the moment unappeased by the apology. "Do you know nothing of gentlemen? Of honor?"

She shrugged. "I know much of the honor of the Afghan. But how should I know of the honor of an English gentleman?"

"You were twelve before you were abducted." He dismissed this quibble with the derision it deserved. "Don't give me that nonsense. You knew your father."

A shadow scudded across the cool green surface of her eyes, and that vulnerability he had seen once before was writ clear upon her face. Before she could banish it, he took her in his arms. "Don't fight me anymore, Annabel." He whispered the plea into the fragrance of her hair, stroking the curve of her cheek with a finger, rubbing her back gently with the palm of his other hand. "Don't fight either of us anymore."

For a second she was unresisting in his hold, then she pulled away. "You had no right to bring me here. I was content where I was."

He sighed. "If you say so. But since you are here, will you come back to the sitting room, at least?"

"As Annabel or as Ayesha?" she asked.

"That is for you to decide." He held the door for her.

"Matters appear to be improving." She moved past him and didn't see the frustration flickering in the gray eyes. But she felt its current surge through his body, rigidly upright in the doorway.

The three men in the sitting room had left the card table in the absence of their host and his other rather more unusual guest, and were standing around the fire, glasses in hand. The abrupt silence that fell as the door opened was clear indication of the intensity and content of their previous conversation.

"We'll be on our way, Kit," Bob declared with an attempt at heartiness. "Pleased to have made your acquaintance, Miss Spencer." He offered a small bow before placing his glass on a side table.

"Yes, indeed," the other two concurred, bowing in turn. "Delighted, ma'am."

"Please don't leave on my account," Annabel said, smiling. "Finish your game. I would like to watch your play." She drew a chair over to the card table and sat down expectantly.

Kit gestured toward the table and the neglected cards. "Come, let us finish. It would be impolite to deny the lady her wish."

"It may not be as exciting as a game of *buzkashi*," Annabel commented, "but it will certainly be new to me."

"This may be also." Kit poured a glass of claret and handed it to her.

She took a tentative sip and her nose wrinkled. "What a strange taste. I don't think I care for it in the least." She held the glass out to him.

"It grows on you," Kit said with a wry smile, taking the glass. "If you give it the chance."

Her eyes held his. "I don't see much point in giving it the chance . . . not at the moment. It can only compound the disadvantages of a disadvantaged position."

"Whose position, Miss Spencer?" William Troughton looked up from his cards and blinked in some bemusement.

"Yours," she replied bluntly.

"Mine?" The blinking became more rapid.

"Never mind, William," Bob Markham said. He regarded Annabel with eyes that no longer bore the least sign of befuddlement. "You mean the British position in Afghanistan, I take it, Miss Spencer."

She nodded. "The hill tribes will flock to Kabul and Akbar Khan now . . . now that you have suffered such a signal defeat and made no attempt to reverse it. If you are besieged in the cantonment, how do you think you will ever get free and clear?"

"Free and clear?"

"You explain the rules of *buzkashi*, Kit," she said.

"I am going to see if Harley will make me some tea."

"What an extraordinary woman," Bob declared once the door had closed on her departure. "How could you ever have thought to give her into Lady Sale's charge, my dear fellow? Lunatic idea!"

"Lady Sale?" Derek interjected. "Miss Spencer goin' to be her protégée? Is that the idea?"

"Not anymore," Kit said. "Look, would you consider me very rude if I asked you to call it an evening?" He made a swift excluding gesture in Bob's direction and his friend nodded in comprehension.

William and Derek were far too polite to do anything but make an immediate departure. Kit watched their stumbling progress down the path, then closed the door. "Damn it, Bob, but I think Annabel's right. How can we possibly see things clearly, make any kind of sensible decisions, in that condition?"

"Is it going to make any difference?" Bob asked, turning back to the sitting room. "Drunk or sober, we're doomed, it seems to me."

"Maybe so, Captain Markham, but maybe not." Annabel came into the room, followed by Harley carrying a tea tray and wearing his customary air of resignation. "But I'll tell you this much. Akbar Khan is going to have all his wits about him. If you don't have yours, you might as well slit your own throats."

"Will you be wantin' supper, sir?" Harley asked. "I've made cabbage soup and potato cakes. There's not much else in the stores at present."

"That will do splendidly, thanks," Kit said. "Supplies are short throughout the cantonment, but our commissariat fort is well held, thank God."

"Unlike the shah's," Bob said, thinking of the beleaguered Colin Mackenzie.

"I wouldn't be too confident of that," Annabel said, pouring tea. "The Afghans have only to occupy the forts of Mahmood Khan and Mahomed Shereef to threaten the cantonment's commissariat.

Their guns can be trained directly onto your supply station.''

"Must you be such a Jonah?" Kit asked wearily.

"I have big ears," she said, "and I've been listening in the right places."

"Are you serious, Miss Spencer?" Bob stared in dismay.

"I wish you would call me either Annabel or Ayesha," she said. "Yes, I am entirely serious. You don't really imagine Akbar and the other sirdars are going to retreat? Permit you to bring in supplies unmolested?" She shook her head in a gesture of exasperation. "You do not seem to understand. I tried to explain it to Kit, but you are all so obtuse!"

"Not obtuse," Kit said, "just trying to look for a ray of hope."

"I'll serve supper in the dining room, sir," Harley stated, having listened to this exchange without a flicker of emotion on his stolid countenance.

Supper was a generally silent meal. Annabel, who had, it seemed to Kit, the enviable ability to concentrate simply upon the moment at hand, ate soup and potato pancakes with the air of one willing to experiment and to be pleased.

"It's a rather peculiar sensation," she announced, finally laying down her knife and fork. "I know these tastes and textures, yet it's been so long since I've experienced them that it's as if they are quite unfamiliar."

"If you're right, they are about to become so again," Kit observed, not sharing her ability to put foreboding aside.

"On which note, I think perhaps I'll bid you good night." Bob rose to his feet. "It's late and I've trespassed on your hospitality enough."

Kit made no attempt to detain him. Annabel offered a friendly good night and went into the sitting room, where she stood gazing down into the fire, waiting for Kit to return from bidding farewell to his friend.

"Where am I to sleep?" she asked directly, as he

came into the room. "There appears to be only one bedroom."

The sharpness of his disappointment took Kit aback. He had not realized how much he had taken it for granted that Annabel's denial of desire was only a temporary performance, one prompted by an understandable but short-lived resentment.

Lest she should see his chagrin, he bent to the fire, throwing on an unnecessary log, before responding with seeming insouciance, "Have the bed. I'll sleep on the couch in here."

She shook her head. "You are at least seven inches longer than I am. I'll be quite comfortable on the couch. I'll ask Harley to find some sheets and blankets."

"If you insist," he said.

She gave him a bland smile. "I do."

She went out, leaving the door ajar, and Kit cursed her obstinacy in an undertone. Irritably thinking that she would need some kind of a nightgown, he went into his bedroom to fetch one of the nightshirts he rarely wore himself.

He was going to have to procure her some more clothes from somewhere. And how long could he keep her hidden? And once her presence was known, how could he preserve the reputation of maidenly innocence she *must* present if she were to make any kind of a life for herself in the society to which she rightfully belonged? And why the hell had he not thought through these seemingly intractable problems before he had acted in that rash and intemperate fashion? He had not thought things through, simply because he had been consumed by a passionate wanting beyond description, a wanting that he had had to gratify without thought for the consequences. And now, he had the consequences and no gratification. It was a fitting penalty, he decided sourly.

"Here, you might have need of this." He tossed the nightshirt onto a chair in the sitting room, where Harley was putting sheets on the sofa.

"Thank you," she said neutrally. "You're very kind." She offered him that bland smile again and his palms itched. No other woman had ever had this effect upon him, had ever aroused these startlingly crude and tempestuous impulses. But then, no other woman had ever really mattered to the Honorable Christopher Ralston, who had taken his pleasure where he found it; behaved impeccably but without much emotion; paid whatever price was set, be it in coin or kind; and gone on his way again, essentially untouched. Even that ridiculous business with Lucy had been prompted mainly by his drunken anger at his so-called friends.

"Good night." He spun on his heel and left the room, closing his bedroom door with a near slam.

"Good night, miss." Harley gave a final straightening tug to the quilt on the couch, before hastening from the room without meeting her eye.

"Good night," Annabel muttered toward the closed door. She undressed and slipped Kit's voluminous nightshirt over her head. Then she went to the window, drawing aside the curtain and looking out into the night. The window was barred like all the others, and it was to be assumed all the outside doors were securely locked.

What was happening in the city? What was Akbar Khan planning now? A graveyard shudder lifted the fine hairs on the nape of her neck. She had always known how vulnerable the British were, how tenuous their hold in this country, but she had known it from the lofty heights of the hawk, hovering over his prey, watching with amused contempt the antics of the pathetic little creature so blind to the threat from above. Now she was caught in the long grass, too, and when the hawk swooped, she would be as much his prey as any of these others, so heedless of their danger. There were women and children out there in that suburban huddle . . . families leading their lives as if they were tucked up in some smiling English village, instead of clinging to an ungiving landscape in the face of a barbarous opponent.

She turned back to the couch, snuffed the candles in the branched candlestick on the table, and lay down in the flickering firelight upon her makeshift bed. It was narrow and unyielding. Cold and lonely. And her body yearned for the comfort, the warmth, and the ineffable pleasure to be afforded by that other body, so freely offered and as desirous as her own, lying cold and lonely on the other side of the wall.

What virtue was there in a pointless self-denial when the very foundations of her existence were crumbling . . . had crumbled? She got off the couch.

Kit was staring into the darkness, his muscles tense with his longing, bitter self-recrimination whirling in his wakeful brain, when the door of his bedroom opened. A white-clad figure glided into the room.

"Salaam, Ralston, *huzoor*." She slipped out of the garment and stood naked by the bed.

"Greetings, Ayesha," he murmured, turning back the covers in invitation. He did not bother to question this visitation but simply accepted it as he had accepted Ayesha that first night . . . a wondrous, miraculous gift of the gods of love and passion.

She slid in beside him, and he felt the coldness of her skin. "Let me warm you." He wrapped her tightly in his arms, holding her against his body. "Oh, if you only knew how my nights have been tormented with the memories of your skin," he whispered. "The scent and feel of you."

She stretched alongside him, twining her legs with his, pressing herself against him while she arched into the hands that touched her with slow and languid pleasure.

"Oh, God," he whispered on a low groan, "I want to spend all night just touching you, feeling your skin dance beneath my hands. It's never been like this for me before."

"Nor for me," she whispered back, nuzzling the pulse at the base of his throat, spreading her body for the hands that moved in a long, exploratory caress that brought every nerve center to piquant awareness. Her muscles in thighs and belly tightened involuntarily as she moved upward into the caress, and the deep recesses of her body melted in liquid arousal.

"I want to make love to you in ways you've never imagined," he murmured, drawing his tongue upward in the cleft of her breasts. "You taste so wonderful." The tip of his tongue flickered against her throat, traced the line of her jaw, tantalized in the corners of her mouth. "Do you like this, my Anna? Tell me what you want. Tell me what gives you the most pleasure."

In the warm, whispering darkness she told him, and he smiled his delight as he loved her in the ways that made her body sing with the pleasure and brought joy bubbling on her lips as she crested, wave after wave. Kit seemed able to continue indefinitely, using his body to ensure her delight was infinite until, surfeited with ecstasy, she fell into an exhausted sleep and he lay wakeful beside her, long past the ability to achieve his own release, but content that it should be so.

When she awoke an hour later, in the first gray light of dawn, he hitched himself on one elbow to smile down at her before kissing her gently. "Good morning."

She reached up a hand to brush aside the lock of fair hair flopping on his forehead. "Did you not sleep?"

He shook his head. "Too keyed-up, I'm afraid."

"Why did you deny yourself?"

"I didn't. I indulged myself," he replied with a chuckle. Then the laughter died in the gray eyes, a deep burning probe in its place. "I had to bind you to me," he said. "It was the only way I knew how."

Annabel shivered at the intensity behind the words. Possession . . . ownership . . . Was he any different from Akbar Khan in what he wanted from a woman? But she knew it was different, and any intellectual attempt to equate the two would simply be a futile effort to protect herself from the intensity of the emotion that bound her to Kit as securely as it bound him to her.

"Come," she said softly, sitting up and pushing him flat on the bed. "I have some skills, too. Let me ease you."

He lay back as her hands moved cleverly over him, massaging the tension from neck, back, arms, and legs; even his toes received careful attention. But when she felt his gradual relaxation, she applied her deft fingers to those other parts of his body, and in his turn he yielded to the extremity of delight. Then they slept the sleep of satiation and recuperation, while the world woke.

Chapter 10

The crackle of rifle fire, confused shouts, the pounding of feet in the street outside ruptured sleep.

Kit sat up just as the bedroom door burst open to admit Harley.

"Eh, sir, those damn savages are firin' into the cantonment," he said, then his eyes fell on the other occupant of the bed. "Beg pardon, sir," he said stiffly. "Thought you'd want me to wake you."

"Thank you, Harley," Kit said as if he had not noticed his batman's discomfiture. "Pass me my clothes." He flung himself out of bed, stretched naked in the cold morning air, then began to pull on britches and tunic as Harley handed them to him.

Annabel sat up and blinked. "Did you say they're attacking the cantonment?"

"Yes, miss." Harley studiously avoided looking in the direction of the bed, where she sat, the sheet pulled up to her neck, her hair glowing bright as polished copper in the early morning gloom.

The sound of hammering on the front door sent Harley into the hall. Kit turned to the bed. "I have to find out what's happening, but I'll be as quick as I can."

"I'm coming too," she said, pushing aside the covers.

"*No*," Kit expostulated. "You cannot show yourself around the cantonment."

"Why ever not?" She picked up the discarded

nightshirt just as Bob Markham's urgent tones came
from the hall.

"Just stay here until I get back," Kit directed imperatively and left the room. "Bob, what the hell's
going on? Is it an organized attack?"

"It's hard to say," Bob replied. "It was all very
sudden. Everyone's panicking—"

"Of course it's not an organized attack," Annabel
broke into the exchange, coming into the hall calmly
fastening the buttons at the neck of the nightshirt.
She threw the river of hair back off her shoulders
with a swift, impatient gesture. "They are not fools
enough to mount an open attack . . . or, at least,
Akbar Khan is not. It's not devious enough for
him. . . . Oh, good morning, Captain Markham."
She smiled. "How impolite of me to ignore you."

It was clear from Bob's expression that the significance of her attire and her emergence from Kit's
bedroom were not lost on him, but he recovered
with admirable speed. "Good morning, Miss Spencer."

"Annabel," she corrected automatically. "I would
imagine this is in the nature of intimidation, like the
attack on the residency."

"You call that butchery simply an exercise in intimidation?" Kit exclaimed.

Annabel shrugged. "I would guess that was how
it started, but it became out of hand." She turned
toward the sitting room. "I wonder if my clothes are
still in here. I will dress directly and—"

"Goddamnit, Annabel, you have to remain indoors," Kit said distractedly. "You cannot wander
the cantonment until we have decided how to explain your presence here. You must understand
that."

"I don't understand it in the least," she retorted.
"What business is it of anyone's who I am or where
I go?"

"Kit is right, Miss . . . uh, Annabel." Bob came
to his friend's assistance. "There are rules, y'know,
and—"

"They don't apply to an Afghan woman." She dismissed the statement with a lofty gesture. "And since I am no longer in an Afghan zenana, I need not abide by zenana rules either. Had you better not both go about your business? I'm sure you must have to report somewhere." The sitting room door closed decisively behind her.

Kit took a step toward the door, then realized that he could not tarry any longer, bandying words with that infuriatingly intransigent woman. With a muttered "Hell and the devil!" he stormed out of the house, Bob on his heels.

"Bitten off more than you can chew there," Bob observed, matching his companion's speed.

"Oh, no, I have not," Kit returned sharply. "All I need is time to explain matters to her. It's just that she's not accustomed to the way things are here. She's used to a quite different way of life."

"That must be it," Bob agreed solemnly. "Once you explain about how Lady Sale wouldn't look with a friendly eye upon a lady livin' under your bachelor roof, I'm sure the lady will understand the need to behave with circumspection."

"Oh, be quiet!" Kit snapped at this uncomfortable reminder of his own responsibility in the matter. He stalked into the headquarters bungalow.

Annabel, meanwhile, had dressed, fastened her makeshift veil of the previous evening, and enveloped herself in the fur-trimmed mantle Kit had taken from Akbar Khan's house. It was almost as concealing as a chadri, and she felt confident she would draw no remark. There were Afghan servants in the cantonment, as well as camp followers and several regiments of Afghan troops, loyal to the British, so she would not present a particularly unusual sight.

Harley had been given no instructions to keep the front door locked on this occasion, and as it was perfectly clear that circumstances had changed somewhat since the lieutenant had brought home his resistant captive, he made no attempt to prevent her leaving the house.

"I am just going to the gate of the cantonment," Annabel told him. "I would have a look for myself at the fighting. I might recognize someone, or something, I don't know, but it might be useful. Tell the lieutenant that I will be back soon, if he wants to know where I am."

"Very well, miss." Harley closed the door behind her, reflecting that the lieutenant's amorous exploits had taken a new turn with this one. Not his usual style at all, and, unless Harley was much mistaken, one likely to lead him hip-deep into trouble. Shaking his head over this gloomy prophecy, he went into the kitchen to prepare breakfast.

Annabel hastened through the streets toward the sound of gunfire. She realized she was the only civilian in sight, and an officer leading a troop at the double toward the gate bellowed at her in halting Pushtu to get off the street. But she simply ducked into a garden until they had passed, then continued on her way.

The gates were locked; behind them and on the earthworks that formed the only defensive structure for the cantonment were massed troops returning the fire of the Afghans below them. Stones flew as well as bullets, and insults and threats were hurled upward. The grim-faced troops on the earthworks took no notice of Annabel as she wriggled between two posts and poked her head over the top of the barrier.

Below her was a horde of screaming, scimitar-waving Ghazis. It was a disorganized rabble, as she had guessed, but nonetheless alarming. Their jezzails cracked with devastating accuracy, and the screamed insults and curses were so redolent with menace that the soldiers around Annabel muttered prayers and imprecations in superstitious self-defense. However, it was clear to Annabel that no serious attempt was being made to storm the cantonment at this point.

She watched for a while longer, but nothing occurred to change her mind about the nature of the engagement so she slid backward between the posts and attained ground level again, brushing twigs and dirt from her cloak.

"What the 'ell are you doin' 'ere?" bellowed a corporal, leading a party of sappers repairing damage to the earthworks. He stared in astonishment at the veiled woman who had suddenly appeared in their midst.

"Just looking to see what was happening," she replied in English without thinking. "I believe it would be sensible for you to tell your commander to hold his fire. The Ghazis will lose interest if they don't have the satisfaction of an opponent at the moment, and—"

"I beg your pardon?" A voice spoke in clipped accents at her back, and she swung around to come face to face with an immaculate colonel with a waxed moustache and the red-brown complexion indicative of long service under the Indian sun.

"Oh, I was just explaining that the Ghazis are only playing games at the moment," she said earnestly. "Terrifying games, of course, but nevertheless, if you ignore them, they will probably go away. You can always tell by what they are shouting. From what I can hear, it's mostly just taunts and they will soon run out of steam. You don't need to worry until the real threats—"

"Woman, I do not know who or what you think you are." The colonel finally recovered from his incredulity and interrupted this blithe exposition. "But I can assure you I do not need your advice."

Annabel threw up her hands in a gesture of frustration. "Feringhee!"

At the clear contempt of that one word, the colonel's color deepened and he laid hands on her. "Who the hell do you think you are, Afghan bint? I'll have you thrown out of the cantonment!"

"Ayesha!" White-faced, his gray eyes smoky with anger and anxiety, Kit came running across the strip of grass toward them. "In the name of goodness, what have you been doing?"

"Lieutenant, is this woman something to do with you?" demanded the colonel, his hands still gripping Annabel's shoulders.

"In a manner of speaking, sir." Kit saluted. "I'm sorry if—"

"Oh, for heaven's sake, Kit, I was only trying to explain to this gentleman that the Ghazis are not about to storm the cantonment, and if they don't have the satisfaction of returned fire they will probably give up and go home. But with typical feringhee arrogance he won't listen to me."

"For God's sake, hold your tongue!" Kit hissed, as the colonel looked more apoplectic by the second. "I'll take her away from here, sir," he offered, hoping that would secure Annabel's release.

"What's an Afghan bint doing talking like an Englishwoman?" The colonel still maintained his hold and stared down at the woman, who reverted somewhat belatedly to the docility proper to her sex and supposed race, and dropped her eyes.

Kit had to swallow the insulting term because to deny it would expose Annabel to a label with much more far-reaching consequences. "She picked it up somewhere, sir," he said vaguely.

"Oh, did she? Well, it seems to me it's gone to her head. I never heard such insolence from a wench. Goddamnit, man! What you do with her in the privacy of your own house is your business, but you'd damn well better keep her there," declared the colonel, finally releasing Annabel. "If I see her around here again, we'll toss her over the embankment to play with her 'playful' Ghazis! And we all know what they do to their women who consort with the enemy." On which Parthian shot, the colonel strode off.

"Come along." Kit, his mouth taut, seized her hand. "I have never been so humiliated!" he bit out, hauling her beside him. "Are you mad to go around spouting your Afghan contempt for the feringhee in this place? You are not in Akbar Khan's fortress, I'll have you remember, but in the heart of the British encampment.''

"But I was just trying to give him some advice only he wouldn't take any notice,'' Annabel protested, stubbing her toe on a large stone in the street and swearing in fluent Persian as she hopped on one foot.

Kit put an arm around her waist, holding her steady as she rubbed her sore toe through the thin slipper. ''How could you possibly imagine a British colonel is going to listen to the advice of an Afghan camp follower?'' he demanded in exasperation.

"But I'm as English as he is . . . or so you keep telling me.'' Gingerly, she put her foot on the ground again. ''But I happen to know things that he doesn't. It's just so silly . . . such a waste of ammunition . . . to scrap with those Ghazis at the moment. They're not an organized group, just a rabble of fanatics.'' She began to walk again. ''What I cannot understand is why your precious commanders would do nothing about the riot and massacre in Kabul, which *was* important, and waste time and bullets playing a silly game at the gate.''

They had reached Kit's bungalow by this time and he pushed her ahead of him into the hall. ''What do you want to be?'' he asked harshly. ''Afghan or English? Because so help me, Annabel, while you're here you must be one or the other and stick to it.''

"I don't understand,'' she said, sniffing the air. ''Harley is cooking something and I am hungry.''

"Then let me explain it to you,'' he said. ''You can have breakfast afterward.''

"I will be much more attentive on a full stomach,'' she declared, making for the dining room.

"No, you won't!'' He caught her arm and swung her toward the sitting room. ''This is important, Annabel.''

"I do wish you'd stop manhandling me. It's getting to be something of a habit.'' She marched into the sitting room, unfastening her veil.

Kit sighed, massaging his temples where an ominous tightness had begun to throb. "I don't mean to. It's just that you're always challenging me. Ever since I first laid eyes on you, when you held that damn stiletto at my throat."

Annabel smiled in reminiscence, tossing her veil and cloak over the couch. "I don't *always* challenge you," she pointed out.

"No." He grinned slightly. "I grant you that. But I can't keep you in bed permanently."

"Oh, I don't know," she murmured, her eyes narrowing as she looked at him. "I think on past performance you might be able to do that very easily."

Kit felt himself slipping, drowning in the sensual promise of that jade gaze. He grabbed the smooth, cool wood of a chair back and gripped it until the ordinary shape and feel of the object returned him to reality. "Listen to me."

"I'm listening." She sat down, toying idly with the diamond-headed pin she had removed from her veil.

"You have to decide whether you are going to be Annabel or Ayesha," he said. "Annabel cannot live here with me, and Ayesha cannot march around the cantonment giving advice and pouring scorn on the feringhee in impeccable English."

"Why cannot Annabel live here with you?" She put the pin on the table and looked up at him.

"Because it would make her a social outcast," he said bluntly. "You cannot be so naive, Annabel, not to know that. You grew up in this kind of society, you told me so yourself. You must remember the rules. As my mistress, you would be beyond the pale. The community here would ostracize you, and would ensure that that continued to happen when you returned to England."

She shook her head. "Do you think I give a fig for their ostracism?"

"But I do." Even as he said it, Kit realized that for the first time in his life he did. He had never spared a moment's worry over how the world viewed his own antics, had laughed at the idea that he should be subject to society's petty rules and insignificant penalties. But he could not mock them where Annabel was concerned. "If you wish to be Annabel, then I will present you to Lady Sale," he went on. "We will tell her as much of your story as is appropriate and I am convinced she will take you under her wing. It's the sort of mission she loves . . . to rehabilitate—" He broke off in confusion. Annabel was convulsed with silent laughter, tears streaming down her cheeks.

"You cannot be serious!" she cried. "You would pluck me from Akbar Khan's zenana and hand me over to . . . to be rehabilitated under the chaperonage of . . . Oh, no, Kit, admit you were only funning."

He stared at her. "I was not funning. How else are you to take your place in society?"

She sprang to her feet, the tears of laughter drying rapidly. "How can you talk such nonsense? Here in this beleaguered encampment you can babble such irrelevant inanities! Even assuming, for the sake of argument, that you all manage to leave Afghanistan and reach India safely, the rigors and dangers of that journey through the passes in the middle of winter are going to strip away every vestige of social propriety. It will be a matter of survival, pure and simple. And who or what I am will be of supreme unimportance in the face of that survival."

Kit absorbed her words and could not argue with them. "That may be so," he said. "But memories are long, and if we do survive, and if you do wish to make a life for yourself in England or in India, then you must still take some elementary precautions." A little flicker of amusement appeared in his eyes. "I did not really expect you to agree to enter Lady Sale's household, but I did want you to understand the way things are. Stay with me as Ayesha." He held out his hands to her. "To tell the truth, I cannot bear to think of parting with you, but in fairness, I felt I had to show you the alternatives."

Her hands lay warmly in his. "Understand this, Christopher Ralston. I will never be able to embrace the customs and attitudes of the feringhee. I have spent too long being taught to despise them, and I no longer acknowledge any inheritance or ties. So if my rehabilitation in your society is important in your agenda, you must be prepared for disappointment. But as a free spirit, as neither Akbar Khan's Ayesha nor the English Annabel, I will stay with you for the moment."

"For the moment?" His hands gripped hers painfully.

She smiled and shook her head slightly. "Until whatever is going to happen happens. That's all I meant." Suddenly she stood on tiptoe, peering with mock gravity into his face. "The Afghans believe that a man's destiny is written on his forehead, but I cannot read what is written upon yours. So who's to say what will happen. Let us live in and for the moment."

"But you will promise to behave with circumspection in the cantonment?" he pressed, releasing her hands.

"With true Muslim modesty and submission, Ralston, *huzoor*," she said, with a graceful salaam. "May we have breakfast now?"

Kit found that he was not entirely sure exactly what had been agreed between them. Whatever it was, it was insubstantial and impermanent, but for all that, it was a platform of sorts. She would stay with him of her own free will, until something happened to take her away or until she decided otherwise. He watched her over the breakfast table. She was concentrating on the business in hand with the single-minded serenity he admired and envied. It was as if the morning's events and their subsequent conversation had not occurred.

Harley entered the dining room. "Excuse me, sir, but there's a message come from 'eadquarters. An ensign says you're to report to General Elphinstone immediately.''

Kit tossed his napkin beside his plate. ''What does the old man want now? I've already had one set of orders for the day.''

''To do what?'' inquired Annabel through a mouthful of toast.

''Supervise inventory-taking of the supplies in the cantonment,'' he told her. ''Not a particularly difficult task since I doubt there's more than two days' supply of anything. Replenishing the stocks is going to be the arduous part, with that screaming horde outside.'' He came around the table and bent to kiss her, flicking a toast crumb from her lips before he did so. ''Why don't you go back to bed and try to get some sleep? It was a very short night.''

''I don't need very much sleep.'' She touched his mouth lightly with a fingertip. ''But I do need a lot of exercise.'' She invested the comment with a mischievous hint of innuendo, and he laughed.

''Let me go and see what the masters want, then maybe I can supply your needs.''

''How about a horse?'' she said suddenly, as he walked to the door. ''Seriously. I can't possibly spend all day sitting around in the house.''

Kit frowned. ''Where would you ride? Around the streets?''

''That doesn't sound very invigorating.''

''I suppose I could try and get you some time in the riding school. You could do some dressage, if you liked. The rissaldar in charge of the school is an accommodating fellow, for all that he's a tough riding master. He'd insist on supervising you, if I couldn't.''

''How would you explain me?''

Kit grinned. ''I haven't the least idea. You're quite inexplicable. But give me some time to see what I can come up with.''

He made his way to headquarters, feeling ridiculously lighthearted. The cantonment lay under a heavy pall of fearful despondency, although the

sound of gunfire had ceased except for an occasional
rifle crack, but Kit could find in his own heart not
the slightest tremor of fear or gloom. There were few
civilians on the streets, but uniformed men were everywhere, hurrying with an air of urgency that Kit
suspected was more in the mind than in fact. So
many conflicting orders were flying around that no
one really knew what was happening or what they
were supposed to be doing.

He discovered rapidly what he was supposed to
be doing when he presented himself to General Elphinstone.

"Ah, Ralston, I've a job for you," the general declared, sounding for once relatively decisive. "One
we feel suited to your particular talents. Sir William
will explain."

Kit turned to the Envoy, who stood in his customary fashion before the fireplace, the tails of his coat
spread wide, his chest thrust out. "Sir William?"

"We have received a message from Akbar Khan,"
Sir William pronounced. "His messenger and an escort arrived at the gate half an hour ago." The Envoy permitted himself a small smile. "The man is
obviously coming to his senses. He expresses great
regret for the riot in Kabul and for the loss of our
men and property, and wishes to discuss how best
restoration can be made."

Kit kept his face impassive. "Indeed, sir."

"Yes, Lieutenant. He explains that his authority
over the other sirdars is not very reliable, and he
cannot guarantee their behavior, but he wishes to
discuss a joint plan of action by which his authority,
the authority of the deposed Dost's son, and that of
the British can be combined to bring the unruly
khans to heel."

The image of Akbar Khan swam into Kit's internal
vision: those piercing blue eyes that seemed to see
so much more than the physical, that incisive mouth,
the passionate and capricious nature, the stocky,
powerful frame, the unquestioning authority of one
accustomed to instant obedience, to controlling with

absolute power the lives of all in his ken, the burning purpose of his life—to rid his country of the invader and to exact vengeance for the invasion.

This was the man Macnaghten and Elphinstone believed was interested in conciliation and reparation.

Kit kept silent.

"Since you have already made the acquaintance of Akbar Khan and had some discussion with him, the general and I decided that you would be a suitable negotiator." Sir William straightened his cravat. "Akbar Khan requests a meeting in Kabul, our representative to go under the escort the sirdar has sent with his own messenger. You may take three men with you. We will leave their selection up to you."

"And what message am I to take to Akbar Khan?" Kit asked.

"At this stage, Lieutenant, you will simply hear what the khan suggests, and express our sincere desire for a cessation of hostilities," Macnaghten said. "Then you will report back."

"Very well." Kit saluted, revealing not a hint of his skepticism. "I will leave within the hour." He went in search of Havildar Abdul Ali, having decided that the company of one who had stood by him so reliably during his previous visit to Akbar Khan's den would be both comforting and sensible.

The havildar listened, nodded stoically, and agreed to select two sepoys from the previous expedition. "D'you think it's a trap, sir?"

Kit shrugged. "For what it's worth, I don't think we'll be in any immediate danger. But you can be certain there's muddy water beneath the surface of the invitation. Akbar Khan isn't interested in negotiation."

This sentiment was echoed forcefully by Annabel when Kit returned to the bungalow to change into full uniform and attend to the ablutions he had not had time for earlier that morning. But she had another concern, one that had not occurred to Christopher.

"Have you thought what will happen if he suspects I am with you?" She moved restlessly around the bedroom as Kit shaved. Harley was laying out the immaculate blue tunic with its gold braid and shining gold buttons, the deep blue britches, the gold sash, epaulets and cummerbund, and the boots so highly polished that the leather seemed to have depth.

"How should he do so?" The razor paused in its careful stroking, but his eyes remained on the mirror.

"He is no fool, Christopher Ralston."

"I am aware of that." The razor continued its work. "But I still don't understand why he should suspect. He did not know I was in Kabul; no one saw either of us leave; no one heard anything. In the chaos in the city that night, anything could have happened."

"He will look beneath the surface," she said. "And he will find you beneath that surface." She knew Akbar Khan had suspected something in the weeks following her night with the Englishman, although nothing had been said openly. But Ayesha was so finely tuned to the khan's responses that she had needed no words to hear his recognition of a change in her.

Kit buried his face in the hot, damp towel handed him by the silently attentive batman. "He can be sure of nothing, Annabel. Besides, he has another agenda at the moment. Do you think he will take the time to force a confession from me?" He asked the question as a joke, but Annabel's response was serious.

"I don't know," she said truthfully. "I would say not, but he is a man of passions and caprices. You know that as well as I do. If the sight of you triggers a certain reaction, he could have your throat cut then and there."

"Gawd, miss, you can't be serious?" Harley was

provoked into responding. He had been listening to a conversation that went some way to answering the questions he did not consider it his place to ask.

"I can, Harley," she replied soberly. "Could you not ask the general to send someone else, Kit?"

"On what grounds?" Kit's fair eyebrows disappeared into his scalp. "Now who's being foolish?" He shrugged into a clean shirt. "Are you suggesting I say to Elphinstone and Macnaghten that as I have stolen Akbar Khan's favorite from his zenana, I really consider it would be imprudent for me to face him on his own territory?"

"You could do worse," she said. "Perhaps if I came with you—"

"If you did *what*?" He paused in the act of stepping into his britches, one leg suspended.

"If I explained the situation to General Elphinstone and the Envoy, and told them what I know and understand of Akbar Khan, then perhaps—"

"Miss!" exclaimed Harley before Kit could catch his breath. "The lieutenant could never ask to be excused a dangerous mission for any reason! Let alone personal."

"Oh." Annabel sat down on the bed. "In that case there's nothing more to be said."

And no one said anything further until Kit had fastened his sword belt and taken up his plumed shako. He gestured toward the door, and Harley took his departure.

"Annabel, sweet, do you have no faith in me at all?" Kit came over to the bed where she sat, customarily immobile.

She raised her head, and her eyes were grave. "It is not a question of faith. This is not a situation . . . you are not dealing with a foe . . . where your rules apply. You say you cannot in honor excuse yourself from this mission. I accept that. But you must not go to Akbar Khan expecting that he will play by your rules. You must play by his."

"Do you remember the *buzkashi*?" He touched her

mouth. "I played by his rules, but imposed my own. Was I defeated?"

She shook her head. "No, you were not. Go swiftly, and come back safely."

She went to the door to see him go, then turned back into the little English bungalow. It seemed to close around her with its assumption of cozy, suburban security, and she knew that she needed to be beside Kit, as he went head to head with the world of complexity and intrigue that she understood so well. Yet she must let him go alone, while she stayed here with Harley and cups of tea.

In the zenana, there had been no shield against the fluctuations and excitements of her world. She had learned to negotiate a path, to recognize dangers, to circumvent them, to plot, to react with speed and stealth. How could Kit possibly expect her to stay here in this sterile, artificial place while he, so much less well-equipped than she, matched himself against the man she had made it her business to know as well as anyone could know the son of Dost Mohammed?

But for the moment, she had no choice. Soon, though, the time for action would engulf them all. She would be ready, then, to take whatever path Destiny dictated.

Chapter 11

Six Afghan hillmen sat Badakshani chargers just outside the gate of the cantonment. Long ringlets hung beneath their skullcaps, and their faces were expressionless as the small party of sepoys and the English lieutenant rode out to meet them.

"*Salaamat bashi,*" Kit said formally.

"*Mandeh nabashi,*" responded one of the horsemen, and immediately turned his horse toward the city.

"Sullen beggars," commented Abdul Ali with classic understatement as they fell in behind their escort.

The two-mile ride was undertaken in complete silence. The Ghazi fanatics who had attacked the fort earlier had mostly dispersed, although a few were still to be seen throwing stones in desultory fashion at the earthworks and occasionally screaming insults. They stared at the party and shouted something at the hillmen. Kit heard the name "Akbar Khan" in the response. Apparently satisfied, the Ghazis turned back to their harassment.

The streets of Kabul were riot-torn, the evidence of a night and day of plundering, fighting, and murder in the blackened buildings, the piles of rubble, and the bodies that had not yet been removed. There were few people on the streets, and they appeared both fearful and defiant as they stared at the feringhee and the sepoys but made no attempt to molest them with either words or gestures.

174

Akbar Khan's house stood as it had done throughout the days of Kit's vigil when he had watched for a glimpse of Ayesha. He was careful to give no indication of familiarity as they dismounted and were escorted within.

"Ah, Ralston, *huzoor,* I had not dared to hope that I would have the pleasure of your company again." Akbar Khan appeared at the head of the stairs. His loose trousers were tucked into the tops of his riding boots, the buttons on his dark green coat glistened, and as before his head was bare. "How fortunate I am that you should be the one to talk with me about this distressing affair. . . . An inestimable honor, as always." He came slowly down the stairs, a smile on his mouth but not a flicker of warmth in his eyes, which held Kit's gaze for an unnerving length of time, as if looking for something. Then he nodded, as if he had found what he sought.

"Please . . . " He gestured an invitation toward a door on the left of the hall. "We shall take a glass of sherbet together. Your men may remain here."

"Is that wise, sir?" Abdul Ali muttered.

"You are my guest, Ralston, *huzoor,*" Akbar Khan said smoothly. "You would not insult my hospitality by mistrusting me."

"Of course not," Kit said as smoothly. "Remain here, Havildar."

"Very well, sir." Abdul Ali stood at watchful attention, one hand resting on his pistol, every inch of him radiating mistrust as the lieutenant and Akbar Khan disappeared behind the door.

There were no other occupants of the room, and Akbar Khan himself filled a goblet with sherbet and handed it to Kit before filling one for himself. "Welcome, Ralston, *huzoor,*" he said gently, before sipping.

Kit inclined his head and sipped in turn. "I understand you have some proposals, Akbar Khan."

The sirdar looked sorrowful. "Such a dreadful business. I wished to express in person my heartfelt regret for the deaths of Burnes, *huzoor,* and the others. I trust you will take the message back to your superiors. But we must now see how we can ensure such a thing is not repeated." He shook his head sadly. "You must understand that my people are most unhappy. And when they are unhappy, they are inclined to be a little . . . impetuous, shall we say?"

"I would have used a stronger term," Kit observed calmly. "Can you guarantee that there will be no repetition?"

"Alas, no." Akbar Khan shook his head again. "I cannot. My authority and influence with the other military leaders is negligible, Lieutenant. They have individual grievances with the feringhee, and what they do about those grievances is a matter for individual decision. Some might agree to come to terms, but others . . ." He shrugged.

"So what do you propose?" Kit prompted, concealing his disbelief of the khan's statement of his powerlessness.

"I think it might be helpful for Macnaghten, *huzoor*, to foster the individuality of the chiefs," Akbar Khan said. "The more divided they are amongst themselves, the less united they will be in their grievances against the feringhee." He stroked his beard in the way that would have put Ayesha immediately on her guard. "I am certain the Envoy has some contacts amongst the sirdars. He would do well to . . . to . . . sow a few seeds of dissension."

"And how is this dissension to be achieved?" asked Kit directly.

Akbar Khan smiled and shrugged. "However the Envoy decides. Judicious rewards, perhaps; a little intimidation elsewhere, perhaps. You may rest assured I will suggest most forcefully a cessation of hostilities and acceptance of Shah Soojah. It is time for such an agreement to be reached."

Kit inclined his head, hiding his conviction that he had just been given the worst possible advice. Suborning the chiefs would not work, for all that the idea would probably appeal to Macnaghten. And why was Akbar Khan pretending this change of heart? He had sworn there would be no concessions while the British remained on Afghan soil, and Kit did not believe for one instant that that had changed. But he kept such thoughts to himself. "If that is all . . . ?" he said politely, turning toward the door.

"Ralston, *huzoor*?" Akbar Khan spoke very softly.

"Yes?" Kit turned back and felt ice enter the marrow of his bones at the unmistakable and deadly menace in the stab of the khan's blue eyes.

"Do you remember the game of *buzkashi*?"

"Vividly."

"Sometimes, when a man has been wronged by another, we play the game a little differently. We do not use the carcass of an animal." He paused. The taut line of his mouth thinned, and Kit saw for the first time the ferocity in the man undisguised. "The offender becomes the prize," Akbar continued without so much as the flicker of an eyelid.

Kit forced himself to meet the man's eye, to keep his own expression impassive. Incomprehension he could not fake, and he suspected there would be little point even if he could. Akbar Khan knew what he knew.

"Of course," the khan said almost pensively, "if full and timely restitution is made by the offender, one is capable of generosity . . . of an understanding of impulse. However—" He looked Kit full in the eye. "We are jealous of our possessions, Ralston, *huzoor*, and unforgiving if one of our own defects. The penalty for such defection is immutable. . . . You understand me, I am sure."

"You talk in riddles, Akbar Khan," Kit said, amazed that his voice was steady in the face of such a clearly pronounced threat.

Akbar Khan smiled, shrugged again. "You may enjoy unraveling the conundrum, Ralston, *huzoor*. It would certainly be profitable for you . . . and for another . . . to do so." He clapped his hands abruptly, the sound startlingly loud in the quiet room. Immediately, one of the rangy hillmen appeared in his long coat and skullcap.

"Escort the feringhee back to the cantonment," Akbar Khan ordered, and without a word of farewell left both the room and his guest.

They rode back in silence. Kit was not disposed to discuss his meeting with Akbar Khan. He could think only of his last exchanges with the Afghan. Akbar Khan had threatened the lieutenant, but more pointed had been his threat to Annabel. If Ayesha did not return, then her khan would assume she had chosen not to do so. And if she had made that choice, then she stood accused and condemned of infidelity. Kit did not know what penalty would ensue, but if he had been threatened with the role of prize in a *buzkashi*, it required little imagination to construct horrors for one accused of disloyalty and betrayal.

At the gate of the cantonment, their escort left them as uncommunicatively as they had joined them. Kit dismissed the havildar and his troop at headquarters and went in to report.

As Kit had feared, Akbar Khan's advice fell on fertile soil. The Envoy rubbed his hands together. "Yes, yes, I think he is quite right. If we are able to sow discord amongst the various factions, then it will weaken the opposition to the shah. If the chiefs fight amongst themselves, they will not be able to fight us."

"But how should we do this, Sir William?" quavered Elphinstone from the depths of his armchair.

"We will employ Mohun Lal. He has the ear of many of the sirdars, but has always been loyal to us. He will know whom to bribe and whom to threaten." Sir William nodded happily. "Indeed, perhaps we can go further than this. If we could achieve the removal of some of the most malevolent leaders, then the opposition would be in considerable disarray."

"How ever is that to be achieved?" asked the general, blinking.

"Why, by assassination, of course," Macnaghten told him. "We will put a price on their heads and you'll see how the bounty hunters will come running."

Kit could not control his exclamation of disgust, and the Envoy regarded him with irritation. "Did you say something, Lieutenant?"

Kit sighed. "Do you really think treachery is the answer, Sir William?"

"We'll beat those perfidious savages at their own game," the Envoy announced. "Why, it was one of their own who suggested it."

"And you would trust the advice of Akbar Khan? Why would he attempt to assist us?"

Macnaghten's annoyance increased visibly. "The man knows perfectly well that he cannot hope to defeat us in the end. Once Major Griffiths reaches us from Kubbar-i-Jubbar and General Nott's brigade arrives from Kandahar and General Sale comes from Jalalabad, we'll put an end to this revolt once and for all. Akbar Khan, quite realistically, does not want to be associated with the wilder factions amongst his people. When this is over, he will want to come out of it on the right side."

"Quite so," murmured Kit. "If you'll excuse me, General . . . Sir William, I have to supervise the inventory-taking."

"Yes . . . yes, Lieutenant." Elphinstone waved him away and Kit left the office feeling contaminated. Since when did the British army stoop to such repellent tactics? But then Macnaghten was not a soldier. He was a civilian politician who thrived on intrigue; a man for whom assassinations and bribery were not in the least dishonorable. And the soldier who should have put an immediate stop to the plan was too enfeebled to do anything about it.

"How did it go, Kit?" Bob Markham hailed him as he made his way to the stores. He listened to Kit's description of his conversation with Akbar Khan and subsequent one with the general and the Envoy. His expression of disgust mirrored Kit's. "Dear God," he muttered. "Have they lost all reason? Military force is the only way to achieve superiority, and he's talking assassination! Mohun Lal is a treacherous bastard, too. It's just the sort of assignment to suit him." He swung his cane in a vicious swipe at the hedge, sending sere leaves flying. "How's the lady, by the way?"

"Restless," Kit said. "I ought to go home and make sure she's not doing something she shouldn't be. She did promise to behave with circumspection, but I don't know whether she really understands what that means here." He scratched his head, a worried frown drawing his eyebrows together.

Bob grinned faintly. "You're becoming uncommon grave these days, dear fellow."

Kit looked rueful. "It's such a responsibility, Bob. How can I be sure she doesn't suffer for this? If Lady Sale and the other old cats get a whiff of who and what she is, she'll never be accepted anywhere. She says she doesn't wish to be accepted anyway, but that has to be nonsense. She doesn't really understand what she's saying, because she can't imagine what life will be like."

"Assuming we get out of here?"

"Yes, assuming that." Kit's frown deepened. He looked upward at the circle of mountain peaks, blending gray and cold with the lowering sky. And he thought of Akbar Khan. "I should have left her where she was, Bob."

"Matters are coming to a pretty pass," commented his friend as they reached the stores. "I don't think I've ever heard you express regret for anything before. What happened to the 'play and be damned' Kit Ralston whom we all know and love?"

"I think I grew bored with him," Kit said seriously. "Look, would you do me a favor, Bob? Take my duty here. I have to go and talk to Annabel."

"My pleasure," Bob said easily. "And the next time I draw the short straw with a patrol, I'll pass it on to you."

"Agreed. Thanks." Kit strode off, suddenly certain of what he had to do.

Annabel was watching from the front window, as she had been doing for the last hour, and as soon as she saw him turn onto the street, she flew out of the house.

"Where have you *been*? I have been quite distracted with worry," she scolded, flinging her arms around him in the middle of the street. "Have you only just got back from Kabul?"

"No," he said. "About an hour and a half ago. Annabel, for God's sake, get back into the house! You've no veil and no cloak. You cannot behave like this in the middle of the cantonment!"

"Oh, rubbish!" she declared, stepping away from him and planting her hands on her hips, her eyes flashing green fire against her milky skin, her heavy copper plait swinging against her back. "How dare you not let me know that you were back and safe!"

"I had to report straightaway," he said, looking distractedly around the fortunately empty street. "Please, go inside. Anybody could be watching from a window."

"Let them! You could have sent me a message. Or did you assume I wouldn't care one way or the other?"

"I am going into the house even if you are not," declared Kit, deciding that removing himself from the open street was the only avenue open to him at this point. He marched into the bungalow with Annabel, still furiously castigating him for his thoughtlessness, at his heels.

"Now, stop railing at me, you green-eyed lynx," he said, once they were behind the front door. "I am not accustomed to having people waiting and worrying about me, so I didn't think to let you know I was back. I apologize, and I won't do it again. Satisfied?"

"Oh," she said, the wind quite taken out of her sails. "I suppose I must be, in that case. Tell me what happened."

"I need a drink first," he said, going into the sitting room. "Or are you going to turn the Puritan again?"

She made no reply, but stood watching as he poured himself a shot of brandy, tossed it back, and reached again for the decanter. Then he took his hand away. "No, one's enough." He turned to face her. "Annabel, you have to go back to Akbar Khan."

Her jaw dropped ludicrously. "I have to do what?"

He tossed his shako onto the couch. "You must go back to Kabul. He knows you're here."

"I told you he would." She spoke very quietly, and was holding herself very still now. "What did he say?"

Kit grimaced. "Tell me, do they really use their enemies as the prize in a game of *buzkashi*?"

Annabel nodded. "It is not uncommon."

"Are they alive?" He didn't know why he had this fascination for all the gory details, but somehow he could not help himself asking.

"To start with," she said baldly. "But not for long. Did he threaten you with that?"

"In a roundabout way," Kit replied. "But that isn't why you must return."

"I do not blame you for being afraid," she said gently. "He is a frightening man."

"You are in greater danger than I," Kit said. He bent to poke the sullen fire into a resurgence of life. "He made it very clear that if you returned to him, then he would be . . . generous, I think was the word. But that if you failed to do so, then the penalty for such defection would be visited upon you."

Annabel scratched her nose absently. "I would not expect less. But he said he would take no reprisals against you, if I were to return of my own free will?"

"Mmmm. He would forgive an impulse."

"That is more generous than I expected." She continued to scratch her nose until Kit took her hand away.

"You'll scratch a hole."

"My nose always itches when I think," she offered with a slight smile. "I had believed that if I left you at the very beginning and returned to Akbar Khan, then he would take no revenge upon me but he would be avenged upon you, which is why I accepted initially that I could not leave you. But matters have now changed between us. If he is saying that there will no vengeance against you, I will return for that reason, and only that reason, if you wish it."

Kit frowned, trying to make sense of the statement. "You must return for your own sake," he finally said. "I should never have brought you here in the first place. It was a piece of complete lunacy. . . ." He pounded one fist into the palm of his other hand. "I have been obsessed by you, Annabel-Ayesha. And I have never learned to govern my impulses. I have always taken what I wanted, and always believed that I did no harm. But I have placed you in the gravest danger, and I would undo that."

She shook her head. "I am here now because I choose to be, Christopher Ralston. I told you that this morning. *I* will decide when or if I should leave you, when it is my own skin at stake. If we are talking of yours, then you may make the decision."

"Are you suggesting that I am in such fear of Akbar Khan that I would send you back to protect myself?" He sounded incredulous.

She heard the anger beneath the incredulity. Her hands opened in a gesture of placation. "I am not suggesting anything. Just examining the issues."

"Oh, no, you weren't just examining the issues. I have told you before that it is time you realized there is some backbone to the race of your birth." His gray eyes held hers in fierce challenge, and finally she was forced to drop her own.

"Make the decision," she said quietly.

"You know it is made." He poured brandy into two glasses. "And we will drink to it, Annabel Spencer." He held out a glass.

Hesitantly, she took it. "A gesture of acceptance?

An act of repudiation?'' Her lips curved in a smile
that was not humorous. "By drinking this, Ralston,
huzoor, I abandon the laws of Islam and embrace
those of your race?''

"Your race,'' he said, and raised the glass. "To
us, Annabel-Ayesha.''

"To us,'' she returned, closed her eyes, wrinkled
her nose, and drank. "Ugh!''

Kit laughed. He fell back on the couch and
laughed until he thought his chest would burst.
"Sweetheart, I will never ask you to take another
drop,'' he promised, holding out his arms to her.

She dropped onto his knee. "Good. There are
some sacrifices I would prefer not to make. Do you
want to finish this?''

"No.'' He took the glass from her and put it with
his own on the side table. His hand slipped beneath
her tunic, caressing the soft, bare skin. "Do you
never wear any underclothes?''

"Corsets and petticoats and drawers?'' She
laughed against his mouth, her breath warm and
sweet as her lips brushed his. "No, Ralston, *huzoor*.
It is not the Afghan way.''

The tip of his tongue partnered hers for a long
moment, flickering between her lips in a tantalizing
dance redolent with erotic promise. Then he drew
back, holding her hips lightly, his hands warmly imprinting the curve of her body beneath her silk trousers. "I think the Afghan way has certain things to
be said in its favor.''

"Must you go back to work? Or could we go to
bed?''

"We could go to bed.'' He tipped her off his knee
and stood up. "Bob is taking my duty for me.''

"Oh, I must remember to thank him when next I
see him,'' she said mischievously. "There must be
some way I can repay him.''

"You'll leave the repayment up to me,'' Kit pronounced.

"But I am sure I could offer—''

"I am sure you could!'' Kit interrupted her mischief. "But I don't find Ayesha's game amusing, Miss Spencer."

"How very prudish of you," she retorted. "I made sure you had a reliable sense of humor."

"I do have, but not where my women are concerned."

"Oh. So I'm one of your women, am I?"

"It would seem so."

"How many have you had?"

"I can't remember. Would you please go into the bedroom?"

"Why do you not have a sense of humor where your women are concerned?"

"Because an ugly joke on that subject landed me in this godforsaken hole," he said shortly, closing the bedroom door after them.

Annabel bounced onto the bed. "Tell me."

"Not now."

"Yes, now."

"It's a tedious tale, Annabel, and there are much more exciting things to do." Catching her face between his hands, he kissed her eyelids, the tip of her nose, the point of her chin, before bringing his mouth to hers.

"Now tell me," she demanded, the minute he drew back.

"I don't think this is the way Afghan women are supposed to behave with their lords," Kit mused, still holding her face. "Aren't you supposed to be utterly accommodating?"

"I will become Ayesha when you have satisfied Annabel's curiosity." Her eyes gleamed a challenge and an invitation.

Kit pursed his lips, wondering which he should accept first. They were both irresistible. "Let's compromise," he suggested. "Take off your clothes so that I can play with you while I tell you."

"But you might not be able to concentrate," she objected, that gleam deepening. "On either the play or the tale."

"You do believe in sailing close to the wind, don't

you," he commented, pushing her backward onto the bed. Slipping his hands beneath the tunic, he found the hip-fastening of the *chalvar*.

Laughing, she tried to push his hands away, wriggling to the far side of the bed. But he flung a leg over her thighs, holding her with his weight as he unclasped the trousers. "Lift your bottom, Miss Spencer."

"Bully!" she accused, but raised her hips so that he could pull the garment down and off. He let the weight of his leg fall across her again and gazed down into her eyes, his arms braced on either side of her.

"You are the most exciting woman," he murmured. "All sinuous promise and challenge." Shifting his weight onto one elbow, he stroked the slender length of her bared legs with his free hand, tickling behind her knee so that she squirmed and he chuckled, using his imprisoning leg to push apart her thighs.

Her eyes no longer held their challenge. As his fingers pit-patted over the satin softness of her inner thighs, naked desire leaped into the jade depths to match the hunger in the gray eyes. Her body shifted on the mattress as he pushed up the hem of her tunic, baring her belly, and a little shiver rippled her skin. He bent to kiss her stomach as he continued to push up the tunic, his breath rustling warmly over her skin, and she yielded to the invasion of his mouth and stroking hand with a shudder of anticipation, the wondrous tension building deep within her as the sap of love rose in moistening expectation.

Lifting her against him, he drew the tunic up and over her head, letting her fall back again on the bed, where the quilted coverlet cooled her heated skin for a second before it absorbed her own warmth. He cupped one breast in the palm of his hand, lifting the nipple with a grazing forefinger before taking it in his mouth, his flickering tongue drawing a whimper of pleasure from her. Long, sensitive fingers opened her, unfurling the velvety petals of her essence, leading her ever closer to that place where the mind holds no sway.

He took her to the brink of that plane and held her there in tormented ecstasy, his eyes seeming to swallow hers as she looked up at him lost in the wonder of her body, half pleading for release, half willing the instant to last for infinity. Then the heated adhesion of his mouth replaced his hand and the enchanted landscape engulfed her, tossing her in a sensual maelstrom, whirling, swirling crimson glory until she was swept exhausted to the bank, there to lie, trembling, awash with languor, until the violent jarring of her heart died. He stroked her body as she returned to life, whispering softly until her eyes recognized him again and a smile quivered on her lips.

"I am sorry," he whispered, "but I have the most powerful need of you now. Have I exhausted you completely?"

"It's been a long time since we were truly together," she said in answer, holding out her arms to him as he undressed with rough haste. "Not since that long night in September. But this time I do not have—"

"I do," he said softly, opening the drawer in the night table.

"I've enough strength to do that for you," she whispered, taking the sheath from him as he knelt beside her. "You are very beautiful, Christopher Ralston." She kissed the powerful hardness of him, and he threw back his head on a shudder of pleasure. "I want you inside me," she said, with an ardent directness that thrilled him. "Come into me."

Sliding his hands beneath her buttocks, he lifted her to meet him as he entered her body, gasping with joy as her velvety softness tightened around him, gripped and released him in a rhythm unlike any he had experienced. He looked down at her in wonder. She lay spread beneath him, her arms flung wide, only the lower part of her body moving in a caress of such wickedly skilled eroticism that he entered unknown and unimagined realms of voluptuous delight. And all the while she watched him, waiting for the moment when his face dissolved in ecstasy. And with the glory of his climax pulsing within her, her body exploded once more in its own glory, the bright bubble of shared rapture bursting around them.

"Dear Lord," Kit whispered when he could begin to feel his separateness again. "You are a magical creature. What are you, Annabel-Ayesha? No ordinary woman, that's for sure." His lips nuzzled her neck as he lay heavily on top of her, still within her.

Her hands rested on his back. She had not the strength to hold him, so they lay limply, flattened against his damp skin. "Afghanistan is bordered by India and Persia," she murmured, managing a tiny chuckle. "Such neighbors have more to offer than Bokhara carpets and Persian silks."

Kit, with a supreme effort, disengaged, rolling onto the bed beside her. He propped himself on one elbow and looked down at her. "Are you telling me you learned . . . Oh, never mind. I don't want to know." He shook his head. "I shall just be grateful."

"Why should it disturb you?" she asked.

"I don't know. It doesn't really, except that it makes me realize anew how vastly different you are . . . how you don't fit any mold that I am familiar with." He smiled ruefully. "And it makes me uneasy."

"I don't see why it should," she said. "If you believe with the Afghans that our destiny is written unchangeably, then what does it matter?"

"Do you believe that?"

Her milk-white shoulders lifted in a light shrug. "Why not? It's a relaxing creed. Whatever's going to happen will happen, and how we behave is preordained, so there's no point feeling uneasy about anything."

He lay down beside her again, his hand resting

on her hip. "It does have some appealing features, I grant you. Particularly at the moment, when I cannot envisage what is to happen . . . to you . . . or, indeed, to me."

"Then stop worrying about it and tell me the story of the ugly joke and the woman."

"I drink too much," he declared.

"I rather thought so," she responded calmly. "But I wasn't sure, since I don't really know how much is too much."

"It's too much when you do asinine things," he said. "Unfortunately, it's all too common a vice amongst the people I know. We start in school and go on from there."

"Why?"

"Boredom, mostly." He turned his head to look at her face beside his. "There aren't too many people like you around, you see, to keep boredom at bay."

"But you're in the army. Surely that isn't boring?"

"Oh, Annabel! It is excruciating."

"Then why did you join?"

"Because every son and heir to the Ralston line has joined the Seventh Light Dragoons for the last hundred and fifty years," he told her. "I would have been happier staying at Oxford, I think, if I'd had any sense, but having been sent down for two terms for some bloody stupid drunken prank, I decided I'd had enough of the ivory tower and followed the family path with a degree of mistaken enthusiasm."

"But you aren't in the dragoons now, are you?"

"No," he said shortly. "I was obliged to resign my commission and accept a transfer to the East India Company's Cavalry."

"Oh, so that's what Harley meant about being a long way from Horseguards Parade, out here among the heathen."

"Did he say that?"

"He did. He also said you had a roving eye, and

it wasn't all that surprising you ended up here with the way you were carrying on."

"Well, I'll be damned!" Kit sat up abruptly. "The cheek of the man!"

Annabel chuckled. "You can't really blame him if it's your fault he's stuck out here."

"He didn't have to come," Kit said. "He chose to transfer with me. God knows why."

"Perhaps he likes you."

He looked down at her, then smiled. "Yes, perhaps he does. I am actually very lucky to have him."

"So are you ever going to tell me what happened?"

"If you insist. But it's not at all a pretty story." Leaning back against the headboard, he propped the pillows behind him. "Come here." Pulling her up beside him, he settled her with her head in the crook of his shoulder. "That's better. Now, if I had a brandy, I should want for nothing."

She looked across at him and saw he was smiling in self-mockery. "Enough of that!"

He nodded. "Once upon a time there was a girl called Lucy who worked in a milliner's. She was round and pretty and a little plump, but very sweet-natured and thought I was the most wonderful of God's creatures."

"That can't have been very good for you," judiciously observed Annabel.

"That is not an encouraging observation. Anyway, as is frequently done in such instances, I set Lucy up in a house in Hampstead, where she was most amazingly happy as far as I could tell, and seemed to enjoy housekeeping and warming my slippers and—"

"Warming other things," Annabel supplied helpfully.

"You could say that. Would you mind keeping your comments to yourself? I do not find them of the least assistance in the telling of this narrative."

"I beg your pardon." She closed her lips firmly.

"Well, as I was saying. Lucy was very content,

and I was perfectly content, visiting her whenever I felt so inclined and the exigencies of regimental life would permit . . . card parties, balls, dinners . . . that sort of thing."

Mockery laced his voice and he stared over the burnished head on his shoulder as if looking into some other world. "I was rarely sober, but then neither was anyone else. We had little need or reason to be. Unfortunately, brandy can bring out the less pleasant side of some people. Three of my brother officers decided one night that my possession of such an enchanting and accommodating mistress was unjustly exclusive."

He brushed a tickling wisp of her hair from his chin where it had drifted. The mockery had left his voice, which was flat, almost expressionless.

"They were all drunk, and I do not think they really intended Lucy any harm. But she was only a shop girl, after all, and for these gods of the aristocracy, fair game, particularly as she had already demonstrated she was not virtuous."

Annabel pushed away from his embrace and twisted to look at him, an expression of horror and disgust on her face. "Did they rape her?"

Kit shook his head. "I arrived just in time, after a particularly unsuccessful night at the tables and an excess of brandy. They were still in the process of . . . of . . . persuading . . . Lucy to accommodate them. She was terrified, poor girl, but quite frankly I think they were all too far under the hatches to have succeeded in anything. But I wasn't thinking too clearly either. An ugly brawl ensued, ending with my issuing challenges to all three of them." He laughed, a short, bitter laugh. "Pistols at dawn."

She stared. "You fought a duel?"

"Three to be precise, one after the other." He lay back against the pillows and closed his eyes. "Madness. Sheer madness."

"Did you kill them?"

"No, of course not . . . just pinked them. But it caused a monumental scandal. One does not fight duels over shop girls, you understand. One should not fight duels at all, but in true matters of honor, the authorities will turn a blind eye. Shop girls are not considered matters of honor.''

"So what happened?''

Kit shrugged. ''I was forced to resign my commission in the dragoons. My behavior was ungentlemanly, you see.''

"It seems entirely chivalrous to me,'' she said stoutly. ''An Afghan would have chopped them in tiny pieces very slowly.''

"This was Horseguards Parade, sweetheart.''

"Well, why did you join the East India Cavalry? I would have thought you'd had enough of soldiering.''

"I had, but my sire had had enough of me.'' Kit laughed that hollow laugh again. ''He had been very patient for a very long time, but this last scandal was too much. And since my way of life was . . . is . . . entirely dependent upon his generosity until I come into my inheritance, I had little choice but to follow instruction and leave the country. And here I am.''

"Yes, here you are,'' Annabel mused, sitting cross-legged on the bed facing him, regarding him with smiling eyes. ''And just think, if none of those things had happened, we would not be in this room together. It's destiny . . . unchangeable destiny. And I would not have it any different.''

"No,'' he murmured huskily, ''neither would I. I am prepared to embrace destiny with open arms.''

•

Chapter 12

❧◦◯◯◦❧

"Captain Mackenzie, the water supply is barely sufficient now to succor the wounded. And we have shot for only a few more hours if we continue returning their fire at this rate."

Colin Mackenzie glanced wearily at the lieutenant who had brought him this grim but predictable report. The air was acrid with smoke and powder, the noise of firing ceaseless, the cries of the wounded a melancholy and relentless accompaniment. He turned to look over the parapet, to where, in the gathering dusk, the enemy pressed ever closer to the gates of Shah Soojah's commissariat fort, pushing their mines forward at an inexorable pace. The captain had been holding his garrison for two days against attacks that increased in ferocity, the enemy seeming to propagate in direct proportion to his own heavy losses.

"I do not understand why they have sent no reinforcements," he said, rubbing his eyes, which were smarting with fatigue and gun smoke. "Don't they know we are under attack?"

The lieutenant accepted the question as rhetorical and made no response.

"How are the men, Bill?"

"Discouraged, sir," the lieutenant replied frankly. "Our losses are so heavy and the wounded are dying like flies for lack of attention. And they're concerned for their families. It's the thought of their wives and children falling into the hands of those savages . . ."

"Dammit! Where the *hell* is Elphinstone?" Mackenzie swung away from the parapet, just as a man came scrambling up the stone steps from the courtyard below.

"They're firing the south gate, sir."

Mackenzie stood silent for a minute, facing the brutal, unpalatable reality. If he was to have the slightest chance of saving his wounded and the families under his protection, he was going to have to abandon his post.

"Very well. Prepare to evacuate the fort. We'll fight our way back to the cantonment." His expression was perfectly composed, and his men could only guess what it cost him to give the order.

A square of infantry fought a last-ditch defense at the south gate, keeping back the screaming, scimitar-wielding horde until the wounded and the women and children, in litters and on horseback, were out of the fort by the north gate, flanked by ranks of cavalry. Then the infantry retreated, fighting every step until they too were out in the open plain.

It was full night now, and the darkness provided some hindrance to their attackers, who seemed less vigorous than the defense, who drew strength from desperation and the possibility that action might bring salvation, and fought with fierce single-mindedness.

"Sound the call to arms," Mackenzie instructed the bugler, and the notes rang out across the plain a rousing call of encouragement. The standard bearer rode in the van beside the captain, who could take some grim satisfaction that even in retreat, his small garrison would behave with gallantry.

Kit was with Bob Markham at the command post at the gate to the cantonment when the first sound of the bugle echoed faintly through the darkness.

"It has to be Colin Mackenzie," Bob said.

"Then let's bring him in!" Kit was already running to the gate. "Light the flares," he commanded the guards, who were peering into the night. "And get the damn gates open!"

He could hear Bob shouting orders as he mustered the troop of sepoy cavalry on duty at the gate. The night was abruptly lit as the great flares went up. Kit flung himself onto his own horse as the troop under Bob's command galloped through the gate.

"Hope you don't mind if I muscle in on this one," Kit said, a laugh of pure exhilaration crackling in the frosty air.

"Be my guest," Bob returned with his own laugh. "By God, we owe Mackenzie something!"

The troop charged across the plain toward the clear and unmistakable sounds of fighting. The bugle continued to blow its repetitive call, vibrant above the ferocious screams of the enemy and the constant crack of rifles. The night-dark yielded to shadowy visibility, sparked by the fire exploding from gun barrels.

With their own inarticulate battle cry born of the days of frustrating inaction and their own savage need to attack, the two officers led their band of sepoys into the thick of the fight. The suddenness of their arrival and the ferocity of their onslaught caught the enemy by surprise, just as it gave one final, necessary spurt to Mackenzie's beleaguered force.

Half an hour later, they entered the cantonment, their reinforcements, not weakened by two days of unremitting attack and the march across the plain, covering their rear, and following them in only when the last exhausted infantryman was safely inside. The great gates clanged shut, the men on the earthworks offering their own covering fire, finally sending off the enemy, who for the first time had met significant resistance.

People poured forth from bungalows and barracks, rushing to offer assistance to the exhausted and terrified women and children in the party.

"You certainly took your time," Colin commented, still sitting his horse as straight as if he had just mounted after a long night's sleep.

"Not for want of trying," Kit said mildly, not taking offense. "Bob went at Elphinstone until he was blue in the face, but—" He shrugged and dismounted.

"Aye. I can guess how it was." Mackenzie rubbed his fingertips over dry, cracked lips. "My thanks to you both, anyway. I suppose I had better go and make my report." He swung off his horse and looked around the barrack square, seething with activity and lit as bright as day from the oil lamps set in windows and open doorways, and held high by servants as surgeons moved amongst the wounded, making examination and disposition. "At least those poor devils will get attention now."

"You look as if you could do with some attention yourself," Bob commented, handing his horse over to a trooper. "You're welcome to share my bungalow if—"

He broke off at a horrified exclamation from Kit. The reason for the exclamation burst upon them, all flashing eyes and swinging copper hair. A cloak flung loosely around her shoulders, Annabel bounced on her toes in front of Kit.

"You have been out there!" she declared in a voice trembling with fury. "Without telling me, you went to fight the Ghazi. You promised you would not again forget to tell me—"

"For God's sake, stop it!" Kit was white, and the men around him dumbfounded, even the more knowledgeable Bob, who could not imagine how his friend was going to deal in satisfactory manner with this appallingly public scene.

"You did not think I would be wondering where you were," she continued, paying no heed to his interjection. "You said you were going to the gate for a few minutes . . . and you have been gone for hours and hours, without a word . . . and I find you have been in danger—" The tirade came to an abrupt halt as Kit, his face now scarlet, gripped her shoulders with bruising purpose.

"*Be quiet!*"

Slowly her gaze ran around the stunned group in their immediate vicinity, and then to the rest of the square where people stood staring. "I am sorry," she said, her voice now low, her eyes wide with contrition. "But I was afraid for you. I forgot everything else."

"Whoever is that young woman?" demanded a matron in piercing accents from the far side of the square. "I haven't seen her before. And whatever is she wearing?"

"Go back to the bungalow and wait for me to come to you," Kit said, controlling his voice with some difficulty. "I will deal with this then."

She went immediately, hurrying through the gaping crowd, drawing the hood of her cloak over her face, keeping her eyes on the ground as if this reversion to Ayesha-appropriate modesty could undo the damage.

"Whew!" Colin whistled softly. "What a tigress, Kit. Who is she?"

"The woman I intend to make my wife if we ever get out of this godforsaken hole," Kit said almost distantly. "If I haven't wrung her neck first, of course."

"Really?" Bob looked at his friend with kindled interest. "I didn't realize that was the way the land lay."

"Neither did I," said Kit, his lips set. "But I should have. Let us go and make our report. The sooner it's done, the sooner Colin can get some rest."

"Look, there's no need for us both to go to Elphinstone," Bob suggested. "Hadn't you better go back and see—?"

"No," Kit interrupted curtly. "She can damn well sit there and wonder what I'm going to do to her when I do get back! It would serve her right if I marched her straight round to Lady Sale and abandoned her," he added savagely, striding toward headquarters.

"Dear me!" Colin murmured. "It's not like Kit to become so exercised. I didn't think anything would ever scrape the surface of that implacable disillusion."

"The lady's a trifle unusual," Bob offered in explanation.

"Yes, I had rather gathered that. You must tell me the details when we've finished with Elphinstone and Macnaghten. It might cheer me up."

The general and the Envoy received Captain Mackenzie glumly. They offered neither explanation nor apology for abandoning him, but were kind enough to commend Captain Markham and Lieutenant Ralston for their swift action in offering reinforcement.

"I wish I knew what is to be done now," the general mumbled. "General Nott attempted to send a brigade from Kandahar, but they were forced to turn back because of the weather. The snows are beginning to fall. I do wonder, Sir William, if we should not consider making terms."

"So long as our supplies remain intact, General, we can hold on throughout the winter," declared the Envoy. "I have written to Mohun Lal with instructions to begin intrigue amongst the chiefs. Matters will soon right themselves."

Elphinstone did not look convinced, but he did not argue; instead, he fixed Lieutenant Ralston with a rheumy eye. "Lieutenant, it was a captaincy you held in the Seventh Dragoons, as I understand it."

"It was, sir." Kit had found reduced rank a matter of small importance beside the greater one of his exile, and now he responded without much interest. His thoughts were far too busy elsewhere.

"Mmmm. Well, I think it only right that you should hold the same rank with the East India Company's Cavalry," the general said. "You have performed sterling service in negotiating with Akbar Khan and in this evening's action."

"Thank you, sir," said Captain Ralston with much the same note of indifference.

"Well, gentlemen, I think that's all for the moment." The general struggled up from his chair. "I will have your promotion posted immediately, Ralston."

"I was wondering when he was going to do something about your rank," Bob commented outside. "It was manifestly absurd, after your years of service."

Kit laughed, but without much humor. "Service is hardly the way I would describe five years on Horseguards Parade, Bob. Anyway, if you'll both excuse me, I have a pressing affair to deal with. If you would care to join me for supper in about an hour, Miss Annabel Spencer will have something to say to you."

"At least Kit's got something to take his mind off this suicidal lunacy," Colin observed, as he and Bob made their way to the latter's bungalow. "And what a something," he added, managing a weary chuckle. "I trust you're going to fill me in."

Annabel had indeed been chewing her nails in a fair degree of apprehension in the hour since her return from the square. The more she thought about her outburst, the more she cringed. She, who for eight years had never so much as raised her eyes to a man without permission, had railed at Kit in front of complete strangers in the most intemperate fashion. And since she could neither explain nor excuse such behavior to herself, her chances of producing a convincing defense to the justifiably furious Kit were remote.

At the sound of the front door, she jumped to her feet and stood facing the sitting room door.

"Salaam, Ralston, *huzoor*," she said humbly, touching her hands to her forehead as he stalked in.

"Don't give me that!" The door shut under a vigorous push. "You *harpy*! How dare you treat me to such an abominable display, like some Billingsgate fishwife?"

"But you promised—"

"No, *you* promised," he interrupted. "You promised you would behave with circumspection in the cantonment. And what do you do? You descend on me, berating me with all the obvious intimacy of someone who has shared my bed, in full sight and earshot of the entire cantonment. The story will be on everyone's lips by the morning, and how the hell am I to explain it?''

"Tell the truth," she said. "I've told you it does not matter to me."

"And I have told you that it matters to me. Quite apart from that, I have never been so embarrassed by anyone, *ever*."

"I am sorry," she said simply. "It was inexcusable. I was just afraid for you, and I have never felt that way about anyone before."

"But how could you forget everything we have discussed?" He tossed his cloak over the couch and ran his hands through his hair, where the lamplight caught deep golden lights. "How, Annabel?"

"I don't know," she said. "I don't understand what is happening to me. I used to have a quick temper as a child, I remember that, but the last time I lost it was with the Ghazi who gave me to Akbar Khan. Since then, I learned to control it absolutely." She turned away from him and stood staring into the fire, her words coming slowly as she seemed to feel for explanation and understanding. "It's as if I've been in some way released from the need to step quietly at all times, to watch my every move and weigh every word."

"You are not released from that," Kit told her bluntly. "The consequences of forgetting may be different in this place, but they're no less potent." Catching her by the shoulder, he swung her around to face him. "And I give you fair warning, Annabel Spencer. If you ever embarrass me like that again, I will return the experience in full measure, most powerfully and publicly."

There was a short silence while they both absorbed the exchange, its causes and what lay beneath those causes.

"Have a brandy," Annabel suggested suddenly. "It might make you feel less annoyed."

"I thought I was eschewing the demon drink," Kit said.

"Just not taking it to excess," she declared, her eyes twinkling at him now. "Will you tell me what happened this evening?"

He gave her a faithful account, not excluding his surprise promotion, and matters were in a fair way to returning to normal between them when the door knocker banged.

"Who's that?" Annabel did not sound particularly pleased at this interruption, at a point when equilibrium was still a trifle fragile.

"I expect that's Colin and Bob." Kit stood up, frowning again. "I invited them to have supper with me. And if you wish to join us, you will damn well apologize for that scene. They were thoroughly discountenanced."

He went to the door. "Come in. Colin, you have not met Miss Spencer, have you?"

"I have not had that pleasure." Captain Mackenzie bowed politely toward the still figure, standing beside the fire.

Annabel stepped forward with an air of resolution. "I owe you all an apology. I behaved abominably, and I most truly beg your pardons for any embarrassment I may have caused you." She looked toward Kit, one eyebrow lifted. "Will that do?" He nodded and she smiled with relief. "Then we can forget it now?"

"*We* can," he said with resigned emphasis. "But I don't think anyone else is going to. You've now made your presence most dramatically felt throughout the cantonment, and God alone knows how I'm going to explain it."

"I shouldn't bother to try," Annabel said cheerfully, moving toward the door. "I'll go and see if Harley needs any help with supper."

"Maybe you shouldn't bother to try," Bob agreed, shrugging lightly. "There's enough going on at the moment to make a nine days' wonder out of it if nothing is said."

"Let us hope so."

* * *

The next morning, however, brought a most unwelcome summons. Lady Sale wished Captain Ralston to wait upon her at his earliest convenience.

Kit received the summons with darkening brow, and Annabel regarded him warily, wondering if his anger were about to be rekindled. "Perhaps it's not about—"

"Of course it is," he interrupted. "Interfering busybody that she is." He pushed back his chair from the breakfast table. "The trouble is she's the bear-leader in this place, and Elphinstone thinks the sun shines out of her . . . " He swallowed the vulgarity and turned his irritation on the cause of the trouble. "We could have pulled this off, Annabel, if you had kept your promise."

"I said I was sorry."

"Yes, but that doesn't help, does it?"

"I suppose not." She played with the crumbs on her plate. "If you really don't wish her to know my history, why do you not tell her I was a mixed-race harlot in the bazaar who took your fancy? There are some, and they might conceivably speak English. Afghan women frequently dye their hair with henna; it's a favored color." She looked up at him. "There's no reason why an unmarried officer shouldn't have someone to warm his bed, is there? That obtuse colonel made that assumption."

Kit sighed. Even if he wished, it was too late to revert to his original plan and throw the pathetic, innocent, rescued orphan on her ladyship's considerable mercies. Annabel had made the nature of their relationship all too clear by her outburst. He was going to marry her, but he was going to do it properly, in St. George's, Hanover Square, with an engagement notice in the *Times*, banns, and congratulations. His intended bride did not know this, of course, and he rather thought it best kept to himself for the time being, but it did mean that for the present she had to assume a different identity for the likes of Lady Sale.

"It will serve," he said. "But I shall have a peal rung over my head on the subject of moral laxity and indiscretion—the latter being the greater sin. If you had been discreet, everyone would have turned a blind eye to what went on under the privacy of my own roof."

"Are you always this unforgiving?" she inquired with a hint of testiness of her own now. "It really doesn't seem to be at all useful. I have tried to offer constructive suggestions, and all you can do is complain about what's past."

Kit smiled reluctantly. "I used to say that to my father, when he would worry away at some past peccadillo of mine until I was no longer in the least sorry and more than prepared to go out and sin again." He shook his head in some bewilderment. "I don't know what you are doing to me, Annabel."

"I wouldn't do anything to you that you didn't want done," she said, leaning back in her chair, amused by the faintly puzzled expression in the gray eyes, the rueful curve of the sculpted mouth. "What would you like me to do to you now?" She stood up with deliberate purpose, her eyes sparking with unmistakable promise. "Or shall I surprise you?"

"I am going to face the music," Kit said, stepping hastily away from her as she came toward him. "Now, don't be wicked, Annabel." The last plea was a groan as she reached against him, molding her body to his, putting her arms around his neck, bringing his mouth to hers, and her hands palming his scalp. She was wearing one of his dressing gowns and as she lifted her arms the loosely tied girdle came undone and the garment opened so that her body, warm and naked, was pressed to his.

He held his arms away from her for as long as he could, but yielded finally, slipping his hands inside the robe, running his palms over the silken curves and contours as his body rose hard and wanting in response.

"There," she said softly, moving her mouth from his. "Now you may go to Lady Sale and tell her that what you do with your harlot from the Kabul bazaar is entirely your business. You will feel more like saying it now, won't you?" Her hand, intimately mischievous, touched him in pointed emphasis.

He looked down at her, into the jade eyes where beneath the naughty laughter swam the shark of passion, as sharp-toothed as his own.

"You are an imp of Satan," he declared, his fingers tightening on the bare curve of her hips. "I do not know how such a one manages to work celestial magic. It is a contradiction in terms."

"But one worth unraveling," she said. "Aren't you going to let me go?"

"I don't know," he said with mock gravity. "I haven't decided whether or not to exact some penalty for this devilment."

"Like what?" The words seemed suddenly to stick in her throat as she caught her breath on a jolt of desire.

He felt the shock course through her body, read it in her eyes, and smiled with smug satisfaction. "Like that." He took his hands from her. "Having done to you what you did to me, sweetheart, I'll leave you to contemplate the frustrations of beginning something you don't intend to conclude."

He left her standing in the middle of the dining room. Ruefully, she ran her hands over her aroused body, cupping her breasts where the sensitive peaks stood out in aching readiness. Then, with a half smile, she refastened the robe, reflecting that she had been given only what she deserved.

Kit, having decided to take the offensive with Lady Sale, offered her ladyship a bland smile as she received him in her drawing room, waving him into a chair, her expression severe.

"I heard a most disturbing report, Christopher," she said without preamble. "I am certain you know to what I refer."

Kit shook his head. "Indeed, ma'am, I am afraid

I do not. I was not aware that I was in any way accountable to you."

"The tone and conduct of this cantonment is my responsibility," she responded acerbically. "Quite apart from my friendship for your mother, I feel obliged to ensure that your behavior is not lowering the tone of our community, or damaging your reputation."

"Which is long past repair, ma'am," he reminded her. "Just as I am long past the age for being hauled over the coals in this fashion. Whom have I offended?"

Her ladyship had begun to look distinctly disconcerted. "I was given to understand that you have a . . . a young person under your protection."

"It is not uncommon," he said gently. "You must be aware that most of the unmarried men, both in India and here, take care of their needs as it seems appropriate."

Lady Sale's color heightened. "I know nothing of such things. What you men do with the natives is nothing to do with me. But to flaunt one of our own women, of whatever class, in full view of the innocent young ladies in this close society of ours is indefensible. It is a gross insult. What is someone like poor little Millie Drayton to make of it?"

Kit frowned and appeared to give the thought some attention. "Well, ma'am," he said finally, "I have no intention of flaunting anyone in front of these delicate maidens. It seems to me it would be in the worst possible taste. Just as it seems to me, if you will forgive me, that your assumptions are somewhat out of line. Who could you possibly imagine I have under my protection?" He looked suitably bewildered. "An Englishwoman? Here? You cannot truly believe that, Lady Sale. And a native woman is, as you say, a matter of no importance."

Her ladyship was now looking very flustered. "Well, I heard—"

"Perhaps one should not refine too much upon what others may have heard," he interrupted, a distinctly chilly note in his voice. He had now realized that he was not going to be obliged to enter into any elaborate untruths, and the knowledge gave him considerable satisfaction. He would confound the self-righteous with his own brand of that defect. "A great deal was happening in the barrack square last night. I find it difficult to believe anyone could have formed an accurate impression of anything." He stood up. "I have duties to attend to. So, if you will excuse me." He bowed.

"Yes, of course," Lady Sale said stiffly. "If I was mistaken, then I ask your pardon. But someone has to regulate matters in the present state of affairs. All standards could be scattered to the four winds if we permitted it, with no one knowing what is to happen to us all, and those savages whooping and leaping outside the gates."

"Quite so," Kit said with another bow. "I bid you good morning, ma'am."

He went out into the cold morning, grinning unashamedly at the ease and satisfaction of his victory. But his satisfaction did not last beyond the front door to the headquarters bungalow.

"Oh, Ralston, I just sent a message to your bungalow." Lieutenant Watson greeted him distractedly, then jumped suddenly to attention and saluted. "Beg your pardon, sir. I forgot about your promotion. Congratulations, sir."

Kit waved a hand in dismissal. "I'm not about to stand on ceremony. What's amiss? More than the usual," he added.

"It seems the rebels are occupying the forts of Mahmood Khan and Mahomed Shereef," the lieutenant said. "They're threatening the southwestern flank of the cantonments, and are blocking our road to the commissariat fort."

"As someone warned us they would do." Bob came into the adjutant's office, raising an eyebrow at Kit, who nodded grimly.

"We're going to have to pay more attention to

those pronouncements,'' he commented. ''So what's to be done?''

''We've just received a message from Warren at the commissariat fort, saying that he's in danger of being cut off. The general has ordered that he withdraw and the fort and its supplies be abandoned. A detachment has been sent to cover the withdrawal.''

Kit stared in horror. ''You cannot be serious. There's but two days' supplies in the cantonment, and no possibility of replenishing them.''

''I think our esteemed commander has decided in his muddled fashion that having erred by ignoring Colin's plight, he won't err again.''

''But this is quite different! Anyway, all Colin needed was reinforcements to continue his resistance. Ignoring a garrison under attack or abandoning it are not the only alternatives. What about fighting back, for God's sake?''

''You tell the general. The commissary officer has been trying to get him to understand the realities for the last half hour.''

''What of Macnaghten?''

''Busy with Mohun Lal, apparently. Plotting their nasty little plots.''

Kit grimaced. ''It makes my skin crawl just to think of it.'' He turned at the sound of running feet. The door burst open to admit a breathless, red-faced ensign.

''Oh, sir . . . sir . . . '' He saluted belatedly at the two captains. ''I have a message for the general, sir.''

''Well, give it to the adjutant,'' Kit said, indicating Lieutenant Watson. ''And take a deep breath, Ensign.''

The youngster did so and said, ''The detachment sent to bring off Lieutenant Warren and his men have had heavy losses, sir, from the Afghan flanking fire and the occupied forts. They have had to fall back.''

Kit nodded. ''I'll take the message to the general,

Watson.'' He knocked on the general's door and
went in on the quavering invitation to enter. Elphinstone listened and sighed.

"I really do not know what to do for the best."

"General, we cannot afford to abandon the commissariat,'' Kit said, glancing at the two other officers in the room.

"As I have been saying,'' agreed the commissary
officer. "With barely two days' supplies in the cantonment, sir, and no hope of procuring more, it
would be madness to yield the fort.''

"It would surely be better to send detachments to
storm the forts of Mahmood Khan and Mahomed
Shereef,'' suggested Kit. "If we can take those forts,
then the commissariat will no longer be under attack.''

"Oh, dear . . . oh, dear,'' sighed Elphinstone.
"Perhaps a message had better be sent to Warren,
telling him to hold out until the last extremity. See
to it, Captain Ralston, will you?''

"Very good, sir.'' Kit saluted and turned on his
heel. "All right, Warren is to hold out to the last,''
he told the occupants of the adjutant's office. "With
any luck, we'll be able to persuade the old man to
attack the opposing forts.''

"I'll send to Lieutenant Warren,'' the adjutant
said.

"I'm on riding school duty.'' Kit glanced at the
chart on the wall. "God knows what good is to be
done by drilling cavalry troops in the finer points of
dressage. They'd do better practicing the arts of the
buzkashi at this point in their fortunes.''

"Life must go on, m'dear fellow,'' Bob said with
a sardonic grin. "Customs and ceremonies are all-
important, are they not?''

"On which subject . . . '' Kit took a moment to
regale his friend with an account of his interview
with Lady Sale. It added a moment of light relief,
but the relaxation could only be of short duration as
the muddled morass deepened and irretrievable opportunities were lost.

Chapter 13

If Annabel had been expecting a lover's greeting when Kit returned to the bungalow, she realized her mistake the minute she saw his face.

"What has happened? Was it Lady Sale—?"

"No." He shook his head. "Amazingly, that went off without too much difficulty, but you were right about the attacks on the commissariat fort."

"Of course I was," she said simply. "Is that what's happening?"

"Yes. The commanding officer has been ordered to hold out to the last extremity, and it's to be hoped he'll get reinforcements soon enough." He paced the small sitting room, a deep frown corrugating his customarily serene brow. "But I think we have to face the possibility of leaving this place under duress."

Annabel sat down and folded her arms, her head cocked on one side, a picture of slavish concentration.

"All right," Kit said. "I'm not telling you anything you don't already know. But what I am talking about is making sensible preparations for any eventuality."

"Speak on, Ralston, *huzoor.*"

The mockery was so faint that he was able to accept it as simply a shadow of their past dealings, even to smile a little. "You're going to need a horse, Ayesha."

209

"A good one," she agreed calmly. "But my own is in Kabul."

"A blood Arabian, unless I much mistake?"

"Yes." She was watching him closely.

"I assume, if you can handle such a spirited filly, that you ride well enough to handle a horse that is up to my weight?"

"Yes. I would imagine so."

"I have a string of horses, cavalry horses, not sporting beasts. You will be best mounted on one of them, but I think you need to learn how to manage such an animal."

She nodded easily. "I did say I would like the opportunity for some exercise . . . of the outdoor variety."

He smiled. "I can't offer you that, but I am on riding school duty for the rest of the morning, drilling a troop of cavalry. I think you had better join them in the ring."

"In what guise?"

"Afghan. You may leave the explanations up to me."

"How am I to ride without boots?"

"If you'll pardon the intrusion, sir, I think I can find miss a pair of riding boots." Harley appeared in the open doorway. "There's an Afghan wench I know, in the mess kitchens, sir. She can lay 'ands on all sorts of things . . . for a price, o' course."

"Then replenish Miss Spencer's wardrobe, Harley," Kit said briskly. "No questions asked, and no shortage of rupees."

"Right, sir. If I could just 'ave one of miss's slippers for the fit?"

"Some enterprising soul with relatives in the bazaar, I imagine," Annabel said thoughtfully, rubbing her one bare foot. "Consorting with the enemy is not considered an offense if it results in extortion. I daresay she has an entire stall behind the mess kitchens."

"Well, if it will supply your needs, I'll not argue its origins," Kit declared. "It might be best if you went later with Harley and bought what you require yourself. You will know better than he.''

''I'm sure I can also bargain better than he,'' Annabel said matter-of-factly. ''And I'm going to have to have some wool and fur linings to keep the cold out. Also a chadri would make life easier. The cloak is all very well, but it's hard to keep oneself completely covered . . . and probably I'll need—''

''Enough!'' Laughing, Kit called a halt to this lengthening shopping list. ''Buy whatever you think you will want; I don't imagine you will bankrupt me. I'm going to the stables to decide which of my horses will best suit you. Then you can both begin to get used to each other.''

He returned in a short while, riding a powerful and surpassingly ugly piebald. Annabel, who was still one-footed, hopped to the front door, declaring with a laugh, ''I would much prefer my Arabian mare.''

''Maybe so, but Charlie here will do you very well. Come and make his acquaintance.''

''I am still missing a shoe.''

Kit dismounted and led the horse to the door, where Charlie and Annabel could examine each other properly. Annabel gently knuckled the animal's nose. ''He's enormous, Kit.''

''But very well-behaved,'' Kit assured her. ''And he's long on stamina.''

''Mmmm.'' Annabel and her new horse regarded each other solemnly, then she stood on tiptoe and blew gently into Charlie's nostrils. The horse wrinkled his velvety nose and rolled back his lips in a responding grin.

Kit nodded his satisfaction. Annabel and horses were clearly well-accustomed to each other.

''I 'ope these will do you, miss.'' Harley came up the path, holding a pair of leather boots of Afghan design. ''Thievin' bint wanted a small fortune for 'em, sir.''

Kit shrugged easily, taking the boots and examining them. "They're sturdy enough. Put them on and we'll get going."

Annabel took them and turned herself into Ayesha, veiled, hooded, and cloaked. Kit tossed her up onto Charlie, who managed somehow to look surprised, as if a fly had landed on his back, but high-stepped amiably enough beside Kit to the riding school.

Within the large barnlike structure, twenty cavalry troopers stood beside their horses. A lean, weathered Indian officer was supervising a lad sweeping the sawdust ring into a smooth surface.

"Morning, Captain," the Indian greeted Kit. "We're about ready for you."

"Morning, rissaldar." Kit returned the salute of the troopers. "Saddles off, please, gentlemen," he said pleasantly, striding into the ring, adding over his shoulder, "Ayesha, you may keep yours."

There were no verbal grumbles at the instruction, but the troopers complied with dour expressions, unsaddling their mounts, occasionally shooting curious looks at the still, veiled figure atop the enormous horse they recognized as belonging to the captain's string.

The rissaldar made no attempt to hide his curiosity. "Got a visitor, have we, Captain?"

"A . . . a friend of mine, you might say," Kit said with a conspiratorial grin. "I've a wager on that I can teach her to handle that horse in the ring as well as any cavalry trooper, so when I'm on school duty she'll be here, too. And if you've no objection, I might send her over to you now and again for a bit of practice."

The rissaldar was too accustomed to the generally dissolute, hedonistic amusements of aristocratic officers to show the least surprise at this explanation. "Does she speak English?"

"A little," Kit prevaricated. "But she understands it very well."

The riding master simply nodded, commenting, "I don't suppose Charlie even knows she's there."

He scrutinized horse and rider with an expert eye. "She's going to have to persuade him without brawn that she means what she says." He shrugged. "But Charlie's a mild-mannered brute."

Kit nodded and turned to the troopers, now mounted bareback. "Shall we begin, gentlemen? A caracole to the right, if you please."

Annabel sat and watched for the moment, realizing instantly why the troopers had looked so disconsolate at the prospect of accomplishing this drill maneuver bareback, encumbered as they were with the long swords that struck her as more ceremonial than useful, and the lances they were required to hold at rest, while their horses executed a series of half turns under the critical eyes of the rissaldar and Captain Ralston.

Charlie began to shift restlessly on the sawdust, as if resenting his separation from his fellows, and she stilled him with a sharp command and a jerk on the bridle. "Just let me see first what we're supposed to do," she said softly, once he had stopped his pawing. "You may know how to do it, but I do not."

She continued to watch, fascinated as much by this new aspect of Kit as by the drill. His voice, light and unfailingly polite, even in his not infrequent criticism and correction, was the only sound in the wooden building as he took the riders through an elaborate ritual that seemed more like a dance than anything to do with battle. But she was in no doubt as to the level of equestrian skill needed to perform the maneuvers, or to the nature of the communication necessary between horse and rider. If she and Charlie could manage to perform together in this fashion, then there was little they could not accomplish elsewhere.

After a while, Kit said something in a low voice to the rissaldar, who took over the drill smoothly. Kit came up to Ayesha, moving with the long, rangy stride of an athlete, the form-hugging cut of his britches and tunic setting off his spare, well-muscled frame to considerable advantage.

"Let's try a half turn to the right," he said briskly. "Unless you want to sit like patience on a monument all morning."

"No, of course I do not," she responded with a touch of indignation, then saw that his eyes were smiling. "I didn't want to make a fool of myself if I could help it."

"You won't, and Charlie knows quite well what to do, but he won't be comfortable if you don't guide him." He began to instruct her in the same pleasant yet authoritative tone he had used to the troopers, and she found it remarkably painless to follow direction and not in the least irksome when he insisted on corrective repetitions with some regularity.

"What a good teacher you are," she commented. "It's a true gift."

"I am complimented," he responded with a twinkling smile. "Are you ready to join the others now? I can't be giving private lessons for the whole session."

"What are they going to think?" She looked uncertainly at the men in the ring.

"They are here to ride, not to think," Kit said evenly. "Are you ready?"

And that seemed to be that. "As ready as I'll ever be." She urged Charlie forward and he went unerringly to a position in the center of the line of troopers.

"I told you he knows what he's doing," Kit said, laughing.

Two hours later, Annabel was exhausted, sweat trickling down her body despite the frigid air in the riding school. It was not hard to imagine how the troopers must be feeling, weighed down as they were with weapons and unsupported by saddle and stirrups.

At last, Kit glanced at his watch. "Very well, gentlemen. That'll do for today. Thank you for your time."

The courteous appreciation was received at face value, his salute was returned smartly, and the troopers walked their mounts out of the barn. The rissaldar went off in their wake, and Kit looked up at Annabel and grinned. "Enough exercise for you?"

"That is not funny," she said with a groan. "I think I'd rather match Akbar Khan along a ravine than—"

"Rather do *what?*"

"It was a game he liked to play sometimes." She swung her leg across the saddle and slipped into Kit's waiting arms. "A test rather than a game," she amended, allowing him to take her weight for a moment as she explained.

"I used to wonder sometimes what would happen if I failed the test and became like all the other women. Would he become bored with me?" A shiver crept down her spine as she realized for the first time from the safety of distance how that possibility had dominated her unconscious fears.

She looked up at Kit and suffered a shock. His gray eyes were adamantine, his mouth set in a grim line. "Feringhee!" she accused softly, having no difficulty reading the thoughts behind the expression. "I've told you before, you cannot judge them by your rules or place your labels upon them."

"I can hold them accountable for what they did to you," he said harshly.

"And what did they do to me?" she mocked gently. "Come now, Ralston, *huzoor,* I have come to no harm at the hands of Akbar Khan."

"Haven't you?" He stared down at her as if he would see into her soul. "Haven't you, Annabel Spencer? Do you really imagine I will believe that? That I could possibly accept that a child from your background, abducted, hurled into a Muslim zenana, taught things that no child should have to learn, fear amongst them, comes out of such experiences uninjured?"

"Changed," she said quietly. "Different, but not necessarily injured. Unless, of course, you consider an inability to return to the previous life an injury. I am certainly so changed that I could never do that."

Premonition stabbed coldly. She wasn't saying anything she hadn't said before, and in much the same matter-of-fact tone, but he had traveled in thought such a long way down the future road of his own construction that he had allowed himself to believe her opposition must now be pure form. "Yes," he said. "I would consider that to be the gravest injury of all, if it should prove to be the case."

Silence shrouded them as they stood in the graveyard cold of the barn, both aware of the chasm yawning between them.

"Destiny," Annabel said finally. "We are in the hands of destiny, Christopher Ralston. 'Tis all a chequer-board of nights and days / Where Destiny with men for pieces plays: / Hither and thither moves, and mates, and slays, / and one by one back in the closet lays.' A Persian poet, one of Akbar Khan's favorites," she said when he looked confounded. "Eleventh century. His name was Omar Khayyám."

"And you truly embrace that philosophy?"

"Oh, I don't know," she said, turning from him with sudden impatience. "What is the point in this discussion, anyway?"

"If you don't know that, I'm not going to tell you," he said, allowing his anger because it masked his hurt. "You had better go back to the bungalow. I have other duties."

She offered him a mock salaam and with a violent exclamation he seized her hands, pulling them away from her forehead. "Why must you make me so angry, Annabel? I could shake you till your teeth rattle!"

"You only become angry like that when I point out the truth as I see it," she said calmly. "But if I don't point it out, then you will begin to believe I view the world with your eyes, and it is not so."

He sighed and released her. "Go with Harley to

his stallkeeper this afternoon. I shall feel easier when you are properly clothed for whatever eventuality your precious Destiny decides to drop in our laps.''

He watched her glide from the building with that graceful, apparently unhurried step that did set her apart from any of the young women of his acquaintance. He didn't know anyone who moved as Annabel did, who was capable of such immobility, such serenity. But she wasn't always like that, he remembered with a flicker of encouragement. She was capable of furious outbursts worthy of any ill-schooled brat . . . shades of her past, as she had admitted, resurrected by the situation in which she now found herself. Perhaps she was not irreclaimable after all.

On that heartening thought, he swung himself astride Charlie and rode him back to his stable.

He returned to the bungalow in early evening, having been working all afternoon on plans for a counterattack on the besieging forts. Harley popped out of his kitchen as Kit stepped into the hall.

''Oh, there you are, sir. What an afternoon I've 'ad,'' he said, following Kit into the sitting room.

''Did you go shopping with Miss Spencer?'' Kit, deciding that his new regime entitled him to the first drink of the day at six in the evening, poured himself a brandy.

''I did that, sir. Lord, you never seen nothin' like it. The two of 'em goin' at it 'ammer and tongs, Captain, jabbering away in this 'eathen language. I didn't know what they was sayin', but miss got the price down from six hundred rupees to two hundred!'' The flabbergasted expression on Harley's usually stolid countenance, combined with his unusual eagerness to describe his extraordinary experiences, offered an accurate reflection of his awe and dismay at the strange shopping habits of women in foreign parts.

Kit grinned appreciatively. ''Did she buy much?''

''I dunno, sir, but it sounded like it. The wench is bringin' it round in the mornin'. Miss said as 'ow the girl didn't 'ave everythin' in cantonments and would 'ave to go to the city fer it.''

The captain's grin faded. "The guards will never let her pass freely. Or at least, they had better not.''

Harley nodded wisely. "Miss said as 'ow the girl 'as a way of gettin' in and out.''

Kit frowned, sipping his drink. It should not surprise him. The defenses were full of holes, and they could not plug them all. "Where *is* Miss Spencer?''

"Havin' a bit of a nap, sir. Seemed a bit tired like, after the ridin' and all that shoppin'.'' He wiped his brow expressively. "It was enough to finish anyone.''

"I can imagine. What's for supper? I'm famished. I've had nothing since breakfast.''

"Couldn't get anythin' from stores today, sir. They weren't givin' out, but the hen's still layin', although she's an old bird,'' he added on a note of foreboding. "We've still got a sack of flour, a few potatoes, and leeks. And a bit o' bacon—''

"Yes, but what are we having for supper?'' Kit broke in, his mouth watering.

Harley looked hurt. "I've made a bit of a stew with potatoes and leeks, sir, in bacon fat. I'll save the bacon for breakfast, if that's all right.''

"You're a prince among batmen,'' Kit said. "I didn't mean to snap.'' He smiled the disarming, crinkly smile that had won him Harley's undying loyalty five years before.

The batman looked a little warm and slipped a finger into the neck of his collar as if it were suddenly constricting. "Well, I'll get on with it then, sir.'' He took himself back to his kitchen, and Kit took his drink into the unlit bedroom.

Annabel rolled over on the bed as he came in, stretched luxuriously, and yawned. "I have been asleep.''

"With good cause, Harley tells me,'' he said with a chuckle, coming over to the bed. "How about a kiss.''

Her eyes shimmered in the shadowy light. "You don't want to shake me anymore, then?"

"Not at the moment," he said on a dry note. "But I'm sure I shall again in the not-too-distant future." He put his glass on the side table and bent over her. "Kiss me, you infuriating creature."

She obliged with some thoroughness, then sat up. "We went shopping. Did Harley tell you?"

"With most out-of-character eloquence." Kit unfastened his sword belt and stretched. "He tells me the shopkeeper can slide in and out of the cantonment with her wares."

"Of course," she responded matter-of-factly. "You don't imagine there are no spies here, surely?"

"I suppose I did." He unbuttoned his tunic. "Although why I should have, I don't know, when Macnaghten has his own spies in Kabul and is setting them to all kinds of nefarious plots."

"Plotting against Akbar Khan?" Annabel swung off the bed and struck a match, lighting the oil lamp on the table. "I'm not sure how wise that is."

"Why not?" He sat on the bed to pull off his boots. "It's tit for tat, surely?"

"That depends. What are they plotting?"

"Oh, Macnaghten has charged one of his agents, an Afghan called Mohun Lal, who is living in the city residence of a Kuzzilbash chief, to offer blood money for the heads of some of our most virulent opponents."

Annabel stared in dismay. "But that is treachery by any standards."

"Your erstwhile khan suggested it himself," Kit declared.

"Akbar Khan suggested that Macnaghten, *huzoor*, organize the assassination of some of the chiefs? I do not believe he said such a thing."

Kit massaged his cheekbones wearily. "No, he did not suggest exactly that, and it is utterly despicable that the Envoy should have decided upon such a course. But Akbar Khan did suggest that if we could sow dissension amongst the various factions, then they would be too busy fighting each other to fight us."

"And you believed that? After everything I have told you of Akbar Khan, and everything you saw and heard in his fortress! How could you have been so stupid, Kit?" She began pacing the room, the length and restlessness of her strides potent evidence of her agitation.

"No, I did not believe it," he snapped, stung by her tone. "But I was merely a messenger. My opinions were not required. I delivered the message and the Envoy—"

"Played right into Akbar Khan's hands," Annabel interrupted flatly. "If the British prove their treachery, their faithlessness, then Akbar Khan will have no compunction in acting any way he pleases."

"But he did put the idea into Macnaghten's head," Kit pointed out.

"But it was up to Macnaghten to make the decision. Akbar Khan was testing him, to see how trustworthy he is. You know how devious Akbar is. He will offer the apple, but will disclaim all responsibility if it is eaten."

"What are you suggesting?" Kit shrugged into a dressing gown of brown velvet, knotting the belt with irritable emphasis.

Annabel felt his weariness, his surfeit of frustration and acrimony. Coming over to him, she slipped her arms around his waist, resting her head on his chest. "I don't really know. Let us not talk of this anymore tonight. You're tired and I would rather soothe you than argue with you."

He stroked her hair as she held him, held him without passion but imparting a gentleness, some of her own serenity that she seemed to be able to draw upon at will, banishing the sharp edges, the rough surfaces, the grating exchanges.

"I expect you are hungry," she said. "Harley has been cooking since we returned. Come into the dining room and I will serve you."

He yielded to the seductive softness of Ayesha,

feeling the tension and anxieties slip from him as
she attended to his wants, served him, poured his
wine, built up the fire, talked of many things, none
of them related to destiny, to battle, to treachery, to
dangerous incompetence. He began to have the
wonderful, magical feeling that he was the center of
her universe, that she existed only to ensure his
peace and comfort, and that sense of wandering in
an illicit yet entrancing wonderland lapped him as it
had done the first night he had spent with her. And
later, in the soft lamplight, she brought that same
peace and comfort to his body, so that sleep crept
up on him and took him without his will or conscious thought.

Annabel stroked the hair from his brow as he
slept, a soft smile on her face as she traced the line
of his jaw with a delicate fingertip, brushed his lips
in the same way. In sleep, there was no sign of that
occasionally disfiguring curl of self-mockery on his
face, or of the dark gleam of disillusionment in the
gray eyes. She wondered what sort of a child he had
been, and her smile broadened. Angelic-looking, at
least, with that shock of curly golden hair and the
disarming smile that he could still produce when he
was forgetting to be cynical or bored. One would
find it hard to withstand the blandishments of such
a child.

Still smiling, she blew out the lamp and snuggled
down beside him, pulling the quilt up to her nose.
Sharing a bed was really very pleasant, she decided,
as sleep hovered. It was not something she had ever
done before, but the presence of another body, particularly such a loving one, was most soothing and
comforting . . . for as long as Destiny left these
pieces where they were on her board. Why was she
so convinced that Destiny was female. . . .

At first the noise beyond the window barely penetrated the world of dreams beneath the nesting
covers, then she sat up at the same moment that Kit
sprang into full awareness.

''What the hell . . . ?'' He leaped naked from the

bed and strode to the window. "Damn, I can't see a thing!" He began to pull on shirt and britches. "I don't hear any firing, so it can't be an attack. What's the time?"

"Three o'clock," Annabel told him, her voice muffled as she pulled her tunic over her head. "Where's my veil?"

Kit opened his mouth to tell her she was to stay in the house, then closed it and tossed her the cravat. "Promise me you won't speak to anyone, or express to the world in general any of your uncomfortable opinions on the subject of feringhee bungling."

"I'll save them until we're back," she agreed, fastening the veil at her ear and picking up her cloak. "Ready?"

Kit nodded and went to the door. Harley was already in the hall, pulling open the front door. "Now what?" he demanded gloomily, looking out at the street where house lights blazed through the early-hours darkness.

"Your guess is as good as mine," Kit replied. "Nothing good, that's for sure." He went out into the street. "Ayesha, stay with me. I don't want you out of my sight, understand?"

"I understand, Ralston, *huzoor*," she said, bowing her head. "I will walk two paces behind you, in the correct manner."

Despite the grim hour and the absolute conviction that yet another nail had been hammered into the British coffin, Kit's lips twitched. He cuffed her playfully. "See that you do."

They hurried to the barrack square, to a scene of massed confusion. Kit stopped abruptly. "God Almighty! It's Warren and his garrison. He's abandoned his post!"

"What post?" She stepped up beside him, staring into the square where horses and soldiers milled, voices raised above the general cacophony, bellowing orders.

"I don't believe it, Kit." Bob Markham separated

himself from the throng and loped across to them. "Warren says he did not receive the message to hold on to the last. Goddamnit, man! Major Griffiths was about to leave with a sizable force to storm Shereef's fort. Warren would have been relieved by dawn." He looked as rumpled as Kit, his hair uncombed, his tunic buttoned awry. "Oh, Annabel, sorry, I didn't see you standing there," he offered in distracted greeting, before continuing, "Warren says the enemy had fired the gate to the fort, but he admits they hadn't effected entrance. But he wasn't waiting for that." Disgust laced Bob's voice. "Apparently, he had a hole cut in the wall of the fort and evacuated that way."

"Of all the bungling idiots!" Kit ran his fingers through his hair so that it stood out in a wiry halo around his head.

"You do him a kindness," Bob said harshly. "I'd call it something else."

"Yes, I suppose I would, too. But maybe he didn't receive the second message. Anyway—" Kit shrugged expressively. "Either we fight or we talk terms now. Unless Elphinstone's prepared to sit back and accept starvation."

The two men seemed to have forgotten Ayesha, and she did nothing to draw attention to herself, standing immobile beside Kit, listening and thinking. Others came over, all expressing the same disgust and concern, and the discussion raged in the freezing air, while she continued to stand there, reflecting that she was as unable to participate in male conversation as if she were still inhabiting a zenana. There were only four men in the cantonment, apart from Kit and Harley, who knew who and what she really was, and since Kit wanted it to stay that way, she had no choice but to subsume Annabel under Ayesha, as she had done for so many years. It seemed ironical in the light of Kit's so fervently expressed determination to resurrect Annabel Spencer and bury Ayesha.

So motionless was she, and so absorbing the conversation, that Kit turned to leave the square, still in the company of his fellows and still deep in talk, without acknowledging her in any way. Wondering how long it would be before he remembered her, she remained where she was, watching them turn out of the square.

Three minutes later, Kit reappeared, his face creased with anxiety. When he saw her still standing in the same place, the anxiety was replaced with puzzlement. He came over to her at a run. "Whatever is the matter?"

"I just wanted to see how long it would take you to realize you had left me behind," she said.

Kit looked stricken as he struggled to deny the charge but couldn't.

Annabel laughed. "Don't worry, I am not in the least hurt or annoyed. It just seems to me that men are the same in essence the world over, whether they inhabit Afghan mountain strongholds or European bungalows. Put them together with an absorbing topic of conversation, and women might as well not exist."

"That's not true," he denied. "Life without women would be insupportable."

"So long as they keep to their place." Her eyebrows lifted quizzically.

"Oh, come along," Kit said. "I'm not standing around here bandying words with you. Your place is in bed, and that's where I want you."

"We're going to have to find some substitute for eating," she said. "I suppose making love will do as well as anything else."

The light banter overlaid their recognition of the disastrous turn events had taken, overlaid it but did not deny it.

Chapter 14

‟**T**he wench is 'ere, miss, with your clothes.''
Harley came into the dining room, where
Kit and Annabel were eating breakfast.

''Oh, thank you.'' Annabel stood up. ''I'll go and
see what she's brought. I'll need two hundred rupees, Kit, if she has brought everything she promised.''

''I'll fetch it,'' he said easily, putting down his
teacup.

The girl stood in the hall. She was veiled, but wore
no chadri, and in her arms was a sizable bundle.
Annabel greeted her cheerfully in Pushtu but received no response. Mutely, the girl held out her
bundle. She had the terrified air of one desperate to
flee, as if she were in danger of contamination.

Annabel looked at the clothes and understood
why. ''There's no payment needed,'' she said in a
flat voice to Kit as he came in with the money. Her
face wore a strange expression and he gazed at her,
uncomprehending.

''Why not?''

She did not answer him straightaway, but said
something in rapid Pushtu to the girl, whose scared
eyes darted around the room above the veil. She
responded in a low, fearful voice, salaamed hastily,
and vanished into the street.

''What's the matter? Why was she to have no payment?''

''These are my clothes,'' Annabel told him, still

225

in that same flat voice. "You do not pay for what you already own."

"You're talking in riddles." Impatience laced his voice, but it was an impatience born of anxiety.

She returned to the dining room and dropped her bundle on the table amongst the teacups. "Akbar Khan has sent me my own clothes."

"*What*?" He stared at her. "I don't understand."

"We were talking of spies last night, were we not?" Her face and voice still carried that strange flatness. "I don't know why I did not think of the logical extension. Of course he would instruct his spies to report on me. He made it clear he knows I'm here, after all."

"So the girl reported to Akbar Khan that you had made contact with her and he chose to supply your needs himself?"

"Can you think of another explanation?" She began to sort through the pile of clothing, cashmere, silk, fur sliding through her fingers. "See, he has even sent my riding dress and boots." She held up the butter-soft leather trousers and fur-lined leather tunic, the highly polished boots that had been molded to her foot. "And the chadri."

"Why?" The one word question was all he could manage as he looked at the clothes, at the glowing richness of the material spilling upon the table.

Her mouth moved in the travesty of a smile, humorless but knowing. "It's just his way of reminding me that I am bound to him, whatever I may do. That I am in essence dependent upon him, and upon his generosity." She hugged herself suddenly with crossed arms. "That his generosity could at any moment be withdrawn." A note of weary resignation entered her voice. "That is why he has sent these things. The hawk will drop upon his prey when he decides he wishes to."

Kit tried to deny the wash of helplessness that seemed to sap him of all energy and determination. But he could not deny the reality of the situation, the horrible sensation of being creatures in Akbar

Khan's vivarium. "I won't let him hurt you," he heard himself say, even as he knew it to be ridiculous.

She shook her head, but the mockery he had feared was withheld. "You will suffer as much as I will, Kit, and I will not be able to protect you any more than you will be able to protect me."

"Return to Kabul now," he said with painful urgency. "I am doomed here anyway, but you are not. It is my responsibility that you are in this position. I want you to return to him."

"But I don't wish to," she said softly. "I told you that I have made my choice. Nothing has changed. And who knows?" She shrugged lightly and her voice became more animated. "Destiny may have something else in store for us. Let us wait and see."

"You and your damned Destiny," Kit said, but for some reason the exasperation he thought he was expressing was not there. He could hear only relief and a strange joy in his voice.

Annabel heard it too and her smile this time held no bitterness. "Well, at least I shan't be cold," she said cheerfully, as if the last moments of intensity had not taken place, as if the shadow of fear could be banished by sheer willpower. "And it will be wonderful to have a change of clothes. I think I shall ask Harley to prepare me a bath." She reached up to kiss him. "Had you not better report for duty? It would be useful to know how long the food supplies can last, and what's being done to replenish them. It's a pity I don't have my hawk," she said, her eyes crinkling with sudden mischief. "Perhaps I should send to Akbar Khan for my peregrine. He could keep us well-supplied with sparrows and field mice."

"I'm not sure whether Harley's culinary skills extend to making such creatures palatable," Kit responded in the same tone. "But the idea is a sound one. I'll take my gun out this evening and see what I can bag." He held her hips lightly; despite the easy tone, his eyes were serious as he scanned her upturned face. "Are you certain?" When she nodded, unsmiling, he kissed the corner of her mouth. "All right. I'd better get moving, but I'll take you over to the riding school this afternoon and you can do some work with the rissaldar."

"I can hardly wait," she said with a mock groan. "I'm sure he's not as polite as you."

"No, he'll bawl at you," Kit told her. "But you'll learn, I promise you that."

He made his way to headquarters, noticing how the atmosphere in the cantonment was even more subdued than usual. A small boy ran out into the deserted street after a ball. Kit picked up the ball and tossed it gently to the child, who caught it in a hug to his chest and gazed wide-eyed at the officer, before an irate ayah swooped down upon him, scolding in Hindi as she bore him back into the garden of his bungalow. The child yelled, furious and imperious, at his nursemaid, and Kit went on his way, wondering whether little Annabel Spencer had been imbued with the same innate sense of superiority where native servants were concerned, even those who were supposed to have some degree of authority over the child in their care. Her upbringing would have been most unusual if she hadn't, he thought, turning into headquarters. They were all the same, these brats of the raj. But what was going to happen to *these* poor little devils? The unbidden question chilled him, and he pushed it away as he went into the adjutant's office.

"Anything new?" he asked the room at large.

"Morning, Ralston." A bewhiskered major turned from the chart on the wall. "I was waiting for you to come in. D'you fancy a skirmish?"

Kit wasn't at all sure he did, but there was only one answer. "Certainly, sir. Where to?"

"The fort of Mahomed Shereef. If we knock 'em out of there, maybe we can reclaim the commissariat," Major Griffiths said. "Someone's got to show some fight around here. Why don't you pick a dozen handy men to follow you? Assemble in the barrack square at dusk."

"Very good." Kit saluted and went in search of Havildar Abdul Ali. The sergeant was his customary phlegmatic self.

"Do my heart good to get my hands on them, sir," he said. "I'll find the right men for you."

"My thanks, Havildar." Kit returned to headquarters, where an atmosphere of enthusiasm reigned for once, inspired by Griffiths's determination and the idea that resistance was both possible and desirable.

"Lucky devil!" Bob Markham said. "Wish I were going."

Kit gave him a twisted grin. "If anything happens, keep an eye on Annabel for me."

Bob nodded in instant comprehension. "I hope you've told her you're going this time."

"Not yet, but I will."

He went back to the bungalow at noon and found Annabel talking to Harley's precious hen in the small back garden. "They do say they lay better if you talk to them," she said, straightening up. "But I fear Harley's right. This scrawny old bird is fit only for the pot."

"I'm not sure Harley really means that," Kit said, leaning against the wall of the house, for the moment banishing everything but his pleasure in the simple sight of her. "He brought Priscilla all the way from India. You do look enchanting in that color."

She was unaccustomed to compliments, and a trace of pink touched the cream-white complexion as she brushed a little self-consciously at her emerald-green tunic. "It was always one of my favorites."

"Women tend to know what suits them," he observed, then continued in much the same tone, "I am joining a detachment with orders to storm the fort of Mahomed Shereef."

Annabel nodded. "When?"

"At dusk."

"That's sensible. Not that they won't be expecting

you, but shadows make good friends when one is on the offensive."

"Somehow, I thought you'd be dismayed . . . cross, even." He offered a rueful smile.

She frowned. "How silly of you. I get cross when you don't tell me what you're doing and I have to sit around wondering. But, of course, you have to fight." She shrugged. "You forget I've lived amongst men for whom the defining characteristic of their existence is fighting."

"Bob will look after you if anything happens," he said directly, accepting that anything less than forthrightness would be foolish with this woman.

"I won't need to be looked after in any way you mean, Kit," she responded with the same directness. "This is my country. I will know what to do if you are killed."

His hands opened in an inarticulate gesture. How did one describe what one felt for a woman who needed none of the supports one expected and wanted to provide, who had her own strengths, who offered those unstintingly, and who now stood smiling with gentle reassurance in the winter sunlight? And he had to leave her and might never see her again.

She stepped toward him, instantly comprehending. "Destiny, love," she said, taking his hands. "Accept it. You will come back this time. I know it."

"How can you?"

"It's written upon your forehead." She traced the frown lines on his brow with a fingertip. "Do what you have to. A man can do no more."

"I have to go to the strategy session." He took her hands in a painful grip. "I wanted to take you to the riding school, but I haven't the time."

"I am quite willing to forgo an afternoon of being bawled at by that riding master," she said. "I shall talk to Priscilla and see if I can coax a few more eggs out of her."

"Sweetheart . . . ?"

"Go, Kit. I'll be here for you when you return."

He stood holding her hands for a long moment, then bent and kissed her, a quick, light brush of his lips, before he turned and left her. She touched her fingers to her lips in valediction as he cast a final glance over his shoulder, and he smiled.

Alone in the garden, Annabel dashed a recalcitrant tear from her cheek and regarded Priscilla with a quizzical eye. "How about two brown eggs, Prissy? Ralston, *huzoor*, is going to want a good breakfast when he gets home."

"We're not making so much as a dent!" Major Griffiths yelled over the rattle of grapeshot from the horse-artillery gun. "The bastards just seem to pop up out of the stonework. Look at 'em."

Kit looked. The enemy was massed on the parapets, the long-range fire from their jezzails mowing down the squares of British troops firing upward with their muskets. Griffiths was right. As fast as the grape riddled the line of Ghilzais, another line sprang up to replace it.

"We need a second gun," Kit said, just as fire shot through his hand. He stared down in disbelief at the blood welling between his fingers. "How the hell did that happen?"

"Here, sir." Abdul Ali proffered a handkerchief. "Bind it up. Must have been a stray ball, just nicked you."

Kit wrapped the wound as tightly as he could, knotting the makeshift bandage with his teeth. All around him, men were falling and the crew at the gun were dropping with exhaustion. Intimations of the wintery dawn were just to be detected in a graying of the night-dark. They had been attacking the fort all night, and with no success. The storming detachment of cavalry under his command was in the rear, ready to move in the minute the artillery fire had cleared the parapets, which so far it had signally failed to do.

"Sound the retreat," Major Griffiths ordered, a sigh of fatigue escaping him. Then he added with renewed vigor, ''But by God, I'm going to take it next time. Ralston, command the gun crew, would you? I'll have you covered as best as I can.''

The bugle's mournful cry sounded above the firing as Kit galloped to the gun and its near-prostrate crew. He directed the limbering of the gun and the harnessing of the team, trying to keep his voice brisk and cheerful, to encourage the troopers as the deadly fire of the jezzails wreaked havoc, even more devastating now that the British gun had been silenced. A square of infantry offered as much protective fire as they could, but their muskets were of little use against the jezzails. At last, however, the precious gun was limbered up, the team harnessed, and the retreat could begin.

The exhausted and much-depleted force staggered through the gates of the cantonment as dawn broke. They were pursued across the plain by a triumphant contingent of Ghazi fanatics, hurling insults and rifle shots, and turning back only at the bridge across the canal, which was held by a troop of cavalry.

''Better get that hand seen to, Kit,'' Griffiths said, dismounting in the barrack square. ''You game for another try tonight?''

''Oh, yes,'' Kit said with absolute truth, no more prepared than the major to accept the wasted lives of the past night as simply contributing to an effort of complete futility. ''But we'll need two guns.''

Even as he spoke, his eyes scanned the square where order was emerging from the seeming chaos as the troops were fallen out, the wounded taken to the hospital, the cavalry horses led off. He saw her standing in shadow on the far side of the square, enwrapped in the white chadri, and he could feel those jade eyes devouring him through the white silk thread of the *ru*-band. He raised a hand in acknowledgment and she salaamed in response before turning and slipping out of the square.

Clearly, she had learned the lesson of discretion, he thought with an inner smile that did much to alleviate his bone-deep weariness. The handkerchief around his hand was so blood-soaked now that it was doing nothing to staunch the unremitting bright welling, but he decided that a visit to the hospital could wait; there were more pressing matters to attend to.

"Any further orders, Major?" he asked formally, dismounting with one-handed awkwardness.

Griffiths shook his head. "Get some rest and we'll tackle it again tonight. Unless that hand is going to give you trouble."

"I doubt it." Kit saluted with his good hand and made his way home with a degree of energy he wouldn't have believed possible after such a night.

Annabel was standing in the open front door as he turned onto the street. "I was going to be very angry if you hadn't come to me immediately," she declared, running to meet him, but her tone belied the words and her eyes engulfed him in warmth.

"I can't hug you in the street," he protested, as she opened her arms to him. "You were beautifully discreet in the square. Don't spoil it now." He kept his injured hand behind his back and flicked her hip with his other, encouraging her return to the bungalow.

"Did you storm the fort?"

"No," he said. "It was a bloody shambles! But we're going to take another crack at it tonight. If we'd had two artillery guns it would have made all the difference."

"Oh," she said. "Did you have many losses?"

A shadow darkened his eyes and his mouth thinned. "Those damned jezzails have such a long range."

"Yes," she said, stepping back as they reached the front door so that he could precede her. "Kit, there's blood all over the path. Where are you wounded?" Her voice didn't sound any different, not a trace of panic, and he wondered why he had been afraid she would faint or fall into hysterics. He was judging her by the wrong standards again.

"Just my hand. It's only a graze, I think."

"Let me see." She took his hand, grimacing at the sodden rag. "That was not at all clever of you, was it?"

"No," he agreed meekly, allowing himself to be pushed into the house. "But I don't really think I could have helped it."

"Oh, my goodness, sir. You're hurt!" Harley looked aghast.

"Fetch some hot water, will you?" Annabel said briskly. "And some thick towels to mop the blood so that I can see how serious it is." She pushed Kit down into a chair in the sitting room and poured a glass of brandy from the decanter on the sideboard. "Here, I think you might put this to good use."

"A skilled surgeon, are you?" he teased, taking a sip as she unwrapped Abdul's handkerchief.

"You'd be surprised," she retorted.

"No, I wouldn't. Nothing about you could surprise me anymore."

She looked up and gave him a quick, glinting smile, before directing Harley to put his burden of hot water and towels on the floor beside her.

"Is it bad, miss?" he asked, anxiety twisting his customarily stolid features.

"It's hard to tell with all this blood." Delicately, she washed the wound clean and examined it in silence, while Kit sipped his brandy and let lethargy creep over him, and Harley continued to wait anxiously. "I think it's a splinter," she pronounced eventually.

"A splinter!" Kit was shaken out of his lethargy. "How mortifying, Annabel. Surely it was a musket ball, or at least a piece of shrapnel?"

"Kit, are you wounded?" Bob Markham appeared suddenly in the sitting room. "The front door was open, so I didn't bother to knock," he explained, coming into the room with long, impatient strides. "How severe is it?"

"It's a splinter," Annabel said without looking up from her probing.

"It hurts like the devil," Kit said, sitting now on the edge of his chair.

"It's a very long splinter," she said comfortingly, "and very deep. Harley, why do you not make us some tea?"

"Very well, miss." The batman took himself off a little huffily.

Kit drew in a sharp breath suddenly. "Dammit!"

"Sorry," she said, softly apologetic, "but if I do not get it all out, then it will mortify. Have some more brandy."

"No, I'll wait for the tea," he said, gritting his teeth. "Just be quick."

"I'm doing my best," she responded with perfect calm. "There now." Triumphantly, she held up a long, very sharp sliver of wood. "If that had gone into your throat, it would have killed you," she said. "It's like a dagger."

"That makes me feel a great deal better," Kit said wryly. "Where the hell did it come from?"

She shrugged, staunching the renewed flow of blood. "A bullet smacking into a tree will scatter splinters to the four winds."

"You seem to know a great deal about such matters," Bob observed.

She looked up at him briefly. "I know a great deal about the way the Afghans fight. They have many tricks like this one." She began to bind Kit's hand with a strip of bandage. "It's only a superficial wound, I know, but it's going to bleed like the devil."

"Annabel, watch your language!" Kit reproved, only half-joking.

"I am sorry. I didn't realize you had such delicate ears," she retorted. "I haven't noticed you modifying *your* language in my presence."

Bob chuckled. "She's got you there, Kit. Can't demand ladylike restraints when you don't watch your own tongue."

Harley appeared with the tea tray before Kit could

come up with an adequate response. "Shall I pour, miss?"

"Yes, would you," she said absently, concentrating on her bandaging. Kit's eyebrows lifted. Some subtle changes were taking place between Harley and Annabel if one were to judge by that exchange. The batman had most definitely deferred to the lady in a domestic matter.

"Must you go out again tonight?" Annabel asked, sitting back on her heels, regarding him gravely. "The slightest jolt will set it off again, and you won't be much good if you're pouring blood everywhere."

"Sweetheart, I cannot plead a splinter as excuse," he said, taking the cup Harley offered him. "Even if I wished to, which I most definitely do not."

"I'm going to find myself a niche in this one," Bob said with determination. "No, no tea, thanks, Harley. I'm off to offer my services to Griffiths. Get some sleep, Kit. You've earned it."

"I won't argue with you," Kit said, burying his nose in his teacup. "But listen, do me a favor later, will you? Take Annabel to the riding school and give her an hour or so of dressage on Charlie."

"Oh, Kit—" she began, but he shushed her imperatively.

"Charlie will only give of his best if he accepts you as his rider, and you're going to need him to give of his best."

Bob looked doubtful. "I'd be happy to, of course. I taught my sisters to ride, but . . . but, well . . ." His hands waved in an inarticulate attempt to explain how he felt about instructing such a one as Annabel Spencer.

Annabel smiled. "I won't give you any trouble, Bob. I will be every bit as amenable as one of your sisters. I shall be completely enveloped in a chadri, will say not a word to you, but will follow instruction without question."

"Are you teasing me?" The mild blue eyes looked suspiciously at the blandly smiling countenance.

"Not in the least. When you are free, come and fetch me. I'll be waiting for you."

"Around noon, then," Bob said and went off to ensure his own place in the coming night's endeavors.

"Come," Annabel said, rising gracefully to her feet. "Harley will prepare you a bath. You're as black as the ace of spades."

"Gun smoke," Kit explained, hauling himself wearily to his feet. "Am I about to discover yet another facet of Ayesha?"

"You are," she nodded firmly. "You are about to discover how an Afghan woman cares for her warrior on his return from battle."

"Oh," Kit said. "I wish I weren't so tired."

"I can promise you it will only add to the pleasure," she said, her eyes sparkling. "Put yourself in my hands, Ralston, *huzoor.*"

"With the utmost willingness. But what of your pleasure?" He followed her into the bedroom.

"It comes in many forms," she said, deftly unfastening his sword belt. "Sit down now, and let me take off your boots."

"This time, you may do all the work." Kit leaned back in the chair, stretching out his feet for her as she bent to seize his boots. "But only because I would conserve my strength for later, when I can promise you, sweetheart, I fully intend to ensure that you don't know whether you are in this week or the next."

"I'll hold you to that." Her eyes met his in a moment of sensual promise that transcended fatigue, before she returned to her self-appointed duties, ministering to him in ways that reminded him of the nursemaid of his childhood—except that the touch of Ayesha was most definitely intended for an adult male.

Had he been less mesmerized, the absurd comparison would have made him laugh. As it was he could only store it up for later enjoyment. "Lie beside me for a while," he murmured, sliding between the crisp sheets.

"If that is what my lord wishes," she responded with a salaam.

"He does," said Kit sleepily, watching through half-closed eyes as she undressed and slipped naked into bed beside him. "Lie on your side so I can hold you." He curled around her, molding his body to hers, his hands cupping her breasts, his breath warm on the back of her neck, and she felt him glide into sleep, his body relaxing, his hands heavy in their possession.

For a couple of hours she lay with him as he slept, sensing that her presence brought him peace and renewal even in the depths of unconsciousness. When she gently disentangled herself, he groaned in protest and tightened his arms. Laughing softly, she wriggled free and out of the bed.

"Where are you?" He didn't open his eyes and his hands groped blindly over the bed.

"Getting dressed. Aren't I supposed to ride Charlie with Bob?"

"Oh, yes." He flipped onto his other side, muttering, "Practice without the saddle this time."

Annabel gave the hump in the bed a somewhat quizzical look and murmured in an ironic undertone, "Yes, Ralston, *huzoor*."

Bob appeared on the stroke of noon, leading Charlie and looking a little nervous. His nervousness dissipated to some extent under Annabel's cheerful greeting, directed both at him and at the horse, who responded with a whicker of recognition and pawed the ground eagerly as his rider landed neatly in the saddle with a helping hand from Captain Markham.

"Does Kit permit you to keep the saddle?" Bob asked as they reached the riding school.

Annabel looked down at him, regarding him through the *ru*-band in her chadri, her eyes clear and surprised. "I am not a trooper, Bob," she said in blithe prevarication. "I hardly think it's necessary for me to drill as if I were."

"No . . . no, I suppose it's not," Bob said doubtfully. "But drilling bareback does ensure a degree of concentration you don't need with a saddle."

Annabel inclined her head in graceful acknowledgment, but said, "For a trooper, maybe. Charlie and I are simply getting acquainted."

Bob still did not look convinced; however, he was far too diffident to argue with her. The riding school was empty, the sounds of gunfire from the earthworks ample reason for the absence of drilling troopers. Perfecting the finer points of equestrian expertise took second place to the need for defense against the sporadic harassment from without.

Annabel found Bob's style of instruction very different from Kit's. He was so chary of sounding in the least officious that she had difficulty differentiating between corrective criticism and praise. Finally, after one particularly confusing comment, she said, "Bob, just say that again as if you were talking to one of your troopers."

He looked at her, startled, then suddenly began to laugh. "Forgive me, I was trying so hard not to sound critical."

"I'm not such a frail reed that I will break beneath a word of criticism," she said. "I understand I was doing it wrong. I could feel Charlie's confusion."

Matters improved after that, and when Kit, looking refreshed and cheerful, sauntered into the building half an hour later, he watched with approval for a few minutes before going over to Bob and inquiring softly, "Did you think she wasn't ready to dispense with the saddle? I had judged her to be perfectly competent."

Bob turned in surprise. "But Annabel said you thought there was no need for bareback practice."

"Artful hussy," Kit observed with the utmost cordiality. "I told her to do without the saddle today. Presumably she didn't care for the idea."

"Kit!" Annabel saw him and came trotting across

the ring, the smile of pleasure that they could not see nevertheless apparent in her voice. "Are you feeling rested?"

"Completely," he said. "Dismount, now. I want that saddle off."

"Oh, Kit. What possible difference can it make?"

"A big difference, as you will discover. Down, please."

"Why must you be such a perfectionist?" Grumbling, she swung herself to the ground and stood glowering as they removed her saddle. "In a minute, you're going to expect me to carry a sword and lance."

"Stop carping." Impervious to her plaints, he gave her a leg up onto Charlie's very broad back. "Now, just for that piece of insubordination, miss, you may give me a series of eights. Lead off by the left, please."

"Heartless brute!"

Kit laughed and Bob, grinning, picked up his shako. "If you can manage without me, I'll leave you to it."

"They're sending foraging parties to the village of Behmaroo," Kit informed him, not taking his eyes off his pupil. "I met Colin as I was coming over here. It seems we can replenish our supplies to some extent from the village. It's a bare half mile out of the cantonment. . . . Annabel, Charlie needs to combine left front with right back. You're confusing the poor beast."

"Sorry," she called back. "But it's the very devil trying to give him commands when I have no purchase. My knees are not strong enough."

"You don't need strength, just skill," Kit responded amiably, receiving a stream of virulent Persian in return.

Bob chuckled. "I'll go to headquarters and see what else is in the wind. If we've eased the supply situation for the time being, matters are looking up."

"I wish I had your confidence." The laughter faded from Kit's eyes. "But maybe, if we succeed

tonight, it might put a brake on 'em. Did you manage to get a place on that junket?''

''I did. Griffiths was only too delighted to welcome anyone who evinced the slightest degree of
enthusiasm. It's as cheerless as the grave over there,
with Elphinstone still wittering and Macnaghten
looking black.''

''Well, I'll see you in the square at dusk. . . .
That's good, sweetheart. Try it from the right now.''

Bob left his friend and his extraordinary lady to
their lesson—a lesson Annabel brought to an abrupt
halt as soon as the school door banged shut on his
departure.

''Kit, I have had enough now,'' she announced,
drawing rein at the conclusion of a right turn caracole.

''Dear me,'' he murmured. ''Are you compound-
ing insubordination with mutiny? The penalties are
severe, I should warn you.''

''I'll risk them,'' she said, suddenly pulling the
chadri over her head and tossing it down to him.
''Just as I'll take the consequences of unveiling.''
She laughed down at him from her perch atop Charlie.

His breath caught as he gazed at her. Her hair
hung in its heavy plait down her back, every lean
and sinuous line of her body delineated in the
leather trousers and tunic, the jade eyes glinting with
mischievous invitation.

''I seem to remember promising you something
earlier this morning,'' he drawled, draping the
chadri over his arm. ''It might be advisable if you
were to dismount.''

''Advisable for whom?'' she bantered, keeping her
seat.

For answer he simply crooked a finger, and she
obeyed the summons with her imp of Satan smile,
in which anticipation and confirmation joined in a
promise of contracts about to be honored.

''Sweet heaven, but you're a miraculous creature,'' he whispered as she came, lithe and light,

into his arms. His hands moved hungrily over the
body wreathing around him, tracing the swell of her
breasts, the curve of her hips. "I'll take Charlie to
the stables. Go home, take off your clothes, and wait
for me." The instruction was a husky throb, and he
felt the current of passion jolt through her as he held
her. Her thighs contracted, hard against his; her
lower body pressed into his, her head fell back, lips
parted, eagerly expectant.

He looked down at her upturned face, where the
rich brown eyelashes lay in luxuriant half moons
against the cream-white complexion. His hold
shifted to her bottom, cementing her against his own
arousal as his head bent and his mouth took hers,
his tongue exploring within the willingly opened
lips. A fleeting thought of the rissaldar, of troops of
cavalry come to drill, flashed and vanished. He had
a promise to keep.

It was a promise Annabel fully intended he should
keep. She moved against him, in response not ini-
tiation, yielding all self-determination to her lover's
orchestration. When at last he released her mouth
and drew back, his breathing ragged, she smiled
dreamily, making no attempt to move out of his
hold.

"I'll be no more than half an hour," he said. "Be
naked for me when I come to you."

She nodded. He took his hands from her and she
glided away from him. "Anna," he called softly,
holding out her chadri. "Better put this on."

The shortening of her name was an anticipation
of fulfillment. Her eyes narrowed, but she said nothing, simply veiled herself before leaving him.

In a fever of impatience, Kit took Charlie to the
stables, praying he wouldn't be waylaid and obliged
to conduct some ordinary conversation or make
some irksome, routine decision when images of
white skin, sensuous limbs, tumbling copper hair,
and lust-filled eyes rioted in his head.

The sound of gunfire had become part of the everyday noises of the cantonment, and he barely no-

ticed it, brusquely handing the horse over to a sepoy
trooper and hastening back to his bungalow.

There was no sign of Harley, whose instinct for
discretion had always been one of his greatest vir-
tues. He entered the bedroom.

Annabel was sitting cross-legged upon the bed,
her only covering the burnished torrent pouring
down her back, drifting over her shoulders.

"Salaam, Ralston, *huzoor*," she said, touching her
hands to her forehead, her eyes glinting in the firelight.

"Greetings, Ayesha." He unfastened his tunic.
"Can you remember what I promised you?"

"That I would not know whether I was in this
week or the next," she answered, watching as he
pushed off his britches, his movements swift and
economical, watching as he came over to her with
springing step, most beautiful in his arousal.

"I always keep my promises," he said, bringing
one knee up on the bed and catching her chin with
his finger. "This time you will put yourself in my
hands."

"Most willingly."

Chapter 15

A kbar Khan stroked his beard. "Ten thousand
rupees for the head of each chief. That is what
the letter offers."

His audience remained impassive beneath their
turbans, smoke from bubbling hookahs coiling in the
air of the council chamber warmed by a potbellied
stove.

"The Envoy's representative, Lieutenant Con-
nolly, has written thus to Mohun Lal," Akbar Khan
continued in the same pensive tone. "He suggests
that Hadji Ali might be bribed to accomplish this
bringing in of heads." The bright blue gaze ran
around the room, encountering stony faces and grim
eyes. "It would seem to me that those who would
employ assassins cannot be trusted to honor any
contracts made with them," the sirdar quietly
pointed out, and a rustle of agreement swelled into
an articulate consensus.

"When Macnaghten, *huzoor*, professes to negotiate in good faith, I find myself doubting his word."
Akbar Khan permitted a smile of derision to touch
the incisive mouth as he gently labored his point.

"It's said that Elphinstone, *huzoor*, is growing
weaker by the moment," one of the sirdars rum-
bled. "That is why Shelton and his brigade were
ordered into the cantonment from the Balla Hissar."

"According to my sources in the cantonment, that
is the case," Akbar Khan said. "I think it's time we
increased the pressure a little. Despite the British

success in storming Mahomed Shereef's fort the other night, our tribesmen are now occupying all the forts on the plain between Seah Sung and the cantonment. I suggest we fire directly upon the cantonment from the Rikabashee fort.''

''And the village of Behmaroo?'' Uktar Khan sipped sherbet. ''How long are we prepared to permit them to replenish their supplies from that source?''

''No longer,'' Akbar Khan said. ''Although they are able to draw barely subsistence rations from the village, it is a lifeline and one that must be cut. And once it is cut, they will have no choice but to negotiate a withdrawal before they starve.''

''The snows are coming.''

''Yes, the snows are coming, and their fuel stocks must be almost exhausted.''

The *shura* broke up on a note of union unusual with this disparate, factious group, and Akbar Khan remained alone, staring into the middle distance in complete meditative immobility.

Ayesha would know what was being planned. How did she feel, impaled in the cantonment amongst the weak and vacillating fools he had taught her to despise, awaiting the end in which she knew she would have to participate? When should he remove her? It would be easy enough to accomplish at any time, the cantonment was so thoroughly infiltrated with his own people. Should he leave her there to learn the pangs of hunger; to experience the dread of inevitability as the collar tightened; to shiver in terror as her imagination, fed by the knowledge of experience, suggested the various fates her khan might have in store for the unfaithful one?

He missed her. Insofar as Akbar Khan ever permitted concerns of the flesh to obtrude in his single-minded purpose, he missed Ayesha's softness, the softness that overlaid that certain sharpness he enjoyed so much, that set her apart from the women to whom he was accustomed. He missed her ready response to his challenges as much as he missed her skill at the art of love. He missed the sense of being tuned to her every thought and twist of emotion. He could only guess at what she was feeling now, and he wanted to know. She had chosen to remain with the feringhee, but had she chosen the whole people, or just the ephemeral joys of Christopher Ralston's bed? The latter he could forgive. He would punish the infidelity, but he would forgive, since the situation was in some part his responsibility. But betrayal was a different matter.

He frowned slightly as he came out of his contemplative trance. He would leave her where she was for the time being. Exploiting the witless treachery of Macnaghten required all his concentration.

"Dear God!" Kit exclaimed, running his hands distractedly through his hair. "The regiment at Kurdurrah has been cut to pieces. And now this."

"What's 'this'?" Colin Mackenzie came into the adjutant's office looking harassed. It was a universal expression in headquarters these days.

"The cantonments at Charikar have fallen," Kit said grimly. "The Gurkha regiment under Codrington did what it could to defend them, but those damned Ghazi fanatics massacred the entire garrison."

"Families?"

Kit nodded bleakly. "Pottinger and Haughton staggered in this morning, the only two survivors, and Haughton's barely alive."

"Sweet Jesus!" Mackenzie went to the window and stood staring out into the deserted street. The winter wind rattled the glass and sent autumn's fallen leaves scurrying before its vicious sweep. Across the country, British garrisons were falling before the Afghan jezzails and scimitars. On the plain outside Kabul, tribesmen were massed, pouring fire into the cantonment with almost derisory ease.

"We should evacuate the cantonment and move into the Balla Hissar," he said. "For once I agree with our esteemed Envoy. It's the only sensible option. It's well defended, and has a relatively commanding position. Down here, we're like rats in a trap."

"Shelton won't have it," Kit said. "I've been listening to the deliberations all morning. He's in favor of falling back on Jalalabad where Sale is holding, and the brigadier is afraid that if we move into the Balla Hissar it will delay the retreat."

"How the hell does he think we're going to get out of here . . . camp followers, women, children, babes, accomplishing seventy miles to Jalalabad under fire?" Mackenzie exclaimed in disgust. "The only way we are going to leave here is with the permission and support of Akbar Khan and the other sirdars."

"Tell that to Macnaghten," Kit said wearily. "He's still firmly convinced that his plan to sow dissension amongst the chiefs will work, and if we can hold out in the Balla Hissar through the winter, all will be well."

"Captain Ralston?"

"Yes, Lieutenant." Kit returned the new arrival's salute automatically.

"An Afghan force, sir, has been sighted moving from Kabul toward Behmaroo."

Kit's short expletive was echoed by Colin as they absorbed the implications of this fresh disaster. "You'd best deliver your message to Brigadier Shelton, Lieutenant," Kit said.

"If only Shelton were more than a good duty soldier," Colin muttered as the lieutenant left. "Someone has to show some vigor and initiative around here. The troops are thoroughly dispirited, fighting this constant defensive battle without adequate rations. I can't get so much as a crisp salute out of them, and I'm not sure I'd trust most of them much further than I could throw 'em." It was a gloomy truth. Morale was so low that it was becoming increasingly difficult to rally the troops in the field.

"It's not all Shelton's fault," Kit pointed out. "In all justice, Elphinstone is not making life easy for a second in command. He's still hanging on to his prerogative of command, although he can't make a decision and can hardly get out of bed."

"True enough." Colin shrugged gloomily.

"Kit, I need a cavalry diversion with a field gun," a hurried voice broke in from the doorway. "I'm told that's your specialty. Ready to march in half an hour."

"Yes, Major," Kit said to the retreating back of Major Swayne. "Since when have cavalry diversions and field guns become my specialty?" he wondered aloud.

"Since the storming of Mahomed Shereef," Colin said with a faint grin. "Quite a reputation you acquired, my friend, during one of our lamentably few field triumphs."

"A reputation justly belonging to one Havildar Abdul Ali," Kit said frankly. "He has his own troop of sepoys and they'd follow him into Dante's inferno. For some reason, Abdul has elected to follow me."

"Well, take care this time," Colin said. "And keep the havildar at your back."

Kit nodded. "I'd better let Annabel know. I'd rather face a Ghazi scimitar than my green-eyed lynx in one of her passions."

Colin chuckled. "You're a lucky bastard, Ralston. Wish I had something of that nature to take my mind off gloom and doom."

For some reason, the remark failed to draw forth the light response Colin had intended. Kit shook his head, his gray eyes shadowed. "It's the very devil, Colin, when you find yourself with hostages to fortune. I can live with the certainty of my own death . . . if not during this fiasco, then at some other time . . . but I cannot live with the certainty of Annabel's. And I am tormented by the knowledge that if I had not with such blind arrogance taken it upon myself to interfere in her life, she would not be in danger now."

"Does she feel that?"

Kit shook his head. "I have tried to persuade her to return to Akbar Khan, but she will not. She has this infuriating Afghan belief in destiny. We all behave in a preordained fashion and the outcome is laid down, so the choices that lead to enjoyment and suffering are out of our hands. You take what's coming to you, and smile when you can."

"There are worse prescriptions," Colin said seriously.

"I suppose so." Kit shrugged. "I'd best be about my business, Colin."

"God's speed."

Kit raised a hand in a gesture of acknowledgment and went out into the street. He saw the glimmer of the white chadri as he turned toward the stables and quickened his step. For some reason, Harley was pushing a wooden barrow in the wake of the white chadri.

He didn't want to call out in the open street. The presence of an Afghan woman under Captain Ralston's roof was now common knowledge throughout the cantonment, but he deemed it best to maintain discretion. The subject was treated with gentlemanly restraint by his colleagues and conspicuously ignored by such arbiters of conduct and moral standards as Lady Sale.

Lengthening his stride, he came up with them in a few moments. "Whatever are you doing?" He peered at the contents of Harley's barrow.

Harley stared straight ahead in a manner that managed to convey his complete separation from his present endeavor. "Miss says the hillmen use dung for fuel, and since we're reduced to burning the furniture, sir, she decided—"

"Dung!" exclaimed Kit, wrinkling his nose at the steaming, aromatic pile. "Annabel, be serious."

"I am," she responded matter-of-factly. "You don't burn it wet, of course. We make cakes of it and dry it. There's no sun, but the wind will do as well. Sheep's dung is better than horse manure, but beggars can't be choosers."

"No," agreed Kit faintly. "Doesn't it stink?"

"Not much. And it creates warmth."

A much-prized quality, Kit reflected. Glancing at Harley, he read the same reflection beneath the batman's apparent lofty disavowal of his odorous assignment.

"The Afghans are attempting to occupy Behmaroo." It seemed simpler to go straight to the point and allow dung fires to go by default.

"Are you going to intercept them?" she asked.

"I have orders to create a diversion for Major Swayne's infantry."

"Christopher!" An imperious hail came from across the street. Lady Sale billowed toward him. "Whatever has your batman got in that barrow?" Momentarily diverted from her errand, she stared in astonishment.

"Makes a satisfactory fire, m'lady," Harley declared stoutly, aligning himself with Ayesha, who had taken one step backward and stood with head lowered, the perfect picture of Islam diffidence and modesty.

Lady Sale ignored the veiled figure. "I am reduced to burning my armchairs. I shall send Ghulam Naabi to the stables in that case. Christopher, is it true that those savages are attempting to attack Behmaroo?"

"Yes, ma'am," Kit said. "But Major Swayne is taking a detachment to intercept them, and I am ordered to provide a diversion with cavalry and artillery. We will secure the village, I have no doubt."

"I do trust so," said her ladyship. "Provisions are scanty enough as it is. No one can remember what it was like not to be hungry." She billowed on her way.

"Doubtless you will secure the village," Annabel murmured from beneath her veil.

"Do I detect a hint of skepticism?"

"Possibly. Have a care, Kit."

"I will. And for God's sake make sure that muck is relatively dry before you start burning it."

* * *

All day they struggled against the Kohistanee garrison occupying the village of Behmaroo. The occupying force had blocked all the approaches to the village, and any attempt to take it by storm was clearly futile.

Kit watched helplessly as his own troopers and gunners fell beneath the enemy jezzails. Abdul Ali had been wounded in the first half hour and on Kit's orders been carried off the field by his own sepoys. Kit felt strangely bereft and vulnerable without his phlegmatic sergeant and the five sepoys who were his invariable companions. The arrival of reinforcements under Shelton offered momentary encouragement, but still they came no closer to their goal and at dusk the recall was sounded.

It was a much-depleted force, grim-faced, eyes shadowed with an emotion akin to despair, who re-entered the cantonment. They had seen their companions mown down, been deafened by the appalling inhuman screams of the wounded rising above the incessant gunfire, and they had advanced not one step toward the village where lay their only recourse against slow starvation during the brutal ferocity of a mountain winter in the midst of a harsh and implacable enemy.

Kit went first to the hospital where Abdul Ali lay amongst the dead and dying. The helpless moans of those whose pain had become an intrinsic part of them were, if anything, even worse than the battlefield screams of the newly wounded. The havildar was fortunately wandering in morphine-induced delirium, a blood-soaked bandage around the stump of his left leg. Kit felt a surge of intense anger, an anger directed at everyone involved in this pointless, murderous, suicidal idiocy.

He left the hospital and made his way to his bungalow, his step dragging with bone-deep fatigue, his eyes filled with a profound depression. Voices rose from the sitting room, and the door flew open just as he laid a hand on the latch.

"I saw you come in through the gate so I knew you were safe." Annabel held herself back from him for a moment, as if giving them both opportunity to adjust to the vanquishment of terror one more time, to savor once again the piercing intensity of relief. Then she flung her arms around him, permitting as always on his return the uninhibited show of emotion she denied herself on his departure.

He held her, drawing strength from her strength, then looked over her head to where Colin and Bob had risen and now stood discreetly gazing into the sullenly smoldering, extremely pungent fire.

"I see you're burning that muck," Kit observed, trying to sound cheerful but not quite managing it.

Annabel subjected him to a swift, all-encompassing scrutiny. "Bad?"

He sighed and dropped the pretense. "Worse than anything before, I think. Unless it's just that one more failure, one more day of wasted lives, seems like one day too many."

"Sit down." She pushed him into a chair and poured brandy. "This is the last bottle, but I think tonight you need it."

"I won't argue. Pass it around."

"No . . . no, dear chap, wouldn't dream of drinking your last bottle," Colin said hastily.

"Oh, nonsense! When it's gone it's gone." Kit waved aside the polite objection. "Have we got anything to eat, Annabel?"

She smiled. "A feast. I invited Colin and Bob to join us. We have eggs and flour pancakes, antelope meat and noodles . . . and best of all, tea."

Kit looked astonished. "What fantasyland is this?"

"No fantasyland," she said smugly. "Very ordinary. I went to the bazaar in Kabul—"

"You did *what*?" Kit sprang to his feet, his face chalk-white, the skin drawn tight across his cheekbones.

"It was perfectly simple," she said, seemingly unaware of the effect her revelation was having upon him. "I bought sufficient for several days, and I will go back when we run out. I cannot imagine why I didn't think of it before."

"Perhaps because you have only just lost your mind," Kit said with a strange calm. "I have wanted to shake you on more occasions that I can count, but this time I think I am about to do it."

"We'll be on our way," Bob said, coughing awkwardly.

"Yes . . . yes, indeed," agreed Colin, making for the door.

"No, don't go!" exclaimed Annabel, when it seemed Kit was going to make no attempt to prevent them. "You are staying for supper so don't take any notice of Kit. He's just tired and wretched—"

"Not nearly as wretched as you are going to be," Kit warned softly. "But it'll wait." He waved a detaining hand at his friends. "There's no need to leave. Stay for supper, since I imagine this is the only household in the cantonment with anything deserving of the name of food."

"If you're sure—"

"Of course he's sure," Annabel said briskly, not a whit disturbed by Kit's threatening demeanor. "I am going to see if Harley is preparing the antelope and the noodles the way I explained. Have some more brandy, Kit. It will help you relax."

The door closed on her departure and Kit inhaled sharply. "So help me, I am going to . . . Did you know she had gone into the city?"

"Only after the event," Colin said. "When she invited us for supper. She's so much an Afghan when she wants to be, looks like one in that chadri, speaks like one, behaves like one, that I didn't think too much of it, to tell the truth. I mean, m'dear fellow, Annabel's not exactly an ordinary woman, is she?"

"No," Kit said, his lips taut. "And Akbar Khan is very anxious to get his hands on her. And Akbar Khan is in Kabul. And Akbar Khan's Ayesha is a

familiar figure in the city. I cannot believe she could
have been so foolhardy!"

"It wasn't foolhardy." Annabel reappeared and
spoke calmly from the door. "You take your life in
your hands every time you go out of the cantonment
on one of these futile exercises in recklessness. My
errand was not futile and I fail to see why I should
be expected to sit here twiddling my thumbs and
starving when a little effort and ingenuity can put
food upon the table. The situation is desperate and
requires desperate measures, so I should stop behaving in this stiff-necked fashion, if I were you, or
your supper will curdle in your belly and then I *will*
have wasted my time."

"You are not to do it again."

"I will do whatever I deem necessary, whenever
I consider it necessary, Christopher Ralston," she
returned smartly. "Supper is ready."

"I once told you you'd bitten off more than you
could chew," Bob commented with a degree of compassion.

"Mmmm," Kit muttered, for the moment unable
to agree or deny the statement.

He glowered for about fifteen minutes, then gave
up the struggle against Annabel's determined cheer-
fulness and the beneficial effects of the first square
meal any of them had had in several weeks. But he
had no intention of abandoning the issue, and once
his friends had left and Harley had bidden them
good night, he marched Annabel into the bedroom.

"Now there's no need to be cross," she said hur-
riedly, trying to pull out his grip.

"There is every need." His hold tightened, as did
his lips.

"Kit, I was just another woman shopping in the
bazaar."

"In a distinctive white chadri, the badge of Akbar
Khan's favorite!" he exclaimed. "How could you
have been so witless?"

"Witless? Me?" The jade eyes flashed with anger
as all thought of placation left her. "I did not wear

the white chadri. Harley managed to borrow a plain dark one from a servant in Lady Sale's house. I slipped through the breach in the earthwork that the mess girl uses, and once out I was completely indistinguishable.''

"You walked two miles to the city and two miles back, unescorted and in broad daylight."

"Yes, I did." She sighed wearily. "In the company of a dozen other women from the settlements along the canal. And I will do it again, when the need arises."

"You will not." The flat statement lay between them, cold and heavy in the angry silence.

Annabel, even through her anger, thought how desperately tired he looked, the day's defeat still etched stark in his eyes. Perhaps his need to control her actions came from the complete inability he or any of them had to check the seemingly effortless ascendancy of the enemy. It came from fear for her, too, that she did know. But whether she could understand it or no, she would not permit it.

"I do not give you the right to dictate my actions, Kit." She broke the silence, keeping her voice low and evenly pitched, her tone reasonable. "I am living under your roof because we both chose that I should. I said I would stay with you until what happens happens. I would not presume to tell you what you may or may not do, and I ask only for the same courtesy."

"I want you to be my wife." He heard his voice coming from the depths of his fatigue and disillusion, speaking at quite the wrong moment the words he had managed so far to bridle, even in the euphoria of passion's fulfillment.

Her reaction was instantaneous. "Don't be absurd!"

"Why is it absurd?" He still held her upper arms, and his eyes now gazed down at her with painful intensity.

Her voice took on the note of mockery that had so dismayed him in the very early days. "You will wave your feringhee wand, will you, Ralston, *huzoor*, and turn the erstwhile inhabitant of an Afghan zenana into a pillar of polite British society?" She twisted free of his hold. "I would rather die."

"You would rather die than be married to me?" He had not known it was possible to hurt so much.

She saw the hurt, heard it in his voice. "No, I did not mean that. I meant only what I have said to you so often before. I could not fit into your world, Christopher Ralston, and I do not wish to. I am happy with the world we have created here, but it is one that has no roots in any other. It belongs just to us, and for as long as we can live in it, then I am content."

"But there is no future there," he said, feeling the hurt fade beneath a resurgence of anger at her obstinacy.

"No," she said firmly. "There is only a present. That is the way it must be."

"I do not accept that." He caught her, swinging her around to face him. His expression was wiped clean of fatigue and disillusion, washed away by the pure light of conviction and the determination to impose that conviction and deny her opposition.

"You will tell me there is no future to this?" He clasped her head and kissed her. There was no lingering tenderness or spiraling passion to this kiss. It was a bruising assertion against which she fought blindly for a minute, but he held her head still as his tongue possessed her mouth. Ignoring the vigorous writhing of her body, he bore her backward to the bed, his mouth still in possession of hers. They fell together and his legs scissored hers into stillness, the weight of his body subduing her struggles. A hand pushed up beneath her tunic to cup the warm satiny roundness of her breasts, and at his touch, the touch that she knew she would crave when it was no longer hers for the asking, her nipples peaked hard and the coiling tension began to build deep within her.

Still she squirmed beneath him in an effort to free

herself, to fight off the invasion that she knew would render her vulnerable to his conviction, because she would not be able to bear the thought of no future with Kit. Her head twisted beneath the capturing mouth, but he simply moved deeper within her mouth so that he seemed to be within her head, a hot, stroking muscular presence becoming a part of her. She tightened her thighs against the hard knee that would force them apart, and his hand left her breast, sliding over her flat belly where the muscles contracted involuntarily at the touch, sliding inside the *chalvar*, reaching down, touching her with deep, intimate persuasion so that finally she yielded and her legs parted, her breath sighed in submission against his mouth, and at last he raised his head.

The gray eyes impaled her, probing the secrets of her soul as his fingers probed the secrets of her body. "No future, my Anna?" he whispered. "How can you tell me there can be no future when I feel you throb with promise, quiver with hunger; when I read the love and the lust in your eyes?"

Her eyes closed, but she knew it was too late to deny the truth, although her head moved on the quilt in a parody of denial. No one but Kit had called her Anna, and he used the private name sparingly, as if its assertion of his special place in her life was too important to be diminished by use.

"You will admit it in the end," he declared quietly, unclasping the *chalvar* at her hip and pulling them down, casting the loose, flowing trousers to the floor. "If it takes me all night, I will hear you say it." His hands ran in a stroking caress down the backs of her thighs as he raised her legs, pressing her knees against her body, and she leaped beneath his mouth and the sweet piercing pleasure of his tongue.

She could no more resist the surging, plunging delight than she could the power of his avowal and his knowledge that she shared it whatever she might say. When he flung off his britches and entered her body in a searing thrust that brought a cry of joy to her lips, she rose to meet him, thrust for thrust, and her eyes were open, candid in their recognition as they met his.

"No future, my Anna?" He withdrew to the very threshold of her body, holding them both poised on the brink of extinction.

Her eyes closed for a second as the myriad sensations of bodily bliss mingled, centered on the point of their fusion, and she seemed to hang suspended in a viscous pool of delight.

"Say it, my Anna," he insisted, moving fractionally within.

Her eyes opened. "Perhaps," she said.

He smiled. "I won't insist on a complete conversion . . . not yet." Then he drove deeply inside her, becoming bone of her bone, blood of her blood, sinew of her sinew, and there was no longer a past, a present, or a future, simply an intermingling in ecstasy of the cells and atoms that constitute separate entities.

It was a long time before they returned to the recognition of their separateness. Annabel became conscious of her tunic clinging damply to her body, of the feel of Kit, soft within her, his breath rustling against her neck, the pungency of their loving hovering in the air. She stroked his head in languid benediction. He raised his head to look down at her.

"You are so beautiful, my Anna. Such a wondrous being."

She smiled, a hint of mischief beneath the residual sensuality. "You were threatening to do any number of terrible things to me a little while ago. If that was what you meant, I must remember to provoke you more often."

Kit groaned in defeat and rolled off her. "I don't want you to go into Kabul. It's asking for trouble."

"I'll be the judge of that." She sat up, pulling her tunic over her head. "I'm all sweaty." Sliding off the bed, she padded barefoot to the ewer and basin on the dresser. "I will promise to weigh the risks with the advantages. Will that satisfy you?"

He watched her as she sponged her body with natural ease, unaware of the grace of her movements as she raised an arm, shifted a leg, handled her own body with a deft familiarity that despite fatigue rekindled the ashy coals of his desire. There was no point arguing the toss with her, he decided, getting off the bed with a purposeful step. And no point postponing present pleasure for a future they might never have.

But his recognition of that fact was one he would keep hidden in the darkest recesses of his soul. Only thus could he deny it.

Chapter 16

❦❦

"In the name of the Almighty! This cannot be happening." Colin Mackenzie stared, sick with horror, at the scene on the plain beyond the ramparts of the cantonment. "They're running like rabbits."

"Better give them covering fire," Bob said curtly, shouting an order to the sergeant in charge of the riflemen lining the ramparts. "Damnation, but they're so intermingled, it looks as if ours and theirs are going to come in together."

It was the following day, a day when Shelton again tried to retake Behmaroo from the Kohistanee tribesmen. News had reached the cantonment throughout the day of the appalling losses he was taking as the Afghan garrison was reinforced, and of how the infantry had refused to respond to the command for a bayonet charge, and the cavalry had sat like stones as the bugle called the charge. But not even the liveliest imagination of the most pessimistic and despondent amongst them had envisaged this panic-stricken rout.

Across the plain streamed the British force in total disarray, infantry scattered, their lines and squares broken, cavalry troopers thundering toward the cantonment; on their heels, so close that it did indeed seem to the horrified watchers that they were mingled with the fleeing British, came their Afghan pursuers, on horseback and on foot, jezzails cracking, khyber knives and scimitars wreaking deadly havoc.

Men fell, to be left wounded on the plain by their escaping comrades, to be cut to pieces with merciless savagery as they lay.

The loud, imperative blast of a trumpet rang out above the incessant, chaotic sounds of battle. The gates of the cantonment were flung wide and a troop of cavalry, swords and lances poised, galloped forth in a wild charge toward the deadly melee.

"Isn't that Kit leading the charge?" Bob squinted through his field glass. "He never misses an opportunity to get out there these days."

"No," Colin agreed, his own glass trained on the line of fire. "It's almost as if he has a personal vendetta. . . . Adjust to the left, Sergeant, seven points."

"Seven points to the left," came the bellowed correction, and the muskets swung accordingly.

"I think he has," Bob said seriously. "Love does the strangest things to people."

Colin glanced sharply sideways. "Love! That's a powerful word."

"I believe it to be true. The impervious Christopher Ralston has fallen victim to Cupid's dart. And he'll kill every Afghan with his bare hands if it will enable him to get Annabel Spencer safely out of Afghanistan."

Colin whistled softly. "I had thought it simply a grand passion, appropriate enough here but completely unsuitable anywhere else. Surely he realizes that?"

Bob shook his head, but further elaboration became impossible as the stampeding troops drew closer to the gates and the range of the covering fire from the ramparts had to be adjusted moment by moment.

"I was hoping to find a friendly face." Annabel scrambled breathlessly up between the two men. "I suppose Kit has gone out there." She was wearing her leather riding dress and boots, her hair knotted at the nape of her neck, a fur-trimmed cloak tossed over her shoulders.

"Shouldn't you be wearing a veil?" Bob asked automatically.

Annabel gazed at the spectacle of catastrophe, absorbing the pandemonium, before observing somberly, "I don't imagine such concerns will be of any relevance now. It looks to me as if you're not going to be able to hold them off. And once they're within the gates—" She left the sentence unfinished. They all had the impression of inhabiting a nightmare reality as the unstoppable pursuit drew ever closer, seemingly immune to the musket fire from the ramparts and only slightly checked by Kit's cavalry charge.

"Sir, I think they're falling back!" excitedly called a sentry.

"By God, I think you're right." Colin put up his glass again. "Yes, look, they *are* falling back." Just when it had looked as if the enemy tide would pour over the fugitives and overwhelm them completely before surging under their own momentum into the cantonment, the Afghan pursuit had inexplicably slowed.

"May I borrow your glass?" Annabel was straining her eyes into the confusion. "Thank you." She took the glass Colin handed her. "It's Osman Khan," she said. "He has called them off. I wonder why. He is no more merciful than any of the other sirdars."

"You know him?" Bob looked at her with interest.

She shrugged. "I know most of them to some extent. There are always antechambers and tapestries for clandestine listeners. I know who the waverers are, and who are the most powerful. Osman Khan is one of the most powerful, and is strongly aligned with Akbar Khan." She handed back the glass. "I think it's time my knowledge was put to some use, do you not?"

"In what way?"

"The fighting is done," she said softly. "You will have to begin negotiations. I know how the Afghan negotiates. I know how their minds work. Such knowledge must surely be invaluable.''

"I'm not sure Kit will agree with you," Bob said. "He's coming in now."

Annabel rested her elbows on the rampart, watching as the anarchic crowd tumbled through the gates. There was no order, no apparent chain of command, only the appalling mortification of panic and defeat. Kit's troop of cavalry stood out as they brought up the rear, holding to an orderly line. But then Kit's troop of cavalry had not been broken under a day of decimating, relentless enemy fire and sudden, violent attacks by armies of screaming fanatics. They had not been thrown again and again against an unyielding target until the murderous pointlessness of it all had swept them into a terrorized stampede for a spurious safety.

Brigadier Shelton rode in through the gate, his posture erect, his eyes fixed on some spot straight ahead as if he had no place in this scene of turmoil and disgrace. He spoke to no one but dismounted in the barrack square and strode off to headquarters.

"Can't help but feel sorry for him," Bob muttered. "He's a damned good soldier, just bullheaded and not inspired. But he doesn't deserve to be implicated in such a shameful business."

"Feringhee complacence," Annabel said suc cinctly. "A little less of it, and that would never have happened. I am going to find Kit."

"I do wish she wouldn't say things like that," Bob declared uncomfortably. "I always feel I ought to argue with her, that it's letting down the side not to, but then if you really think about it . . . "

Colin frowned. "It's not the sentiment, it's the manner of expressing it that rankles. No one enjoys hearing home truths from the bloody enemy, and that's what she sounds like sometimes. I'm off to headquarters to hear Shelton's report."

"I'll come with you." The two men left the ramparts where desultory fire continued behind them in the gathering dusk.

On reaching the square, Annabel strode boldly across to where Kit was dismissing his troop. She stood to one side until he had completed his business, then stepped out into the light of an oil lamp.

"Are you well?" The soft question startled him and he swung around.

"What are you doing here?"

"The world and his wife are here," she replied, gesturing at the scene. "I have been on the ramparts with Bob and Colin."

"Why are you unveiled?"

Her eyes met his steadily. "There seems little point in further charades, Ralston, *huzoor*."

He said nothing for a minute, then shrugged acceptingly. "No, you are right. We have reached the end here." He looked around and shook his head in an inarticulate gesture of disgust and disbelief. "Shelton said all along that the troops were not capable of such a battle. They're dispirited, weakened by poor provisions, exhausted by this constant defensive fighting. You can't really blame the poor buggers. But, dear God, I never thought to see British troops turn tail like that."

"To have left the Kohistanee in command of Behmaroo without a fight would have been tantamount to a request for a negotiated withdrawal," Annabel pointed out.

"Which is all that is left to us, anyway," he said, suddenly harsh. "Maybe there would have been an element of dignity in a strategic acceptance of the inevitable."

"I would like to talk to the general and the Envoy," she said directly.

"No," Kit said.

"There are things I can tell them, things I know that they do not."

"No."

"Why not?"

"Because I will not have you exposed to mess gossip and drawing room tittle-tattle."

"I thought we had agreed the time for charades was past."

"But not the time for discretion."

"Kit—"

"No!" He turned on his heel and left her standing in the square, a remarkable figure with the coloring of the feringhee and the garb of an Afghan. She watched him go, a deep frown between her eyes. Then she, too, left the square, her stride for once long and impatient, the cloak fluttering behind her as her leather-clad legs hastened through the cantonment.

"Young woman!" At the imperious hail, she slowed, looking toward the piercing tones she recognized as those of Lady Sale.

"Ma'am?" She realized instantly that her automatic response had given her away. If she had continued on her way, as if she had not understood the summons, the charade would have been preserved. It was too dark in the street for Lady Sale to see anything but the bright hair and the familiar Afghan costume.

"Come over here." Her ladyship beckoned imperatively from her front garden, and Annabel crossed the street. Lady Sale raised her lorgnette and scrutinized her in the thin light thrown by the lamplit window at her back, missing not a detail of her unusual coloring, revealed for the first time now that the familiar figure was without chadri or veil. "I thought as much," she announced. "I do not know what is going on here." The statement was made in tones of disbelief, as if such a happenstance had been hitherto inconceivable.

"There has been a rout, ma'am," Annabel said, willfully misunderstanding her. "The enemy pursued your troops across the plain—"

"That is not what I am talking about," interrupted Lady Sale. "And why would you say 'your' troops? You are as English as I am, are you not? And

clearly from a good family, judging by your voice.
But I will tell you that those clothes are a disgrace.''

"Unfortunately, ma'am, they are the only ones I
possess.'' For one absurd moment Annabel was
transported to her mother's drawing room in Peshawar, when as a little girl in muslin frock and frilled
pantalettes she had made her curtsy and responded
politely to the catechisms of her mother's guests,
and tried not to wriggle when kissed by avuncular
whiskered gentlemen smelling of brandy and cigars.

"I knew Christopher was prevaricating,'' her ladyship muttered, frowning fiercely. "I've known
him too long for him to pull the wool over my eyes.
Where do you come from, gal?''

"Peshawar,'' Annabel said blithely.

"Nonsense! I know all the families in Peshawar.''

"Ma'am, I don't wish to be discourteous, but I am
not convinced I am obliged to answer your questions,'' Annabel said gently. "But I can assure you
that where I do answer, I tell only the truth.''

Lady Sale drew her cloak tighter against an icy
finger of wind, laden with the promise of snow, and
demanded bluntly, "Are you livin' under Christopher Ralston's roof?''

Annabel gave the question due consideration.
"Yes, ma'am.''

"Then you're no better than a camp follower.''

"If you say so, ma'am.''

Her inquisitor stared at the blandly smiling young
woman, whose speech was of the carefully modu-
lated brand of the upper class, whose jade eyes were
carefully expressionless, yet they stood out against
the milk-white complexion in a curious, involuntary
challenge.

"I do not understand this at all,'' her ladyship
pronounced. "But I intend to.'' She turned back to
her front door.

"I beg your pardon, Lady Sale, but I think there
are more important matters requiring your attention
at present.''

The older woman stopped, looked over her shoulder to where Annabel still stood at the gate. Her frown deepened as she seemed to consider something, then she asked abruptly, "Do you think we'll come through?"

"I don't know," replied Annabel, as if the strangely confidential question were not in the least inappropriate in the light of their conversation. "But whatever strengths we have, we will need. And those who lead must be seen to do so."

There was a moment's reflection, then Lady Sale nodded. "You may be a shameless hussy, miss, but your head appears to be straight. I bid you good night."

"Good night, ma'am."

Annabel waited until the servant had admitted Lady Sale to her bungalow before continuing on her way, wondering whether to tell Kit of that encounter. He was bound to hear of it from Lady Sale, anyway. It would undoubtedly annoy him, but it had had the strangest effect on herself. Something had crystallized, and she was not sure she wanted to face that something. She was beginning to belong behind these ramparts. Her fate was inextricably tied to that of the inhabitants of the cantonment, but it was not simply by virtue of her physical presence here.

It was not simply by virtue of her physical presence here.

Her swift step faltered as the implications of that realization crept beneath her skin. How had it happened? That subtle sliding from Afghan contempt to alignment with the supposedly contemptible enemy? Was it just that she was aligned in love with Kit? In friendship with Colin and Bob? In understanding with Harley? Or was it something more fundamental? The legacy of her childhood springing anew, vigorous, bursting through the overlay of Akbar Khan's teaching, so that Ayesha became the construct and the essential Annabel renewed herself in the soil of her growing?

It was a profoundly disturbing concept, yet

strangely exciting. And it was one that informed her determination to put the knowledge she had to best use. If these were her people, then she owed them her loyalty and the benefit of her experience. No one else in the cantonment knew what she knew, and it was inconceivable, in the light of the day's disaster and the present hopeless position, that they would reject what she had to offer.

Deep in thought, she went into the bungalow. Harley's anxious "Is the captain all right, miss?" brought her out of her reverie.

"Yes, Harley. Did you hear what happened?"

The batman's stolid countenance took on an expression of grim disgust. "Yes, miss. A bloody disgrace, it was, beggin' your pardon, miss."

"I shouldn't judge too harshly," she said. "We might all face a Ghazi scimitar soon."

"They'll not see *my* back," Harley declared, and stomped off to his kitchen.

It was late when Kit returned. "I understand you had a frank discussion with Lady Sale," he said without preamble, sniffing hungrily at the bowl of antelope stew Annabel placed before him.

"However did you discover that so soon?" She looked at him in surprise.

"I was waylaid by her servant on my way home from headquarters," he told her aridly, "with the request that I pay her a short visit." He took an appreciative spoonful of stew. "This ought to stick in my gullet, knowing how you acquired the ingredients, but for some reason it doesn't."

"In the circumstances, you would have to be very foolish to permit such a consideration to spoil your appetite. Everyone else is going hungry to bed," she responded smartly. "What did the lady have to say?"

"She wanted to know who you were. I gather you weren't too forthcoming." He raised an interrogatory eyebrow.

"I was very polite," Annabel said. "But she seemed to doubt that I came from Peshawar. She

did, however, say that she had known you too long
for you to be able to pull the wool over her eyes,
and she hadn't believed you when you denied having an Englishwoman under your roof.''

Kit shrugged. ''Well, I am afraid I told her that it
was none of her business, so we did not part
friends.''

''Oh, dear. I suppose it was my fault.''

''You could say that.'' His voice was as dry as
before.

''But how can such silliness be considered important now?'' she exclaimed in genuine frustration.

''Forms and ceremonies take on a great importance when the fabric of life is disintegrating,'' Kit
said quietly. ''Customs, rituals, standards become
all that is left. Once they are destroyed, then for
people like Lady Sale and others, hope and energy
are also destroyed.'' Even as he spoke, it occurred
to him that a few short months ago he would never
have made the least attempt to understand, let alone
defend, the needs and attitudes of those he had so
freely declared prehistoric fools and bores.

''Lady Sale, for all her stuffiness, is a woman of
considerable energy,'' he continued. ''It's in everyone's best interests that she maintain that energy.
There are too many women in the cantonment dependent upon her leadership and strength.''

''I realize that,'' Annabel said. ''And I said as
much to her.''

It was Kit's turn to look surprised. ''Did you indeed?''

''Yes, and she did not seem to take it amiss,'' she
responded stoutly. ''She even said that, although I
was a shameless hussy, my head was on straight.''

Kit laughed. It was not a very hearty laugh, but it
was a step in the right direction, Annabel thought,
refilling his teacup.

''What is being decided?'' she asked, changing the
subject to one of much greater interest.

Kit frowned. ''Nothing at the moment, just wails
from Elphinstone and trumpeting from Macnaghten

and tight-lipped anger from Shelton. I'm going back as soon as I have finished eating."

"Let me come with you," she said urgently.

"Oh, don't be ridiculous." He pushed back his chair. "The last thing anyone needs at this point is you, confusing things even further."

"That is so hurtful, Kit. How would I confuse things?"

The effort he was making to control his impatience was clear on his face and in his voice. "Sweetheart, I am not going to present you as an erstwhile inhabitant of Akbar Khan's zenana. I refuse to go into the intimate details of your history, and unless I do so they are not going to believe your pearls of wisdom. They would see in you only my mistress and hear from me only the rambling championship of some besotted fool. Macnaghten would laugh in my face, and Elphinstone would probably become extremely stiff-rumped about the questionable behavior of a cavalry officer who kept such an exotic creature under his roof."

She shrugged and turned aside. "Very well. I think I'll go to bed in that case."

He stood for a moment irresolute, hating to leave her hurt and annoyed, yet somehow too tired and depressed himself to make the effort to placate her. "I don't know how long I'll be," he said, rebuttoning his tunic.

"I'm sure I shall be asleep," she replied stonily. "Good night." Brushing past him, she left the dining room.

"Damn!" He took a step after her, then shook his head as if dismissing the irritation. It was one last straw that he didn't think he could pick up tonight.

Throughout the long night of an endless discussion, when acrimonious words flew in the tobacco fug of the general's office, and suggestions were made and discarded as frequently as blame was accorded and denied, he found he had little mental energy for worrying about Annabel's hurt feelings. And when, in the early morning, a message for the

Envoy arrived from Kabul, the weariness engendered by the staleness of the night's debate was banished.

Sir William read the letter. "It is from Osman Khan," he announced.

"The chief who called off the pursuit yesterday," Colin said.

"How did you know that, Mackenzie?" The Envoy looked both surprised and displeased at this interjection.

Colin glanced uneasily at Kit, who stared at the ceiling and offered no help. "I seem to remember hearing someone say it," he said eventually.

Macnaghten huffed a little, then said, "Well, according to his letter, Osman Khan maintains that if he had permitted his force to follow up their successes, the loss of the cantonments and the destruction of our force would have been inevitable." He glanced around the table and met only a grim acknowledgment of the Afghan claim. He continued. "It is apparently not the wish of the chiefs to go to such lengths. They wish only that we should peacefully leave their country to the rule of their own sirdars and the king of their own choosing."

Silence lay heavy in the smoke-wreathed room as the winter dawn broke beyond the window. General Elphinstone, from the depths of his armchair, wheezed plaintively. Sir William cleared his throat and said formally, "General, is it your opinion that we have the military strength to retain our position in Afghanistan?"

"It is not feasible to maintain our position here, Macnaghten," the general said, sounding relatively strong for once. "I suggest you avail yourself of the offer to negotiate forthwith."

Now that the inevitable decision had finally been expressed, relief settled on every face. At least there was now a plan, even if it was the worst-case scenario, and the futility of false hopes was now a thing of the past.

"Then I will suggest we talk terms with their deputation," the Envoy said.

"Eggs, butter, onions, and two lamb breasts, Harley," Annabel announced, setting her basket on the kitchen table. "It should keep the wolf from the door for a couple more days."

"Yes, miss," Harley agreed, making no mention of the shouting match that had occurred that morning when miss had announced her intention of going to the bazaar for fresh supplies. In fact, if the captain and his lady were not shouting at each other these days, they seemed to preserve a stony silence. Occasionally, the captain would try cajoling, but his efforts were met with a mocking, taunting tone that sent him scowling and slamming out of the bungalow, and miss would take herself off to the riding school where she would spend hours practicing intricate maneuvers with Charlie.

The front door banged and Harley saw Annabel stiffen, turn toward the kitchen door with the old eagerly welcoming expression on her face, then it was wiped clean and she resumed unpacking her basket. Kit came into the kitchen. "Oh, there you are."

"Back safe and sound, as you see," she said, managing to make it a taunt. "I picked up some interesting titbits in the bazaar, but I don't suppose *you* would find them interesting. The feringhee is far too certain he knows what he's doing to acknowledge a more informed opinion."

Harley coughed uncomfortably and began to clatter saucepans at the stove. Kit jerked his head imperatively to the door, his lips set. Annabel swept past him into the sitting room.

"Don't talk to me in that tone in front of Harley," Kit said furiously, slamming the door behind them.

"It upsets your consequence, does it? The servants must not be permitted—"

"Stop it!"

She fell silent and they stood glowering at each

other for a long minute, then Kit sighed. "How long is this going to continue, Annabel?"

"Until you listen to reason." She perched on the arm of the sofa beside the pungently smoldering fire and regarded him steadily. "First of all, Macnaghten peremptorily rejects terms proffered by the deputation of chiefs—"

"He had no choice but to do so," Kit interrupted. "They were too humiliating to be considered."

She inclined her head in acknowledgment. "Maybe so. But then what happens? He is finally forced to reopen negotiations. He takes a draft treaty to another meeting outside the cantonment, agrees to evacuate Kabul within three days in exchange for a supply of provisions and safe passage for the entire force and its followers to India. He agrees to the return of Dost Mahomed to the throne and the removal of Shah Soojah in exchange for amnesty. He agrees to the evacuation of the Balla Hissar and all forts under British occupation in the vicinity of the cantonment. Tell me that those conditions were not humiliating."

Kit winced but could not deny it.

Annabel continued forcefully. "And now what is happening? The three days have passed and no attempt has been made to evacuate the cantonment, although the Balla Hissar and the other forts have been given up. The enemy has not honored its agreement to supply provisions, nor have they supplied the transport animals for which they were given ample sums of money. And what is Macnaghten doing now? Instead of insisting that the terms of the treaty be honored by both sides, he is continuing with his devious attempts to subvert the chiefs. Does he think they are not aware of what he is doing? I have been listening to the talk in the bazaar. Why do you think they are just sitting back, watching and waiting?" She sprang to her feet on a surge of impatience. "Does he think they've lost interest . . . or momentum . . . or something? Of course they have not. The weather is on their side, there's almost no food or fuel in the cantonment, and they are waiting for Macnaghten to hang himself. And with your damned obstinacy, Ralston, *huzoor*, you won't permit me to tell him that."

Kit was silent. He could not deny anything she said. The troops were living on half rations, transport cattle were dying of starvation, camp followers were eating carrion, and there was no possible way of replenishing the stores. While Elphinstone and Macnaghten went over and over the same issues, concocting and discarding plans, the Afghans had destroyed the bridge over the Kabul river and the British in the cantonment sat and watched.

"The Envoy believes that since the chiefs have not honored their side of the treaty, he is no longer bound by it himself," he said at last, sighing heavily. "I have told him what you think, but he won't listen to me."

"But he might listen to *me*," she said vehemently.

Kit looked at his impassioned green-eyed lynx with the swinging copper plait, the lean sinuous lines of her body accentuated by her Afghan costume, and he thought of that derisive tone investing her voice whenever she met opposition to her opinions. He thought of quavering Elphinstone and the self-important, pompous Envoy listening to a scornful diatribe from this extraordinary creature, and he shuddered. "I will tell them what you heard in the bazaar," he said. "I have never before attributed my opinions to an informed source, but now I will do so. Will that satisfy you?"

She shrugged. If he would not permit her to help in the only way she could, then she would have to live with her frustration. But it was so hard, when she could hear Akbar Khan's voice, see his face, read his mind. He would be sitting there waiting for Macnaghten's treachery to become manifest, and then he would strike with a clear conscience. There would be no mercy for those who had broken an agreement, and Akbar Khan would deny absolutely that he himself had done so. He would say simply that when there were no indications that the British were preparing to leave the cantonment, he had assumed bad faith on their part and decided not to provide the promised supplies.

Kit laid one hand on her shoulder, catching her chin with his other. "Please, let's cry peace, Annabel. We are all depressed . . . at a low ebb . . . and it seems such a crying shame that you and I should dissipate the time we have left together in this wasteland of storms and silence."

It was the first time he had openly admitted to himself, let alone to anyone else, his belief that he and Annabel were living now on borrowed time. The jade eyes met his calmly, acknowledging his statement as if she had been waiting for him to make it.

"I don't wish to quarrel," she said. "But I am so frustrated, and you are being so foolishly blind. As if it could possibly matter who knows where I come from! If there is to be any hope of extending our time together, some correct decisions have to be made."

"And what happened to Destiny?" he said, trying to sound lightly teasing but failing miserably. "I thought you believed it did not matter what one did."

"The outcome may be preordained, but we are still required to make the choices," she replied earnestly. "And there are always sensible choices and foolish choices."

Kit shook his head, baffled. "Sometimes I do not understand you at all. You say one thing but seem to mean another."

"No, feringhee, it is not me you do not understand, it is the Afghan."

"We have now come full circle," Kit said, releasing her chin with a sigh of defeat. "You may know Akbar Khan, but I know Elphinstone and Macnaghten, and I know that no good will come of my presenting you to them as an informed source. They will see only a woman with a dubious past and even more dubious present, and they won't take unpalatable truths from the lips of my mistress." He turned to the door. "I don't know when I will be back."

"That is hardly unusual," she replied without expression. The door banged on his departure and she swore softly. Perhaps Kit was right, and she would have no credibility with the Envoy. But he could at least let her *try*. It was so ironical; here she was now, firmly aligned with the idiot feringhee, and no one would let her do anything to help.

Kit marched over to headquarters, wondering if perhaps he was being simpleminded. He did not know whether Macnaghten would pay any heed to Annabel; possibly he would. But Kit could not face the prospect of exposing her to public scrutiny, of having to explain that her knowledge came from her time as an inhabitant of Akbar Khan's zenana. Those of his intimates who knew her secret treated it with absolute discretion, but the minute it became more widely known, her name would be on every gossip's tongue, her story the subject for prurient speculation in mess and bungalow throughout the cantonment. He had given up concerning himself about her future reputation. His grand design of finding Annabel's family in England, of presenting her to his parents, of a wedding in St. George's, Hanover Square, he now recognized as a mere pipe dream. As usual her pragmatic clarity had been proved right. They would have no such future. But while the present existed, he would keep her to himself, protect her from unkind tongues, and let anyone who wished to worry away harmlessly at the identity and history of the mystery woman under Captain Ralston's roof . . . except that in the harsh climate existing between them at the moment, there was little satisfaction to be gained from this exclusivity, he reflected gloomily as he reached headquarters.

Within the hour, all such considerations became irrelevant. Emissaries arrived from Akbar Khan with a proposal that Sir William Macnaghten found most appealing, and that Kit, fresh from Annabel's analysis, heard with horror. Akbar Khan proposed that the British should remain in cantonments until the spring, when they would accomplish their own withdrawal. Akbar Khan would present the head of Ameenoolla Khan to the Envoy in return for a certain sum of money, and an undertaking by the British government to make him a present of thirty lakhs of rupees and an annual pension of four lakhs.

"There now," declared Sir William, presenting this proposal to the assembled officers. "The man is as greedy and self-serving as I have always believed him. I see no reason why we should not agree to his proposals immediately, and accept his invitation for a conference tomorrow morning."

"Sir William." Reluctantly, Kit accepted his obligation to speak up. "They are saying in the bazaars that Akbar Khan suspects treachery. If we accept his offer of Ameenoolla's head, we will confirm that suspicion."

"How d'you know what is being said in the bazaars?" demanded the Envoy.

Kit glanced at Bob and Colin, who offered him shrugs of resigned sympathy. There was nothing further to be gained by pretense. He told the Envoy in full how he knew what was being said in the bazaar.

"This woman . . . who . . . " The general waved his hands and discreetly left the description hanging. "This Miss Spencer, you say, knows Akbar Khan personally?"

"Yes, sir," Kit said woodenly. "She lived under his protection from the time that she was twelve until quite recently."

"When she moved under yours, I take it," bluntly said the Envoy.

"In a manner of speaking," Kit said.

"Perhaps we should hear what she has to say," suggested one of the Envoy's staff officers. "If Ralston is willing, that is."

"She has been most anxious to give her opinion

for several weeks," Kit said dryly. "Her opinions are generally delivered in somewhat forceful fashion, I should warn you." He glanced toward the Envoy and received a dour nod of consent. He went next door to the adjutant's office. "Ensign, go to my bungalow and ask Miss Spencer to accompany you back here."

The ensign saluted and tried not to look surprised. He knew, as did everyone, that the captain had an Afghan wench in his house; but who was Miss Spencer?

The discussion in the general's office was somewhat desultory as they all awaited the arrival of Captain Ralston's lady. The Envoy contributed little, concentrating instead on reading and rereading Akbar Khan's proposals. After about fifteen minutes, the door opened and Annabel was shown in.

She stood in the doorway, only her eyes moving as the jade gaze ran around the room, seeming to assess the reaction on every face. Kit felt the power of her self-possession, a self-possession earned in a school harder than any around this table could imagine, and his heart jolted with love and a bone-deep sense of loss as he thought how in another time and place he and she could have enjoyed a lifetime's happiness . . . if Destiny had chosen to play these pieces differently.

"Annabel, let me introduce you." He stood up with the rest of the men and held out his hand to her. She moved to stand beside him, acknowledged the introductions with a salaam that somehow seemed entirely appropriate, invested as the gesture was with her own grace and confidence. Then she took the seat next to Kit, hastily provided by the fascinated ensign.

"I understand you have some personal knowledge of Akbar Khan," the Envoy began.

"I know him as well as any, I believe," she replied simply.

The Envoy coughed and there was a certain shuffling of chairs which Annabel appeared not to notice. She remained regarding Sir William attentively as he read to her the message from the emissaries. "Perhaps you would be good enough to give us the benefit of your opinion, Miss Spencer?" he said ponderously at the end, folding the paper and sitting back in his chair.

"It's a plot," Annabel said calmly. "You will release Akbar Khan from any need to honor his obligations if you accept his offer of Ameenoolla's head. He is aware of your machinations with Mohun Lal, and wishes simply to prove your perfidy."

"You accuse me of perfidy, miss?" Sir William sat up abruptly, glaring at her.

Kit touched her foot beneath the table in an appeal for circumspection and she cast him a quick, almost amused, sideways glance.

"I think, sir, that you would be foolish to compete with Akbar Khan when it comes to cunning," she said. "He is a past master at such tactics."

"You are suggesting that we ignore these proposals?" The Envoy looked incredulous. "I have every intention of meeting with Akbar Khan in the morning."

Annabel was about to retort that she could not, in that case, imagine why she had been summoned here, but Kit kicked her ankle imperatively and she swallowed instead. "Do not offer Akbar Khan money," she advised. "He has no need of it, and he would never take a rupee from the feringhee dogs."

There was a sharp indrawing of breath around the table, and she realized that her voice had assumed the intonation of Akbar Khan's.

"It does smell of treachery, y'know, Sir William," said Elphinstone.

"I understand these things better than you," snapped the Envoy, effectively closing the general's mouth. "I will not agree to pay blood money, but I will suggest a plan whereby our troops will cooperate with Akbar Khan in the capture of Ameenoolla Khan. We will accede to all his other proposals." He

stood up briskly. "That closes the discussion, I believe. Captains Lawrence, Trevor, and Mackenzie
will accompany me to the conference in the morning. Miss Spencer, I thank you for your contribu-
tion." He bowed and left the office.

Kit turned to Annabel, reluctant resignation on his
lips. But she was looking across the table at Colin
with a chilling intensity. "You must not go, Colin."
The injunction fell leaden into the despondent wake
left by the Envoy's departure.

"You know I must," he said, half-smiling.

She continued to look at him, long and hard, as if
she would read his destiny in his face. Then she
shook her head. "If you say you must, you must.
But you walk into a trap." She turned to Kit. "You
have no further need of me?"

He shook his head. "You said what you wanted
to."

"I said what I had to," she corrected quietly.
"Even if it didn't do much good."

His hands opened in a gesture of acceptance, then
he gently eased her from the room. "Peace, Anna?"
he questioned softly as they reached the street.

"I have never wished to be at war," she replied
as softly. "But I felt this overpowering need to offer
what I could. And you would deny me."

"I wished only to protect you."

"From death? From Akbar Khan's vengeance?"
She smiled, but there was no mockery. "My love, I
need no protection from anything less than those
things . . . and from those there is no protection."
She looked up at the sky. "It is going to snow, Kit."

Chapter 17

Akbar Khan sat his horse atop a small hill sloping down to the bank of the Kabul river. He was looking across the snow-covered plain toward the cantonment. The men around him, accustomed to his silence and stillness, made no attempt to intrude on his contemplation as they waited for the British contingent to come out to meet them.

Just where behind those ramparts was Ayesha? Akbar Khan pondered. And what was she doing at this moment? He wondered if she were afraid, knowing as she must the inevitable outcome of this struggle. If she knew of Macnaghten's clumsy attempt at treachery, then she would know how Akbar Khan would react. She would know that the Envoy was walking into a snare carefully spread for him. How could he possibly be foolish enough to imagine that Akbar Khan would sell himself and his honor to the feringhee dogs? That he would cooperate with them, as the Envoy had suggested in his return proposals, in betraying one of his own confederate chiefs? Just the thought that the Envoy did believe it was enough to bring a savage fury bubbling in the sirdar's veins, to pierce his meditative calm.

It was time to bring an end to this business, to drive the invader from his land once and for all . . . and it was time to reclaim Ayesha from Christopher Ralston. What changes had been wrought by her sojourn with the feringhee? How long would it take him to eradicate those changes? And how should he accomplish that? Akbar Khan had not yet decided what he was going to do with his Ayesha when he reclaimed her, and he was content for the moment to let that decision rest upon what he found in her.

"They are coming," one of his companions said softly, indicating with his whip the small party riding out from the cantonment.

Akbar Khan dismissed thoughts of Ayesha and concentrated his mental energies with a cold ferocity on the man who was coming to this conference with his head full of treachery and the conviction that Akbar Khan would betray his fellow Afghans for a British stipend. He watched as the escort of soldiers drew rein some way from the hill, as had been agreed, and four gentlemen dismounted, advancing on foot upward to the meeting place.

Akbar Khan dismounted, as did the other sirdars, and they stood waiting under the snow-laden sky, with the gray river below them, and the jagged snowcapped mountain peaks as backdrop. This was their land and its innate unfriendliness was one of the strongest weapons in their armory.

Colin Mackenzie tried to control his unease as they approached the group of Afghans, all of whom were armed to the teeth. Akbar Khan stood slightly to the forefront, his fur-trimmed cloak open despite the cold to reveal a brocade tunic, loose trousers tucked into the tops of his riding boots. A saber was thrust into the sash at his waist. From beneath his fur hat, his blue eyes stared with a frightening impassivity and there was not the slightest hint of softness about his mouth.

This was the man with whom Annabel had grown to maturity, Colin thought. On the rare occasions that he had heard her mention him, she spoke always with a mixture of awe and genuine liking, although she freely admitted that she had lived on the edge of terror for much of those years, in the contemplation and understanding of the absolute power wielded by one of such a passionate and capricious temper. There was nothing about the man to reassure this morning. And there was nothing about the

crowd of warriors massed upon the hill to reassure
either. Just why did Akbar Khan have an armed escort, when the political officer and his staff of three
military officers came alone? Not a comfortable question.

Macnaghten had been brought to admit the danger of their present enterprise, but he had dismissed
the threat with a lofty impatience. "Let the loss be
what it may, I would rather die a hundred deaths
than live the last six weeks over again." Now, as
the armed hillmen moved almost imperceptibly to
encircle the four British officers, Colin felt his sense
of foreboding blossom into full-blooded certainty of
imminent peril. His hand went to his pistol butt and
remained there.

"Are you ready to carry out the proposals as
agreed last night, Macnaghten, *huzoor?*" Akbar Khan
spoke in flat, expressionless Persian.

"Why not?" responded the Envoy shortly.

Colin wondered if he had imagined the tongue of
fury flickering in the khan's bright blue gaze, it was
extinguished so swiftly. Captain Lawrence stepped
forward, indicating the fiercely armed circle surrounding them, suggesting mildly that it did not give
the impression of friendly negotiations. Two of the
confederate chiefs made vaguely dismissive gestures
with their whips toward the bristling hillmen, who
took no notice.

"It does not matter," Akbar Khan said, apparently casual. "They are all in the secret so there is
nothing to fear."

What happened next was so sudden it was much
later before Colin could properly piece together the
sequence of events.

Akbar Khan was transformed. But perhaps he
wasn't. Perhaps the calm, casual man of the last few
minutes was the act and the near-diabolical ferocity
he now evinced was the real man. His voice rang
through the frigid morning air. *"Begeer! Begeer!"*
Obeying his own command, he grasped the Envoy's

left hand. Sultan Jan followed the order to seize Sir William and held him fast by the right hand.

The three staff officers stood stunned for a second as the Envoy was dragged, bent double, down the hill. They could hear Sir William's voice in astonished plea, calling upon God, *"Az barae Khooda,"* and caught a glimpse of his expression of horrified bewilderment. Then they leaped forward, swords in hand, only to be engulfed by the circle of hillmen.

Colin struck out with his sword, hearing the steel ring off the blades of khyber knives and scimitars as the ferocious horde pressed closer. He saw Trevor struggling desperately to break through the circle and reach the Envoy, then Trevor went down beneath his attackers, lost to all help as knives slashed and a dreadful gurgling cry came from the melee. Screams and yells filled the air with fearful menace, and the two staff officers left standing fought for their lives, knowing even as they did so that they could not hope to break free from their attackers, and it was but a matter of minutes before they too would go down, to be hacked to pieces on the snow-carpeted plain.

They fought with the ferocity and savagery of those facing certain death, but Colin could feel his strength ebbing just as a huge black charger reared through the press. The Dourani chief upon his back leaned down, bellowing an urgent instruction at Colin, who reacted blindly, grabbing the hand and leaping upward out of the fray, seeing in a blur the flashing teeth, savage eyes, slashing knives fall away as the charger leaped out of the circle. Behind him, he was aware that another mounted chief had offered Lawrence the same means of escape. As they pounded across the hilltop, he looked down the far side, to where Macnaghten had been dragged. He could see only a pushing, thrusting mass centered on one spot on the ground. It required no imagination to guess what was happening, and he felt a nut of nausea lodge in his throat even as he wondered what his own fate was about to be. Had he been inexplicably rescued, or was this simply a temporary reprieve before fresh horrors?

The escort, left too far away to intervene in timely fashion in the abrupt violence erupting on the hill, streamed back to the cantonment, pursued in somewhat desultory fashion by a troop of Ghazi fanatics. They brought a confused tale of the wholesale slaughter of the four British negotiators, and Colin's friends in the cantonment listened and grieved for his loss.

"I don't know why Akbar Khan would have murdered them all," Annabel said, huddling over the meager fire, cold and empty with loss and the sense of futility at such a pointless and demeaning death.

"But you said it was a trap," Kit pointed out. "You warned Colin not to go."

"I know. I knew there was danger, but it does not make sense that Akbar would have them massacred. I believed that he would take them hostage, perhaps, and use them as leverage to force the withdrawal here, but he gains nothing by their blood . . . unless . . . " She shivered.

"Unless—" Bob prompted gently.

"Unless he decided he was due vengeance. He would not have plotted the murders in cold deliberation—he is too cunning for such simple violence to offer solution—but if he was suddenly swept with fury, then—" She shrugged. "He is a man of great passions, as I have said. And occasionally they will rule his head." She looked bleakly at Kit, and he returned the look with grim comprehension.

But Colin and Lawrence were for the moment safe under the friendly roof of Mahoomed Zemaun Khan in Kabul. They watched in sick disgust from a window as the wildly excited throng paraded the mutilated bodies of Macnaghten and Trevor through the streets, finally hanging them from butcher's hooks in the great bazaar.

"Not a pleasant sight, is it, gentlemen?" A soft

voice spoke from the doorway of the room where they had been confined. Akbar Khan entered the room, followed by two servants bearing trays of food and a bowl of honeyed sherbet. "I much regret this morning's violence," the khan said calmly, dismissing the servants once they had shed their burdens. "The death of Macnaghten, *huzoor*, was most regrettable."

"You had not intended the murder?" Colin asked, an eyebrow raised incredulously.

"Goodness, no," Akbar Khan said, stroking his beard. "Please, eat, drink . . . you are my guests. No," he continued, "I had not intended the death of the Envoy. I wished merely to lay hands upon his person; but he was a very foolish man to dabble in treachery, and one might say was deserving of his death. There was little I could do to control the tribesmen, once their blood was fired. The Afghan, sirs, does not take kindly to bad faith."

Colin bit back the retort that in Afghanistan the likes of Macnaghten had had good teachers when it came to treachery. Somehow, he didn't think Akbar Khan would appreciate the statement, any more than he would appreciate skepticism at his stated inability to control the bloody fervor of the tribesmen.

The khan had seated himself before the food and was looking expectantly at the officers. Colin and Lawrence sat down, both ashamed of how their mouths were watering at the rich aromas coming from the covered dishes. But their empty bellies yearned for decent and plentiful nourishment, the first in weeks, and the horrors of the day seemed not to have the least inhibiting effect.

Akbar Khan maintained a gentle flow of civilized conversation throughout the meal, but his sharp scrutiny never dropped. "It was fortune, indeed, that we were able to bring you safe from the mob," he commented, belching with formal satisfaction at the meal's close. "You will convey my deepest regrets to General Elphinstone and my desire that we should reopen negotiations without delay?'' Despite the questioning intonation in his voice, his audience was in no doubt that it was simply form. They would, of course, convey whatever message Akbar Khan wished.

Colin indicated their agreement and then waited. There was something about the way their host was frowning and stroking his beard that seemed to suggest he had not concluded his business with them.

''You are, of course, acquainted with Christopher Ralston,'' Akbar Khan said finally.

Annabel, Colin thought. ''Yes, he is a good friend of mine,'' he said neutrally.

''Ah . . . then, doubtless, you are aware he has a guest.''

Colin met the bright blue gaze steadily. ''Yes, I am aware of that, sirdar.''

''Then you will not, I trust, object to being my messenger in one further matter.'' The khan rose and left the room. When he returned in a very few minutes, he held a small carved rosewood box. This he placed upon the table, opened, and drew forth two identical bracelets of elaborately chased beaten silver. The clasps were intricately worked and as the two men watched he took a tiny key from the box and unlocked the clasps. He then replaced the key in the box.

''Would you be good enough to present these to Ayesha?'' he said calmly. ''Do not close them. As you see, they can only be opened again with the key, and the key remains in my possession.'' A thin smile touched the incisive mouth. ''There is no further message. Ayesha will understand perfectly.''

Colin felt a cold finger march up his spine. There was something almost barbarous about the bracelets . . . something primitive and forbidden, it seemed to him. They seemed to speak of a different culture and different rules, to give off an aura of illicit promise both exciting and sinister. He raised his eyes from the bracelets and looked directly at the khan, who

met the questioning gaze with the hint of a comprehending smile.

"We all have our customs," he said softly. "The
feringhee does not easily understand those of my
people. I am certain Ayesha will explain it to you."
Then he became all brisk business. "You will leave
now with an escort to the cantonment. I will await
a response from General Elphinstone, which I trust
will not be long delayed."

An hour later, Lawrence and Mackenzie arrived at
the gate of the cantonment with an escort of silent,
well-armed Ghilzais. The guards at the gate greeted
them with expressions of astonishment and relief,
but it was nothing to the joyful reception they received at headquarters, where their friends had been
maintaining a dismal vigil, listening to the sounds
of riotous disturbance carrying from the city.

The two survivors of the morning delivered Akbar
Khan's expressions of regret and desire for a renewal of negotiations, and Elphinstone quavered
and wheezed, alternating expressions of acute dismay at the fate of the Envoy and Trevor with bursts
of outrage at the murdering, treacherous Afghans.
But the outrage was not translated into action, except to have the garrison put under arms and maintain defensive positions continuously.

"Major Pottinger must take over the negotiations
now that poor Sir William is gone," Elphinstone
muttered. "We must come to an agreement without
delay. There's not a sack of grain in the cantonment,
I understand."

Colin felt a pang of guilt for his full belly, satisfied
at the enemy table, but he dismissed it as too nice a
reaction in the face of calamity.

"Annabel will be glad to see you," Kit said softly
as they left the general's office. "We all believed you
dead."

"I have a gift for her from Akbar Khan," Colin
said. "I do not understand what it means, but he
said she would." He looked at his friend gravely.

"It struck me as somehow sinister, but I don't know why."

"Anything from Akbar Khan would be sinister at this point," Kit responded, looking grim. "I have felt like a mouse being toyed with gently and with infinite care ever since I first made his acquaintance. And I can't do a damn thing about it, Colin. Annabel is just so . . . so . . . fatalistic about it. I know she expects the worst in the end, believes that there is no protection from Akbar Khan's long reach when he decides to close his hand over her, and no protection from the death we all face in this godforsaken land. But I refuse to accept that so tamely. There has to be something we can do."

They had reached the bungalow as he said this and the door burst open. Annabel, hair flying, came hurtling down the path. "You are safe, Colin."

"As you see," he mumbled with some embarrassment as he found his arms full of this warm, lithe body. "It did not suit Akbar Khan, apparently, that Lawrence and I should be cut down also." His hands drifted awkwardly over her, as if seeking some safe spot to touch as she clung to his neck. "You know, Annabel, this display is very gratifying, but it is a little public in the open street."

Laughing, she released him. "You English are all the same. You think there's something wrong with displaying affection."

"And what, pray, are you, miss?" demanded Kit.

Her eyes glinted mischievously. "Neither one thing nor t'other, Ralston, *huzoor*. Come into the house where we may be as frank as we please without drawing unwelcome attention. I wish to hear everything about this morning. Maybe it will give me some idea of what Akbar and the other sirdars intend now." Linking arms with both men, she hustled them into the bungalow.

"I am charged with a message for you," Colin said as they reached the sitting room.

She released his arm and stepped away from him,

her body suddenly vibrating with tension. "From Akbar Khan?"

He nodded and in silence drew forth the bracelets from his coat pocket. "He said you would understand." He held them out to her.

For a moment she did not take them, but stood looking at them instead with the fixed fascination in her eyes one might exhibit before a cobra, reared to strike.

"What does it mean?" Kit asked in low-voiced urgency as the tension radiating from her still figure seemed to set the air humming.

"He did not send the key?" she asked, although it was clear from her voice that the question was rhetorical.

Colin shook his head, still holding out the bright silver objects, gleaming richly in the dim light of late afternoon.

At last, she took them, hesitantly as if afraid they would scorch her fingers. "They're very beautiful," she said softly, "and very valuable. Ancient Persian craftsmanship, he told me, when he first showed them to me."

"What are they for?" Kit asked insistently. "Why would he send you such a beautiful and valuable gift at this juncture?"

She smiled, a wry, almost mocking smile. "Akbar Khan has a love of symbols." She slipped the bracelets onto her wrists, where it was clear that once the wide silver bands were closed, they would fit as tightly as if they had been made on her. "Once I close the clasps, I cannot remove the bracelets without the key. He holds the key." She looked across at him. "Do you understand now? They are a mark of ownership."

Colin felt that cold finger on his spine again as he understood what it was about these undoubtedly beautiful bracelets that had given off that strangely barbarous aura.

"Take them off!" Kit said with sudden violence, grabbing her arm and wrenching the unclasped band

from around her wrist, then doing the same with
the other. He dropped the silver manacles on the
table with a gesture of disgust, as if they were contaminated. "I cannot endure this!" he declared with
the same violence. "The man is playing with us . . .
they are all playing with us, standing gloating outside this stockade watching us starved into submission, waiting for the first real snow to fall—"

"Peace, love." Annabel laid a hand on his arm.
"Railing hysterically isn't going to achieve anything."

"And sitting back accepting the whims of your
damned Destiny *is*, I daresay," he snapped, his raging frustration turned abruptly upon her. "That attitude is simply an excuse for cowardly inaction and
I cannot stomach it, on your lips or anyone else's,
so don't let me hear it again, do you understand?"

Annabel flushed and bit her lip fiercely, trying to
bring under control her anger at being spoken to in
such fashion and so unjustly in front of Colin, who
was looking extremely uncomfortable. Absently, she
picked up one of the bracelets, running her finger
over the intricate chasing on the silver.

"Put that down!" Kit snatched it from her, his
face set in livid lines, the gray eyes as hard and life-
less as pebbles. "I have had as much as I can take
of Akbar Khan's goddamned symbols. Don't touch
them again."

It was too much, to be dictated to in such peremptory fashion, as if she were somehow responsible for
rather than the victim of Akbar Khan's unplayful
games. Her anxiety was subsumed under a wash of
temper that with a certain perverse and flagrant enjoyment she made no attempt to bridle.

"They are mine," Annabel asserted vigorously.
"Just as my attitudes are mine. I do not give you
the right to tell me what I am to touch and what I
am to believe." With a gesture that Colin could only
describe as blatantly provoking, she picked up the
other bracelet and slipped it around her wrist. "And
if I choose to wear these, I will, Christopher Ral-

ston!'' For one horrifying moment, it looked as if
she were about to snap the clasp, and Kit sprang at
her with an exclamation of incoherent fury. Annabel
squealed and leaped for the door, the outraged Kit
on her heels. The bedroom door slammed.

It couldn't hurt to have such an outlet for depression and anxiety, Colin thought with an envious
sigh, going into the hall. Even anger, when it was
the other side of passion's coin, had to provide relief
from this deadening reality.

''Dear me, sir.'' Harley popped his head round
the kitchen door. ''Has miss upset the captain?''

''I think it's rather a case of six of one and half a
dozen of the other,'' Colin said wearily. ''There's
not a pin to choose between them.''

Harley nodded sagely. ''It's usually the case, sir.''

''I'll be on my way,'' Colin said, picking up his
cloak from the hall table. ''Tell the lovebirds . . . or
fighting cocks . . . or whatever they are now, that
I've gone in search of some rest.''

Within the bedroom, Annabel was bouncing on
the bed, dancing out of Kit's reach as her impassioned lover lunged for her. Annabel found that she
could not help herself as she continued to taunt him
with her semi-braceleted wrist. She thought they
had slipped back from the edge of anger and into
play, rough play certainly, but sometimes there was
a necessary place for such deflection, when tensions
and tempers ran as high as they were at present and
one lived on the brink of desperation.

Kit suddenly caught her ankle, tumbling her onto
the bed, her hair swirling, her cheeks flushed, eyes
bright with the spirit of the game or the residue of
anger or the promise of passion, or all three intermingled. ''You damnable, green-eyed lynx,'' he
said, bearing her backward with his weight, seizing
her wrist in a grip verging on the painful as he tore
Akbar Khan's bracelet loose and hurled it across the
room. ''How could you make a game of that?'' His
hands circled her throat, thumbs pushing up her

chin. "You fill me with such confusion sometimes, I could as easily smack you as love you."

Her eyes looked up at him as she struggled to catch her own breath, and they contained not a flicker of alarm at the infuriated assertion. Although the pulse at the base of her throat beat fast against his hand, it was an emotion other than fear that set her heart speeding.

"Which do you want to do now?" she asked.

"I don't know." Kit groaned. "The whole house of cards is collapsing around our ears, and you start playing the most appallingly provoking game over something which is not in the least amusing!"

"Maybe that's why I had to make a game of it," she said. "It was too deadly to take seriously."

"Maybe there was a little of that," he said, "but there was a devil of a lot of pure mischief. Admit it, you wretched woman."

"You provoked me first," she offered in partial admission. "And I could just as easily hit you as love you."

Kit laughed, reluctantly at first, then he yielded to the seduction of amusement. "We are an admirably suited pair," he declared. "Clearly a match made in heaven. Let's settle for a kiss, shall we?"

"With the greatest of pleasure. So long as it doesn't stop there . . . "

That evening of violent emotions and crazy loving was one they would long remember. It was the last time in the cantonment when they were able to annihilate catastrophic reality in the fires of passion.

It began to snow in earnest and negotiations continued. Major Pottinger, the senior political officer, was a different kind of man from his predecessor, a soldier rather than a politician, but he was obliged to accept majority rule in headquarters. And majority rule decreed unconditional acceptance of the terms laid down by Akbar Khan and the confederate chiefs, however humiliating. Pottinger produced letters maintaining that reinforcements were on their

way from Peshawar and Jalalabad; he urged the
reoccupation of the Balla Hissar, or a forced military
retreat through the passes, abandoning baggage and
all encumbrances in the cantonment, as preferable
to a surrender which failed to guarantee safety and
ensured the loss of all honor. The council decreed
that those alternatives were impracticable, and Major Pottinger perforce assumed the miserable burden
of negotiating the release of the army and its de-
pendents from the cantonments.

He was forced to agree to pay huge sums to the
chiefs for their efforts in supporting the treaty, since
only on that agreement were supplies sent into the
cantonment. He agreed to the surrender of all significant artillery, and then came the demand for hostages, four married officers and their wives and
children. A circular was sent around the cantonment
asking for volunteers in exchange for the promise of
a substantial stipend. But no volunteers were to be
found, and Pottinger was obliged to beg the sirdars
to excuse the women from remaining as hostages.
The sick and wounded who were unable to march
were sent into the city under the care of two surgeons, and on New Year's Day a ratified treaty was
sent into the cantonment.

The British garrison at Kabul undertook to evacuate the cantonment under the protection and escort
of certain chiefs, within twenty-four hours of receiving transport animals.

Annabel stood on the ramparts, snow sticking to
the hood of her cloak. The snow had done nothing
to inhibit the now-familiar throng of townsfolk and
Ghazi fanatics yelling their taunts, throwing stones,
jeering at the rigid gunners lining the ramparts beside the muzzles of the loaded guns they were forbidden to fire. She could feel the deep, fulminating
resentment of the soldiers denied the right of repri-
sal, and she stared down at her adopted people and
cursed them in their own tongue with a virulence
that shook her.

She knew that the undertakings of the chiefs were

not worth the paper they were written upon. She
knew it, and so did everyone else, but they were all
mired in the slimy tendrils of hopelessness and
helplessness. What could they do but what they
were doing, whether it was profitable or not? Mohun Lal, loyal still to his British paymasters, warned
that if the British did not insist on taking as hostages
the sons of the sirdars, they had no guarantee of
safety during the retreat; but how could they demand such a thing when they were completely pow-
erless, and had voluntarily yielded all power, both
material and emotional?

The snows fell, as relentless as the excruciating
night frosts which destroyed any residue of morale
amongst the semi-starved troops, shivering in their
barracks empty of fuel. And still the chiefs failed to
provide transport animals.

Annabel knew why they were delaying. Every extra debilitating day of fruitless waiting, every extra
inch of snow in the passes would augment the torture of the journey that lay ahead—a journey to be
undertaken by some eighteen thousand souls, the
elderly and infirm, babes in arms, children, women
newly recovered from childbirth and those great
with child—a journey reasonably to be undertaken
only by the hale, even if they were well supplied
and were to be permitted to make it unmolested.
And Annabel knew that they would not make the
journey unmolested.

Her fingers circled one wrist. When would Akbar
Khan fulfill the promise of the bracelets? How far
would she be permitted to travel with the people of
her birth on their journey into near-certain death?

On January fifth, the military authorities ordered
the engineers to throw down the eastern rampart,
creating an exit from the cantonment wider than that
provided by the gate. They were still without the
promised escort, without adequate supplies or
transport, but evacuation could be postponed no
longer.

Chapter 18

At nine o'clock on the morning of January sixth the great exodus began. The advance force was mostly sepoy infantry, ill-clad and debilitated by weeks of semi-starvation, their thin-soled shoes offering little protection from the thick snow covering the plain. The cavalrymen fared a little better, and Annabel, sitting astride Charlie as she watched them go, recognized the weather-beaten face of the rissaldar commanding his own troop. She thought of those sessions in the riding school and wondered if the rissaldar was remembering them now as he rode out of the cantonment beneath the drooping banners that seemed somehow to exemplify the brooding foreboding in which they were all enveloped.

"We ride with the main body under Shelton, moving out as soon as the advance is through." Kit rode up to her, his voice curt, but she did not take the tone personally. "The ladies, invalids, and sick all will be with the main body, but you may ride in the van with me. I will be accompanying Elphinstone as staff officer. You are known to everyone at headquarters, so it will cause no remark."

"Less than if I were to be cast amongst the ladies," Annabel commented dryly. "I'm sure they would not welcome me."

"Probably not, but it seems of minor importance at this stage. More relevant is that Charlie will carry you well, for all that he's somewhat skinny these days." Kit leaned over and patted the horse's neck,

296

as if the gesture would expiate the guilt he felt at the mute sufferings of his animals. "He'll be more at home with the cavalry horses than the camels and ponies."

Bob rode up, looking pale and distracted. "Wouldn't you know it! That damned temporary bridge the sappers were supposed to have completed over the river is not yet in place. The advance has had to halt on the bank. God knows how long it will be before they can cross."

Annabel looked behind her at the milling, seething scene. Camels lifted their elongated necks in disconsolate fashion, their howdahs occupied by the officers' wives and children, their drivers shivering in the freezing air as they stamped their feet on the icy ground. Litters and palanquins crowded the square, their bearers yelling at each other, the female occupants peering out and giving conflicting orders. Children were wailing and whining, in fear and cold and bewilderment. Pouring into the square, getting underfoot of beasts and soldiers alike, were the skimpily dressed camp followers, some twelve thousand of them, who could not be forced or persuaded into the rear with the baggage, but insisted on mingling with the main body. The sharp crack of whip leather, the exasperated bellows of officers, the whinnying of horses, the cries and protests of all and sundry made a hellish din, redolent with chaos and frustration.

She glanced at Kit and shook her head in a gesture of helpless resignation.

"I know," he said. "Not a chance."

"Not a chance."

"Hey, less pessimism, if you please!" Bob attempted a jocular tone of voice but the shadow of his own knowledge left a jagged edge. "The general's so weak, I wonder if he'll manage to sit his horse," he said, dropping the pretense. "Are you riding with him?"

"Yes. If he fails, there's a litter prepared. It'll slow us up, but then I hardly imagine speed is going to be the order of the day. Annabel, are you going to be warm enough?''

It was a seeming nonsequitur, but they all knew it wasn't.

''Warmer than most,'' she answered and didn't add *Thanks to Akbar Khan*. Her leather trousers were lined with cashmere, the tunic with fur, and over the tunic and trousers she had a sheepskin, fur-lined jacket, and over that the fur-trimmed hooded cloak. Her leather gauntlets and boots were also fur-lined. She was a great deal better protected than Kit and his colleagues, and was immeasurably better off than the vast majority of those attempting this journey. But then she was dressed as an Afghan, one who made her life in this inhospitable land and was prepared for its savagery. Akbar Khan had not intended she should start this journey ill-prepared . . .

''They are beginning to move out,'' she said abruptly, veering away from that train of thought. ''Should we join the general, Kit?''

As they left the cantonment through the wide gateway prepared by the engineers, a triumphant crowd of Afghans poured down from the city, forcing their way into the cantonment as the evacuation continued. ''Dear God,'' muttered Kit. ''They can't even wait for us to get out before taking possession.''

Exultant yells filled the air in complete contrast to the grim silence of the retreating force, and from the residential areas of the cantonment flames shot up as the victors plundered then fired the bungalows, destroying the suburban enclave until the pathetic facsimile of an English village was reduced to ashes.

It was well after noon when the first lines of the main body crossed the temporary bridge in the wake of the advance party. Behind them the rear guard was massed between the ramparts and the canal, offering what protection it could to the vast procession of camels slowly clearing the cantonment. Baggage, already abandoned as too cumbersome once the reality of the freezing march had become apparent, lay heaped outside the ramparts, rapidly disappearing under the thickly falling snow. And within the cantonment the riotous plundering and destruction continued to the frenzied yelling of the marauders.

Once the joys of plunder had palled, the Afghans within the cantonment turned their jezzails onto the trapped rear guard, who were obliged to remain in position beneath the vicious fire from the ramparts until the last camel, the last camp follower, the last baggage mule had passed them. It was twilight before they were able to turn and follow the main body, leaving one officer and fifty men dead in the snow.

At the head of the main body, Annabel could hear the sounds of confusion, the screams of triumph, the continual crack of rifle fire from the rear carrying through the crystal-sharp air.

"What the hell's going on?" Kit muttered, craning over his shoulder. But he could see only the column weaving into the fire-shot distance behind him.

Annabel swung Charlie away from the line. "I'm going to see," she called.

"Annabel, come back here!" Kit yelled imperatively, but she waved at him and galloped down the column. "Goddamn it!" Kit exclaimed, unable to go after her without abandoning his post at the general's side. "It must be all of three miles to the end of the column."

"She'll be all right," Colin reassured him. "That horse isn't going to let her down, and if you can't see her face she still looks more like an Afghan than an Englishwoman."

Kit didn't look particularly reassured, but there was nothing he could do except wait for her return and reflect that his Anna was not without a well-honed sense of self-preservation.

Annabel rode hard down the column. Men were already falling out on all sides, collapsing with fatigue and cold by the wayside, lying apathetically amongst the heaps of abandoned baggage. Afghan plunderers swarmed over the baggage, turning their knives on the fallen sepoys as they searched for booty. A woman lay in the snow, a baby wailing thinly beside her. A Ghazi fanatic stood above the supine figure, knife raised.

"Son of swine!" Annabel rode at him, screaming abuse in Pushtu with the virulence of any Ghazi. He turned, his eyes glaring at the insults. His khyber knife arced through the air, aiming for the underside of the horse's neck, and Charlie sidestepped as neatly as if they were practicing in the riding school. The knife fell harmlessly and before he could lift it again, Charlie had turned on a sixpence and reared high above him, every hoof as powerful a weapon as any knife. The Ghazi gave up the unequal struggle; there was easier prey elsewhere.

Annabel dismounted cautiously, well aware that the minute she was on the ground she would be vulnerable to attack. She carried a stiletto, Kit having acceded to the request to find her one with no more than a grim nod, but she was under no illusions that the slender dagger would deflect the sweep of scimitar or khyber knife.

The babe's mother, clearly a camp follower worn down by the deprivations of the last weeks, was beyond help, her eyes staring sightlessly at the gray bowl of the sky, darkening now with the approach of evening. The babe was blue with cold, thinly wrapped in a blanket, its piteous wails trembling on cracked lips. Annabel picked it up, wrapping the blanket more securely around the tiny frame, and wondered how she was to remount. In the past, there had always been someone to give her a leg up onto the enormous Charlie, but out here on the frozen plain there were no helping hands and she was hampered by the babe in her arms.

An abandoned chest lay a few feet away, and she led Charlie over to it. Using the chest as a mounting block, she scrambled onto his back, the babe tucked securely in the crook of her arm, and surveyed the scene anew. The column still trudged through the snow, the rear guard now following, groups of Ghazis cutting into them with merciless persistence, hampering the march with their repeated deadly forays that the troops could not beat off. The whole ghastly scene was illuminated by the raging conflagration from the abandoned cantonment, where the flames showed violent orange and crimson against the grim, gray desolation of the winter twilight, and the crackles of destruction sounded like some species of satanic laughter.

Sick at heart, yet knowing that she should have expected nothing less, Annabel rode Charlie back to the front of the line. The three miles seemed much longer this time, and she realized that the column had now slowed to such an extent that it was spread out much farther than before. The march was impeded by the bodies of those who had yielded the frozen, exhausting struggle, and by the endless piles of discarded baggage. If but half a day could produce such disintegration, what would the expected six days to Jalalabad bring?

Kit greeted her return with a furious diatribe to which she listened quietly, making no attempt to answer back. She was too chastened by what she had seen and too well aware of Kit's justifiable fear for her safety to offer defense or protest, even at the embarrassingly public nature of the reprimand. "That is the last time you will leave my side without permission, is that clear?" he finished, finally running out of steam in the face of her complete lack of response.

"I don't imagine there will be any reason to," she replied. "See what I have found." She drew forth the baby from the warm folds of her cloak. It had ceased wailing some time earlier, either through exhaustion or because her body warmth had offered some comfort. "What should we do with it?"

"Where on earth did it come from?" Kit stared in dismay.

Annabel told the story as briefly and unemotionally as she could, making as little of her encounter with the Ghazi as was consonant with veracity, but she could see Kit begin to whiten as his imagination filled in the details.

"Charlie and I partnered each other very well," she said calmly. "That was the point of all those hours in the riding school, wasn't it?"

Kit sighed in defeat. "When we bivouac, take it to one of the ayahs. One child more or less will not make much difference to them."

She nodded and they continued in silence as night fell. Finally a solitary bugle signaled a halt. "We cannot have traveled more than six miles from the cantonment," Annabel commented.

It was not necessary to expand the statement. Seventy miles to Jalalabad could not be accomplished in six-mile stages, as they all knew.

Harley, who had been riding at the rear of the general's staff, came up with them as the lines broke to make some kind of camp on the frozen wasteland. "There's a stream over yonder, sir," he said. "I've sent one of the carriers to fetch water." He unfolded a small tent from his saddlebag and looked for a suitable spot to pitch it.

"Where the hell did that come from?" Kit demanded.

"Miss found it, sir," Harley said. "Found our provisions, too." He drew forth dried antelope meat, *talkhan*, and a bar of tea. "If we can get a fire going, we'll manage tonight."

"You were too busy to worry about such matters," Annabel said, seeing Kit's dumbfounded expression. "I knew we would not be able to rely upon the regular provisions with the baggage train." She shrugged. "There's sufficient to go round, and the tent will probably sleep eight or nine if no one minds being cozy." She glanced around the grim landscape and the confused milling of beasts and people. "Pitch the tent over there, Harley, against that rock. It will provide some protection from the wind."

"I do not think we can have advantages denied others," Kit said slowly.

"But we already have one inestimable advantage that is denied everyone else," she pointed out. "I know this land and I know how the Afghans live and survive their winters. I have traveled with the nomads during the snows. Would you pretend I do not have that knowledge? Surely it is better shared than denied."

"Annabel's right, Kit," Bob said. "To whom are you going to give the supplies and tent?" He gestured at the milling multitude. "Are you going to pick one of those poor devils?"

Kit shook his head. "No. I daresay we had best put her foresight to good use amongst ourselves. It'll not be an advantage we'll have for long. Are you going to find someone to look after the baby, Annabel?"

"I suppose I had better," she said, looking down at the scrap still wrapped in her cloak. "I would keep it, but I have never cared for a baby before and I really do not know what to do with it. Would it drink tea, do you think?"

"Too small, miss," said Harley authoritatively. "Give it 'ere, and I'll take it to Mrs. Gardner's ayah. The poor lady only 'ad her own child five days ago, so they're bound to 'ave the right things with 'em."

"Five days ago." The thought of making this journey a mere five days after childbirth was horrendous, sending chills up her spine. But then Mrs. Gardner was not the only invalid, many of whom were traveling in litters and palanquins in the vicious cold, wearing only their nightclothes. She handed over the baby, putting grim speculation from her. "I will make some tea. There are some cakes of dung in my saddlebag to make a fire. Kit, can you light it?" Her tone was slightly hesitant as if she was unsure, as indeed she was, whether pampered cavalry captains were capable of undertaking such a lowly chore.

"Yes, ma'am," Kit said solemnly. "I think I might

find myself equal to the task, although you are putting us all to shame, I fear.''

She smiled nobly at his brave attempt at lightheartedness, but no one was deceived. They drew some comfort from the warmth of the tea, passing around the little saucepan as they huddled in their cloaks over the tiny smoldering flame of the dung fire.

Annabel remembered that other time when she had been so desperate for tea in the *aksakai*'s hut, and it would have been denied her but for Akbar Khan's vigilant thoughtfulness. Where was he? She looked up at the mountain peaks all around them, deep whitecapped shadows against the night sky. Was he up there somewhere, watching this murderous fiasco from some lofty spot, watching and waiting for the moment when he would intervene? She knew he would intervene at some point, but in what way she could not guess.

''Come.'' Kit touched her shoulder. ''It's time for bed.''

They managed to squeeze ten people into the tent. Kit and Annabel took up the space of one body, so tightly did he wrap her in his arms, covering her with his body so their breath mingled warmly and the killing cold was kept at bay.

Out in the open, soldiers and camp followers froze to death in hundreds. Others deserted, sliding off in the night across the snow, searching for some shelter away from this doomed progress through the mountains. Sepoys, severely frostbitten and no longer fit for duty, mingled with the noncombatants, adding to the confusion as dawn broke and the column sluggishly dragged itself onto the march again.

Annabel did not need Kit's sternly reiterated injunction that she was to stay at his side. The savage cold bit through her clothes, despite fur and wool, and she crouched on Charlie's back in a numbed torpor, her hood covering her mouth, leaving only her eyes visible. The rear guard struggled against harassment from their Afghan pursuers, who seemed unaffected by the temperature and the continuously falling snow.

"Anna . . . Anna, sweetheart!" Kit spoke urgently, breaking into her lethargic trance.

"Mmmm? What is it?" She blinked at him in the gray-white light.

"I am taking a troop up to the lateral heights," he said swiftly. "An Afghan force has charged into the baggage column and is threatening to cut off the rear. They need reinforcements to clear the pass from above."

"God go with you," she said simply, and he nodded before wheeling his horse and disappearing into the blanketing snow.

She couldn't worry about him, Annabel found. In many ways it seemed that a swift death from a Ghilzai bullet or a Ghazi knife would be preferable to this slow disintegration of body and spirit. It might be a defeatist reflection, but she couldn't seem to care about that either.

Up on the ridge, Captain Ralston and his men fired down onto the track where the Afghan force massed, blocking the advance of the rear guard. At last, the enemy moved away from the thoroughfare and the rear of the column was able to catch up with the main body.

Kit and his men rejoined the column as they approached Boothak. Ten miles outside Kabul, this settlement was always the first halt on the road from Kabul to Jalalabad.

At Boothak awaited Akbar Khan.

Annabel saw him sitting astride his Badakshani charger on a ridge above the track where the column painfully wound its tortuous way. He was surrounded by Ghilzai tribesmen, three of whom separated themselves from the circle and galloped down the ridge toward the approaching column.

General Elphinstone struggled upright in his saddle and his staff closed around him. There was no threat apparent in the newcomers' demeanor, but there was arrogance in the way they drew rein and ran their cold dark eyes over the confused and distraught multitude.

One of them began to speak in Pushtu and the general replied that he did not understand them.

"He is saying, General, that Akbar Khan had agreed to escort the column to Jalalabad, but you left the cantonment prematurely, so he was unable to offer protection from the Ghazis," Annabel translated quietly, somehow knowing that this role had been allotted her.

The Afghan, with no sign of surprise, waited until she had finished. Then he resumed.

"Akbar Khan insists that the column halt here for the night," she said, receiving a nod from the tribesman when he paused. "He will send in supplies in the morning, but he demands fifteen thousand rupees immediately."

The man began to speak again and this time the names of Lawrence, Mackenzie, and Pottinger were distinguishable. Annabel glanced at the three men. "Akbar Khan demands that Major Pottinger and Captains Lawrence and Mackenzie be given over to him as hostages," she said without expression.

"Tell them, Miss Spencer, that I accede to Akbar Khan's demands," mumbled the general, amid a whispering rustle of outrage from those around him. "Dear God," he said in agitated defense, "what else can we do? Someone tell me what is to be done."

Without a word, Major Pottinger drew his sword and dropped it to the ground. Colin and Captain Lawrence did the same, then they sat their horses, unarmed, stony-faced with the mortification of obeying such an order, waiting for a signal from Akbar Khan's messenger.

Annabel waited also, but the expected summons did not come. The Ghilzais moved to enclose their hostages and the little party rode off up the ridge, the three British officers not looking back.

So she was to be left squirming, hooked but as yet in the water, for a while longer. With an internal shrug, Annabel turned aside, but not before she had caught a glimpse of Kit's expression, where stark despair stood out in every line as he, too, faced the absolute knowledge that they danced on the end of Akbar Khan's line. He would reel it in whenever he was ready, and until then they must endure this appalling, degrading helplessness.

They passed the second night of horror. The snow lay a foot deep on the ground and access to the stream for water was prevented by Afghan snipers firing with devastating effect on the carriers, who rapidly gave up the attempt. The tent and their entwined bodies again afforded Kit and Annabel the shelter that stood between life and death, and the morning dawned, for all those still living, with the same bitter realization of the extremity of their plight.

Jezzails were pouring fire into the rear of the bivouacking column and the camp followers hurtled to the front, stripping the baggage animals of what remained of the supplies and taking off the animals in a desperate attempt to escape. The ground was littered with ammunition, household goods, the private possessions of the Kabul garrison.

Annabel was too stiff to clamber onto Charlie's back, despite Kit's cupped palms beneath her booted foot. Catching her by the wrist, he lifted her with some difficulty until she could grasp the pommel and haul herself astride the saddle. "I don't know why I'm so feeble," she apologized. "I'm not sure I have the right to be. There are so many so much worse off."

"You'll loosen up," Kit said, brusquely because he was afraid for her. She was so wan, the jade eyes dominating the drawn face, an alarming fragility suddenly manifest in the usually lissom, sinuous frame, cracks appearing in that previously indomitable spirit. He knew he could not bear it if she were to give up the fight.

"Sir, this should help." Harley appeared clutching a tumbler of tawny liquid. "I know miss doesn't take strong drink, but they're givin' it to the children back there." He held up the tumbler. "Even Lady Sale 'as had a glass. She said as 'ow it warmed her somethin' powerful, miss."

Annabel took the tumbler. "What is it, Harley?"

"Sherry, miss," the batman responded. "You drink it up, now. If a cup don't bother the kiddies, it's not goin' to bother you."

In any other circumstance, Annabel would have smiled at this invigorating encouragement, but now she simply took a tentative sip. The taste was unpleasant, but the effect was instantly restorative.

"They're distributin' the mess stores, sir," Harley explained. "Shockin' it is back there. The bearers 'ave all died or deserted and they're puttin' the ladies in panniers on the camels. Right in the line of fire, they are."

"What happened to Akbar Khan's escort?" Kit demanded harshly of Annabel, as if she should somehow have the answer. "He had his fifteen thousand rupees and his hostages! So what the hell does he want now?"

"I don't know," she answered quietly, holding the half-full tumbler out to him. "You have need of this, also . . . but I do not think he will be satisfied with less than total humiliation. You must do what he says in the hope that he will keep faith with you, but whether he chooses to or not is entirely up to him." She looked behind her at the chaotic, panicked melee. "There is the Khoord Kabul pass ahead."

The men around her said nothing. The Khoord Kabul gorge was five miles long, with steep cliffs rising on either side, a raging torrent at its floor, layered ice and snow edging the river.

"I think this is our escort," Bob said suddenly, gesturing toward the ridge where half a dozen horsemen in the garb of Afghan chiefs were riding toward them, behind them a substantial force of tribesmen.

The chiefs ranged themselves at the head of the

column, beside the general and his staff, their followers falling in behind.

The column approached the entrance to the pass. Annabel looked up at the heights. They were lined with Ghilzais, jezzails aimed down at the floor of the gorge. "The jaws of death," she said softly, remembering the Ghilzai name for the Khoord Kabul.

Kit turned at her whisper. "What did you say?"

"Look," she said, pointing upward.

"I saw them," he said grimly.

The escorting chiefs shouted something to their followers, who bellowed up at the tribesmen on the heights.

"They are telling them to hold their fire," Annabel said. But just as the first line of the advance entered the pass, a volley of shots rang out from above as the tribesmen from a range of fifty yards fired down at the now-trapped troops.

They could do nothing but press on, running the gauntlet of the deadly fire, while the harassment of their pursuers continued to cut into the column. Tribesmen poured down the steep cliffs, swords in hand, to charge at soldiers and civilians alike. Camels fell under jezzails' bullets, their passengers scrambling free only to be cut down as they struggled onward on foot. Children screamed as they were swept up by the enemy, some snatched from their mothers' arms, and Annabel was suddenly paralyzed, frozen in time as she relived the deeply buried horror of the attack in the Khyber pass eight years earlier.

Akbar Khan watched impassively from a peak near the exit to the defile. Would Ayesha die in that orgy of slaughter? If it was her destiny that she should die from a Ghilzai shot in the Khoord Kabul pass, then he must accept it. It was a risk he had taken by not including her amongst the hostages yesterday. But he wanted her to come to him, as he knew she would eventually, when she emerged from whatever dream she had been inhabiting and once again acknowledged reality.

"Will you call them off, sirdar?" The question came from a turbanned warrior, who had just ridden along the edge of the ravine.

Akbar Khan shrugged. "How can I? They are beyond control now."

Behind him, Major Pottinger said softly to Colin, "Mackenzie, remember if I am killed that I heard Akbar Khan at the very beginning shout 'Slay them' in Pushtu, although in Persian he called out to stop the firing."

Colin nodded, his expression an accurate reflection of the shocked nausea churning in his belly at the cold-blooded treachery of Akbar Khan, who promised protection, demanded and received payment for providing it, then incited wholesale murder. The sirdar sat and watched the massacre without a flicker in those bright blue eyes or a twitch of that incisive mouth.

One minute Bob Markham was riding at Annabel's side, the next his riderless horse was plunging and cavorting, blood spurting from the main artery in its neck. Bob had died cleanly from a bullet to the head. Annabel found that even this death had little impact on the nightmare.

Kit had no opportunity to grieve for his friend, recognizing in the timeless hollow of the present hell that grief for so many would fill his days and nights later, if he survived. For the moment, Annabel was his only concern. He did his best to shield her with his body as he fired without cease, picking a face—any face—from amongst the seething, surging mass of the enemy and taking a deadly aim, and there would be a cold satisfaction as he saw the man fall, and then he would pick another, all the while pushing his horse toward the exit from this death-pit.

Then they were out of the shadows and into the open plain where the snow-whiteness momentarily blinded and the silence deafened after the violent reverberations of rifle fire and screams bouncing off the rock face.

"Stay with the general's party." Kit spoke urgently to Annabel. "I have to go back, take a detachment to cover those poor devils still trying to get out. Promise me that you will not move from here."

She looked at him blankly, as if she did not see or hear him. Then her eyes focused and she nodded. "Do what you have to."

He rode off, back to the pass, commandeering a detachment of the forty-fourth infantry who were milling around, directionless and stunned. But they rallied and followed him to a rocky outcrop at the head of the exit. From there they commanded the exit and maintained a steady fire into the enemy, checking the pursuit until the last straggling survivors of the rear guard had emerged and were drifting toward the campground.

Five hundred soldiers and over two thousand five hundred camp followers died that day in the gorge.

The misery at the campground was of such a depth that Kit could only feel that the dead were perhaps the more fortunate. The general and his staff, those who had emerged from the jaws of death, were huddled in despairing conclave, the chiefs and tribesmen who had offered such ineffective escort sitting their horses to one side. Of Annabel there was no sign.

"Where is Annabel?" He tried to keep the frenzy from his voice but could hear its edge nevertheless.

"With the ladies," an exhausted captain told him, as he struggled to staunch the blood from a wound in his thigh. "Lady Sale took a bullet in the hand and there are others in great distress. Miss Spencer went to their assistance."

Kit looked around where figures lay in the snow, in various attitudes of defeat. He wondered why the Afghans did not come and finish them off now, so utterly without resources as they were. Again he thought of the cat torturing the mouse, allowing

it to drag itself painfully away from the claws, to
feel for a minute that escape might be permitted,
before batting at it again with the casual, seeming
indifference of the predator.

He found Annabel with the women. She was
binding Lady Sale's hand and did not immediately
look up when he spoke her name. All around,
women and children sat on pieces of baggage, or
just lay where they had collapsed in the exhaustion
of terror. Lady Sale, despite her pallor, was sitting
upright and maintaining a continuous flow of encouragement to all and sundry. The company and
assistance of the shameless hussy who shared
Christopher Ralston's bed Lady Sale clearly accepted without question in this extremity.

Annabel straightened up from her task and regarded Kit quietly. Her face bore the expression of
one who has delved deep in despair, searched for
and reached the only possible decision, one that
now afforded her the serenity of resignation. "I am
going to Akbar Khan."

His heart jolted sickeningly. "Do not be absurd," he said.

"It has to be done." She gestured at the desperate scene around them. "I realized it in the pass
. . . It was so like the other time . . . the noise . . .
the sights." She began to walk away from the
group and Kit caught her arm. "That other time, it
led me to Akbar Khan. Things have now come full
circle." She stopped and looked up at him, her eyes
intense in their anxiety that he should understand.
"It is Destiny, Kit."

"Damn your Destiny!" he exploded in agony.
"What possible good would it do anyone for you
to give yourself up to that treacherous swine? Least
of all yourself?"

"I will have to go in the end," she asserted softly.
"We both know that. And I know that he is waiting
for me. Perhaps, if I go to him of my own accord,
I will have a chance of interceding . . . for the
women and children, at least. I have to try, Kit;

surely you understand that? There is no one else who would have the access to him that I have. I know him, in as far as it is possible for anyone to know him."

"But what of us?" he said, even as he already mourned her loss, touching her face in his desperation as if he would imprint its shape on his hands.

"Oh, Kit," she said. "There is no future. There never could have been. I will return to him. There is possible death there, and certain death here. But I believe I may work some good before whatever happens happens."

She had said to him, in another land and another time it seemed to him in his anguish, that she was only lending herself to him, that she would stay with him until "whatever happens happens." And now that time had come. His hands fell from her face and he stepped back.

She nodded slowly and turned and walked to where Charlie stood, his head hanging in exhaustion. Kit watched her take from the saddlebags Akbar Khan's silver bracelets. She slipped them on her wrists and without hesitation closed the clasps. Then she looked up at him. "I must have a veil, or else I will offend."

Silently, he unbuttoned his tunic and removed the cravat from his neck.

She took it and fastened it around the lower part of her face, inhaling the scent and warmth of him, swallowing the tears that filled her eyes and clogged her throat.

He stepped forward, placed his hands on her waist, and lifted her onto Charlie for the last time.

"Say good-bye to Harley for me," she said. "He came through safely. I saw him just a short while ago."

"I will."

"And . . . " But there was nothing more to be said. Their eyes held for a moment in memory of shared joy, in acknowledgment of a future of shared loss, then Ayesha turned the weary Charlie and urged him toward the ridge above the Khoord Kabul where the Afghan force was massed, watching with the patience of the cat who knows the mouse has no refuge.

Chapter 19

A kbar Khan watched the approach of the solitary figure on the enormous piebald. He felt a surge of pleasure which surprised him, springing as it seemed to from the simple prospect of seeing her again, rather than from the satisfaction of her submission.

He gestured to the men around him that they should fall back, and he sat alone awaiting her.

She rode up to him and salaamed, the cuffs of her gloves pushed back as she lifted her joined hands to her forehead, so that the dull gleam of the bracelets caught his gaze. Her own eyes she kept lowered while she waited for permission to speak.

"So, Ayesha, you have returned," he said calmly.

"Yes, khan." She knew she must not raise her eyes, not here in front of so many men, but the habits of the last two months had created carelessness and it required all her concentration to maintain the posture.

"Do you bring a message from the feringhee?" he asked.

She shook her head. "No, but I would ask your mercy. There are women and children, babes in arms . . . what purpose will be served by their deaths?"

"What purpose will be served by their lives?" he countered.

"Magnanimity from a position of supremacy can only augment power," she said.

"Did you think I was not aware of that fact, Aye-sha?"

"No, khan. I thought simply to express it my-self."

"You will return to the feringhee commander in the morning and tell him that I will take under my protection the families of the officers." He paused and let his gaze drift over the bleak landscape, up into the gray sky where a great eagle soared over the mountain peaks. "On condition that their hus-bands accompany them as hostages."

Annabel found again Ayesha's immobility. Akbar Khan was virtually cutting off the head of the British force by this condition. Most of the senior officers were married and had their families with them. He was slowly, humiliatingly, compelling the surrender of the British command. Why did she no longer sympathize with his driving need to stamp the ar-rogant invader underfoot? Because she now knew the invader in all his weaknesses, his humor and his anger, his strengths. She knew the invader as indi-vidual . . . as Colin, Harley, Bob, General Elphin-stone, Lady Sale . . . . And she knew in the invader passion and love beyond description. But she still understood Akbar Khan's need, even if she could no longer identify with it. Maybe therein lay the rack upon which she would lie for the rest of her life.

"As you wish," she said.

"There are no women to care for you here," he said. "You will keep apart from all but myself until you take my message in the morning."

Her lowered eyes fixed on the intricate silver man-acles circling her wrists. "As you wish."

"Come, I will take you to my tent. You have need of rest and food. Your horse, also, requires atten-tion."

Ayesha followed him to the cluster of black no-mad tents pitched in the snow. There were no fires here, either, but there was order and discipline, strangely at odds with the frenzy of blood lust in-dulged in the day's slaughter. She wanted to ask about Colin but dared not jeopardize her reassumption of Ayesha by an inappropriate interest.

"Your horse will be fed and watered," Akbar Khan said as she dismounted unaided outside the tent where he drew rein. "It's an ugly animal, but has stamina, I can see." He ran a knowing eye over Charlie. "One of Christopher Ralston's, I presume."

"Yes," she agreed, handing the reins to a hillman groom, hearing her affirmative sound steady and noncommittal.

"Remain within the tent. Food will be brought to you."

She slipped through the narrow aperture. It was still freezing, but there were additional furs piled on the rough carpeting laid over the snow and an overpowering drowsiness hit her without warning. Whether it was the fatigue of despair, of exhaustion, of terrified memory she neither knew nor cared. She simply crawled into the warming, comforting heap and slept, her last waking thought of the strong circling arms that had held her through the last bitter nights, warding off both cold and danger in symbol if not in reality.

Akbar Khan came into the tent some two hours later and stood looking down at the curled, unconscious mound beneath the furs. She had eaten nothing, but presumably her body knew what it needed most. Tendrils of copper hair wisped beneath the hood of her cloak. Her eyelashes lay straight and thick on her cheekbones. All else was concealed with due modesty.

He knew she had slipped away from him . . . had known it from the moment she had come close enough for him to sense her spirit. Ayesha herself was no more, for all that she knew how to play the part and would do so if it were the only way to achieve her aims. But did he want her to play the part? Could he be satisfied with the appearance and form of Ayesha, when the reality was lost . . . gone from him forever?

He left her in sleep and went out into the bitter night, where for the moment only the cold was the enemy and it bit both pursuer and pursued alike.

Ayesha awoke at dawn, bewildered at her extraordinary warmth. Then memory returned, sharp-etched and lacerating. The tent flap fluttered and a disembodied hand pushed something inside: a bowl of soured milk, a flat round of bread spread with goat cheese. It was rough nomad fare to which she had been long accustomed, but it tasted strange now, although her appetite was such that she would have refused nothing.

When she had eaten, she adjusted the makeshift veil, drew her hood well over her face, and left the tent.

Akbar Khan was mounted, Charlie standing in well-trained patience at his side. The horse looked refreshed, Annabel noted. But then he would have been well cared for by these people who recognized the value of a good animal. Her heart lifted for a second as she saw Colin and his two fellow hostages behind Akbar Khan. They looked drawn, their eyes filled with the dull anger of frustration, but they appeared unharmed. Dropping her gaze modestly, she walked across the snow toward the waiting group, racking her brain for a way to mount her horse without a helping hand. No Afghan would offer such assistance to a woman.

She salaamed and waited for Akbar Khan to acknowledge her difficulty and rule upon it.

He looked over his shoulder, requesting in English, ''Would one of you gentlemen be good enough to assist Ayesha to mount?''

Colin moved forward with telltale speed, but as he approached her eyes lifted fractionally, signaling caution. He wiped all expression from his face, bent, and offered his cupped palms. She went up lightly and settled herself in the saddle.

Akbar Khan spoke clearly in Persian. ''You will tell the feringhee general that I most sincerely deplore the condition of the ladies and children in the party and offer my protection, on condition that their husbands accompany them. You will tell him that I pledge myself to offer escort through the passes in the rear of his force.''

A pledge that was not worth the air it was spoken upon, Ayesha knew, but she merely nodded and prepared to leave.

''And Ayesha . . . '' Something in his voice sent a shudder of apprehension creeping over her skin. ''You will number Ralston, *huzoor*, amongst the hostages.''

For a second, apprehension was banished by a surge of happiness. Even if she were never to lay eyes upon him, just the knowledge that he was in her vicinity would be balm. She had not been able to face the thought that she would never know how or when he met his death, as he surely would if he remained with the retreat. Then fear returned. Akbar Khan would do the man who had stolen his possession no favors. So what game was he going to play with them?

''As you wish,'' she said in customary neutral docility.

''Go.''

She rode off down the ridge toward the forlorn huddle on the plain. Those who had not frozen to death during the night were slowly pulling themselves out of their snowy lairs to face the third day's journey into death.

Kit saw her coming and wondered if he had slipped over the edge of sanity into the world of delusion. He tried to run, but his muscles were locked after the night's intense cold, and he stumbled to his knees in the snow. Cursing, he dragged himself upright and limped over to the group shivering around the general.

''General, I bring an offer from Akbar Khan,'' Ayesha said without preamble. She removed her veil and her eyes in love sought Kit's. She smiled softly and his blood flowed warmly again and strength returned to muscle and sinew. He strode over to her,

lifted his arms imperatively, and Annabel slipped off
Charlie into his embrace.

"What is this?" demanded the general.

"My apologies, sir," Kit said, although he could
not stop smiling, like some half-witted buffoon, he
thought joyfully as he held her in his arms and
whispered in wonderment against her cheek. "I did
not think I would ever see you again."

"What is this offer?" Brigadier Shelton spoke
brusquely.

Annabel turned, still in the circle of Kit's arm.
"Akbar Khan offers his protection to the ladies and
children, on condition that their husbands accompany them into his camp."

A babble of shocked protest ran around the
group, all of them recognizing the cunning ploy
that would rob the force of its senior officers. General Elphinstone sighed heavily. "Gentlemen . . .
gentlemen . . . " he said, "your protestations do
you credit, but we cannot deprive the ladies of the
slightest chance of succor. Take your families in
honor and God go with you."

"Akbar Khan also demands that Captain Ralston
give himself up as hostage," Annabel said quietly.
She felt Kit stiffen beside her and looked up at him.
"I do not know what he intends. It may be worse
for you than remaining here. . . . Worse for both of
us," she added, more to herself than to him. "But
if you refuse, he may be avenged upon the other
hostages."

"Do you imagine I would not come?" His voice
was suddenly sharp, anger flashing in the gray eyes,
as if she had impugned his integrity. "What species
of coward do you think I am, Annabel?"

"No coward," she said. "I intended no insult.
Suffering comes in some form with either choice."
She stepped out of his encircling arm. "Akbar Khan
also pledges safe escort from the rear through the
remaining passes to Jalalabad, General. But I do not
know how much you may rely upon his word in that
matter."

"Or in any matter," Shelton declared viciously but with absolute truth.

"What choice do we have?" Elphinstone asked. "We must accept his offer."

"I will tell him." She refastened her veil and it was Ayesha who turned again to Kit. "This was just a moment," she said. "I do not know why he permitted it, but there will be no others. I belong to Akbar Khan again, and am isolated according to custom." She spoke without expression, laying out the facts that they had faced the previous evening and that for one dizzying instant of delusion he had thought somehow commuted.

For a moment, he thought he would not be able to contain his pain, so deeply did it slice into his very core. He could not bear to touch her in farewell. He could find no words to express the inexpressible. So he walked away from her in his agony, leaving her to seek assistance in remounting from other hands.

When she attained the ridge again, she was conscious of a weariness that transcended the merely physical. When Akbar Khan told her softly that the matter lying between them would be dealt with when they reached the fortress of Budiabad, where he intended to house the hostages, she could summon no concern about her fate that would then be decided. He told her that except when they were riding, when she would keep at his side, she was to remain in the tent away from all eyes, just as if she were back in the zenana. In many ways, the order for seclusion brought relief. Alone with herself, she could perhaps find again the strength of acceptance that had served her so well in the past.

Fifty hostages followed Akbar Khan and the line of retreat. The sirdar kept his promise to provide a rear escort, but it was not a protective escort and the starved, frozen, despairing remnant of soldiers and those camp followers who had stayed with the re-

treat were attacked in every pass by Ghazi fanatics
and vengeance-hungry hillmen.

Kit rode with his friends through the Tunghee
Tariki gorge, where the majority of the main body
of the column lay massacred; they rode on through
the Tezeen ravine where bodies lay stripped, hacked
to pieces, cut in two; and they rode through the valley and up the steep incline to the peak of Jugdulluk
where the tribesmen had blocked the path with
prickly brushwood and under a heedless moon had
completed the destruction of the British retreat from
Kabul. It was here that he saw the body of Harley,
lying as he had fallen, sword in hand, beside him
the twisted body of a brigadier at whose side he had
fought.

One more death of a friend.

At Jugdulluk, the weary, blood-sickened hostages
found Brigadier Shelton and General Elphinstone,
now ''guests'' of Akbar Khan, forced to offer themselves as hostages after the massacre at Tezeen as
the only chance of saving the remainder of the force
. . . the force subsequently destroyed amongst the
rocks of Jugdulluk. Only one military survivor of the
retreat from Kabul reached Jalalabad to tell the tale.

The following day, Akbar Khan set off to the north
with his flock of hostages to the Laghman valley and
the fortress of Budiabad. Beside him rode the
swathed figure of Ayesha, who had set eyes only on
the British dead during this journey, the living being
kept from her.

Chapter 20

The great gray fort of Budiabad sat in a mountain valley, overshadowed in the north by the massive peaks of the Hindu Kush. The hostages had not been told where they were being taken, once they had left the grisly remnants of the retreat behind. For four days, they had ridden through the snow, the ladies and invalids carried in camel-panniers, thankful simply for the cessation of murderous assaults and an adequate if not plentiful supply of food and water.

They were surrounded by an escort of impassive Ghilzai tribesmen, who led the camels, encouraging the beasts to maintain a considerable speed.

"I wonder why they're in such a hurry?" Colin commented.

"I expect Annabel would know," Kit replied, staring ahead as he always did these days, as if he could distinguish the slender figure amongst the sizable force of tribesmen riding with Akbar Khan in the distance. Charlie had been returned to him without a word spoken, and he had spent long enough with Annabel to understand the significance of the gesture. Akbar Khan looked after his own, and a feringhee horse was no suitable mount for one of his own. When they made camp, they were still surrounded by their escort, and any attempt to move out of the confines of their designated spot toward the huddle of black nomad tents where Akbar Khan and his entourage were housed brought harsh directives enforced with the threat of a khyber knife.

Colin glanced at his friend in silent sympathy. He knew the agony of frustration and anxiety Kit was suffering as his imagination ran riot with speculation on the form Akbar Khan's vengeance would take upon the woman who had left him. For himself, Kit seemed not to care, even if he was to play prize in a *buzkashi;* after the horrors they had witnessed, the friends who had been so hideously slaughtered, such a fate seemed to have lost its sharp edge of atrocity. But Akbar Khan had been most lucid in his threat toward one of his own who defected. The penalty was immutable, he had said that day in Kabul, and Kit trembled for Annabel, even as he raged at his helplessness.

An unmistakable rustle of enthusiasm ran through their generally dour escort. One or two pointed with their whips and called out to their companions.

"It seems we've reached journey's end," Brigadier Shelton said, gesturing toward the edifice squatting on the plain, watchtowers standing sentinel on either side of the iron gateway.

"Friendly-looking place," muttered Colin.

Ayesha would have agreed with the ironic sentiment had she been with them to hear it. She had been to Budiabad once before, when Akbar Khan was traveling the land raising an army in the very early days of the invasion. It was a bleak spot, even in summer, and in the middle of January would be desolate in the extreme.

She cast a furtive glance at Akbar Khan riding beside her. He had said nothing substantive to her since they had left the Khoord Kabul, in general ignoring her as completely as she was ignored by his men. She was aware that this isolation was an indication of prisoner status. The prodigal's return had not been accepted as ending the matter. Judgment would be made and sentence passed at some point. She could die in the stoning pit for her offense, if Akbar Khan decided she merited the full punish-

ment decreed by Koranic law. And what of Kit? They
could die in that manner together, if it was so decided. Or some other, more ingenious penalty could
be planned for him.

They turned through the great iron gates into the
central courtyard of the fort. Two shrouded women
appeared from a low doorway in the north wall and
hurried across to Ayesha. The reception did not surprise her. An alerting message would have been sent
to the fort to ensure that her present irregular position without women attendants could be remedied
without delay.

She slipped from the sturdy mare she had been
given to replace Charlie and went with the women
without so much as a covert glance of inquiry at the
khan. What would happen would happen.

The hostages entered the fort an hour later. They
were shown to an interconnecting group of five
rooms on the ground floor of the fort. Five filthy,
sparsely furnished rooms for fifty men, women, and
children. There was a moment of utter despondency
as they stared around at the quarters they were to
occupy for an indefinite time. A child's piercing wail
was heard announcing it didn't like this place. It
was cold and dirty and there were creepy-crawlies
everywhere, and why couldn't they go home?

The wail served to galvanize the able-bodied
amongst them. Rooms were allocated, leaders appointed, and a deputation gathered to make representation to their captor.

Kit was elected to the deputation, together with
Major Pottinger, Mackenzie, and Lawrence. The
general was now so physically enfeebled, the disintegration of his spirit finally completed by the mortification of being forced to abandon his command,
that authority amongst the men by default devolved
upon Brigadier Shelton. Amongst the women, Lady
Sale, despite her wounded hand, took energetic
control.

Kit silently debated turning down his election on
the grounds that his inclusion in the party of hos-

tages had had a personal component that might
serve him ill as a negotiator for improved conditions, but decided that he must behave as if there
were no woman between himself and Akbar Khan.
There was nothing he could do to alter that situation
until Akbar Khan revealed his hand. Until then he
was simply another soldier torn in his innermost soul
between a natural relief at his temporary safety and
a deep self-disgust at the disgrace of imprisonment
and the manner of their surrender.

Where in this grim prison was Annabel? Did she
know where he was? Was she standing at some window somewhere, looking out, her heart as empty as
his of all but loss?

As the deputation was escorted across the courtyard, his eyes searched the ungiving walls, the tiny
blank windows, his nerve endings raw with tension
as all his senses strained to catch a hint of something
he could identify as an indication of her presence.
They passed a group of black-clad women drawing
water from a well. The women's chatter ceased as
the men went by and they turned their heads to the
wall, away from the forbidden sight of feringhee
men.

They walked through gloomy stone-floored corridors, all as much in need of a broom and water as
the rooms allocated to the prisoners. He glimpsed
inner courtyards, and in one women were hanging
clothes upon a washing line. His heart lurched violently as he recognized the emerald-green tunic that
went so well with the copper hair and the jade eyes.
He felt the most absurd urge to snatch the garment
from the line, to bury his nose in the soft linen to
try to catch that elusive scent that was just Annabel,
a melange of cinnamon and roses that in memory
was driving him to distraction.

Akbar Khan received them in a winter-dark presence chamber, where candles of sheep fat gave off a
noxious stench to mingle with the fumes of the dung
fire. "Our accommodations are somewhat humble,
I fear, gentlemen," he said pleasantly. "If it had

been possible, I would have housed you more comfortably in one of my other fortresses." His eyes rested on Kit for a moment. "Captain Ralston will vouch for the comfort to be obtained there."

"Indeed." Kit bowed slightly. "Your hospitality, khan, was generous in the extreme."

"Yes," murmured the khan. "I begin to think it was." He shuffled some papers on the broad plank table before saying, "You have some questions, gentlemen?"

"It is customary for prisoners of war to negotiate the terms and conditions of their imprisonment," Pottinger said stiffly

"I am willing to do all in my power to ensure your comfort," Akbar Khan said with the appearance of utmost sincerity. "But I am constrained by the place." He gestured expressively. "The fort has been neglected and is inhabited by the poorest of hill-people during the winter. I daresay the standards of cleanliness are not what you are used to."

"Vermin," declared Colin succinctly. "The ladies are most uncomfortable."

"But at least they are alive and sheltered," the khan mused as if to himself. No one responded.

"Whatever you require to improve your circumstances I will be happy to furnish, if it is in my power to do so," he suddenly said genially, as if the previous sotto voce comment had not been made. "You will wish to take exercise, I am certain, and should feel free to do so within the main courtyard." He smiled the benign smile Kit had seen before. "I shall be leaving here myself quite soon, once I have attended to a small but irritating matter." The heavy-lidded eyes narrowed, hiding their expression from his audience. He stroked his pointed beard. "Major Pottinger speaks some Pushtu, I understand. He will be able to make your needs understood in my absence, I trust . . . unless, perhaps, Ralston, *huzoor*, you have learned a little of the Afghan language in the last few weeks?"

Kit met the bright blue gaze with a cold clarity of

his own. "I remember no occasion when it was necessary for me to speak any but the language of my birth, Akbar Khan."

Reflectively, the sirdar nodded as if examining the gauntlet before deciding whether to pick it up or not. Then he smiled. "At some other time I should be most interested to hear your views on certain aspects of birth and adoption."

"I would imagine they differ from yours."

"I would imagine so," he agreed with apparent affability. "If that is all, gentlemen—" An eyebrow lifted in query. "The guards will provide you with whatever you need to make your quarters more habitable."

After diplomatic expressions of gratitude and disclaimer had been exchanged, the door closed on his visitors and Akbar Khan sat frowning, the geniality wiped clean from his face. Then he pushed back his chair with a harsh scrape on the stone floor and strode from the room.

The women's apartments were situated on the north side of the courtyard, and like everywhere else in Budiabad were cold, dirty, and primitive. The women who occupied them were the slovenly, brutalized wives of the hill peasants, a far cry from Ayesha's usual attendants. But Ayesha, according to instruction, was secured in a small room behind a locked door.

Akbar Khan stopped outside the door and softly moved aside the wooden shutter over a tiny aperture that permitted the occupant to be observed from the corridor. Ayesha was sitting on the floor before the fire, motionless, staring into the dully smoldering hearth. The candle flickered under a finger of wind probing into the room through the high, ill-fitting window slit. Despite her inhospitable surroundings, she was warmly dressed and furs were piled thickly upon the narrow cot against the far wall.

He stood watching her for a long time, trying to decide whether her mood was one of dejection, apprehension, or simply contemplation. She had ample reason to feel the first two, but he knew also how she drew strength from introspection and guessed she was seeking that resource as she prepared herself to face him when he decided to deal with the matter that loomed, waiting, barely mentioned yet of paramount consequence, between them.

Drawn to her without volition, he laid a hand on the latch, then abruptly withdrew it. Turning, he made his way back to his presence chamber. ''Have Ayesha brought to me.''

The guards received the command in silence, and Akbar Khan sat down to wait.

When they brought her in, she was veiled, her eyes lowered. When she salaamed, her posture was neither abject nor defiant; she held herself as if she simply accepted the reality of her predicament. He dismissed the guards and sat regarding her in silence.

''I could not have done otherwise,'' she said at last, her voice low but steady.

''You were held in the house of Christopher Ralston by force?''

She shook her head. ''No, but I could not have done otherwise.''

''You know that the stones await the unfaithful?'' he said softly. ''I gave you ample opportunity to return to me, just as I told Christopher Ralston that if timely restitution were made, then I could be generous.''

''I knew those things . . . but I could not have done otherwise,'' she repeated with the same steadfastness. ''I could not untie the 'master-knot of human fate.' ''

''You misuse the poet, Ayesha. He was referring to the ultimate destiny of humankind, not the immediate fate of an individual.''

Her head bowed in acknowledgment, but she said, ''Nevertheless, I thought it not inapposite.''

He said nothing for a minute, secretly enjoying

her wit which he had fostered, as he had fostered
the courage that enabled her to stand before him
exhibiting no fear, despite the threatened sentence.

"Will you plead for mercy, Ayesha?"

She shook her head. "Not for myself. But for
Christopher Ralston." Gracefully, she slipped to her
knees on the hard, cold stone. "I would petition for
him."

"He is a man. Can he not plead his own case?"

Her eyes lifted. "You will not permit him to do
so, Akbar Khan, because he is a feringhee who has
transgressed your laws. You would not consider him
qualified to present a defense against a system of
laws that he does not understand. He is condemned
because he is an infidel." She knew she was riding
the edge of the ravine again, matching her courage
against the standard Akbar Khan had set for her long
ago. To show the slightest hesitation, the merest hint
of a faint heart, would lose Akbar's interest. And
once that was lost, he would give not a straw for her
fate . . . or that of Kit.

"And you chose to forsake the true believer for
the infidel, Ayesha," he pointed out. "You would
not say that *you* did not understand the system of
laws and the punishment attendant upon their in-
fraction."

"No, I understood. But who *am* I?" she asked, as
quietly as ever but with an underlying throb of intensity. "Can you tell me truly, Akbar Khan, who I
am? Am I not in essence also an unbeliever?"

"Ah." His eyes narrowed. "It has come to that,
has it? Stand up."

She rose to her feet with the same fluid grace. Her
body was vibrating with tension, every nerve
stretched as she fenced with Destiny in the shape of
Akbar Khan.

"Do *you* know the answer to that question?" he
asked. "Have you discovered it during your sojourn
with the feringhee?" He thought he knew the answer and now waited to see if she would dissemble.
But Ayesha was too skilled in the ways of Akbar

Khan to attempt anything but the truth. "Sometimes I think I know, and at other times I do not."

Surprise flickered for a second in the blue eyes. "Do you hunger for the body of Christopher Ralston or for his soul?"

That question brought her head up, and she showed him the surprise in her own eyes. "Both."

"Ah." Abruptly, he stood and clapped his hands. The guards appeared instantly. "Return Ayesha to her room."

They took her away and he went to the window, staring into the snow-flecked night. He had thought that if simple lustful passion had informed her defection, he would be able to excuse it, but he would not be able to excuse a treacherous alignment with the feringhee. Now it did not seem so straightforward.

With sudden impatience he swung away from the window. What did it matter in the end? She was only a woman and the man was a dog of an unbeliever! Why should motives concern him? They had both betrayed him. Now he had to continue the struggle for his land. He had to march to Jalalabad, still held by General Sale and his force. Jalalabad must pass into Afghan hands, as must Kandahar, before victory could be complete. He would have the feringhee Ralston hanged in the morning. Ayesha would remain a prisoner for the moment. He could not bring himself to order her death. Later, when he had less on his mind, he would decide what was to be done with her.

The decision, once made, should have ended the matter. But for some reason it didn't bring the expected peace of mind. Why did it trouble him so much, that declaration that she felt more than simple lust for Christopher Ralston? Love was not an emotion Akbar Khan permitted himself, so why should it concern him that Ayesha felt it for another man? The puzzle niggled, disturbing his firm dismissal of further interest in the affair, his resolution to deal summarily with the feringhee and leave Ayesha's fate for future determination.

What were they like together? How did the intensity of love affect the ordinary process of passion? Why should he not satisfy his curiosity? The idea took a pleasing shape. He would reenact a little play. It would be a fitting close to a business that had begun four months ago, and when all was said and done, a condemned man was entitled to one last night of pleasure. A capricious smile touched his mouth as he went to give the necessary orders.

Ayesha regained her cell, and as the door closed on her she began to shake violently, every muscle now aching as if she had been holding herself tightly clenched for hours. She wanted to weep . . . to scream . . . to collapse in an exhausted, beaten heap on the floor and yield the struggle. Why had this happened? Why had it happened to her? The monstrous injustice engulfed her and she sank into the morass of self-pity, letting the tears flow as they would as she screamed in silent rebellion at an unjust fate that had propelled her into this abyss of loss and fear. Every vestige of the careful control she'd built inch by inch in the last eight years was demolished under an outburst worthy of the Annabel Spencer she had once been. And then, when the storm subsided, and she thought of those others, in their own imprisonment somewhere in the fortress, some who had seen their children snatched screaming from their arms or cut down before their eyes, her own plight settled into perspective. It had happened.

One thing is certain, that life flies; one thing is certain, and the rest lies; the flower that once has blown for ever dies. The words of Omar Khayyám brought the comfort they had always done. Maybe to some they would not be comforting words, but to Ayesha, who had absorbed their philosophy for so many years, they brought the peace of acceptance. She washed her face in the cold water in the chipped basin in the corner of the room, soothing her swollen eyes. She let down her hair and brushed it with strong, rhythmic strokes that lulled her into a meditative calm, then she knocked imperatively at the locked door.

It was opened by a shambling black-clad woman with gnarled hands and a back bent with years of carrying burdens. She looked blank-eyed at the young woman, her toothless mouth slightly open. She was probably no more than thirty, Ayesha thought.

"Bring me food and tea," Ayesha commanded, the imperiousness of Akbar Khan's favorite not a whit diminished by imprisonment. "And the fire needs more fuel."

The woman mumbled an assent before locking the door again. Ayesha could hear her slippered feet shuffling down the corridor. She sat down in front of the fire again and gave herself up to dreams, weaving her own destiny, playing at planning a future.

In the hostages' quarters, candles flickered and fires smoked, but it was the first night in an eon, it seemed, that they had spent within walls and under a roof. The children were quiet; invalids slept or lay in relative peace close to the fires. They had been given a huge pot of broth and thick rounds of wheat bread. Shiny dollops of fat from the fat-tailed sheep glistened on the surface of the broth, and Kit remembered Annabel's telling him that the nomads prized the tails of the sheep because they provided for many of them the only source of meat during the long winters. No one had grimaced openly as they swallowed the thin, greasy brew—memories of near-starvation were still too vivid—but later they discussed preparing their own food, as much for hygienic considerations as gastronomic.

The discussion was in full swing when the door was opened and three armed Ghilzais stood, turbans over ringlets, staring at the group. "Ralston, *huzoor.''* There was no expansion. They simply waited.

Kit rose slowly to his feet. The eyes of his friends were upon him, and he knew they were telling him that if he chose to fight whatever this was, then they were beside him. Except that they had no weapons, not even a stick or a stone with which to resist the scimitars, rifles, and daggers of their captors.

"I am Ralston," he said. "What do you want with me?"

Wordlessly, they stepped aside and gestured to the door.

"A reckoning?" Colin murmured.

"Perhaps." Kit smiled grimly. "But it's a trifle dark for a *buzkashi.* I wonder what else he has in mind." He flung his cloak around his shoulders. "I can but discover." He offered a mock salute to the room at large and stalked to the door, his escort falling in behind him as he stepped into the bitter night.

They ushered him across the courtyard, through a door in the north wall. Instantly, he was aware of something rarefied in the atmosphere . . . something hushed, secret. They saw no one, but once or twice Kit could have sworn he heard a rustle of material, caught a glimpse of black cloth fluttering into a doorway at the sound of their booted feet. He glanced at his escort. They were staring straight ahead with a rigid determination, as if to look to right or left were forbidden. When deliberately he slowed at a half-open doorway and made a movement toward it, he was grabbed roughly by the shoulder, hard brown eyes glared savagely, and involuntarily he took a step backward before a violent stream of Pushtu invective. As he had guessed, they were walking through the women's apartments. He bowed his head in a gesture of conciliation and apology, and was spun around hard, a knuckled fist pressing into his back, pushing him ahead. He bit his lip on his anger at the manhandling, and continued on the designated way.

Evil-smelling torches stuck into sconces against the

wall cast a yellow flicker of light. The freezing air
stank of grease and unwashed bodies and mildewed
clothing. They stopped outside a door set into the
stone wall where beads of moisture had frozen into
pearly ice-drops. Kit wondered if he were afraid and
decided numbly that he wasn't. He seemed to have
gone beyond fear.

The heavy latch was lifted. The door swung on its
hinges. The knuckled fist in the small of his back
propelled him forward with unnecessary violence so
that he stumbled, catching onto the doorframe to
save himself.

He was in a small room, as primitive as any he
had seen, except that the fire was brighter, the candles, although equally smelly, were more numer-
ous, and the stone floor was covered with a goatskin.
The door clanged shut behind him.

"Salaam, Ralston, *huzoor*," she said.

"Greetings, Ayesha." He stepped toward her,
arms reaching to enfold her, for the moment not
troubling to question this amazing turn of events,
accepting it as he had done in the past as a wondrous, miraculous gift of the gods of love and passion . . . of Destiny.

She came into his arms, every warm throbbing
inch of her, and he caught his breath at the familiar
enchantment of her body under his hands. They had
not made love, it seemed, for an eternity, and here,
in this dim prison chamber, with horror behind
them, a conundrum in their present, and an unknown fate ahead of them, passion blossomed,
wildly urgent, consuming all thought.

A week ago he had believed he would never see
her again, yet he was holding her, inhaling her
scent, feeling the rich silky burnished copper of her
hair against his cheek, the soft mounds of her breasts
against his chest, the firm curve of her backside beneath his palms as she pressed against him; her
hands, on their own voyage of reexploration, moved
over his frame and the words of hungry desire whispered between her lips as she stood on tiptoe and

nuzzled his mouth, trailed her tongue over the line of his jaw, nipped his bottom lip with fiery little bites.

"Wait, sweetheart, just one minute," he said, his breathing ragged as the buttons of his tunic flew apart under her peremptory fingers.

"No," she said. "I want you now."

He groaned, but caught her hands in one of his and reached sideways to the cot, grabbing up a pile of the furs. He threw them to the floor before the fire and she sank onto them, her hands reaching up for him as he yanked off his boots, pushed off his britches, and dropped down beside her.

With a moan of need, she took his hardness in her hands, reacquainting herself with the feel of him, her body trembling with anticipation at the thought of taking him within herself again. He stripped the *chalvar* from her and her hips lifted, her thighs parting as he came over her. Then he was giving her what she craved, driving deep to become that indissoluble part of her, filling her loins as she closed around him and they left the squalid prison far beneath them, soaring on their own ecstatic flight.

"Dear Lord!" Kit whispered on an exhausted exhalation, falling heavily upon her. "How is it that that can happen? How can one be consumed with such a desperate hunger, engulfed in such wondrous satisfaction?" He rolled off her with a groan of effort and turned sideways, propping himself on an elbow to run his hand over the long length of her exposed thighs. "How is it that one person can love another as much as I love you, my Anna?"

"It just is," she said, smiling, lost in the radiance of her own love, shifting languidly on the furs as his fingers played idly in the curly tangle at the apex of her thighs.

"Why have we been given this?" His playing did not cease, but there was gravity now in the quiet voice.

She knew he referred to the moment, not to the miracle of shared love. "I am not sure. I'd rather not question.'' A shiver prickled her skin, and a mist of apprehension encroached on the warm enclave of desire, clouded the peace of fulfillment.

''What do you mean?'' He moved his hand upward so that it lay warm and flat on her belly, simply a presence, no longer an instrument of pleasure.

Her head moved in negation on the furs, as if she did not wish to speak of it.

''What do you mean, Anna?'' he insisted, sitting up, reaching for a candle and bringing it closer, so that her face was illuminated and she could no longer take refuge in the shadows.

''Let it alone, love,'' she said, turning her head to look into the sullen fire. ''Don't let us waste what we have. Why should it matter why we have it?''

''Oh, no,'' he said, catching her chin. ''That will not do, sweetheart. You will tell me what you suspect . . . know . . . and you will do it now. This is not something we bear separately.''

A ruddy glow from the fire bloomed on her cheek, caught the deep luster of her hair massed on the dark fur, but the jade eyes looked up at him with a frightening emptiness. ''You know of the condemned cell,'' she said. ''Of the last wish of the condemned prisoner.''

''Sweet Jesus!'' Kit stared for a moment, dumbstruck. ''He would plan such a callous, savage . . . ?''

A humorless smile touched her lips. ''Need you ask? After what you saw in the passes?''

There was a moment of silence, then Kit, with an expression of quiet concentration, lifted her against him, sliding the tunic up and over her head so that she was naked, the smooth, clean-limbed whiteness of her body gleaming, diminishing the mean reality of their surroundings.

He eased her onto the furs and with the same concentration ran his hands over her breasts, touched each sharply delineated rib, stroked the jutting hipbones with his thumb, a thoughtful frown drawing his eyebrows together. ''You have become extremely thin,'' he remarked casually.

"As have we all," she responded, waiting to see where this conversational turn would take them. Kit was behaving as if the words had never been spoken to throw a shroud over loving.

He nodded. "Turn over."

"Turn over?" She looked askance.

He nodded again. "On your belly."

With a tiny shrug, she rolled onto her front.

"Now, let me see if I have learned anything from you, Ayesha, in the last months," he whispered, kneeling astride her prone form, pushing aside her hair, his fingers moving strongly on the column of her neck, down to her shoulder blades, trying for the clever, deft identification and release of knotted, muscular tension that she had so often offered him.

He felt her gradual relaxation, as if it had crept up on her, and he smiled, knowing that he had succeeded because her reaction was exactly as his had been under her own ministrations. She stretched, arched, catlike, and he bent to kiss her ear, sliding backward to kneel astride her ankles so that he had room to move downward, pressing hard massaging thumbs into her spine, into the indentation of her pelvis, moving his flat palms in a circular sweep over her buttocks, kneading her thighs, softly stroking in the vulnerable spot behind her knees, moving strongly over her calves, finally lifting her feet, feeling for the spots on the soles that he knew from his own experience would communicate the reflex sensations of pleasure and relaxation to other seemingly unconnected parts of her body.

"Such joy," she whispered in wonderment. "No one has ever given me that before."

"I am glad," he answered, sliding his hands beneath her loins, drawing her onto her hands and knees. "Glad that no one has eased you in that way before." Holding her hips, he slipped in gentle delight within her opened body. Her head and shoulders dropped, her cheek resting on the slightly scratchy furs, touched by the minimal, fingering warmth of the fire, as she surrendered herself to this loving, giving her body to his direction, receiving the gift of love as she offered her passivity.

Outside, Akbar Khan softly closed the shutter over the small window in the door. The lovers had been too enmeshed to notice the tiny aperture that gave access to the voyeur's eye and ear. The game he had intended to play had somehow misfired, he reflected, drawing his cloak tight against the freezing air in the corridor. He had thought to satisfy his curiosity by observing the conduct of Ayesha and the man she claimed to love. He had thought to derive some satisfaction from knowing that they performed for him, unknowing of the fate he had decreed.

He had received satisfaction in neither instance. Ayesha had guessed his plan, had communicated it to her British captain, who had received the knowledge and proceeded to behave as if it were of no significance. And Ayesha had yielded her fears to her lover's direction.

He had derived no satisfaction either from observing their lovemaking. He had certainly satisfied his curiosity about the difference loving made to the gratification of lust, but it was not a knowledge that pleased him in the least. Indeed, for one who had believed sexual gratification to be the only dimension worth considering, it left him feeling bereft.

He returned to his own quarters, deeply thoughtful.

Chapter 21

❦

It was not a night to be spent in sleep. It was a night to be spent in lingering enchantments, wandering in the fields of passion where ugly thoughts of the morrow had no soil in which to grow, and fears withered beside the strong, flourishing flowers of joy.

When the sound of booted feet in the corridor, the grating scrape of the unoiled lock, penetrated the lovers' dreamland in the freezing dawn, they drew apart with no words, just the barest delaying instant when their bodies touched, hands loitered, drifted, then parted.

The door was pushed ajar, but the escort remained in the corridor, issuing a harsh command that Kit, although he could not understand the words, had no difficulty interpreting. He dressed rapidly and turned to look down at her where she lay in the furs, copper and white and deep jade. She smiled and he smiled back. Then he walked to the door.

It closed behind him and Ayesha lay very still, summoning every resource of spirit and body she possessed to bridle the hideous imaginings of what he might be going to. Would she ever know what befell him? When Akbar Khan pronounced her own sentence, would he also tell her what fate he had decreed for the feringhee?

She was alone with her fears for a long time, before the black-clad woman shuffled in with a bowl of curds and a round of bread for her breakfast. The food brought some renewal of strength, and when she had eaten she dragged the cot below the high window slit and stood on it, squinting down into the main courtyard. Akbar Khan, astride his charger and with a sizable force around him, was preparing to ride out.

She stared in astonishment, standing on tiptoe as if to verify the scene. Was he just leaving her like this? She had heard him discussing his plans during the ride from the Khoord Kabul, so she knew he was intending to march on Jalalabad, joining up with the other sirdars and their armies in the siege of the city. But what was to happen to her? What had happened to Kit? Had he dealt with the feringhee transgressor and decided to leave Ayesha to the torture of dreadful unknowing in her prison cell?

It would not be beyond the cruelty of which she knew he was capable. And since she had returned to him he had exhibited none of the softness, the humor, the understanding with which he had in general used her in the past. She had expected to be punished, but after the gift of such a night, there was a barbaric refinement to this carefully engineered ignorance and isolation that went beyond anything she could have anticipated.

She stepped off the cot, shivering with more than the bone-deep chill in the stone chamber. She had neglected the fire in her hours of reverie since Kit had been taken away and now turned resolutely to rekindle the sullen flame. She had no employment to pass the weary hours, no books, no writing materials, no domestic tasks. She had neither horse nor hawk . . . not even the freedom of the zenana. What was she to do in the weeks of Akbar Khan's absence? And it would be weeks.

The gloomy reflection was enough to cast her into the depths of despondency. She began to recite Omar Khayyám's rubaiyat to herself, attempting an elegant translation from Persian into English, exercising her mind in the effort of memory and linguistics even if she could do nothing for her body. But she was weary after her sleepless night, and eventually lay down on the cot beneath the furs to seek renewal in sleep.

She had been asleep for no more than half an hour when the door creaked open and her attendant came in, leaning over to shake her shoulder. Ayesha blinked dopily at the ruined face hanging over her.

"Men are coming to fetch you," the woman said. "You must veil yourself."

Fetch her for what? Ayesha sat up, shaking the sleep from her brain. It seemed orders had been left regarding her fate. She could find no alarm in her heart, only relief that something was about to happen. Nothing could be as terrifying as the prospect of being confined for an indefinite period without access to any outside stimulation or information.

"Tell them they must wait," she said. The woman stared incomprehending at such an instruction. Women did not tell men anything.

"Tell them I will be ready shortly," Ayesha said gently. These men, of course, would not be accustomed to the the unusual license granted Akbar Khan's favorite. But then, since Akbar Khan's favorite was a prisoner in this primitive fortress, one could hardly blame them for failing to accord her her accustomed civilities.

The woman shuffled out and Ayesha swung herself to the floor, splashed the sleep from her eyes, and fastened her veil. Kit's cravat had been taken from her early on and a conventional veil procured. Her head spun suddenly at the memory, and the scent of Kit, the feel of his body warmth, filled the air around her as powerful and palpable as if he were beside her.

"Tell her to hurry. We cannot be kept waiting on the whims of a woman!"

The harsh tones from the corridor returned her to her senses. The scared eyes of the veiled attendant appeared in the doorway. "Please hurry," she whispered.

"I am ready." Ayesha stepped past her into the

corridor, debating whether to assume a confident stance with the three tribesmen standing without. But Akbar Khan was not here to lend credence to such an act and she had no idea what orders he had left for her treatment. She bowed her head before the men and salaamed.

"Come with us, woman."

She followed three paces behind as they marched through the zenana, women fleeing at their approach. Were they taking her to the stoning pit, to the flogging post, to the scaffold? Would Akbar Khan have condemned her to suffer his sentence in his absence? Somehow, she did not think so.

They emerged in the main courtyard and the three men closed around her, marching her toward a door in the south wall. She heard the voices before the door was pushed open. They were the high-pitched voices of English children, reciting a lesson in unison. A clear voice rose above them, the voice of Mrs. Anderson, she recognized from the days of the retreat, instructing the class.

She stopped, looking askance at her escort, who gestured brusquely that she should enter the building. "You are to talk with the women and discover what needs they have," she was told.

"Those are Akbar Khan's instructions?"

"It is not for you to question. Enter."

She entered and stood in the dimly lit room where a group of children sat in a semicircle, Mrs. Anderson standing before the fire, other women arranged around the room.

"Please don't let me disturb you," she said quietly. "Where will I find Lady Sale?"

"Why, Miss Spencer . . . ?" One of the younger women stood up and came toward her. "We were wondering what had happened to you."

"I have been sent to interpret your needs to the guards," she said carefully, glancing over her shoulder to where her escort stood, making no attempt to hide their contempt for the feringhee women who evinced no modesty in dress or bearing in the presence of men.

"Annabel?" Colin Mackenzie's voice rang out in joyful surprise. He came into the room from one of the inner chambers. "I thought it had to be your voice."

"Colin!" Forgetting herself, she stepped toward him.

Instantly, a furious command, a hand grabbing her shoulder fiercely, reminded her of her position. She was an Afghan woman amongst the feringhee. She salaamed, murmuring in hurried conciliation, and the man released her, glowering around the room.

Colin had gone pale as if for the first time he really understood that she belonged to the Afghan. "I will fetch Kit," he said, keeping both face and voice expressionless.

Her head shot up, her eyes alive with hope, then at a threatening movement behind her, she bowed her head, speaking in a low, rushed voice. "He is safe?"

"Yes, but in an agony over what may have happened to you," he replied.

One of her guards made harsh protest at this continued conversation and she said, "They will not permit me to talk directly with men. I will say what I can indirectly, through conversation with the women."

"Ah, Miss Spencer. Laurie told me that you were here, but I could scarcely credit it." Lady Sale billowed into the room, her bandaged hand in a sling, her voice as piercingly energetic as ever. "You are to act as liaison, I understand."

"I believe so, ma'am," Annabel said, greeting her ladyship's arrival with relief. It would provide some distraction for her grimly alert escort. "Akbar Khan has left, but I am told that I should talk with you about what you might need." She looked around the room where the children and the other women were staring and listening, wide-eyed and big-eared.

"You should talk with Major Pottinger as well,"

her ladyship announced. "He is the senior political officer."

"I will not be permitted to do so, ma'am," Annabel said swiftly. "I do not understand exactly what Akbar Khan ordered or why, but I must behave as an Afghan woman for the moment. If you will conduct me around your quarters, I could perhaps make some suggestions as to how you could improve matters within the constraints of this place. The people are poor and have no understanding of European comforts or even of basic cleanliness. I imagine that is why Akbar Khan has deputed me to act for you." She smiled a little bitterly, but no one could see her mouth. "I understand both sides of the coin, you see."

Kit stood in the shadows of the inside doorway, behind Lady Sale. He stood and he looked at her until she felt his presence. She continued to talk to Lady Sale, keeping her head bowed, but her eyes over the veil held Kit's and a deep peace entered her. He was safe and she was safe, and they were under the same roof. The cat had left the mice for the time being.

But he had not left them in a position to play. And he had not left them with their fears permanently eased and fates resolved. However one should be grateful for the small mercies, temporary though they might be.

Annabel winked at Kit and her lips beneath the veil formed her imp of Satan smile that he knew so well. She saw his mouth curve in recognition, both of the smile and of what it stood for. They were not yet defeated. Then he melted into the shadows and she became briskly businesslike with Lady Sale.

They walked through the five rooms, Annabel with her vigilant escort. Whenever a man approached, a guttural but unmistakable order was issued that sent them into another room.

"This is most uncivilized," muttered Lady Sale. "You are an Englishwoman when all is said and done, even if I do not approve of the manner in which you have conducted yourself with Christopher Ralston. Why do these savages consider they have the right to treat you like one of their women in purdah?"

"Because that is what I am," Annabel explained patiently. "We are all prisoners, are we not? The terms of my imprisonment simply differ from yours."

"Well, I really do not understand it at all. How did you fall into this situation in the first place?"

"Kit will tell you," she said. "We have more important matters to discuss. The men will become impatient soon and mistrust our conversation. Then we will have achieved nothing."

"Imperious gal, aren't you?" declared her ladyship, and then began to reel off a list of requirements and complaints, all of which Annabel noted, decided which could be supplied and remedied and which were beyond the limited scope of Budiabad and its peasant occupants.

She was just leaving the quarters when Brigadier Shelton and Colin strode casually into the room behind her. "It would be interesting to know where Akbar Khan has taken himself off too," the brigadier said in carrying tones.

Annabel turned to Lady Sale who had accompanied her to the door. "He has gone to Jalalabad to join with the other sirdars to lay siege to the city," she said in the same conversational tone she had employed throughout. "I will learn what I can, but I am kept in such close seclusion I can promise little."

"Anything will be better than nothing." It was the brigadier who had spoken, as if to Colin. "Even if you consider it of no importance, it may have significance."

"I understand," Annabel said. She turned to the guards, salaamed, and said in Pushtu, "When am I to be permitted to return here?"

"When they ask for you," one of them said. "You must leave now."

"I understood what they said." Major Pottinger had joined the brigadier and Colin at the rear of the

room and spoke casually as if to his companions.
"We will ensure that you are a frequent visitor."

She made no reply because to do so would imply
a conversation. She wanted to look over her shoulder, to see if she could catch a glimpse of Kit, but
did not dare to jeopardize her chances of returning.
The guards hustled her out into the courtyard, where
she passed on the hostages' requirements and was
then returned to her prison chamber.

Later that day, the sounds of voices raised in
laughter reached her from the courtyard below. She
stood up on the cot again and peered down. A game
of blindman's buff was in progress amongst the hostages, adults playing as energetically as the children.
She watched as a blindfolded child of about ten
grabbed Kit with an exultant shriek. Kit, laughing,
swung the child into the air before removing the
blindfold and putting it on himself.

Annabel felt lonelier than she had ever felt in her
life.

So it continued. She would be taken once a day
to hear the hostages' requests and complaints, frequently spurious but her guards did not seem to
guess that they were excuses to enable her visits.
She would catch a glimpse of Kit. She would watch
them playing backgammon and draughts on boards
they had constructed for themselves. She would listen to the children in their makeshift schoolroom.
She would tell Lady Sale whatever titbits of information she had picked up from Zobayeda, her attendant, and from the guards when they escorted
her on the walks she was permitted to take for exercise: that Shah Soojah had been murdered in Kabul; that General Pollock had marched from
Peshawar and had relieved the garrison at Jalalabad
and was now camped on the Jalalabad plain facing
the Afghan forces; that the British in Kandahar had
expelled every Afghan inhabitant because the situation there had become so menacing; that the Afghans had doubled back on Kandahar and were
attacking it in force. Good news alternated with bad

and moods swung accordingly. She would watch from her prison window as the hostages played hopscotch and blindman's buff with the children. On Sundays, she would hear the church services they rigorously kept, hear the hymns and the psalms and the prayers bursting through the physical confines of their squalid prison. And she would ache to be a part of that community, close-knit now in the forced intimacy that commonly experienced hardship created. She knew that the purely conventional polish of polite society had been rubbed away. She heard a plainness of speech that would be unthinkable amongst ladies and gentlemen in any other circumstances. And she wept in her loneliness more hours than she would ever admit to.

Then, on a soft day in early April, when the promise of spring seemed to touch the valley, the news came that Akbar Khan had suffered a signal defeat on the Jalalabad plain and had been forced to retire.

The jubilation of the hostages rose in direct proportion to the gloom of their guards. The expectation that General Sale would now be free to march to their rescue became the subject of their waking hours, and Annabel permitted herself the luxury of speculation. If the hostages were rescued, then, unless Akbar Khan removed her, so would she.

In the euphoria engendered by this possibility, she committed a grave error. Kit always positioned himself leaning against the doorway when she made her entrance into the hostages' quarters, so that she was obliged to brush past him. They never looked at each other, so as not to draw attention to the position, but just that instant of proximity was sufficient to buoy Annabel's spirits for the rest of the day. But on this occasion, she stopped in front of him, raised her eyes, and said softly, "Salaam, Ralston, *huzoor.*"

"Greetings, Ayesha," he replied, smiling, reaching out a hand to touch her.

A curved knife slashed, and blood spurted from his hand. Annabel turned on the guard with a cry of outrage. He drew back his fist, then one of his fellows called a warning. Instead of hitting her, he caught her wrists behind her back, wrenching them upward so that she inhaled sharply with the pain. He propelled her across the yard just as British officers emerged from the building, surrounding the injured Kit, turning furiously on the remaining guards, who all drew their knives. Other guards boiled into the courtyard at the sounds of commotion, knives and scimitars drawn. The high wail of a terrified child soared through the soft air.

Annabel, petrified that her foolishness was about to precipitate a massacre, tried to pull back against her captor's hold. The guards' mood had been ugly since the news of Jalalabad, and she had sensed that it would take little to tip them over the edge into a violent revenge for their sirdar's defeat. But she had also heard the other guards' warning reminder that it was against Akbar Khan's orders to offer Ayesha any violence, and the knowledge emboldened her. "Is this what Akbar Khan ordered?" she demanded, ignoring the pain in her arms. "Did he order a massacre of the prisoners? If he has lost the field at Jalalabad, then he is going to be even more anxious to have negotiating power. Do you think he will thank you for murdering them?"

The man reviled her for a worthless, deceiving piece of female flotsam, but he abruptly released his grip on her wrists so that she stumbled and nearly fell to the ground. He yelled over his shoulder at the seething, furious mass behind him, and they drew away from the unarmed hostages who were backed against the wall with nothing but their bare hands for defense.

Annabel searched anxiously for Kit and saw that he was still on his feet, although blood dripped from the knife wound in his hand. It had been her fault. An act of self-indulgent thoughtlessness at such a volatile time. And she knew that she had now denied herself the daily visits which alone seemed to preserve her sanity. Furious with herself, she ac-

cepted the penalty as entirely justified, and when
she was pushed ungently into her cell and the door
clanged shut with a more than usually vigorous
slam, she allowed the angry tears to flow un-
checked. What if Kit's wound were to mortify? Med-
icines and bandages were in short supply as she
knew, having been responsible for procuring those
they had. There was still dirt and vermin everywhere . . . it would take little for gangrene to set
in. . . . She continued with her merciless self-
flagellation until exhaustion took over and she lay
down in utter dejection upon her cot.

The commotion outside had died down and a
deep, brooding silence settled over the fortress and
its occupants. As evening fell, the silence was shat-
tered by shouts and the clatter of horses' hooves.
Annabel leaped up with a renewal of energy and
stood on the cot to look out of the window.

Akbar Khan had ridden into the courtyard with a
sizable entourage.

She stared down, trying to gauge his physical
condition and his frame of mind, but it was hard to
read anything at this distance. She thought he dismounted with a little less than his customary vigor,
wondered if perhaps his shoulders were less rigid
than usual, if there was less spring to his step as he
crossed the yard and disappeared through a door
beneath her window.

She climbed off the cot and began to pace the small
room, trepidation now her companion. He would
have plans for the hostages. Would he have plans
for Ayesha, or was she to be left languishing here?
Death by stoning would be better.

She sensed the approach of a visitor before she
heard the clack of booted feet. During the weeks of
imprisonment, she had become adept at hearing beyond the immediate sounds of her environment, listening on some deeper level. In a sudden panic, she
realized that her cheeks were tearstained from her
afternoon's weeping, her eyes red and swollen, her
hair disordered. Feverishly, she splashed cold water

on her face just as the door opened and Zobayeda came in.

"You are to be taken to Akbar Khan," she said in the tremulous tones of one who had pronounced the name of a divinity. "I will help you prepare."

Annabel accepted her help willingly enough. In any other place and any other circumstance, when Akbar Khan returned and asked for her, her preparations were lingering and meticulous; hot scented baths, warm oils, the softest silks to clothe her body, her hair brushed and braided and threaded with flowers for the moment when he would remove her veil. Here, there was only cold water, crude soap, and the well-worn clothes that had formed her small traveling wardrobe on the retreat from Kabul. But they did the best they could and at least she felt relatively clean as she was escorted by her usual guard to the presence chamber.

Akbar Khan was sitting at the table, arms folded in front of him, eyes fixed on some spot in the middle distance. As she came in and the door closed behind her escort, the bright blue gaze focused and he looked at her in silence for a minute.

"You look tired," she said involuntarily, before she had been given permission to speak.

A slight smile touched his lips. "A not inaccurate observation, Ayesha."

She stepped toward him, saying with sudden compassion, "May I ease you?"

He shook his head. "No . . . no, not yet." Propping his elbows on the table, he rested his chin on his clasped hands, regarding her somewhat quizzically. "Remove your veil."

She unfastened the pin, letting the soft gauze fall aside.

"Take it off."

She drew it away from her head, and the candlelight fell on the swinging copper braid, caught the luminous jade glow in her eyes, dark-shadowed yet startling against the extreme pallor of her complexion.

"You do not look as if you have derived much pleasure yourself in the last weeks," he observed.

"I do not care to be a prisoner," she replied.

That smile touched his lips again. "No, neither would I. But your seclusion gave you ample time to reflect upon the question to which you were unsure of the answer when last we spoke."

Who am I? she had asked. *Am I not in essence also on unbeliever?* She had not known the answer to the question. She stood quietly, waiting.

"Do you know the answer now?"

Slowly she nodded, aware that the truth would condemn her if he chose to see betrayal, yet knowing that she had no choice but to tell it. "I am not truly of the feringhee anymore, and never could be again after the years I have spent with you, but in essence I belong with them."

"In essence," he repeated pensively, stroking his beard. "It does not sound a very comfortable position, Ayesha, to belong in essence yet not to be of them."

"But it is a position you put me in," she said boldly. "If you had not played your game at the very beginning, I would never have rediscovered my essence in the feringhee. I would have been content with the life I had. I felt I was Ayesha."

"But you are not," he stated, making no attempt to deny her accusation.

"It seems not," she agreed simply. "But I am not what I understand Annabel Spencer ought to be, either."

There was a moment's silence, then he commanded abruptly, "Veil yourself." When she had done so, he clapped his hands and the guards reappeared. "Take her away," he said, pushing back his chair and walking to the begrimed window, turning his back on her as she stood for a moment irresolute, wondering if there was anything she could say to recapture the strange ease, the sense of their old companionship, of a few minutes before. But a hand jerked her roughly to the door, and a voice ordered her out in accents no one would have used to her in Akbar Khan's presence in the past.

The favorite had certainly fallen from grace, she reflected, casting one backward glance at the stocky figure gazing out into the night, before she was shoved from the room and returned without ceremony to her prison.

Now what? She looked down at her wrists, still encircled by the silver bracelets. Spiritual essence or no, in essence she still belonged to Akbar Khan.

Zobayeda brought her a bowl of chicken stew and rice. Chickens were luxurious fare during the winter months, so Annabel could only assume this delicacy was in honor of the khan's return. She ate without appetite, then went to bed to lie sleepless throughout the night, wondering about Kit's wound, about what Akbar intended to do with the hostages who must now be of even greater importance to him as bargaining counters. She found to her surprise that she could no longer summon up the least interest in her own destiny. What would happen would happen.

Across the courtyard, Kit sat in the open doorway of the outer room. The night air was chilly, but the vicious snow-laden bite of winter was absent, and the freshness was a welcome change from the frowsty interior, where too many none-too-clean bodies cohabitated with the fleas. His hand throbbed, but he had been lucky not to have lost a finger in that savage slashing. He thought of the daggerlike splinter Annabel had removed with such skill from his hand in a time when the despair of hopelessness had not tightened its jaws.

"I wonder what she said to prevent our being cut down to a man."

Kit looked over his shoulder, not surprised that his friend had been following some part of his train of thought. "Lord knows, Colin. But she and I should have known better. It was a bloody stupid thing to do."

"I don't know how you can bear it," Colin said
frankly, squatting down beside him. "It's difficult
enough for the rest of us, but—" He shrugged expressively. "At least we're all in it together. Hus-
bands have their wives, women their children. Even
in hardship, there's comfort in sharing."

"In knowing!" Kit said with sudden savagery.
"It's not knowing what's happening to her, or
what's going to happen that I cannot endure, Colin.
Sometimes I think I will go mad . . . that I *am* going
mad." He pointed across the courtyard. "I am almost positive that that window, second from the left,
is hers. But I cannot be certain. . . . " His hands
opened in a gesture of futility. "*Why* can we do
nothing?"

Colin made no response. It was the hardest thing
for them all to bear, brought up as they had been in
the absolute conviction that they ruled wherever
they walked. They imbibed the conviction with their
mother's milk, were taught it as they were waited
upon hand and foot, deferred to from toddlerhood
by adult men and women whose only function as
far as the child was concerned was to gratify his
whims and ensure his comfort. In school, superiority was beaten into them, the hierarchy of the priv-
ileged established forever. When one's turn came,
one did unto others what had been done unto one,
confident that one was inculcating through established means the values and standards of the ruling
class. And a British gentleman *never* expected to find
himself helpless, in bondage to the whims of a lesser
being. But short of mass suicide, Akbar Khan's
hostages had no choice except to surrender to reality.

"I'm for bed," Colin said finally. "Why don't you
turn in too? Brooding won't help."

"True enough, but someone in my room snores
most powerfully." Kit did what was expected of him
and banished the moment of weakness. He grinned
up at Colin. "I very much fear that it is Mrs. John-

son, so I daren't mention it. It's a most unladylike sound."

Colin chuckled. "No, best preserve a chivalrous silence on the subject." Then he said soberly, "I wish someone could do something about little Betsy Graham. She has the most dreadful nightmares night after night. Her mother does what she can to keep her quiet, but a man can't sleep, listening to that terror."

"I wonder if they'll ever get over it," Kit said.

"Annabel did."

"Did she? I am not convinced of that, my friend."

Akbar Khan spent the night in contemplation . . . in contemplation of defeat. His battle with the feringhee invader was not over, for all that he had suffered a major reversal, but he needed to formulate new strategies. The hostages were vital to his plans and must be moved farther from Jalalabad, where the enemy was now in control. No, it was too early to cry defeat in that area . . . but in the other matter?

He had lost. Only one question remained: what should he do about it? He could take whatever vengeful action he chose. They were all pawns on his board. But the prospect of simple vengeance held no appeal. Once, in the first flush of anger it had, but now it seemed an empty gesture . . . one conferring neither honor nor satisfaction.

He could simply send Ayesha under escort to Madella, where they could resume the previous pattern of their congress once this war was finished. And if he did not wish to resume in the old way, then she could lead a pleasant enough existence in the zenana. He would not deny her her horses and hawks, or her books. She would have the companionship of other women. His wives were perfectly satisfied with less freedom than he would permit Ayesha.

Or he could . . . But he could not be seen to yield to the feringhee . . . not in this, or in anything.

He paced his presence chamber, stroking his beard, and contemplating a means by which defeat could take on the appearance of victory: a solution which would require quick thinking and ingenuity on the part of Ayesha and her lover if they were to win their freedom, and one that would show no weakness on his own part.

When dawn broke, he thought he had the answer.

Chapter 22

❦❦ **A** yesha! Ayesha, quickly, you must wake up.
They have come for you." Zobayeda's
frightened voice, her hand roughly shaking, brought
Annabel wide awake.

"What time is it?"

"Past dawn," the woman said. "You must dress.
They have come for you."

Annabel sat up, swinging her legs over the side
of the cot. She reached for her tunic and *chalvar*, but
Zobayeda said in the same frightened voice, "No,
you are to wear these."

Annabel stared blankly at the coarse black homespun trousers and tunic. "But those are not mine."

"It is ordered," Zobayeda said.

There could be only one interpretation. The day
of judgment had arrived. For a moment, Annabel
was terror-struck, the peace of a philosophical belief
in Destiny vanquished under the rioting images of
possible fates awaiting her. She put on the clothes,
her skin shrinking with distaste. She had never worn
such garments before and the rough material
scratched. She wondered to whom they belonged.
Such garments of the peasant kind were not to be
found spare when people lived so close to the edge
of subsistence. She shuddered, recoiling at the
thought of the unwashed body they must have
clothed a few short hours ago, even as she realized
how foolish such a fastidious discomfort now was
in the scheme of things.

"You are to be veiled but no chadri," Zobayeda said. "And barefoot. It is ordered."

Veiled, so there would be men at the sentencing, but no chadri so she would have no way of concealing her reactions to whatever humiliation and disgrace awaited her, and barefoot in the manner of the condemned. Only now did she realize that in her heart she had not believed Akbar Khan would exact the full penalty from her. How wrong could one be? And if he would not spare Ayesha, he would not spare Kit.

The veil was black also: the color of the brutalized slave-wives of the hillmen; the color of the disgraced women of the khans. Dressed in these clothes, she noticed almost abstractedly how her entire demeanor seemed to change. Keeping her head bowed, her eyes on the floor, her shoulders drooping was suddenly second nature. She felt drab and despised, and the contempt in the eyes of the guards as she emerged from her prison struck her as only reasonable.

She walked behind them, the entrenched cold of the oozing stone floor striking through her feet, upward through her body.

When the troop of guards burst into the hostages' quarters just after dawn, the first impression of all those awake enough to think was that the massacre averted yesterday was about to take place. Children began to cry at the sight of the armed warriors with their pronged helmets and drawn knives. Women hustled the wailing youngsters aside as if to hide them in the shadows or behind their skirts. Those men who slept in the outer room, as conscious as ever of their defenselessness, gathered themselves together, ranging themselves in front of the women and children.

"What do you want at this hour?" Major Pottinger spoke in his halting Pushtu. "Are we to leave this place?"

"That is for Akbar Khan to decide," one of the

tribesmen replied. "We have come for Ralston, *hu-zoor.*"

Kit stepped forward from an inner room where he had his own bed space. "I am here."

"What do you want with Captain Ralston?" demanded the major. "He is an officer in Her Imperial Majesty's cavalry."

"Not a very impressive status at present, Pottinger," Kit said dryly. "But my thanks for trying." He straightened his tunic, shabby and well-worn now, and did up the button on a threadbare shirt cuff. For some reason, it seemed to matter that he should face his fate in as good an order as could be achieved with such unpromising material. He could not get used to the absence of the sword at his belt, however. It made them all feel naked, both mentally and physically.

"Gentlemen?" He gestured to the ferociously glaring guards. "I am ready."

"Kit . . . ?"

"Thanks, but no, Colin," he said, swiftly forestalling his friend who had stepped forward, his face dark with anger and determination. "Nothing will be achieved by your death, and the sooner I get these savages out of here, the sooner the children will stop crying." He strode to the door, his escort falling in behind him.

As they crossed the courtyard, he looked up at the great bowl of the sky contained within the jagged, ice-tipped peaks of the Hindu Kush. Small clouds scudded across the pellucid blue of an early spring morning. The air held a tang of snow from the mountains, softened with the pasture-scents of the breeze ruffling his hair. It was a beautiful day for a *buzkashi.* Everything seemed etched clear on his senses; he was conscious of every part of his body; of the way he walked, each muscle group moving in that miraculous automatic fashion; of the blood flowing in his veins; of the steady thump of his heart.

They reached a door on the far side of the courtyard. The rank, cold, damp odor of ancient stone imbued with poverty and misery wafted from the doorway, sullying the fresh promise of the morning. He stopped before stepping into the gloom and looked around him, as if imprinting the scene forever on his memory. Did one carry a memory into death? Better not, he thought distantly. Memories would only make the reality of "never again" so much harder to accept.

One of his escort made a threatening move, and he stepped inside before they could touch him. He knew he could not bear with restraint any physical contact . . . not until it was forced upon him, by which time he would be beyond caring.

They entered Akbar Khan's presence chamber while Kit's eyes were still accustoming themselves to the dank dimness after the bright outdoors. There were men lining the walls, turbanned or wearing steel-pronged helmets, knives thrust into studded belts, one or two holding lances or broadswords. They were a fighting force, not horsemen dressed for sport. Akbar Khan was standing on the small raised dais at the far end of the room; the table had been pushed against the wall behind him. The sirdar was dressed in chain mail, a turban on his head, a sword in his hand.

"Good morning, Ralston, *huzoor*," he said in English.

"Good morning, Akbar Khan," Kit heard himself reply as if this were a perfectly ordinary morning.

Akbar Khan gestured to one side below the dais, and Kit's guard ushered him to the designated spot. The sirdar maintained his commanding position over the room and its occupants.

Kit stood very still, wishing he had Annabel's skill at immobility. He did not think anything was expected of him at this point, and he could expect of himself only that he appear calm and unafraid. If only he knew what had happened to Annabel.

The door opened and six more Ghilzai tribesmen entered. Behind them walked Akbar Khan's Aye-

sha. For a moment, Kit did not recognize the drab,
bowed figure. Then he could feel the pulse in his
temple throbbing as he wondered what they could
have done to her to bring her to this attitude of complete subjection. It was only with the greatest difficulty that he maintained his outward calm, sensing
that a violent expression of his outrage would play
right into their hands.

Akbar Khan gave an order in Pushtu, his voice
harsh and resounding. The men with Ayesha suddenly seized her. The room swam before Kit's eyes.
He knew he took a step forward, an oath on his lips,
and then he felt the sirdar's bright blue gaze fixed
upon him. He could not read the message in the
gaze, but it was sufficiently powerful to bring him
to a standstill.

Ayesha was pushed brutally across the room to
stumble to her knees at Kit's feet. He stared down
at her, dumbfounded, as her guards, having disposed of her, moved back against the wall with the
air of men who had performed a duty well.

Akbar Khan began to speak, or rather orate, in
Pushtu. Kit could not understand a word that was
being said. Around him, the Ghilzais' faces grew
grimmer if it were possible. Then suddenly he became aware of a whisper, swift and fluent. Annabel
was speaking to him in urgent English, still on her
knees, her head still bowed, the words rustling from
beneath the black veil.

"He is giving me to you . . . it is an insult, not a
gift. He finds me unworthy and has no further use
for me, so he would cast me to the feringhee, who
deserves no better than the discarded worthless possessions of the Afghan. You are obliged by the laws
of hospitality to accept this gift, and by the laws of
the land to assume responsibility for my existence
. . . to assume Akbar Khan's responsibilities for
something he has discarded. However, by those
same laws, you may use me as you please. I am
nothing."

Kit listened, incredulous. Akbar Khan's words

continued to ring through the room, dripping with contempt and loathing, occasionally taunting, producing rumbles of amused mockery from the audience, relishing the insults. Then he became aware that the whispering rustle at his feet had begun again. Without looking down at her, he strained his ears to catch the vehement instructions.

"You must be angry at the insults, or there will be no satisfaction for them. Say you will reject such a gift . . . that the pride of your race will not permit you to receive something that your host considers worthless. . . . Think like an Afghan!"

Urgency pulsed in the last instruction. *Think like an Afghan.* Dear God Almighty, how did an Afghan think? What code of honor and insults was operating here? A man could not refuse the gift of hospitality, he remembered that from the first occasion, when Akbar Khan had given him Ayesha for the night. He could not have refused that gift without having his throat cut. While he had understood the underlying insult embodied in that gift, it had been offered within the code of compliments—a man shares his most precious possession with a favored guest. Then he realized: for some incomprehensible reason, this exhibition was not for Akbar Khan; it was for the Ghilzai tribesmen. They would believe what they heard. They must see him forced into accepting the insult that would redeem Akbar Khan's pride and legitimize the khan's merciful action in not passing the death sentence. For these men, death was preferable to humiliation, particularly over something as intrinsically expendable as a woman.

Think like an Afghan. Well, he'd always had a talent for the dramatic.

He raised his head, the gray eyes blazing. "You would insult me, Akbar Khan," he said in slow, careful Persian. "You would give me this . . . " He touched the kneeling figure contemptuously with the toe of his boot. "This that you find worthless."

A rustle ran around the room, a murmur of satisfaction, even as the men laid hands upon their weapons. Even for those who did not speak Persian, his meaning was clear.

"You would refuse the gift of hospitality?" Akbar Khan demanded in Persian, swiftly repeating himself in Pushtu. The audience became more watchful, and Kit had the unmistakable impression that they were waiting for the order to fall upon him.

"A gift that is given in insult," Kit snapped, nudging again at the bowed figure. A quiver shivered through her, whether of fear or tension or indignation at the gesture, he could not tell. Never could he have imagined a situation more appalling, more barbaric, more volatile. Akbar Khan might be offering them a way out, but if Kit made a mistake, the sirdar would have no hesitation in abandoning them to the blood-lusting Ghilzais. "You would oblige me to accept in the name of hospitality a woman you have discarded? To assume responsibilities you have cast off?"

"You accept the insult or death, Ralston, *huzoor*," Akbar Khan declared. His hand lifted, tossed something toward him. A sliver of silver arced through the dimness, fell with a metallic tinkle at his feet. It was a key.

Kit stared down at it, for the moment bewildered, then Ayesha at his feet moved an arm and he caught the glimmer of the bracelet at her wrist. It was the key to the bracelets. If he picked it up, he indicated that he had swallowed the insult. He would leave here humiliated in the eyes of these men, a defeated enemy not worth further consideration; and Akbar Khan would emerge from the situation the victor, his own honor intact.

He was really becoming quite adept at thinking like an Afghan, Kit reflected, bending to pick up the key.

A sigh whispered around the encircling men. Kit pocketed the key, glanced down at the kneeling figure, commanded curtly, "Come." Then he spun on his heel and walked to the door, his spine crawling at the expectation of a dagger in his back. But he heard only the soft pad of Ayesha's bare feet as she followed him, her eyes resolutely on the ground.

They walked unescorted, unmolested, through the stone passageway and out into the courtyard. The sun shone. A sparrow hopped across the stones and offered them a beady-eyed, cocky glance before taking off over the wall.

Kit stopped. Annabel stopped behind him. "Did what I think just happened, happen?" he asked in a strangely flat tone, not turning to look at her.

"Yes," she replied. "Do you understand why—"

"I think so," he interrupted. "He could not simply give you back to your own people. It would be an admission of defeat."

"Exactly. Not so much for himself, but for the others who follow him. A khan cannot show weakness."

"Is there anywhere we can go in this place without being observed?" They were still standing apart, Kit in front, the veiled, black-clad Afghan woman the correct number of paces behind.

Annabel thought, remembering when she had been here last, not as a prisoner. "Behind the stables, perhaps," she said tentatively. "To the left of the far outhouse."

"Will we be prevented? I do not think I could endure patiently another confrontation at this point."

"I don't think so. Wound-licking is considered appropriate and permissible after such a beating."

Kit grimaced. In that respect at least the Afghan code was not dissimilar from his own. He wondered why he felt as if he had died and had not yet been reborn. He followed her soft directions as she walked behind him, maintaining the charade for any knowing eyes, and they found themselves at the rear of the low stable building. They had encountered a few curious glances, had been aware that there were those who watched them, but no one attempted to interfere with their progress.

It was cold and shadowy between the wall of the

fortress and the stable wall, the ground hard-ridged mud, the air insalubrious.

Ayesha unfastened the black veil, and Annabel sighed with relief as her mouth and nose were freed from the stale-smelling cloth. "I was so afraid that you would not be able to manage it," she said, leaning against the wall of the stable. "I did not know whether you would understand properly what was going on."

"Ye of little faith," he said sourly. "I have never participated in a more disgusting affair."

"Oh, feringhee," she taunted. "Was it too subtle for you? Or was it too painful to play the Afghan game? Did it hurt your pride so very much? Surely it was better than being the prize in a *buzkashi?*"

Kit closed his eyes on his anger. He knew what it was, why it had erupted between them. The dreadful fear of the last months should have gone, but it was like an amputated limb: one still felt its pain. They had somehow to establish a communication that would permit the newness between them, the knowledge that they now had each other and only each other. And he must make the effort to understand that for Annabel, the final, irrevocable loss of Ayesha could not be accomplished with indifference.

He pulled the still-draped veil from her hair and took her in his arms. "Sweetheart, we mustn't quarrel . . . not now. I can imagine the fear you endured in the last hours simply by remembering my own." He brushed a coppery tendril of hair from her forehead. "But it is over and we must build anew. You belong with us now."

"Do I?" Her voice sounded strangely flat, lacking in her usual confidence. "I do not know what is to happen now. I do not know what I am to do. How can I live in such close quarters with the others? I am not really of them. I do not belong with them or with the Afghan. Everything that has happened since Khoord Kabul has served to accentuate that. And they know I do not belong."

"You could trust me," he said with a quizzical smile. "I will look after you."

Her chin lifted and that mocking gleam appeared in the jade eyes. "You agreed to do so, of course, Ralston, *huzoor*. To take responsibility for my existence according to your own lights, as Akbar Khan has done these last eight years. I belong to you. You have the key." She lifted her hands, turning them so that the bracelets caught a finger of sunlight poking into the shadows.

Abruptly, Kit decided that maybe anger had a purpose. Annabel seemed bent on provoking him, for some reason of her own—a not unusual occurrence, as he well knew—and in the aftermath of the last hour he had little energy to resist provocation. Indeed, on one level, he would welcome the cleansing fire.

He took the key from his pocket, opened her hand, and slapped the little object onto her palm. "The key is yours. The bracelets are yours. You wear them or not as you choose." He closed her fingers hard over the key. "I give you fair warning—I have had as much as I can take of this Afghan mockery, swallowed enough insults in one morning to last a lifetime, so if you want a fight, Miss Spencer, you may have one with the greatest of pleasure."

The gray eyes glared at her as she stood in her rusty black peasant's garb, her hair shockingly bright, her eyes overly large in her pale face. "I ask your pardon," she said. "I don't wish to have a fight."

Kit took a deep breath. "Good. Because I have to say, sweetheart, this really does seem both an inappropriate time and place to choose for one." Catching her chin, he tilted her face and very gently kissed her. Her lack of response alarmed him. "What is it, love?" He smiled, touched her cheek.

"Nothing," she said without expression. "I just do not know what I am to do now."

Since when had Ayesha-Annabel been at a loss for either words or actions? Then Kit realized with a shock that she suddenly seemed to have lost some inner spring, as if she had wound down, her last reserves used up in that desperate battle to bring them both out of the presence chamber alive. Without her interpretation and instruction he would have failed to understand what was required of him, would have made the wrong move, and they would both have been lost.

It was time he took over. She was in his world now, more so than she had been in the cantonment when her presence was something she had chosen, her wholehearted involvement withheld, and it was his turn to bear the brunt of the responsibility for making and implementing the necessary plans that would make sense of their new situation.

"Right," he said briskly, taking her hand. "You may not know what to do, but I do. I have endured enough of your adoptive rituals, my Anna. And I am sick to death of being conducted through them like a bewildered recruit at an induction ceremony. You are now going to participate in some of my ceremonies—one in particular."

Pulling her behind him, he set off at a fast lope, back across the courtyard toward the hostages' billet.

"What do you mean one of my rituals?" Annabel demanded, hanging back. "I do not wish to go in there just yet, Kit."

"How would you describe that barbaric ceremony, if not one of your rituals?" Kit said, jerking her up beside him. "Now you are going to experience one tradition amongst the people of your birth, Miss Spencer."

"Kit, thank God, man, we never expected to see you again." Colin, with the brigadier and two others, came running out of the building as Kit and his seemingly reluctant, black-clad companion approached. "Who the hell—" Then Colin gaped. "Annabel?"

"Yes," Kit said shortly. "And don't ask me to describe what happened, Colin, because I don't think I could do so without committing murder. Where's the padre?"

"I wish you would talk in plain English," Annabel declared, digging her bare heels into the cobbles, her voice sounding considerably stronger than before. "All this half-witted muttering about rituals."

"Weddings," Kit said, turning to face her. "That's what we do where I come from, miss, when a man agrees to take responsibility for the welfare of a woman. And that's what we are going to have now."

"A wedding?" exclaimed Lady Sale, appearing in the doorway. "Goodness gracious, Kit, whatever would your poor mother say?"

"I rather imagine she would view the prospect with some relief, ma'am." Kit's voice was as dry as the desert wind.

Lady Sale looked uncertain. "I fail to imagine how you could find this a laughing matter, Captain Mackenzie," she said in stern rebuke.

"I do beg your pardon, ma'am." Colin was doubled over with laughter. "But you must admit the opportunities for amusement are few and far between these days."

Lady Sale's lips twitched. "Perhaps so . . . perhaps so. But if there is to be a wedding, then it must be done properly. There's to be no hole-in-the-corner affair under my jurisdiction. What's the poor gal to be married in, for heaven's sake?"

"What does it matter what she wears?" Kit exploded, forgetting the courtesies for once in the face of this absurdity after everything that had gone before.

Lady Sale drew herself up to her most dignified amplitude. "Christopher, if you are intending to make an honest woman of Miss Spencer, then I can only applaud your belated sense of responsibility. But you will not deprive the members of this group of the opportunity for a celebration by behaving in a rash and haphazard fashion."

Annabel slipped slowly to the cobbles, utterly de-

feated. Here she was, having narrowly escaped the
stoning pit, dressed in the garb of the meanest hill-
woman, insignia of a condemned adulteress, released from the zenana yet still Akbar Khan's
prisoner, thrown without preparation or resources
amongst a close-knit group of people with whom
she wanted to identify but couldn't, and they were
arguing wedding clothes as if it were the most important subject under the sun.

"Damnation!" Kit dropped to his knees beside
her. "Sweetheart, how could I have been so
thoughtless? Are you ill?"

Lady Sale, who had not flinched at his language,
evidence of the erosion that captivity had had upon
the conventions, pushed him aside. "The poor girl's
quite exhausted, I shouldn't wonder. I don't know
how we would have managed without her these last
months . . . and it must have been so lonely for
her."

"I am quite all right, Lady Sale," Annabel said.
"Just a little bemused." She held out a hand imperatively to Kit, who took it and pulled her upright.
"I have to take off these clothes," she said abruptly.
"My skin's crawling. I wonder if I went back to the
zenana, Zobayeda would find me my own garments."

"Don't talk nonsense. You cannot go back in
there," Kit said forcefully. "You do not belong there
anymore, Annabel. Was that not made sufficiently
clear to you?"

She bit her lip. It was true. She would enter an
Afghan zenana as an interloper now. There was no
possibility of keeping a foot in the old life; Akbar
Khan had ensured that. Why, in her confusion, was
she not grateful? She had prayed for release, begged
Destiny and the gods for just the chance to be united
with Kit. So why did she simply wish to weep and
flee to the seclusion of her prison cell? How could
she live with these people with whom she had nothing in common, in these cramped conditions with
no privacy, when she was accustomed to the soli-

tude and peace of her own company? Then she remembered her loneliness as she had watched them playing with the children; as she had heard them conducting Sunday service; whenever she had left them after her daily visits, entertaining each other, conversing, disputing maybe, but a sharing community. Wasn't this what she wanted?

She turned away with a whispered apology and went to sit in the sun a short distance from the doorway. Kit, stricken, took a step toward her, but there was something forbidding . . . or did he mean forbidden . . . about her posture. He knew with absolute certainty that he could not intrude upon her privacy.

"Come, Kit, we will discuss the wedding with the padre," Lady Sale said, briskly encouraging. "There must be something we can do to make a special occasion of this. We have little enough, to be sure, but if we all contribute something . . . " Chattering in this bracing fashion, she went inside.

Kit followed her because for the moment he could think of nothing else to do. Colin and the brigadier stood for a minute, looking at the still, black-clad figure who seemed so out of place in their little enclave, then they too left her and went inside.

"Ayesha?"

At the sound of her name, Ayesha came out of her reverie. "Why, Zobayeda, what are you doing here?"

The enwrapped servant, her eyes darting fearfully around as if she expected some demon in feringhee form to jump out at her, put a bundle on the ground beside Ayesha. "Your clothes . . . but I'm to take back the ones you're wearing. They belong to the goatherd's mother."

That answered that question. "Just a minute." Picking up the bundle, Annabel went to the outhouse that served the hostages. She stripped off the loathsome garments of disgrace and dressed in her own worn but comfortable linen *chalvar* and tunic, slipped her shoes upon her feet. The effect was instantaneous. She felt herself again. Whoever herself was. Suddenly the question seemed to embody excitement, the prospect of discovering the answer quite intoxicating. She stepped out into the April sunshine, handing the waiting Zobayeda the hill-woman's clothing.

But as she walked into the dim outer room of the hostages' quarters, that flash of confidence faded. The people grouped in the cramped space were deep in a discussion and form of communication that was alien to her. Men and women huddled together in consultation over common cause, the ability to understand each other as essential as the air they breathed. Conversation ceased at her appearance, in a manner that indicated she had been the subject of discussion. "I do beg your pardon, I didn't mean to intrude," she said, turning back to the door.

"Miss Spencer . . . ?" Brigadier Shelton spoke hesitantly. "There's no need for you to leave."

Annabel gestured in vague, what she hoped was polite, dismissal and took her confusion toward the door.

"Annabel." It was Colin's voice, quietly arresting. When she continued with her retreat, he repeated her name imperatively. "*Annabel.*"

Kit said nothing, simply kept his seat on the broad stone windowsill. Annabel must come into this group of her own accord, believing that she was welcomed. His assurances would prove nothing.

"Come and sit down, dear." Mrs. Anderson spoke up comfortably, patting the bench beside her. "We were just talking about your wedding. . . . Such excitement!" She rubbed her hands together and beamed. "All the little girls want to be bridesmaids."

Annabel turned and smiled effortfully. "You are very kind, but I don't see—"

"Oh, do come and sit down, sweetheart." Kit picked his moment, permitting just the hint of impatience in his voice. "Quite apart from anything else, we need your views on what Akbar Khan intends, after his defeat at Jalalabad.''

''Yes, indeed, Miss Spencer,'' agreed the brigadier. ''Your opinion would be most valuable.''

This was Ayesha's territory, an area in which she was accustomed to contributing. Maybe it could help to bridge the gap. ''I do not think he will permit you . . . us . . . to stay so close to Jalalabad,'' she said, taking a step into the room but still not accepting a seat. ''He will need to keep his bargaining counter in case of reversals. I would imagine you . . . we . . . will be moved farther into the mountains.''

''Soon?'' Major Pottinger asked.

She nodded. ''Very soon.'' She glanced at Kit. ''They were armed and ready to move this morning, were they not, Kit?''

''I judged so,'' he agreed somberly. ''How did you get your clothes back?''

''Zobayeda brought them,'' she answered. ''Apparently the goatherd's mother wanted her own returned. I can't imagine why.''

Kit stood up suddenly, as if he had come to a decision. ''Excuse us, ladies and gentlemen, but Annabel and I have a few matters to discuss.'' He got up and strode across the room toward where she stood just inside the doorway. His voice was low but assured. ''Come, responsibility of mine. Let us walk in the sunshine.''

She allowed him to ease her out into the courtyard. ''What do we have to discuss?''

His eyes narrowed. ''A very great deal, it seems to me. Now you have your clothes back, I find it easier to grasp what has happened. We are free, Annabel.''

''But not clear,'' she replied.

''Oh, you are such a Jonah!'' Kit exclaimed, exasperated. ''I had intended we should be married in St. George's, Hanover Square, with your family—once we had found them—and mine, and an escort from the Seventh Light and—''

''I may be a Jonah, but you are completely un-

realistic," she interrupted. "What a cloud-cuckoo-
land you've invented. Apart from anything else, I
haven't decided whether I wish to be married yet.
In essence I may belong with you, but I am not of
your kind. I do not know what I am yet."

Kit's expression darkened. "My sweet, if you
think you have the slightest choice in the matter
now, then you must rethink your position rather
rapidly. Marriage is the only option, now that your
place for better or worse is with us. You have to
abide by our rules."

She kicked idly at a loose stone on the ground. "I
don't think there's much point discussing it at the
moment. See who's coming."

Kit followed the direction of her eyes. Coming
across the courtyard toward them was Mohammed
Shah Khan, Akbar Khan's lieutenant. He was accompanied by the usual armed escort.

Annabel raised her hands to her forehead automatically at his approach. Then she felt Kit's hands,
warmly insistent, taking her arms and putting them
at her sides. "You don't do that anymore," he said
quietly. "Look him in the face."

A quiver rippled her slender frame, but she raised
her eyes and looked boldly at the Afghan, asking in
Pushtu, "Do you bring news, Mohammed Shah
Khan?"

"The prisoners are to leave here. You have an
hour in which to prepare yourselves," he said without expression.

"Where are we to be taken?"

"That is not for you to know."

She inclined her head and turned with Kit back to
their quarters. "A wedding, Ralston, *huzoor*? When
and where?"

He gritted his teeth, reminding himself that for
Annabel the irrevocable loss of Ayesha could not be
a matter of indifference.

Chapter 23

The cavalcade trekked through the spring sunshine, their worldly goods for many of them no more than could be wrapped in a towel. Annabel was once again riding Charlie, the children and most of the other women in camel-panniers or on ponies. Their escort was fierce and silent, and the shadow of an unknown destination destroyed the harmony the group had achieved in their community at Budiabad.

At Tezeen, the hideous remnants of the January slaughter in the passes lay in grim reminder. The war was far from over, their fate as uncertain as it had ever been. Victory at Jalalabad brought them no closer to deliverance. At Tezeen they also left General Elphinstone, who was now too close to death to continue. Colin and Major Pottinger were ordered to remain with the general, a loss to the company that none felt more keenly than Kit.

In the mountain village of Zandeh, the party halted. Annabel looked around at the squalid huddle of dirt-walled huts, their windows barred against brigands, the customary watchtower clinging to the mountainside. It was a village of the kind she had often stayed in on her travels with Akbar Khan, but she rather suspected that her fellow travelers were going to be in for yet another shock.

"We are to stay here?" Millie Drayton's dismal question spoke for them all. "But it's worse than the fortress."

"It's the way they live, feringhee," Annabel muttered under her breath. Somehow, she didn't have the patience to listen to the complaints of discomfort. The whole party made them to a greater or lesser degree, some serious, some with a redeeming note of humor, but only she seemed aware that what they grumbled at was the immutable lot of the majority of the Afghan people, struggling to scratch a bare subsistence in the short span allotted them between birth and death. There were times when the moans and incredulous criticisms irritated her beyond bearing.

Kit heard the undertone and sighed, wondering for the thousandth time why the joy and relief they should have felt were so conspicuously absent, wondering what had happened to the passion and commitment of that night in Ayesha's prison cell. Lovemaking was denied them in present circumstances—there was neither privacy nor opportunity—but they were together in this adversity and surely some closeness could come from that. But Annabel was distant and preoccupied. She treated her fellow prisoners for the most part with a degree of absentminded contempt that was all too reminiscent of Ayesha. And it was driving Kit to the edge of distraction, as much as anything because she seemed to treat him in the same way, as if he were an irrelevance to whatever preoccupied her. Had he been mistaken? If they emerged from this captivity, was it going to be possible for Annabel Spencer to return to the life she would have had but for a violent abduction? Was it even realistic for him to expect her to? And if it wasn't, then what was realistic for either of them?

She had dismounted and was engaged in discussion with their escort. He watched her, noticing how, while she no longer kept her eyes lowered when she spoke to them, she still behaved with a hint of deference. It angered him, as much as anything by the comparison with her attitude to her own people.

"Six of the villagers have been instructed to give up their houses for us," she said to Brigadier Shelton. "It will cause them and their families considerable hardship, so I suggest you accept the shelter with appropriate gratitude."

"How long are we to be here?"

She shrugged. "They will not say. I expect they do not know. It depends on how matters are going with Akbar Khan. The villagers have also been instructed to feed us, something I don't think they are too happy about it, since it's the product of the sweat of their brows that's to go into feringhee bellies, and they have little enough for themselves. I suggest you tell your people to behave with circumspection while they're here."

Kit felt the last strand of patience and understanding tolerance snap as he saw the brigadier's palpable annoyance at being spoken to in such fashion. He swung off his horse. "I apologize for Annabel, sir," he said stiffly. "Standards of courtesy in a zenana obviously fall somewhat short of what we are accustomed to."

The brigadier murmured some disclaimer as Annabel flushed to the roots of her copper hair with anger and embarrassment. "How dare you apologize for me?" she demanded.

"It's time," he said grimly. "Past time. Let's get this over with, shall we?" Taking her by the elbow, he hustled her down the narrow dirt track running through the center of the village toward a group of stunted, wind-deformed trees at the edge of the huddlement. The escort cast them a look of indifference. There was nowhere for two unarmed pedestrians to go up here in the mountains.

The hostages looked around the circle of sullen, dull-eyed men of Zandeh, who were staring with hostile incomprehension at their unwelcome infidel visitors. There were no women in sight, although they were all conscious of unseen eyes upon them. It was not an audience to dispel unease.

Well out of earshot amongst the deformed trees, Kit and Annabel faced each other.

"I have tried to be understanding," he said. "But I seem to have run out of patience. What do you want, Anna?"

"Want?" She turned from him with a gesture of dismissal. "What has want to do with anything?"

"Don't turn away from me, you arrogant green-eyed lynx!"

She swung around to face him again. "I did not mean to offend, Ralston, *huzoor.*"

"Oh, no," he said softly. "Never again will you call me that, and never again will you throw 'feringhee' at me. Now, what do you want of me?"

"Of you? Why should I want anything of you? Why should I want anything of anyone?"

"Because I love you, you provoking woman!" He took her by the shoulders and shook her as he had so often wanted to do. "And when people love each other, they want and expect things of each other, and they want and expect to give things to each other. Do you understand what I am saying?"

"It's not easy to understand anything when my head feels as if it's about to leave my shoulders," she cried. "Please stop."

"Oh, God!" He pulled her against him with a violence akin to the shaking. "I knew one day you were going to drive me to that." He pushed her hair away from her forehead, ran his flat palm over her face, molding her features against his hand in a gesture of rough need, as if he had to reacquaint himself in haste and desperation with a temporarily lost intimate. "Anna . . . my darling Anna, you must help me. Tell me what I can do to make things right between us."

She heard his desperate unhappiness, and slowly the recognition of how selfish she had been filtered through her self-absorption. Locked in her own little world of confusion, she had ignored Kit's confusion. It had seemed to her that he had no right to feel confused, since he was where he had always been, with the people who formed his customary framework. She was the one wrenched from the familiar, forced to make a place for herself with people diametrically opposed to those who had formed her customary framework. And in some perverse fashion, it seemed to her that she had not asked for any of this to happen, in which case Kit was to blame for her bewilderment. She appeared to have lost her lofty belief in Destiny, and was laying the blame for her present distress squarely at the door of the most convenient target . . . and the one most undeserving of her unkindness. So she had pushed him away and treated her fellow travelers with a contemptuous indifference that ignored their justified fears and miseries and hurt Kit abominably.

"I think perhaps you'd better shake me again," she said with a rueful smile. "I don't know how you've put up with me . . . or why. I've been horrid."

He drew back and regarded her quizzically. "Now what game are you playing?"

"Oh, unjust!" she cried. "I apologize and you accuse me of game-playing."

"Well, you must admit it's a trifle sudden," he said, continuing to scrutinize her expression. "If a little judicious violence can achieve such an about face, what would a little equally judicious loving achieve, I ask myself?"

"Perhaps you should try it and see," she said softly, putting her arms around his neck, standing on tiptoe as she brought her mouth to his.

He held her for a moment, then said as softly as she, "I never refuse a challenge, responsibility of mine. If we have an audience, to hell with it!"

She laughed, a low sensual chuckle of excitement, and her eyes glimmered their imp of Satan smile as she went down to the grass under his peremptory hand.

"The grass is damp," she murmured in mock complaint as he stripped off her trousers and her

bare backside and thighs made contact with the
ground.

"Easily remedied," Kit returned, kicking free of
his britches and coming down beside her. Slipping
his hands beneath her, he rolled her on top of him.
"There, better now?"

"Much." Her tongue touched her lips as she knelt
astride him, running her hands up and under his
tunic, whispering wickedly, "Supposing someone
comes looking for us?"

"For God's sake stop dawdling, then, you impossible creature!" he ordered, then drew in his breath
with sharp pleasure as she shifted backward, raising
her hips to take the hard impaling shaft deep within
herself.

"I hear and obey," she murmured, that same
impish smile in her eyes. "Shall we see how fast we
can be?"

He closed his eyes and gave himself up to the
swift, febrile, spiralling glory, his hands gripping her
buttocks as she moved with ever increasing speed,
bringing them both to a climax that sent delighted
laughter dancing in the air.

"Oh, my Anna," he said on a sigh of bone-deep
contentment. "How I've missed you. What a miracle worker you are."

"Not just a horrid, selfish, bad-tempered, un-
grateful female?"

"Well, that too," he teased, lifting her off him.
"But not all the time, fortunately. Hurry and get
dressed. We've taken enough chances for one day."

He pulled on his own clothes and then stood
watching her for a minute as she straightened her
tunic, tucked a recalcitrant wisp of hair into the
heavy braid. "Annabel?"

"Yes?" She glanced up, then frowned. "You look
very stern. What is it?"

"I am about to issue an ultimatum," he said.

"Is that wise?" She was standing very still again,
the jade eyes calm pools, hiding whatever she might
be thinking.

"I don't know whether it is or not. But I do know that there will be no peace for me otherwise."

"So?"

"A wedding," he said. "Now."

"And if I say not?"

He sighed and rubbed his eyes wearily. "Then I will know that the love I have for you is not reciprocated. I cannot live with you with less, Annabel. But if that is the case, then I will promise to do all I can to help you establish yourself when . . . if . . . we get out of this hole."

"You will not renege on your responsibilities, in other words," she said, a smile quirking her lips. "In the manner of all good English gentlemen." She turned the bracelets that she still wore on her wrists. "Take them off for me."

"Give me the key."

She took it from the pocket of her *chalvar*. "Here." She held out her wrists and he unlocked the clasps, sliding the bracelets off.

"Is that your answer?"

"In a manner of speaking."

"What a complicated creature you are. Let us go and find the padre."

Lady Sale regarded them with shrewd eyes when they rejoined the other members of the party, who were dismally surveying their accommodations. "I trust you have come to an agreement."

"You could say that, ma'am . . . Annabel, where are you going?"

"To talk to the *aksakai*," she said. "I may be able to smooth matters a little."

"The brigadier has already talked to him," her ladyship said, discreetly averting her gaze as Kit lunged for Annabel in the manner of a huntsman laying hands on escaping prey.

"Yes, but he may not have understood fully," she said. "Kit, I will be back in a minute."

"Lady Sale, do you know where I may find the padre?" Kit asked, maintaining his hold. "There are some words I want spoken without delay."

"Well, I do think it's about time," said her ladyship, having no difficulty understanding what the
captain intended. "But I do wish we could have
made a little ceremony of it. I feel I owe it to poor
dear Letty."

"I think my mother would understand the circumstances," Kit reassured her soothingly. Her ladyship pursed her lips but did not look displeased
as she hurried off to set matters in motion.

"Annabel, if you keep trying to wriggle away, we
are going to have a falling out." Kit tightened his
grip on her wrist as she attempted a second plunging bid for freedom.

"Another one?" She wiped her brow with an exaggerated gesture. "Heaven forbid." But her eyes
smiled and there was much more than mischief in
the smile. "I'm not running away, love. Where do
you think I would go, even if I wanted to?"

"And you don't want to?"

"Have I not said so?"

"In a manner of speaking," he tossed back at her,
but released his grip on her hand. "I am afraid
something will happen to prevent this. I can't help
it, Anna."

"Nothing will prevent it," she reassured him.
"What happens afterward is more uncertain."

"I'll worry about that afterward. I am going to get
this organized. Just make sure that when I need you,
I can find you."

"Yes, Ralston, *huzoor*," she teased. "Your bride
will be waiting for you. Unfortunately, I don't think
I can find a veil."

"That," Kit said bluntly, "is a joke in very poor
taste."

Annabel laughed and swung off down the track.
If a wedding would make Kit happy, what right had
she to deprive him simply because *she* didn't need
a wedding to underscore love? In the scheme of
things, it could make little difference. It was just a
convention that mattered to Kit. But she knew Destiny had not finished with them yet. They might

have the freedom to be together, but they were not clear. Something more than the simple fact of captivity was still outstanding, although she couldn't put it into words yet.

She looked up at a great snow peak dwarfing the calm, indifferent mountain to which their village clung. A small ivory butterfly with gray wing markings danced against a clump of spring primulas. The delicate, tranquil evening light bathed the village, transmuting the ugliness and squalor, banishing the miseries of cruelty and poverty. It was a fine evening for a wedding.

She picked a handful of white daisies, threading them into a coronet, remembering her girlhood when she had done this at the summer house in the mountains above Peshawar. Then she turned and made her way back to the village.

There was considerable commotion, but it was not of the distressed variety. Lady Sale was vigorously giving orders, mostly to Kit who appeared not to be taking any notice. The padre was offering soothing murmurs. The rest of the community was expressing varying degrees of excitement.

"But where is the bride?" Brigadier Shelton was heard to ask above the hubbub.

"Here." Annabel walked toward them, the crown of daisies wreathed into the bright burnished copper of her hair, released from its braid to cascade down her back.

Wordlessly, Kit held out his hand to her and she stepped beside him, smiling.

A curious hush fell abruptly over the group. The villagers came out of their huts to stare in fearful incomprehension at the strange antics of the infidels. The setting sun caught alight the dominating snow peak, spilling fire down the mountainside, setting the village awash with a gentle reflecting glow.

The padre spoke clearly in the mountain stillness, the words redolent of promise and hope in a shared future. The celebrants made their responses with the same clarity, and if Annabel cast a swift invocation to Destiny, it was between themselves.

That night, Christopher Ralston lay down decorously and legally beside his wife in a crowded, vermin-infested mud hut. Annabel, blessed with the ability to ignore such discomforts, fell asleep almost immediately, and Kit lay staring into the darkness. St. George's, Hanover Square! The absurd comparison brought a hastily suppressed choke of laughter to his lips. Slipping an arm beneath the peacefully sleeping figure at his side, he rolled her into his embrace beneath the threadbare scrap of blanket they shared, and fell asleep, counting flea bites and his blessings.

Two weeks later, Annabel came into the hut that served as a general common room. "It seems we are to be moved again," she said matter-of-factly. "The guards have received a message from Akbar Khan. Apparently, he is gaining the ascendancy in Kabul and we're to be taken closer to the city while he waits to see what the British generals at Jalalabad and Kandahar intend."

"Anything has to be better than this place," Mrs. Armstrong declared for them all. "When are we to move?"

"Within the hour," Annabel said. "If we can be packed up by then." The pleasantry was received with wryly appreciative smiles.

"Shir Muhammed was talking about the fortress of Abdul Rahim," she said. "It is about three miles outside Kabul, and if it is to be our destination, I can think of many worse places."

"Clean?" demanded Lady Sale.

"And commodious," replied Annabel with a twinkle. "With access to the river and pleasant gardens. I do not think Akbar Khan wishes you to be uncomfortable if he can avoid it." She realized her slip too late to correct it unobtrusively so let it lie. You . . . us . . . me . . . it was still hard sometimes, and Kit seemed to understand. He was smiling at her in the special way, indicative of secret pleasure that he had developed since the wedding, as if he had pulled off a coup of some magnitude. It made her want to pat his head and kiss his eyelids as if he were a little boy who had won a prize.

They set off again, thankful to be leaving Zandeh behind and hopeful that their new quarters would be an improvement. Strangely, they no longer thought of their captivity as temporary, the prospect of freedom the be-all and end-all of their existence. Their goals were simply the day-to-day ones of adequate and palatable food, the struggle against dirt and disease, the endless battle to maintain some standards of courtesy and conduct, setting an example to the children, some of whom were beginning to run wild.

Much to Annabel's amusement, Kit had taken one particularly obnoxious little boy under his wing. The child's mother was ill, his father dead at Khoord Kabul, and sturdy little Edmund Marten had managed to alienate weary adults and fractious children alike. The more friendless he became, the more unpleasant he became.

Finding him in the act of tormenting a fragile child with a particularly thorny piece of bramble, Kit had cuffed him soundly and carted him off, screaming ferociously, to the small area he and Annabel called home.

"Someone has to take on the miserable little tyke," he said, sounding somewhat apologetic, when Annabel had raised an inquiring eyebrow. "It doesn't do any good to treat him like a pariah."

"No," she agreed serenely, regarding the child who was kicking and spitting with what could only be called ingratitude against the hand that held him fast by the collar. "What do you suggest?"

Kit looked at her and his lips twitched. "I have this horrible feeling that I might have turned out just like him, in similar circumstances."

"Oh, no, surely not," she said in exaggerated disbelief. "You must have been angelic, with all those golden curls."

Kit looked rueful. "That was the trouble. I was spoiled rotten, and I dread to think what would have happened if the attention had been withdrawn as it was for this brat. Apart from anything else, I think he's terrified. Stop bawling, Edmund, I can't hear myself think."

To their amazement, Edmund's bellowing ceased. He sniffed and wiped his nose with the back of his hand. Since handkerchiefs were a long-forgotten commodity, no one made any objection. "You hit me," he accused. "I'm going to tell my mother when she's better."

Kit smiled. "Yes, so you shall. But you asked for it. Why don't you come with me now and we'll see if we can catch a fish in the stream?"

"I'll come too," Annabel said.

"Ladies don't fish," Edmund stated.

"That's how much you know, Master Edmund," Annabel retorted.

"Ladies don't wear trousers, either," he said.

Annabel laughed. "Now there you may have a point. But who's talking about ladies?"

From that afternoon, they formed an unusual threesome. Edmund ate with them, slept in their corner, and followed Kit around like some small snub-nosed puppy. When he became disagreeable, Kit brushed him aside as if he were an irritating fly, and gradually the child became cheerful and confiding. Annabel was both intrigued and moved by this new side of Kit. He'd told her how children had always bored him, how the prospect of setting up his own nursery had filled him with gloomy trepidation, although he'd assumed at some point he'd have to fulfill the obligations of the son and heir. This Kit, she rather thought, would reveal some surprising talents in the realm of fatherhood . . . if such a realm lay in his destiny.

Now, as they rode away from Zandeh, Edmund was riding with Kit, chattering with the single-minded egoism of an eight-year-old. Annabel listened with half an ear. She had the conviction that circumstances were going to change, but whether for the better or not she couldn't sense. Some resolution of the conflict had to be in the offing. If Akbar Khan was truly gaining ground, then their imprisonment would probably be of short duration. If he was losing ground, then he would hold on to them to the bitter end. But bringing them to Kabul seemed to indicate the former situation. Maybe they would leave Afghanistan alive after all. And then what would she do? Mrs. Christopher Ralston at the vicarage garden party? Paying morning calls in her barouche? Attending soirees? Where did she belong? Until she discovered that, the sense of something still outstanding would not be laid to rest.

"Deep and dismal thoughts?" Kit's voice, light yet with a note of anxiety broke into her musings.

"Not in the least," she denied.

"Liar," he said.

"Why's Annabel lying?" Edmund piped up with sudden interest.

"I am not lying," she said firmly. "I was just wondering what it will be like in the new place."

"Liar," Kit mouthed.

She didn't bother to defend herself this time. Strictly speaking, she had been thinking of a new life in a new place.

The sound of gunfire, the first they had heard since leaving the retreat at Khoord Kabul, reached the weary cortege as they came within sight of Kabul. Akbar Khan's forces were firing at the Balla Hissar where Shah Soojah's son, as his successor, was struggling to maintain a losing position.

"It's hard to believe that we've come full circle since January," Kit commented. "I never expected to see those walls again."

So much death lay between the journey out and this return, Annabel thought. Perhaps they were destined to wander this land endlessly. But she only thought that when she was weary in spirit.

The fort of Abdul Rahim was as she had promised. The zenana was given over to the prisoners,
with its pretty private garden and series of comfortable, well-appointed chambers. They were allowed
free access to the river, flowing behind the fortress,
and after the exigencies of Budiabad and Zandeh,
they seemed to be in paradise. Edmund's mother
began to recover her strength and the Ralstons found
the child to be a less frequent third party, although
Kit kept a vigilant eye on the boy and was quick to
express his displeasure whenever Edmund showed
a not unnatural inclination to take advantage of his
mother's convalescent frailty.

On a hot August morning, Akbar Khan came to
Abdul Rahim's fort. Annabel was in the garden,
teaching elementary Persian to a group of the older
children, when Mohammed Shah Khan summoned
her to the khan's presence chamber.

Her first thought was one of panic. What could he
want with her? The manner in which he had discarded her surely prohibited any further congress
between them. And then came the blinding illumi-
nation. It was this that remained outstanding: the
sore, like a cut that would not heal, that had rubbed
raw against any peace she might have found. Only
Akbar Khan could close the wound . . . could set
her both free and clear.

How should she go to him? As Ayesha or as Annabel? It was Ayesha he had discarded, but he had
never acknowledged Annabel. She felt Kit's eyes on
her. He stood behind Akbar Khan's lieutenant, saying nothing, but his silence was more eloquent than
any speech. She was married to him . . . Akbar Khan
was nothing to her now . . . or was he?

"You will give me a few minutes to prepare myself," she said to Mohammed Shah Khan, rising
from the stone bench and hurrying inside.

Kit followed her into the cool, shuttered seclusion
of the zenana. "Annabel, you are not obliged to obey
that summons."

"You know that I am." She had reached the room

they shared with two other families. "We are still his prisoners."

"But he no longer has any claims upon you," Kit said. He stood by the door, holding himself away from her, trying to keep from his face and voice his desperate longing that she would refuse to obey the call. "If he wishes to discuss the affairs of the hostages, then he should do so with Shelton."

She turned to face him. "Kit, I must go to him." She spoke with difficulty, trying to say what she had to without its sounding threatening. "I do not think he has any further claims upon me, but I feel there is unfinished business between us. I must hear what he has to say."

"Very well. If you must, you must." His voice sounded flat. "But you are my wife, and I claim the right to come with you."

A deep frown drew her eyebrows together. "That is absurd. Akbar Khan will not hurt me. What are you afraid of?"

How could he tell her, when he didn't really know how to say it to himself? He still wasn't sure of her. He wasn't confident that the chains that bound her to him were indissoluble. They hadn't had sufficient time to discover, no time for private explorations and the intimate negotiations out of which grew shared and lasting goals and commitment. They didn't know, for God's sake, whether shared and lasting goals and commitment was even a realistic aim. And the chains that bound them had been forged in such a passionate inferno. Supposing the metal had cooled and weakened in the air of everyday?

He turned back to the door. "You must do whatever you wish, Annabel."

"Yes, I think I must," she said quietly. "May I borrow your cravat?"

At that he swung around on her, his eyes as coldly piercing as the winter wind. "No, you may not! My wife will not go veiled before a tribal chieftain!"

She bit her lip. "Kit, I wish simply to observe the courtesies. This is Akbar Khan's land and his customs rule. I do not consider I have the right to offend against those customs. If the feringhee had accepted that in the first place, matters would be very different now.''

''You go to Akbar Khan if you must, Annabel, but you go as a feringhee . . . as my wife . . . with your eyes raised and your head bare. You may be as polite as you please, but so help me you will stand up and be counted as one of us. If you do not, then there is nothing for you and me, and never can be.'' The words sickened him, yet he knew they were true. He saw her face whiten at the ultimatum, shock springing into the deep green eyes. Without another word, he left her, the door swinging forlornly behind him.

Annabel stood still for a long moment. If Akbar Khan still had a hold upon her soul, then it was time to find out . . . time to break it. The hold he had was based on the molding of the child growing to womanhood. There had been dependency and fear, and liking, also—a most powerful combination. But Kit was right. She must now stand up and be counted, face down the person created by that combination and allow Annabel to be herself . . . allow the essence to shine free and clear.

She brushed her hair and walked back to the garden, where the lieutenant was waiting for her. ''I am ready.''

Kit stood in the shade of a juniper tree and watched her walk out of the garden, moving with that fluid grace he had loved from the first moment, her hair glowing unfettered in the sunlight, her back straight, her head up. Would he win?

The lieutenant pushed open the door to the presence chamber, a comfortable room of silken carpets and tapestried walls and upholstered divans. Akbar Khan was sitting on a divan beneath the open window. The bright blue eyes missed none of the significance as she walked slowly across to him, her bare head high.

''*Mandeh nabashi*, Akbar Khan.''

"Salaamat bashi, Ayesha."

"You look unwell," she said softly.

"I am weary," he replied. "But what of you? Are you managing to tread the wire, to belong in essence yet not to be of them?"

"I am of them," she said.

"Ah." He stroked his beard. "You have found happiness with Ralston, *huzoor?"*

"In as far as it is possible to find happiness in such uncertainty," she said truthfully, taking a seat on the ottoman at his feet as if it were the most natural thing in the world, as indeed it was.

"The British are intending to march in strength on Kabul from Kandahar and Jalalabad," he said. "This will be over soon. We have expelled Shah Soojah's son from Kabul and the British puppets are no longer enthroned. I imagine there will be negotiations at Kabul . . . negotiations which will eventually lead to the departure of the British from this land." A smile quirked his mouth. "I am certain they will wish to exact some retribution before conceding."

"What is to happen to us?"

He shrugged. "I have no interest in harming any of them. Whether they will be rescued or surrendered remains to be seen."

"You say 'they,' " she said hesitantly. "What of me?"

"Ah, Ayesha, it is simply a case of old habits dying hard," he said. "You do not belong with me. But I will tell you this." Reaching down, he took her chin, turning her face toward him. "You will never truly belong to the feringhee, either."

"So I must find my own place."

He nodded. " 'Some little talk awhile of *me* and *thee'*—"

" 'And then no more of *thee* and *me,'* " she finished, rising gracefully. "Is this farewell?"

"Yes, Ayesha. Remember the words of Khayyám. They will help you to find your own place."

She left him, a hard, sad knot in her throat, yet she knew that she was now free and clear, the past within her, intrinsic to who she was, yet in no way binding her.

Instead of returning to the zenana, she went down to the river. It flowed over large stones gleaming whitely through the clear water. Golden buttercups glimmered in the thick moss on the sedge-lined bank. There was no one around, but she didn't think she would care if there were. She unfastened her slippers and slipped out of her *chalvar* and tunic, then twisted her hair into a rough and heavy knot on top of her head before wading into the river.

She had been expecting the cold. These waters flowed from the mountains, and not even the summer sun could do more than take the ice off the surface. Nevertheless, she yelped, and Kit, who had followed her at a discreet distance, chuckled involuntarily, despite the anxiety that had kept him in the shadows outside the presence chamber and that had driven him in her footsteps, afraid to confront her truth, yet knowing he must.

He stood enjoying the sight as she waded thigh-deep in the water, holding her hands outstretched, summoning up the courage to take the plunge. Then she dived forward, a bare white arm cleaving the water cleanly, at the height of its arc catching the sunlight.

It was how he had first seen her. He stepped over to the pile of clothes on the bank, his back to the water.

The freezing clasp around his neck took him by surprise for all that he had been waiting for some reaction. "Do not move, feringhee," she said in that fierce voice.

With a swift movement, he swung his arms behind him and clamped her wet, naked, ice-cold body against his back. "This time you do not have a stiletto." He chuckled, then shivered. "But I think you could probably freeze me to death! Are you mad, Annabel?" He released his grip and turned to face her.

"I just felt like it," she said. "I wanted to wash things away."

"What sort of things?"

Her bare shoulders lifted in a tiny shrug. "Murky bits and pieces that were lurking around."

"Are we free and clear now?" His eyes held hers.

"Oh, yes, Christopher Ralston. Free and clear, the *jorchi* has sung for us." She laughed and grabbed his hand. "Come run with me so that I may dry off in the sun."

Pulling him behind her, she set off at a merry gallop along the bank, her hair bouncing free of its knot to tumble down her back as she ran naked as a river nymph, and he laughed aloud.

Eventually, she stopped, panting for breath, and flung herself onto the mossy bank, patting the ground beside her in invitation. Kit dropped to his knees, regarding the lean, lissom, glistening length of her with narrowed eyes.

"I have been thinking," she announced. "And I have had an idea."

"Oh," he said. "Would it distract you too much if I were just to stroke you a little while you tell me about it?"

"It might," she said, her eyes glinting at him. "But it might distract you as well."

"Oh, it's bound to," he agreed cheerfully. "But I think we'll take the risk. Say away."

"Well, when we leave this country—"

"You think that will happen?" he interrupted, a finger poised over the rosy crown of one full round breast.

"Yes," she said with quiet confidence. "Akbar Khan says that the time is not far off now. Whether we will be rescued or surrendered is the only issue, as far as I could gather."

"So, when we leave this country—" he prompted, unable to hide the joy that was filling him as if he were a porous vessel that has been too long empty and absorbs into its dry surface the moisture of life. She was talking as he had never heard her talk, with confidence and acceptance of a future they would share away from this land.

"I would like to visit all the places I have always wanted to visit, even when I was little," she said, closing her eyes dreamily. "China and Tibet and Egypt. And I would like to go again to Persia and maybe even Africa—"

"Sweet heaven!" Kit groaned. "I have married a nomad."

"You do not like the idea?" Her eyes opened and she made as if to sit up, but his hand slipped to her belly and held her down.

"Of being married to a nomad?"

"No, I did not mean that . . . well, perhaps I did by extension. There's so much to discover in the world, so many different peoples to understand. I want to understand them all." Her arms swept wide in an all-encompassing gesture. "Does it not appeal to you at all?" Her eyes were now anxious.

"Lady Hester Stanhope has clearly found a successor," he observed wryly. "Do nomads have babies?"

"I suppose they must," she said with mock solemnity. "Otherwise, how would there be lots of little nomads to make big ones? Anyway, I do not think we should have ordinary children, do you?"

He grinned. "I think it would be impossible."

"So does the idea not appeal to you in the least?" she persisted.

Kit thought for a minute, then he said, "Yes, it does." Kneeling beside her, he looked gravely down at her. "But have you no desire to visit England, my Anna?"

"Not yet," she said. "I don't think it's my place, Kit. If you must, then I suppose I will—"

"No, you won't," he broke in. "I did say visit, not live, sweetheart."

"Oh." This time she pushed against the restraining hand and sat up, resting her chin on her drawn-up knees. "Well, I suppose I would like to visit it, since I have never been. And I daresay your parents will wish to see you from time to time.''

''I daresay they might,'' he agreed with the same gravity. ''I expect they will wish to make the acquaintance of my wife, also.''

''Oh, dear.'' She sighed. ''Could we go to Tibet first?''

''Wherever you wish, my sweet, just as long as we go together.''

''That's all right, then,'' she said, lying down again. ''Shall we try now to go to the very top of that mountain up there, where the golden eagles have their nests?''

''Close your eyes,'' he said, ''and I'll see if I can take us both.''

Her arms went around him as he came down beside her. ''You have never failed me yet, Ralston, *huzoor*.''

''And while I have breath, my green-eyed lynx, I never will.''

Author's Note

At noon on September 17th, 1842, the British hostages passed into the guardianship of Sir Richmond Shakespear, who had been given the task of ensuring their liberation. The Afghan resistance was technically defeated by reinforcements sent from India, and in retribution the British destroyed the principal bazaar in Kabul, where the bodies of Macnaghten and Burnes had been exposed. On October 12th they left Afghanistan for India, harassed again through the passes by Ghazi tribesmen, who, it might be said, had the last word. Dost Mahomed returned to his previous position, and all traces of the British invasion were obliterated.

Thus ended what is regarded as one of the worst examples of nineteenth-century imperial interference. The entire episode was so mismanaged that its catastrophic conclusion was inevitable. A few of the military participants in the debacle shared this view but were ignored by the decision-makers. I have presented the historical facts from this viewpoint.

The character of Akbar Khan remained an enigma for contemporary chroniclers as well as later historians. His fanatical detestation of the British invaders was both understandable and unquestionable, but his kindness and courtesy to the hostages is well-documented, as is his brutal attitude during the disastrous retreat from Kabul. Opinions differ as to whether he could have influenced the tribesmen during the massacre and deliberately chose not to.

They also differ as to whether he cold-bloodedly planned the murder of Macnaghten, or whether it was accomplished in an impassioned moment of blind rage at the political officer's treachery. I have obviously fictionalized the character of Akbar Khan, but have attempted to incorporate the paradoxes of his nature into my portrait.

Colin Mackenzie was one of the few heroes of the fiasco to survive. The events in which he participated I have recorded as accurately as possible; however, I have taken certain liberties with a temperament that I suspect was too stern and highly principled to have permitted him to accept with equanimity Kit and Annabel's situation.

General Elphinstone, Sir William Macnaghten, Sir Alexander Burnes, Lady Sale and others are shown to the best of my ability as history has presented them to us.

The exploits and characters of Kit and Annabel are entirely fictional.